D0398578

Don't Mean Nuthin'

Books by Ron Lealos

Pashtun

No Merci

No Direction Home

The Sixth Man

Jaw of the Traitor

www.ronlealosbooks.com

Don't Mean Nuthin'

A Military Thriller

Ron Lealos

Skyhorse Publishing

This is a work of fiction. Names, characters, places, and incidents either are the product of the author's imagination or are used fictitiously. Any resemblance to actual persons, living or dead, events, or locales
is entirely coincidental.

Skyhorse Publishing books may be purchased in bulk at special discounts for sales promotion, corporate gifts, fund-raising, or educational purposes. Special editions can also be created to specifications. For details, contact the Special Sales Department, Skyhorse Publishing, 307 West 36th Street, 11th Floor, New York, NY 10018 or info@skyhorsepublishing.com.

Skyhorse® and Skyhorse Publishing® are registered trademarks of Skyhorse Publishing, Inc.®, a Delaware corporation.

Visit our website at www.skyhorsepublishing.com.

10 9 8 7 6 5 4 3 2 1

The Library of Congress has cataloged this title as follows:
Lealos, Ron.
Don't mean nuthin': a military thriller / Ron Lealos.
pages; cm
ISBN 978-1-62914-572-3 (hardcover: acid-free paper) 1. Vietnam War, 1961–1975—Fiction. 2. Special forces (Military science)—United States—Fiction. 3. Assassins—Fiction. I. Title. II. Title: Don't mean nothing.
PS3612.E2193D66 2015
813'.6—dc23

2014035415

Cover design by Ashley Lau

Ebook ISBN: 978-1-62914-926-4

Printed in the United States of America

1969

The 727 from McCord to South Vietnam. Blue-clad stewardesses in tight skirts and cute pillbox hats patrolled the aisles, nylons "swishing" as they squeezed past, handing out chicken cutlets, Coca-Colas, and wilted salads. The faint tang of Lysol lingered from the Freedom Bird's last cleaning after touching down on its return from Da Nang. Three hours into the flight, the loudest sound was murmured prayers.

Benzedrine made the grunt on the right lick dry lips. The yellow pills he dropped earlier forced the corners of his mouth to battle each other when he tried to smile. A tune danced in his head, and no one else had the beat. He snapped fingers and every few minutes smashed the back of the seat in front with a clenched fist. A quick look back and the cherry in the seat ahead knew it was terminal to say a word. When the song finished, the grunt stroked a deerskin pouch hanging from his neck by a leather braid. No one dared ask him what it held. On his wrist, a crude peace sign, carved with a knife, charcoal for ink. He reeked of beer, sweat, and vomit, and his green fatigues were a year in the bush from my tan, pressed uniform.

The grunt chuckled. A private joke, punch line only he knew.

Staring straight ahead, he said, "Listen up, cherry, I ain't one ta give ad-vice, but hope ya' ain't thinkin' yur here to protect yur momma from the dinks comin' ashore in Los An-gel-ees. LBJ's 'maintainin' democracy' crapola is bullshit. We're here for the party." He rubbed the pouch like it was the smooth skin of a firstborn. "There's only one rule. Keep yur balls covered. And get to the chow line before all a' them other assholes."

The plane roasted, the cooling system not able to keep pace with the calories burned by fear. I wiped the sweat on my forehead with the sleeve of my tropical uni.

The man stared at the folded tray table in front of him. Every few minutes, he kicked the frame of the forward seat and hissed, "Freekin' slants." Maybe he was cursing the North Vietnamese. Or a cheating woman.

The cherry in the aisle seat to his left moaned.

"Hear that?" the grunt asked. "You boys'll be whimperin' like baby-sans once we set down in the 'Nam. First, you're gonna think the air's been run through an F-4 engine and pumped inta yur cherry lungs. That ain't even the worst. That Jesus fella' a yours, he done added to the heat with what them college girl LTs call 'hum-id-it-y.' Feels like ya' got yur face tied in a plastic bag full a' boilin' water. Rots out yur skivvies and makes yur balls think they're in the swimmin' hole."

The cherry started to shake.

Turning to his left, the grunt said, "Ah, hell with it, boy. Don't mean nuthin'."

The cherries wore fresh uniforms, butch haircuts, and clean shaves. They were awake, some with hands steepled in prayer, and sat inspection stiff, every few minutes wiping the sweat from their eyes. The grunts were sprawled in their seats, snoring. Lights were dimmed, and the stewardesses covered the snorers with blankets. The 727 didn't carry enough air freshener to veil the terror stench.

A new tune finished in the grunt's head, and he looked at my chest.

"Morgan," he said. "That right?"

The name was printed in white letters on a black patch above my pocket. I nodded.

He looked away.

"Ain't gonna be no formal in-tro-duc-tion, cherry," he said. "Don't care and don't wanna know. Just before I shipped back to The World, met another cherry named Jazinsky, or some such shit. He was only around a coupla' days. Took off his helmet to get a drink a' water in the creek. Gook sniper blowed his brains back ta Poland."

Three rows in front, a boy sitting at the window, who didn't look out of high school, began to sob. A blond stewardess bent over the two cherries between her and the boy and whispered something in the crying one's ear. He sobbed louder.

Someone in the back of the plane had a nightmare. He screamed, "Dink motherfuckers. Don't want no more stinkin' rice balls." Nobody said a word.

A cherry passed, stumbling toward the head. He smelled like puke, and there was a stain the size of a canteen on his uniform blouse.

"Now lookee there," the grunt said. "Cherry musta eaten too many greasy cheeseburgers back in The World." He laughed. "Soon, he'll be thinkin' a solid shit is a blessin' from the Lord. Most a' the time, it just runs down yur leg."

He slammed the seat again.

"Hey, Morgan," he said. "You ain't laughin'. You one a' them gung ho, straight arrow, un-i-vers-i-ty cocksuckers? You look too old ta be ridin' with this buncha draftees."

The muted lights flickered like the power was going out. I looked at my watch. Two o'clock p.m. Seattle time.

"Twenty-three," I said. "Spent some time in college. My old man's a colonel, and there was no way I could run to Canada."

He slapped his forehead.

"Well, ex-cuuu-se me, troop," he said. "Didn't know I was sittin' next to no pencil dick officer's brat. Suppose yur gonna enjoy your tour behind a desk by Au Tau Beach. Workin' on yur tan after ya' get sucked off by the mama-sans."

No way to answer. Already condemned. But it was enough for the grunt to stop. He took a baggie from his pocket and gently removed three red pills, washing them down with the last of his coke. Within minutes, the grunt was asleep.

Five hours later, the Freedom Bird touched down in Da Nang. The line of cherries and grunts moved slowly down the stairs into air thick as C-rat mashed potatoes. A band played "The Star-Spangled Banner," sweat rolling from their faces and dress uniforms drooping in the sun, the last notes ending in a long sigh. A line of slicks ferried bodies to the evac hospital across the melting tarmac. In the distance, the boom of 155 mike-mike shells landing in the hills. A DC-6 was parked next to the Freedom Bird, green body bags waiting to be loaded.

The only thing I knew was there was no direction home that didn't include a journey through Vietnam.

The old woman had white hair. Two black crooked teeth were all that remained in her constant smile. A blanket sewn from pajamas held a sleeping baby snug to the old woman's thin back. Her brown skin was wrinkled and creased, but didn't stop the corners of her mouth from curling into the grin of a wise woman. A woman who had seen great joy. And great sadness.

Around the old woman, two small, naked boys played a game with bamboo sticks in the red clay of the Delta, jumping and dancing to the rules of a game that was foreign to me. The old woman understood. She clapped her bony hands and made clucking sounds of encouragement through sun-cracked lips. Sores, running white with ooze, covered the bare legs of the boys. Grunts called them "gook sores." Most Vietnamese peasant children had them, not as a consequence of the war or a plague imported by the white devils. The sores were part of the Delta's history and hardship.

The earth smoked in the afternoon sun. Paddies in the distance held ghosts of booby-trapped legs, trip wires firm in the swaying rice shoots. Reflections of the sun streaked from the muddy water below palm trees that drooped in another day of lung-searing heat, the humid air making each breath weigh a thousand pounds.

Three scrawny chickens pecked in the red soil around the huts near a sleeping pig tethered to a hardwood pole. By the door, behind the old woman, clay pots stood as sentinels. A black metal drinking cup made from an old C-ration can sat on the top of the brown pot closest to the bamboo door. Usually, in other vils, the pots held rice or water. Sometimes grenades and Kalashnikov ammo. Or trip wires that made future handshakes a dream.

Water bugs zipped around a puddle in a bomb crater left by a B-52 Stratofortress strike from thirty thousand feet in the sky. The raids were called Arc Light missions, but the grunts named them "Whispering Death." Five hundred pounds of high explosives per bomb, more than one hundred death whispers on each plane.

The trees scattered through the vil were scarred and blackened by the air strikes but still waved gently in the breeze, wounds healing in the tropical sun. Broken, rotting coconuts littered the ground below many of the trees. A ditch behind the hootches served as the latrine, and the smell drifted through the palms. Rats scampered into the jungle, white coconut meat between their sharp teeth.

The old woman didn't sweat like everyone in the recon patrol I led. We were crouched in the bush, waiting for this scene to turn into something sinister so we could destroy the peace with our ArmaLites and flamethrower. Intel claimed there was supposed to be a rendezvous between local Viet Cong leaders in this vil today.

The baby moved, and the old woman slid the pajama backpack to her front, cooing. She tickled the baby's chin and smiled as though the world was at peace. Not full of bloody stumps.

The head of the meeting was said to be a Sorbonne-educated woman named Liem Tran, accused by the Phoenix program commanders of being the most important cadre chief in this sector of the Mekong. If I didn't punch Liem's ticket today, I was ordered to grease her later while she slept in a villa ten klicks south. A firefight this afternoon would have a higher enemy body count, much preferred by Military Assistance Command Vietnam, MACVN, in Saigon.

The two boys ran behind the old woman, sticks in their hands. They formed a chorus of sweet talk aimed at the baby. One of the boys raced into the hut and came out with a piece of black plastic. He took the baby's fingers and pressed them around the handle from a busted M16. The baby's hand was too small to hold the toy.

Only the one hootch looked occupied. Fresh palms covered the roof, the hardwood supports leaning much less than the other abandoned huts. Chipped plates and silverware made from shrapnel surrounded the smoldering cook fire. An uneaten rice ball, nearly black with a covering of flies, decomposed in the middle of one of the plates.

A young woman walked toward the vil on a dike between the paddies, a woven basket on her shoulder. The sun beat on her back, outlined by the next grove of trees in the distance. Behind her, a water buffalo grazed. A conical grass hat covered her head and the top of the long, black hair that hung to her waist. As she entered the vil, the two little boys screeched and jumped in the air. They ran to her side and tugged on the wet pajamas that almost reached the young woman's bare feet.

The old woman slowly stood and tottered toward the young woman. Her smile made long furrows in leathery skin. The baby whimpered. The young woman handed the basket to the biggest boy and took the baby. She nuzzled the baby-san and walked toward the shade of a palm tree on the edge of the vil. The young woman sat and pulled up her pajama top. She fed the baby and shushed the two prancing boys. The old woman squatted next to the young one, watching.

The patrol had been in position for three hours. The jungle, again, was alive with the sounds of birds, monkeys, rats, insects, growth, and slow decay. Fumes from the small cook fire in front of the hut mixed with the rotting fruit and vegetation to make the ever-present sweet, smoky smell of Southeast Asia. A smell that coated every inch of cloth and skin. Coated the red earth itself. Coated the greasepaint that helped us blend into the bush.

A dog barked from behind one of the huts. It ran into the cleared area in front of the hootches and skidded to a stop, turning around and yapping back in the direction in which it had just come. The mongrel was the brother to every other dog in 'Nam. Long legs, pointed snout, yellow teeth, ribs pressed against short, wiry hair, scabs, and milky eyes.

A tap on my shoulder. A finger pointed to the jungle behind the huts. Figures in black pajamas moved slowly through the bush, rifles searching. Ammo belts crisscrossed their chests. Soviet RKG grenades hung from the rope around their waists. The grenades were shaped like longneck beer bottles, but held no joy. Not one of the VC was over five-foot-four or weighed as much as the average housewife back in The World.

Two more high-pitched yips and the dog ran off into the bush. The young woman covered herself and rocked the baby. The old woman moved closer to the young one, and the creases in her face no longer formed a smile. Huddled behind the women, the boys stared toward the approaching VC. The pig awoke from the nap and pulled its tether as far away from the soldiers as it could manage. Now, silence in the jungle, and the sun dropped behind a cloud shaped like Puff the Magic Dragon.

The VC spread out and inspected each one of the huts. No one spoke. They used the barrels of their rifles to poke and prod at sleeping mats and the few belongings of the villagers. Two of the squad were women, black hair cut almost as short as the men. No one wore shoes. Mud caked their feet like tight slippers. None looked older than fifteen.

If our intel was right, another squad would soon arrive. The mission was to blow both units into the soil of 'Nam. Take no prisoners. Burn the vil to the ground and set it free to make an example that would spread through the huts of the Mekong. Don't fuck with Uncle Sam or he'll be sure your relatives get to attend another cremation. Burn the vil to set it free. Pacification.

The VC dispersed under the shade of the thatched porches of the huts. Didn't bunch up. One grenade meant the end of the party. Canteens came off belts. Murmurs traveled across the open ground. AKs leaned against thighs.

My breathing became as quiet as the centipede crawling across the jungle floor in front of me. The wind that had kept the flies away died. The buzz in my ear joined the nervous chatter in my brain.

The young woman gently stroked the baby's head while the old woman chewed and watched. The two boys peeked from behind the young woman.

A VC, AK across his chest, walked to the young woman. He barked something and waved the rifle in her face. The young woman looked down at the clay, and the soldier grinned and kicked her foot. The baby cried.

Another VC came out of the nearest hut carrying a doll made of elephant grass and pieces of red and blue cloth. He threw the doll into the air and sliced its head off with his knife before it hit the ground. The squad laughed.

One of the VC women passed out cigarettes, in her hand a silver lighter that must have been liberated from a "running dog" GI grunt's dead body. After each light, she flipped it shut like James Dean and marched to the next soldier. The bandoleers across her chest and back made the woman move with a slight stoop.

The soldier who had been questioning the young woman squatted next to the cook fire. He took a letter wrapped in plastic from his black tunic and began to read. By his interrogation of the young woman and the ability to read, he was probably the squad leader. The first to die. I was sure the ARVN Rangers behind me had already marked the soldier in the sights of their M16s.

My escort for the day's mission was a squad of Luc Luong Dac Biet Special Forces, better known as Rangers, the elite force of the South Vietnamese Army. The LLDB troops were only 5 percent of the ARVN and were as merciless as any soldiers in-country. Better paid, better trained, better equipped, and better housed, they were macho killers of their own countrymen. The detachment was permanently assigned to the Phoenix program to help in assassination missions and spread terror. They weren't my buddies.

For the next hour, we watched the VC smoke and chat. AKs were never more than an arm's length from their bodies. Bandoleers and grenades didn't leave their belts. The VC continually scanned the jungle, as though they expected enemy contact. One of the VC used a folding shovel to straighten the banks of the bomb crater, using it for a bunker. A Chinese-made Chicom Type 56 light machine gun lay on top of a pile of dirt next to the bunker.

When they had to piss, they used a hootch. If the VC had to shit, they used "chieu hoi" propaganda leaflets for toilet paper. The leaflets were folded in their packs and encouraged VC guerrillas to surrender in five different languages. Chieu hois littered South Vietnam like hotdog wrappers at Yankee Stadium after the World Series. If a Vietnamese held up a chieu hoi, it was a white flag. Sometimes they weren't shot.

The peasant women and children stayed under the palm tree away from the VC. When the baby cried, the young woman raised her pajama top. The boys clung to the women, black eyes wide and frightened. The old woman tugged on a wisp of silver hair that grew on her chin, her mouth moving slowly like a cow chewing its cud.

More and more, the gangrene of conscience blackened my soul. Every mission brought doubts, especially this one. An old woman and a young one, with three small children, alone in a deserted vil. No men in sight. VC chiefs meeting in broad daylight. A possible woman leader. One pig, three chickens, and one water buffalo. Too much merchandise for these solitary peasants. Props for an ambush. Nothing made sense. Even if we waxed these VC, there were ten more to replace them. They were everywhere. Like snipers in the trees.

One thing I was sure of, if we could surprise Charlie's party, the firepower we packed would waste a regiment. The Rangers carried two M60 "pig" machine guns and enough ammo to fire until the barrels melted into the clay. In seconds, the 7.62mm slugs, a full metal jacket, would rip the vil to shreds twice over. Nothing would survive from the short distance from which we would be firing. If the pigs didn't end it, the M79 grenade launchers would. We had three of these "bloop guns" loaded with forty-five flechette darts in each round. The flechettes went in so fast that a hit body didn't even bleed. When combined with the pigs and a steady rain of well-aimed M16 rounds, the bloopers brought beaucoup hell to the paddies in a flash. After we went in for the body count, we'd light their fire with the flamethrower to sanitize the vil.

Another tap on my shoulder. This time the finger pointed me to the line of trees that bordered the rice paddies. A dozen VC walked toward the vil. The Rangers behind me tensed. Almost showtime. The ARVN silently spread out in the jungle on both sides to give a clear field of fire. The leaves stuck in the webbing of the Rangers' helmets and camo fatigues made them invisible even when they moved.

No one would shoot until I gave the order. Disobedience didn't go down well with Rangers. It was an on-site death sentence with no right to appeal.

The rain began as the second unit entered the vil. Drops as big as eyeballs fell from the green canopy and ran down the back of my fatigues. In the Delta, this time of year, it was either wet or wetter. Today, the rain might help. The VC would probably take shelter under thatched porches, shrinking the field of fire even more. The monsoons would drown any noise my detachment made.

All twelve VC men in the second squad wore black-and-white checkered scarves around their necks above the black pajamas. Combat boots were thick with mud. AKs at their waists, the VC spread out slowly through the vil. They were obviously well-trained regular troops, not the "volunteer" army of locals made of farmers and merchants. The VC already in the vil stood at attention.

If the intel was right, I would soon see a woman take charge of this get-together. But neither of the two women in the first cell was likely to be Liem. They were too young. No women were in the second group of VC.

The Rangers waited for my hand sign while the rain sounded louder than on the roof of a two-poncho night bivouac in the bush. Across the paddies, a brilliant rainbow marked the distance. The peasant women and children stayed huddled under the palm tree, puddles forming at their feet. Smoke from the cook fire turned gray as the rain sizzled on the coals. Behind us, a monkey shrieked at the wet that spoiled his afternoon nap. Steam rose from the warm soil barely dry after the last shower. The flies disappeared into the mist.

Finished with their recon of the vil, the VC greeted each other with bows in two of the hootches. No salutes. No jive handshakes. No smiles.

I raised my right fist. Lock and load. M16s, bloopers, and pigs were aimed at the two huts. I turned to the pig operator on my left and pointed to the furthest hootch. The pig on my right was already focused on the nearest hut. The Rangers didn't need more signals. They would wait until I fired my M16.

The plastic on the handle of my rifle was slippery with rain. I sighted in on the VC who was doing most of the talking. He had a thin mustache and Alfred E. Neuman ears. A fresh, pink scar ran from the corner of his mouth to a right eye that drooped out of its socket. His AK dangled from his shoulder by a ragged leather strap, muzzle pointed to the clay. Two RKG grenades were stuffed into the ammo belts crisscrossing his chest. I aimed at the one over his heart and fired.

Bamboo, palm thatch, hardwood chunks, clay pottery, chicken feathers, dirt, and body parts exploded into the cloud of rain. Both the hootches took direct hits from the bloopers. The pigs shredded everything still in solid form. M16 bullets rat-a-tatted into bodies as they vanished into the ozone. The noise was louder than a 105mm howitzer barrage. But it only lasted a few seconds. I signaled cease-fire with my hand. No return fire. The VC were vaporized. The mist turned red with swirling blood. Nothing moved but the smoke and scraps that danced on the wind current from the grenades. The only sound was the loud whimpering of the peasants under the palm tree.

The Rangers followed me out of our hiding spots in the canopy and into the Armageddon of the vil, M16s on full auto. We searched for any survivors or documents the intel analysts could use. A blackened fingertip lay next to the head of the doll. Nothing but scraps oozing flesh. I motioned for the flamethrower to burn the huts in the back that still stood. As I watched the Rangers torch the hootches, four quick shots snapped from behind. I turned in time to see the peasant women and children fall to the clay, blood seeping from holes in the middle of their foreheads. The baby-san cried. One more bullet and it was quiet. We moved out.

* * *

On the march south to Liem's villa, I tried to understand the afternoon's action. Intel had also said the villa would be the secondary target. The VC had gone to a lot of effort to make the deserted vil seem alive. Stock it with women, children, food, and animals. Have them work the paddies. Props to convince the Americans that it was just another innocent, worthless vil. No threat. But Charlie must have been using it for a meeting spot. That meant the women were VC too. Somebody high up in the National Liberation Front's local command must have ratted the position. The Rangers figured it out in an instant, and the women and children died for their supporting role in the drama. Intel was right about the vil. But the Phoenix program had become Murder, Inc., doing the bidding of every corrupt ARVN general and South Vietnamese politician with a hard-on for gore. Civilians were killed for being overdue a few piasters on the latest bribe or smiling at the wrong mistress. In Hue, a barber was executed by Phoenix operatives because his trembling hands nicked a general's scalp. No telling what crime Liem had really committed.

The squad made it to the villa before midnight. Being in Indian country slowed us, but the Rangers knew the shortcuts. We hunkered down in the bush that surrounded the crumbling French mansion and watched. Since Liem hadn't been caught in the slaughter at the village, plan two was for me to put a silenced bullet in her head. We waited.

The garrote fit snug in my hands, grooved plastic handles cool on my mud-caked fingers. Kerosene lamps lit the old French villa fifty yards in front of my squad. No one had passed the windows in the decaying villa for more than an hour. It was almost time to move out. The Beast, what black grunts named the US war machine, needed to be fed.

The carbon fiber of the garrote slid as smooth as a round down the barrel of an M1 mortar. The boys at the CIA lab inside Fort Monmouth, New Jersey, had made murder by strangulation much easier. Steel rusted in the jungle humidity. Carbon was lighter and just as strong. Wood handles rotted and got coated with sweat. And blood. Besides, steel was too sharp. The objective wasn't to decapitate the target. Too loud and messy. Just crush the jugular and Adam's apple, strangling the victim fast. The retractable carbon line avoided stuffing loose, bloody wire into a fatigue pocket. Phoenix operatives called the garrotes "bow ties."

"Did you wear your bow tie to the dance last night?" The answer, "Right on. Got two twists and a herky jerk."

Crickets and night birds played the jungle symphony. Wild pigs and dogs scavenged in the bush. Yellow eyes peeked through the leaves like mini-flashlights with low batteries, and kraits slithered across the jungle floor in search of mice. The moon was covered by clouds, and the smell of the night's rice and fish ball dinner lingered in the trees.

Next to me, First Lieutenant Thieu whispered to one of his squad of Hoa Hao Rangers. The op called for the Rangers to detail on the other side of the villa in the rubber plantation where there was sure to be VC. Westmoreland had given a general order Vietnam-wide. No firefights in the rubber plantations. No shooting into the rows of trees. Rubber was off-limits, but not tonight. The plantations were thick with VC tunnels, and the ARVN weren't bound by Westmoreland's order. The Rangers would create a diversion while I waxed Liem. We would meet up here and ricky-ticky back to base camp.

"*Tot di san*," Thieu said. Good hunting. No smile. No warm embrace.

The Rangers moved out, Thieu at point. They were as silent as the little green lizards that crawled into my pack in search of Hershey bars. Ten yards away and the squad was invisible.

The jungle here wasn't thick. Not the dense foliage around the vil we had taken off the map earlier in the day. Slaves of the French colonialists who built the mansion must have thinned the bushes that were, again, getting the upper hand. The night gave the cover we needed.

Fifteen minutes and I was on stage.

A fire ant nibbled on my leg. Shit, if there was one, his brothers would soon be feasting on my flesh. Another bite. Three more. I mashed as many as I could and moved quickly to the base of a palm tree fifteen yards to my left. Already, the little fuckers were making my skin a dartboard, injecting their poison into my blood. Another minute and I'd have to move again or the bastards would be back. Still, the ants were better than the slimy, cocksucking leeches. In the daylight, in ambush position, I would have had to let the sons of bitching ants have their way. Not tonight. There were no patrols out.

Things didn't add up. If Liem was really a local honcho, there would be guards and patrols. Not enough to raise suspicion, but more than zero. VC chiefs rarely lived in mansions. They were in the bush with other little people soldiers. Or holed up in tunnels. The Sorbonne? Foreign-educated Vietnamese were always suspected by the VC. Tainted by capitalism. Spies. Executed. Women were allowed to pack rifles and supplies. To die. Few were in command positions. Could be counterintelligence to prove that the intel was right by having us blow away a mock vil used for VC powwows. A cover for the real target. Liem.

The bounty on my head was a hundred thousand piasters. The VC knew of the assassins run by Phoenix, and the VC hung posters of a face that looked something like me on barbiturates in towns all over the Delta. But, to the Vietnamese, all long noses looked the same. They knew my MO. My name was "*gan con ran.*" Night Snake. Sector commanders, or anyone else my masters picked out, had a tough time catching z's unless they were hidden in a tunnel. I'd never greased a woman with a silenced bullet. A gook with no legs, okay, but not a mama-san. Besides, that Charlie was in his wheelchair drinking tea and working on map coordinates when I pressed the Hush Puppy to his neck. The papa-san was in the hootch next to his bicycle shop that served as the communications center for civilian VC. Or so I'd been told.

Little dink fucker shit his pajamas. My dreams weren't of heads with mangled brains and holes at the base of the skull, but of naked faceless yellow people drenched in shit jamming me against the clay walls of a pit lined with shit-dipped punji sticks. The smell woke me gasping for air in the night and squeezing my nose shut.

A shadow moved across the porch of the villa. Vines and Rangoon creepers grew to a rotting roof and blocked a clear view. The shadow was outlined by the lamps. A match flared. The face of a shirtless man.

Ten minutes till showtime. The green dials on my watch shown like Day-Glo. Time to get up close and personal. The man had to be wasted first. Liem or anyone else who got in the way next. I propped my M16 against a lime tree and started toward the villa. The sparse bush and moonless night hid my silent approach.

A skill drummed into me at Benning and in the jungle of the Mekong was how to move like a hunting tiger. No boot touched ground without the foot transmitting an "all clear." I could walk for hours on the balls of my feet, heels never feeling the clay soil. No sound. All senses on receive. It was as natural to me as a stroll in Central Park.

The man's elbows rested on the porch railing, cigarette in his right hand. Smoke curled above his greasy black hair with each drag. He stared toward the muddy road that led to Pha Than. Glasses, frame held together by dirty, white tape, sat on the bridge of his nose. I could smell his sweat from my position three feet away and just below the rusted iron railing.

The Hush Puppy was jammed into my ammo belt, the garrote in my left hand. I slid closer. In one motion, I pulled the carbon wire from the handles and looped it around the man's neck, overlapping my wrists and twisting. The cigarette fell into an orchid bush. The man's hands went to his throat. I jerked down, but not enough to pull him over the railing. Just enough so he wouldn't kick his feet against the mahogany boards of the porch.

Noise was the enemy of the assassin. That's why I didn't use the Hush Puppy. Even the *pphhuupp* sound of a silenced bullet was like thunder in the peace of a jungle night.

Our noses touched as the man fought to suck in a breath. I balanced his body on the railing while his feet flailed in the last death kick. A mole sprouting black hairs on his cheek. A wad of white sleep scum was lodged in the corner of his eye. As his hands loosened and his body went slack, I heard the shit trickle from his pajamas. The foul smell coated my nostrils. Back in the dream. I shook my head and let the man drop slowly before the noise awoke the villa. The garrote went in my pocket. The Hush Puppy came out. Five minutes.

Moving silently through the jungle was second nature. Walking quietly through a villa, decaying in the tropical humidity, without the creak of a rotting board was dicey. Every footstep had to test whether it would bear weight without a groan. Doors had to open without a squeak, Hush Puppy leading the way.

The villa smelled of mildew and cooking oil. In the dim light, sheets on the furniture looked like dirty robes on Buddhist monks. Silverware and plates sat on the dining room table next to empty wine glasses, waiting for a breakfast that wouldn't be served.

The first two bedrooms were empty. One more at the end of the hall. I moved like a krait. The door was open a few inches. Inside, a muted lamp burned to the side of a bed covered in mosquito netting. Long, black hair was splayed across an embroidered pillow. A porcelain washbowl and a white towel sat on a wooden table next to the canopied bed. Paintings of the French countryside dotted the walls. Cracks zigzagged across the plaster ceiling. Two geckos crawled slowly up the far wall. The smell of kerosene replaced the dead man's shit. I walked softly on the frayed rug.

A young woman slept, a flowered sheet over her body. Her skin was light brown and shined smoothly in the dim light. A small nose came to a rounded tip. Full lips were turned up in a slight smile. Black lashes were closed below thick eyebrows. Simone Signoret chin. No wrinkles. No scars. No drool. Drop-fucking-dead gorgeous.

Two minutes. The muzzle of the Hush Puppy easily parted the mosquito netting. I pushed the barrel into the woman's throat and asked "Liem?" Her eyes blinked open. "*Vang*," she said. Yes.

The eyes. Emerald green. No fear. Not even surprise.

"*O tren*," I said. Up. "*Mau le*." Quickly.

The Hush Puppy still at her throat, I grabbed her hair with my left hand and jerked her from the bed. I was breaking every commandment of special ops. Liem should already be dead. But I couldn't do it. Not in bed. Not another one.

Silence. "*Lam cho*," I hissed in her ear as I dragged her toward the door. No struggle. No noise. Lamb to slaughter.

In the hall, I moved Liem in front and nudged her toward the door, pistol to her skull. The Gerber fighting knife usually strapped to my calf was in my left hand. We walked out the front door and down the steps of the porch to the start of the bush.

Two grenades went off in the rubber plantation, followed immediately by M16 rounds and the tearing sound of trees being ripped apart by the pig machine guns. AK-47s answered. The house was backlit by fire from the rubber trees.

I shoved Liem to the ground. Flames danced in her green eyes. She smiled. Liem's long, thin nightgown rode up on her thighs. Small breasts poked through the silk. She lifted her head and looked at me. A red bruise was already starting where I had jammed the Hush Puppy into her neck. Her legs were curled under her hips. A strap fell off her shoulder, and black hair covered the left side of her face. I put the end of the silencer between her green eyes. Liem smiled.

It wasn't a plea. "*Cam on*," she whispered. Thank you. It was forgiveness.

The rhythm of the firefight picked up. Short bursts of the Soviet-made RPD light machine guns answered the death sentence of the pigs.

The Hush Puppy shook in my hand. Bone and skin rubbed against the tip of the silencer. My knees felt like they couldn't support the weight of all the killing tools on my body. A drop of sweat, blackened by greasepaint, fell on the breast of Liem's white nightgown. I blinked, but the green eyes were still there.

"*Lam long*," Liem whispered. Please.

The tip of my bush combat boots touched Liem's calf. Through the nylon webbing, I could feel Liem's relaxed muscles. I flexed my knees to keep from falling. The fighting knife hung slack at my left side. Shadows from the fire in the plantation flickered through the orchid bushes and banyan trees. Cordite fumes drifted across my face.

"*Lam long*," Liem whispered again. Only her mouth moved. Liem's hands lay on the flatness of her stomach. A glitter of orange flame reflected from a gold band on her finger.

Within seconds, Thieu would be back.

"*Nay*?" Why? I asked. Sometimes, I could still feel goodness. Not even the evil that surrounded me every day could dull the sense. Liem was good.

"*Buddha goi*." Buddha calls, she said. Now she smiled—the look I had seen on the face of a monk before he lit the gas that soaked his robes.

The Hush Puppy made a crunching sound as I pushed the barrel harder against her teeth.

"VC?" I asked. Stupid question that came from my conscience. And I knew it even before she answered with another smile.

Raising the pistol to her forehead, I pulled the trigger. *Phfffupp*. The bullet went into her brain. Her head slammed into the ground. Liem's eyes stayed open, looking straight into mine, the smile still on her lips. No muscles jerked. No blood came from the hole in her forehead. No shit ran down her legs. She looked like she was resting, daydreaming of a welcome lover. Liem's green eyes wouldn't let me go. But I went. It was all duty.

The M16 was against the tree where I left it. As I picked the rifle up, Thieu and his squad hustled by. Shouts and an occasional AK round came from the rubber plantation. One of Thieu's men was dragged by another Ranger, blood on a limp right leg. I followed the squad into the darkness of the jungle.

* * *

"*Bo di*," I said two hours later to the Ranger on the trail ahead of me. Stop. The message passed up the line, and the squad melted into the bush that surrounded us. Over the last two hours, we had been moving as fast as the jungle and rice paddies allowed. The squad had avoided the dikes that were always booby-trapped and gave a target to snipers and patrols even in the dark. The Viet Cong owned the night.

"Lieutenant Thieu. *D`ay*," I said to the soldier. Here. The Ranger whispered to the man next to him. While I waited for Thieu, I tried to cut the fucking leeches off my legs with the Gerber. At least I could get part of their slimy bodies off without firing up a cigarette, suicide at night in the middle of the Mekong.

Leeches meant I had been in the water too long. The sewage that floated in the paddies gave me jungle rot. Or made the case I already had worse. I moved my toes. The green skin that was left barely covered the bones. They ground together like chopsticks.

No matter where my mind tried to go, it jumped back to green eyes and the smile of a dead woman. I shook my head and tried to focus on anything but the feeling that I had done something terribly evil. But there were just more faces. A gallery of evil. Like Thi Myong, the veterinarian in Chau Doc. I killed him at a meeting of the local GVN, Government of Vietnam, council. An old man, Myong was never alone. Phoenix agents claimed he was a tax collector for the NVA. Myong's death was designed to be a message for everyone on the council, but I would need time to escape. The Chau Doc council was certainly infiltrated by the VC. I went to the meeting as the new liaison between the US military and the local government. I brought an ice pick sharpened to a needlepoint and a folded red handkerchief.

Three hours of squabbling in Vietnamese, most of which I didn't understand. Should Chau Doc declare itself a "neutral zone"? The ceiling fan barely moved the dense air in the tin-roofed building. Would the VC and Americans respect the neutrality? Sure. For the time it took a Zippo to light off the first hut with a suspected VC. Or just for grins.

Time for an ice-cold *bia*. Beer. Myong stood against the plaster wall, no one beside him, white safari shirt hanging over his belt and the beginning of cataracts making his black eyes gray. I walked toward Myong with a smile of greeting, hand in my pocket. The other councilmen were gathered around the tub of beer. When I reached Myong, one quick jab to his chest with the ice pick and he slumped to the wood floor. The handkerchief over the tip stopped any blood from spurting. "Heart attack," I yelled. "I'll get a medic." I jogged out the door and into the night while the others went to Myong. The move was called "quinella" because you picked a winner.

* * *

Thieu appeared next to me through a clump of liana vines that hung from the trees like black, wooden stalactites. He squatted in front of me, the butt of his M16 on the decaying leaves that covered the jungle floor.

"You get the feeling that something's up?" I asked. "We're only a klick from base, and it's too quiet. No artillery. No flares. No crickets. No patrols. Better keep alert."

A drop from the afternoon's shower fell on the shoulder of my flak jacket. I rubbed my finger in the water and licked it. It tasted the same as the rainwater I used to drink out of the barrel under the eave of my uncle's cabin back in The World.

"*Vang*," Thieu said. "Men say same. We go slow. Two minutes." Thieu stood and slid into the dark.

Thieu and his men were Hoa Hao Buddhists. They hated the North Vietnamese and anyone on the NVA's side. The Hoa Hao sect was a minority in South Vietnam that worshipped the Healing Buddha of Tay An. It was a Mekong Delta farming sect. Their beliefs were focused on a love of the land and agriculture. The Hoa Haos had Four Great Debts of Gratitude that drove their religion. Great Debt number three was we "must be ready to sacrifice ourselves for country when required." The North Vietnamese were invaders who had persecuted the Hoa Haos and their country. Death did not scare the Hoa Haos. They were as fierce as the Nung mercenaries and the Montagnard tribesmen.

We moved back onto the trail, Thieu on point, me on trace.

Unexplainably, a dry palm leaf brushed my fatigue, making the sound of paper rubbed together, an anomaly in the monsoons. *Phung Hoang*. The VC posters drew the Phoenix program as a huge eagle with a snake in its mouth, always flying above a poor, defenseless peasant. The GVN printed a comic book that was distributed all over South Vietnam called *The Ba Family*. In it, the *Phung Hoang* was said to "provide security and prosperity to the people." The Ba family was praised for turning in two new neighbors as NVA tax collectors. The comic didn't say what happened to the NVA after they were arrested, but the Ba family got a written commendation and a public thank-you. Rumor had it that all nine of the Ba family, women and children included, were decapitated by the NVA. Their heads were mounted on Vespa motorcycle handlebars and given a joyride around the city square. Luke the Gook knew how to get revenge.

The only sounds were the water drops from the trees. No wind to rattle the leaves. The moon came out from behind the clouds every few minutes, and the speed trail was well traveled and muddy. Smoke tree branches tickled my face. The path was made for Little People.

A booby trap exploded in front, sounding like a .50-caliber toe popper. The trail was lit up by AK-47 and light machine gunfire. A pineapple grenade went off twenty yards in front of me. As I dove into the bush, bullets ripped into the trees over my head, and Rangers fell to the trail in death throes, arms and legs dancing like broken dolls, without firing a shot. The noise was worse than a Huey landing next to me. It would be over in seconds. I had to di di mau out. Now. My knees scraped on roots and dead branches as I crawled away on all fours as fast as I could, for the moment, not caring how much racket I made.

Ricky-tick, boy, or you'll be rat food and some zipperhead will be one hundred thousand piasters richer. We were so close to base, I knew I'd only have to hide for a while. The VC wouldn't risk staying here in case the marines charged to the rescue. But no radio to call in the arty. *Phung Hoang* assassination teams were on their own.

The firing stopped. I was only twenty-five yards off the trail and without the M16 that was now the prize possession of a VC. My hand touched a banyan tree. The monsoons had made a hole between the foot-wide roots of the tree. Palm ferns surrounded the hole. I crawled in and pulled leaves over my body, brushing as much rotted vegetation and mud on top as I could reach. I waited.

VC moved slowly through the bush, quiet as wild boars. "*Lai di, gan con ran.*" Come out, Night Snake, a VC said.

Fuck. It was an ambush, and I was the target. The VC were anxious or desperate enough to call out my name in the bush.

"*Gan con ran,*" the soldier said, "we send you Hanoi Hilton. *Lai di.*"

The VC would have to put their sandals on my face to find me. The NVA didn't issue flashlights. I closed my eyes and practiced the slow breathing learned at Benning.

The straps of the nylon-aluminum flak jacket pinched my right side. I was in a fetal position, webbed helmet covering my face. Something crawled into the gap between my camo shirt and pants and slowly made its way toward my balls. Dead branches poked my arms. The bush was alive with muted sounds of VC. They were close. But close was only good with horseshoes. And grenades.

"*O dau, gan con ran*?" Where are you? The ferns next to my head rustled. The thing in my pants bit a chunk out of my crotch. A bayonet poked into the dirt six inches from my arm. The sour-milk smell of VC filled the hole. I held my breath. The bayonet jabs moved away.

In the distance, the 105s restarted their nightly bombardment from the base.

"*Di di mau bay gio,*" a VC barked. Go now. VC moved quickly through the bush. My flak jacket loosened as I let out a long breath and sucked in the decaying earth smell of the Delta.

The voices drifted away, and now I was alone. Alone, unable to move, buried in a hole, and something unknown gnawing on my flesh as it slowly chewed its way closer to the vital part of my crotch.

Once, at Fort Lewis, the engineers were building new officer quarters near our house. I was six and out for a late-afternoon escape from the Colonel. While looking down a black hole dug for drainage, I slipped and fell nearly fifteen feet. Knocked out for minutes. Squirmed to my feet. Headache. Sticky stuff on my face. Smooth round walls. No ladder. Smell of wet cement and piss. Walls close enough to touch without extending my arms. Spiders. Dark. Screams. Hours of screaming. Echoes. Night. Stars. More screams. Tears joining the blood and drips of water pooling around my tennis shoes. Throat rough as a grenade. Voices. Mom. Flashlight. Sobbing. A rope and I was out.

Tight dark places. Major fear. Must keep the tremors from shaking the dirt and leaves that covered me from falling off. Or into my mouth and nose. Eyes closed, I quieted the screams in my head with discipline instilled by the Colonel and the Company. Fuck. Let me out. I'll face a squad of NVA tanks. Just let me out. Slow it down, troop. Try to get why you're quaking in this hole and who put you there. Go to that angry place instead of overwhelming fright.

After an hour of silence from the jungle, I crawled out of the hole, convinced there were questions that needed to be answered. The answers had been building in my mind for months in this shithole country, but I needed one final confirmation from Viper. Maybe I needed to become someone other than Frank Morgan, the Night Snake.

Cherries flew into Da Nang nearly every day in 1970. The Boeing landed, and the doors opened to the steam bath of 'Nam. Sweat began before the new grunts stepped onto the tarmac. And didn't end for a year—unless the trip back to The World was inside a sealed plastic bag or to a hospital for training on how to use a wheelchair. I flew in with the newbies. And a grunt beside me for entertainment. The CIA had already taken my file and trained me to be a "floater," not assigned to any of the Provincial Reconnaissance Units, PRUs, established for terrifying the local populations. My brief was to be a one-man assassination team, answering only to a man nicknamed Viper. His direct boss was Robin Comer, the cowboy honcho of Phoenix. I was intended to be the poster child of Phoenix, leaving my signature countrywide with a silenced 9mm bullet.

Special Ops school at Benning taught me the skills I needed to sneak into bedrooms or hide in jungle ambush. Graduating at the top of the class gave me a ticket to stardom and a bounty on my head. Officially, Phoenix was supposed to use the Rand computer to classify South Vietnamese according to risk levels a, b, c, or d based on intel provided mostly by local agents or Government of South Vietnam authorities. But it didn't always work that way. Phoenix based its philosophy loosely on an old Chinese saying, "To frighten one hundred monkeys, shoot one sleeping monkey in the back of the head." I shot a whole clan of monkeys.

On my first in-country training mission, I accompanied Collingsworth into the basement of a Saigon bicycle shop. We were there to question a suspected VC who had been snitched by an unnamed spy in the Choi Lo neighborhood bureaucracy. Every South Vietnamese man over fifteen was required by law to have an identity card and be fingerprinted to feed the ravenous Rand computer. This man didn't have a card, condemning him to whatever might happen. But it was no mystery. Within minutes, Collingsworth went beyond level-one interrogation techniques and skipped to "jam a hand shovel into the left ear, making sure to penetrate the brain by hearing the sound of skull fragments crunching like you just stepped on a broken Coke bottle." Actually, the law in South Vietnam said any suspected VC could be held for two years without trial, representation, bail, or the ability to question the accuser. Not murdered. Phoenix never cared much about laws or the Geneva Conventions, except the one that said, "Scare the monkeys out of the trees."

Back then, I believed. None of the men and women we greased would soon be invading the beach at La Jolla if we didn't stop them. But they would surely spread the evil plague of Communism to places like Thailand, Laos, and Cambodia. Then, move across the Indian subcontinent and eventually drool on Europe, just a seven-hour flight from the boardwalk of Atlantic City. I knew this because LBJ told me it was so.

In Vinh Lan province, the CIA used an abandoned VC tunnel for interrogations. It was surreal how every one of these chambers in all forty-four provinces was underground and gave even more of a feeling of the Inquisition. The CIA mantra wasn't "Bleed them for Jesus." It was "Kill a Commie for Christ." Innocence didn't play a role. All gooks were the enemy, especially after a smiling five-year-old tossed a grenade from her basket of flowers. Collingsworth started this interrogation by putting the man's hand in a cage full of starved rats captured in the tunnel. He didn't even ask the naked man a single question. When the first hand was stripped of its meat and the bones were licked white as the sand on China Beach, he switched to the other hand and then the man's feet, all the time laughing and indicating that the prisoner's cock and balls would be next. As far as I could tell, the man wasn't asked one question before I left to the squeal of the rats fighting over the last chunk of flesh. Before I reached sunlight, I heard a shot from a Colt pistol. Within seconds, Collingsworth joined me at the surface, gibing me about being a "pussy."

The official method of recruiting locals to snitch on their fellow hamlet citizens was piasters. That didn't mean Phoenix was above other techniques. Blackmail, kidnapping, and terror weren't in the written rules of procedure, if they ever existed, but those routines were more popular than giving money to the monkeys. Snatching a suspected VC's daughter from the schoolyard had a certain elegance that Phoenix bosses appreciated.

Collingsworth was a loser. Over a Tiger beer, he let slip that he had been stranded on the Cuban shore during the Bay of Pigs farce and was lucky that he was able to steal a boat and get back to Miami. Almost all the older operatives in 'Nam had that fiasco in their portfolios. Phoenix liked to force the transfer of SEALs and Green Berets into the program, too. Sleeping most days on a cot inside a base or a hotel room was coveted duty. The nights were spent crawling into bedrooms, not in the mud. If they wanted to keep their jobs, Phoenix teams had a kill quota of fifty Vietnamese per month. That didn't mean the victims had to be VC, just have the right ethnic background and skin color to be tallied.

Not long after we met, Collingsworth was shipped back to The World because of the My Lai massacre. Phoenix was trying to distance itself from that wholesale slaughter of men, women, and children rumored to have resulted from intel Collingsworth provided. And the example. Phoenix operatives invalidated that opinion as "comsymp" propaganda. Communist sympathizer. Just like the misguided efforts of politicians like Senator Eugene McCarthy back home who tried to have Phoenix investigated. Of course, the budgets and actions of Phoenix were part of the "Black Ops" brief. Information was not divulged under the guise of "national security." If Eugene only knew that a fantasy drinking game amongst Phoenix agents was to have the winning hand rewarded with a trip to Minnesota to put a silenced bullet into the traitor's ear. The prize was called a "McCarthy."

Over the first months of detail, I learned that Wilson Bringham was our daddy, using many of the talents he groomed in the Cold War to birth Phoenix in 1967. His major successes were in gathering intel on Soviet missile silo complexes. Many of the strategies we were ordered to carry out were developed in Budapest and East Berlin. Now, Bringham had an office in the annex of the American embassy in Saigon.

* * *

After wasting Liem, I snuck back to base camp from my hidey-hole in the mud, figuring my behavior lately was the reason Viper wanted me dead, though not before Liem fertilized the clay. There must be two motives for the ambush. A politically charged assassination that had to be kept quiet at the cost of a doubting agent had double benefit. It could be that recent demands to see the dossier on my next victim were getting under Viper's slimy skin. It could be questioning the execution of so many sleeping men and women wasn't tolerated. It could be the night I called Viper a "psychopathic serial killer in the same league as Manson." It could be that the untreatable Saigon strain of clap that caused the front of Viper's shorts to have a constant wet spot was decaying his brain as fast as his dick.

Could be the ambush was coincidence. Coincidence in 'Nam was more likely to mean that you or your buddies arrived at the gate from a night enjoying the boonies still able to count to ten on your fingers. Coincidence was if a suspect emerged from the darkness of a Phoenix interrogation center. But that never happened. Besides, the VC knew my name and didn't hesitate to whisper the fact. Maybe a VC counteragent knew about the mission to kill Liem and was trying to cover his tracks and collect the bounty on my head. Viper would know.

The password at the gate was changed every day. That was mostly for the night, since it was clear in daylight that even a filthy white man without insignia on his fatigues was probably not a gook. I didn't know today's, so I hid in the jungle until sunrise before approaching.

Hungry, I craved one of my favorite treats. But thoughts of food were full of land mines. A grunt nicknamed S'more. He had nearly the same color skin as Liem, just a shade darker. His chubby stomach made him look like a dark marshmallow. On Memorial Day, he used C-4 and some napalm requisitioned from the ammo dump to cook us a barbecue of steaks and franks. One of S'more's other talents, beyond brewing the best grilling sauce in 'Nam, was shaping C-4 inside a piece of steel pipe. Plenty of stuff was around to make fireworks for the night's celebration. He mixed stolen food coloring from the PX and a dash of salt and pepper and put the loaded stick into the neck of an empty bottle of Jim Beam. Better than the nightly display from the 155 howitzers. S'more was one of the few black grunts who refused to join the Vietnam chapter of the Panthers or sew a Black Power fist to his fatigues. I guess his brothers were tired of the Oreo cookie metaphor and settled on S'more. He carried a seventy-pound M40 pig machine gun, with bandoleers of ammo, through the bush like it was made of bamboo. On an op outside Cần Thơ, he went into a hootch. With the barrel of his pig, he pushed up the lid of a thatched basket that held a few weeks' supply of rice for a squad of Cong. The VC knew the white devils enjoyed destroying food that might reach their bellies. They left a gift. And pieces of S'more ended up riding a slick back to base.

Agent Orange had killed all the vegetation the bulldozers missed within a quarter mile surrounding the base. I walked on a path I knew wasn't mined, at least not yesterday, and connected with the road to the gate, joining a squad of grunts limping toward the entrance. We were waved through. I didn't have to report in and headed for the Special Ops compound to ask Viper a few questions. Or fit him for a bow tie.

Viper's right hand crept toward the KA-BAR on his belt. His shaved head was as round and smooth as an M26 "wake-up" grenade. Red Man tobacco juice ran from the corner of his death's-head mouth, his teeth brown like a Montagnard hill tribesman. Betel nut brown.

"So, pussy," Viper said, "lost your appetite for cappin' gooks?"

The Gerber fighting knife in my right hand was sharp enough to sever his spine without stopping for a smile.

"You fuckin' pogue assholes just give the orders," I said. "And I ain't greasin' anymore dinks because you fuck-ups tell me to."

"I got my orders," Viper said. "You got yours, Morgan."

Bodies of headless kraits hung from the crooked bamboo beams of the sweltering Phoenix program command hootch, their dead black-and-yellow snake skins limp like baggy prom dresses. The sagging hootch was outside the perimeter of the Special Forces camp in the Mekong Delta, but still inside the firebase. Ho Chi Minh watched our dance from a stained poster on the bamboo wall. Blackened ears were pinned to the sides of Uncle Ho's head. A nail on one of the banyan support posts held a broken stethoscope and a dirty, white operating room mask.

"Orders?" I asked. "You fuckin' spooks don't even have names. It's just a game with you gung-ho Phoenix motherfuckers. Where'd you get the intel that Liem was VC?" The chinstrap on my webbed helmet chafed my neck. I loosened the leather. "Crank a little extra juice during Bell Telephone Hour? Some peasant's nuts fryin' while you called his number on your field phone?

Did he squeal loud enough for you to get your rocks off, Viper? Or whatever your fuckin' name is."

The dirt on the hootch floor scraped under my bush boots as I slid closer for a strike to Viper's throat. A jagged piece of a broken, pitted mirror was nailed to a post behind Viper. Morning humidity made the greasepaint on my face streak. An Indian in from a night of massacre in the bush. Sweat caused my camouflage fatigues to cling like Saran Wrap. The smell in the hootch was a mix of filthy armpit and crotch, along with the ever-present jungle decay. And rotting flesh.

"Now I get it, Morgan," Viper said. "You fell for that slant bitch. You a double veteran now? Did she call you 'sweet papa-san' while you fucked her? Or did she save all the nice-nice for when you zapped her?"

The Gerber stopped a centimeter from Viper's throat. My left hand pinned Viper's KA-BAR tight to his side. Gray chest hair tickled my wrist from the open neck of Viper's Hawaiian shirt. Small drops of blood pooled on the blade of the knife.

"Hear about the lieutenant in Charlie Company who got fragged while he was takin' a shit last week?" I asked. "Blew his balls through the latrine roof and into a banyan tree, still in one piece. The vultures had a number one meal. Now that's a set of nuts. You think yours are that big, Viper?"

"Fuck," Viper said, "you ain't gonna wax me. You'd spend your days back in The World at Leavenworth. Always knew you didn't have the guts to hump it over here."

"Maybe you're right," I said. "Damn straight I'm not gonna ice another woman because you psychos order it. Seein' your bald head roll across this hootch might be the R&R I need."

"Drop the knife and I won't rat you out to Comer," Viper said. "You need to di di mau to China Beach. Knock some white meat off a few doughnut dollies." It would take a crowbar to pry the shit-eating smile off Viper's face.

I jammed my knee between Viper's legs harder. Viper stiffened as if he'd taken a hit in the back from a VC sniper. The heels of his unlaced tennis shoes lifted off the red dirt. I slid the Gerber a centimeter right. Fresh blood surged across the blade like the gentle waves at Au Tau Island.

The field radio squawked. "Heavy incoming at LZ 39. Charlie's murdering us. Dust-off now. Got casualties. Get them Jolly Green's here. *Now.*"

Grunts were caught in a firefight in Bravo sector. The muffled rat-a-tat of AK-47s, M16s, and exploding Soviet-made pineapple grenades was the background music. On the spool table next to the field radio, Viper's transistor crackled with Jimi Hendrix singing "All Along the Watchtower," courtesy of Armed Forces Radio, Saigon.

"Need some intel from you before I make up my mind whether to feed your nuts to the rats," I said. "Who told you Liem was VC? And you better not say it was those ARVN assholes. Last week they raped and butchered the mama-san who did the laundry for Alpha squad. The ARVN security goons claimed she was washin' the secrets out of A squad's maggoty shorts."

Behind Viper, a yellowed map of the Mekong was dotted with red pins. Each one the obituary notice for an assassinated supposed VC sympathizer. A spider web connected the dots in the southeast quadrant.

The sweet smell of Laotian green drifted through the cracks in the bamboo walls, mixed with the acrid smell of shit burning in kerosene. Morning in Vietnam. A joint with the cowboy coffee. Fill your lungs with weed and black smoke from the torched two-holer. Pick the grounds out of your teeth with a stem from the dope. If the weed didn't give the right charge, drop a white for a kick of adrenaline. Groove to the sound of the Doors on the Akai reel-to-reel tape deck while you check if you scored a chocolate pudding in the C-ration breakfast. Get pumped for another day of blood. Or boredom.

"What would you do if I told you, Morgan?" Viper asked. "Grease 'em? You're a professional. Where'd this conscience bullshit come from? Why give a shit about some dink cunt?" The stubble of Viper's beard rubbed against the top of my knuckles. When he swallowed, I could feel his Adam's apple move above the Gerber blade. Viper's breath was a mix of chew and rot. The ugly, insane smile still bent his lips. I knew Viper would welcome death in this killing field as much as me. Fear wouldn't make him talk.

"Conscience?" I asked. "The story I heard was that you waxed a whole family of gooks with a garrote, including the little girl who woke to her mama-san's last breath. A LURP patrol found you wandering in the bush with her scalp on your ammo belt, muttering about 'eyeballs in the trees.' They say you're crazier than Charles Manson. That's why you're stuck in this hellhole. Nobody wants your disease. Perfect for Phoenix."

"But now I don't have to do the killing," Viper laughed. "I get naive cocksuckers like you to do it for me. I just write the death warrants. You get the nightmares."

"You and Comer made me what I am," I said. "Payback's a bitch." I moved closer. My nose touched Viper's. "Now we're gonna quit rappin' and you're gonna tell me who ratted Liem. Or I'll liberate your dickface head from your body." The hand on the Gerber tightened enough to start another fresh flow of blood. "You'll be diddy boppin' around this hootch like one of them mangy chickens the villagers decap."

The bamboo hut creaked in the morning sun. Dust motes floated in the humid air from the drying thatched-palm roof. A streak of light from the open window settled on Viper's Colt semiautomatic pistol. The Colt hung in its leather holster from the back of a rattan chair under a blowup of Ann-Margret dancing in a pink miniskirt and white go-go boots. Bob Hope licked his lips in the background.

"If you put the blade down," Viper said, "I'll tell you. Not because I'm wetting myself 'cause of a candyass chickenshit like you. But I heard something interesting about your dead girlfriend. Maybe you smoked the wrong bitch."

Everywhere I looked in 'Nam was green. Green jungle. Green elephant grass. Green fatigues. Green fungus from the rot between my toes. Green mold on the tuna in my C-rations. Gangrene. Except when the clay ran red with blood. Like the red that flooded my eyes.

A twist of my left hand on Viper's wrist caused the joint to pop. The sound a white phosphorous smoke grenade made when it marked the LZ for the Hueys. "Fuck, boy," Viper said. "I said we can talk this over." The shit-eating grin vanished from his face. "I'm havin' too much fun to be medevaced to the Land of the Big PX with a pissant broken arm."

"If you can figure a way to tell the truth once in your fucked-up life," I said, "I'll let you go. First, I gotta relieve you of your KA-BAR and that Beretta I feel in your pocket. You gonna bullshit me?"

"Nawww, Morgan," Viper said. "Maybe I'll confess all my sins. But I don't think confession will keep either of us from roasting in a napalm hell."

Viper tried to nod his head but the Gerber at his throat made it a bad idea.

"I'll be a good little scout," he said.

The 9mm Beretta Tomcat fit easily into the palm of my left hand, the silver handle cool to the touch and moist from Viper's sweat. I tossed the dainty pistol and the KA-BAR into the corner next to a pile of dog-eared *Playboy* magazines.

"That cute little gun fit well in your purse, Viper?" I asked. "Down on the deck, hands on your knees." I used the tip of the Gerber to prod Viper to the dirt floor. "You might need a Band-Aid for that cut on your neck. Should leave a nice scar you can tell lies about."

Viper used the corner of his shirt to dab at the blood that dripped onto his hairy chest. On his left hand, a bone ring carved from a dead VC skull said he was married to the dark side. The sun-bleached ring was a badge of honor worn by the spooks in the Phoenix program.

"Now that we're cozy," I said, "tell me about Liem." Broken pieces of the rattan chair poked through the ass of my camo pants. Viper squirmed below me. The Gerber was aimed at Viper's left eye. A cloud of jungle steam lazed through the open windows and door. Armed Forces Radio played "Sympathy for the Devil." Mick Jagger's gravel voice was backed by static and the distant *thump, thump* of slicks ferrying grunts to the boonies. The field radio was silent.

"Have you heard about the new local ARVN Special Branch commander?" Viper asked. I shook my head no. "Name of Colonel Hoang. Badass motherfucker. Smile like a cobra. Seems he took a likin' to your girlfriend. Rumor has it she wouldn't put out."

"So you send me to grease her?" The Gerber nicked the blond hair on Viper's eyebrow. "Because she wouldn't fuck? I oughta pop your eyeball in the dirt, you sorry piece of shit." A drop of blood fell into Viper's eye. He didn't blink, he smiled. "Was it Hoang's men who wasted Thieu and his squad? I'll bet you didn't figure on seeing me again."

"Hey, Morgan, you hear about the bitches in Dogpatch outside the gate to Firebase Echo? They stick razor blades up their holes so stupid grunts can go stateside without their luggage. Two greenbacks, couple a humps, and they're callin' you Sheila."

"You practicing some of that psy ops shit they sling at Benning?" I asked. "Spit in the interrogator's face? Show him you're hung like a water buffalo?

How many dinks have you had me ice? Twenty? Thirty? Lost count? You think I give a shit that your skin ain't yellow and I won't carve that smirk off your turd-eating face?" My right hand held the Hush Puppy I used to kill Liem. The silencer was pointed at Viper's balls. "What about Hoang?"

"I'm thrilled you stopped by this morning, Morgan. It was stacking up as just another boring day in paradise."

"Hoang, shit head."

"A worldly man like you knows the pursuit of pussy has lots of twists. Seems Hoang's blue balls pissed him off. Told us Liem was the local VC cadre chief, in charge of finishin' the tunnels to the Ho Chi Minh Trail and supplying the VC with rice and bullets. But, surprise. Yesterday, just after you left to smoke her, a patrol from Bravo Company captured the command tunnel for this sector. Papers they grabbed said the real number one was Jin Nguyen, a barber and surgeon in Vu Thi, ten klicks down the road. Gotta think old Colonel Hoang was shittin' us."

"You guys never checked Hoang's intel on Liem?"

"The watchword around here is *cooperation*. Now, how would it look if we questioned info that came from the very top papa-san? We're tryin' hard to have a relationship built on trust."

The crooked smile never left Viper's face. I figured he didn't believe I'd kill him. Maybe fuck him up a little. Stall until somebody came to the rescue. Viper forgot that everyone avoided this hootch like it was surrounded with claymores. Grunts called the mines with their little green legs "toe poppers," and a visit to the Phoenix hootch could mean a future missing a lot more than a few toes. The stench of death from the palm fronds woven in the roof of Viper's hut poisoned anyone who passed. No one dropped by to rap uninvited.

"Heard anything about Liem before Hoang?"

"Nope."

"I thought the policy was that no one got capped until you had backup evidence."

"Boy, you're shittin' in the wrong jungle. Can't you see we're losin' this police action? Just the scent of VC and you're rat food."

"So now it's policy to wax anybody who doesn't smell right?"

"Don't it make you proud to be an American?" Viper asked. "Hey, Morgan. Came up with the best scam yet to get free pussy. Wanna join in? See that busted stethoscope on the nail by Ann-Margret? Got it from a Second Battalion medic. Put the mask on, hang the scope around your neck, and go into a vil. Tell the gooks you're a doctor on a mercy mission. The dink women line up for their exams. Get their legs spread and jam it in. Boom-boom time. What're they gonna do? Scream? All you gotta do is say '*Bac-si, bac-si,*' Vietnamese for doctor, and the bitches come runnin'."

"Shut the fuck up." The Hush Puppy bucked in my right hand as it jammed into Viper's balls. A sharp hiss came from his mouth, but the smile stayed. "I only wanna hear about Hoang. Where's he headquartered?"

"Why should I tell you? You gonna grease him, too? That would be against United States Military Law and the Geneva Conventions. And would certainly fuck up LBJ's Hearts and Minds policy. Besides, I hear you're at your best killing gook women in their beds."

The sound of the Doors singing, "Come on, baby, light my fire," muffled the quiet *thhuupp* of the Hush Puppy. The sound-suppressed bullet missed Viper's balls by a quarter inch and slammed into the dirt behind him. He jumped back. The Gerber stayed pressed against Viper's eyebrow. The smile was gone.

Viper swept his right leg at my feet. At the same time, he grabbed the arm that held the Hush Puppy, rolling left and pushing the pistol toward the thatched roof. The Gerber opened a six-inch cut across Viper's forehead. I jerked my arm away and let him go. As he crawled to his feet, wiping the stream of blood from his eyes, I shot him in the thigh. Viper fell backward against the bamboo wall, ripping off a VISIT GAY, HISTORIC VIETNAM poster. The poster showed a handsome Vietnamese couple strolling down a sunny boulevard in front of a cathedral in Saigon. The woman carried a yellow umbrella. Both of the happy citizens smiled with straight, white teeth.

"You son of a bitch," Viper hissed. He used both hands to try to slow the bleeding. "You're gonna spend the rest of your short life in the stockade at Long Binh. Until they hang you."

"Now why would that be? I came in here this morning and found you dead. Obviously you were tortured before you died. I hear there's a bounty on you Phoenix pricks. Just like the SOG boys. Some lucky Charlie just bought himself a year's supply of rice. Took your ring finger with the skull on it, since you spooks don't wear dog tags." I wiped the blade of the Gerber on my camo pants. The Hush Puppy was pointed between Viper's eyes. "Hey, what the fuck. Seems Langley's got an endless supply of dirtballs like you. You won't even be missed."

Killing came easier to me than handling the constant dysentery. The backside of my fatigues was always stained black from the sweat-and-shit cocktail that seeped from my ass. Shooting Viper would be the one murder that was absolutely right. His face wouldn't be in the jury of victims that condemned me in the nightly dreams. But I'd think of his dead, smiling face when the green shit dripped into my pants.

"Fuck, that hurts," Viper said. The blood from his forehead fell onto the hands that clutched the gunshot wound. A cockroach scurried past his foot.

"If we rap for a couple days, the maggots will start eating the infection in your leg. That's nature's healing process at work. But you're not gonna be around to feel it, Viper. The maggots don't care if the host is alive or dead. You're gonna be dead unless you tell me more about Hoang."

A puddle of Viper's blood turned black when it mixed with the clay floor. Viper squeezed his wound with both hands and tried to smile. His fingers made squishing sounds as they tightened.

"He holes up in an old villa at the abandoned rubber plantation outside Vin Khe. His office is downtown. It's about twenty klicks southeast. He's got a squad of ARVN Rangers protecting him. Uses the wine cellar to torture the locals. I heard he's even better than you with a knife."

The soft jacket bullet went into Viper's head between the eyes and sloshed around in his brain, ripping pieces into stew. Behind Viper's mangled head, a scorpion dashed for a new hidey-hole.

No one saw me go into the hootch. No one saw me leave. Barry McGuire sang "Eve of Destruction" as I went out the door and blended into the jungle, Viper's ring finger in my pocket. That night, I visited Colonel Hoang.

The slit in the bargirl's short skirt ran from above her knee to her purple panties. A brown and black bruise tattooed her thigh. Breasts the size of M26 grenades peeked from the scoop of her yellow-and-green flowered dress. Pink makeup failed to cover the mortar craters that pocked the bargirl's face and stained the tips of the black hair that hung to her bare shoulders. The dark-red lipstick on her mouth was thick and smeared.

"Good ruck to you, GI," the bargirl whispered in my ear for the hundredth time in the last hour. Her name was Dom. "Drink." Dom raised her glass and looked across the Formica tables at the bartender.

On the stage, a woman in a black leotard and a white T-shirt jammed with three Vietnamese men in jeans. They were practicing for the night's stage show. If I closed my eyes, the band could be the Beatles. "Ruv, ruv me do, you know I ruv you." The woman's pageboy haircut and voice was pure Paul McCartney.

The sign above the thatched canopy outside the front door read HOLLEYWOOD. Across the busy street, shirtless men in shorts patched the walls of an old French building that used to be headquarters for the local colonialist government. Vin Khe had been shelled for three days during the Tet Offensive, and the building had craters that gaped above the surrounding banana trees. The three-story building was the daytime home to Colonel Hoang.

This afternoon, the biggest danger to me was the MPs. Phoenix agents didn't carry military ID or dog tags. Dom was on my lap and I sat on a vinyl chair against the wall in the shadows of Holleywood. If the military police walked in, I hoped I looked like any other horny bush rat in from the boonies, hunting for beer and pussy.

At least my fatigues were clean. After the ambush, it took five piasters in a village two klicks outside Vin Khe, and a toothless mama-san washed my uniform and gave me a bath. The Hush Puppy and the fighting knife sat next to a bar of soap a foot from my hand while she scrubbed my back. Greasepaint and mud made the bathwater black. The red tint came from the leech wounds and gook sores that dotted my legs.

From the chair, I had a clear view of Hoang's home and office. Two ARVN soldiers stood at attention alongside a wrought-iron gate, M16s across their chests. Jeeps carried uniformed soldiers, both Vietnamese and American, into the compound after a brief ID check. Sandbags were piled twenty high against the parts of the wall without mortar holes.

The street between Holleywood and the building was busy with smoking motorcycles, peasants in pajamas, bicycles, young women in colorful ao dais, and merchants hawking chickens and snakes. Kids chased each other through the crowd. Carts, pulled by oxen or water buffaloes, fought for a place on the road with Citroens, trucks, and jeeps, while the motorcycles zipped through the traffic with mechanical whines. A thirty-foot red billboard stood to the right of Hoang's building. COCA-COLA was written in English and Vietnamese in white letters. Exhaust fumes mixed with the smell of overripe fruit and meat, sewage, and piles of steaming garbage. Honking horns, motorcycles without mufflers, and people cursing echoed through Holleywood's open doors.

"You rike fucky-suck?" Dom asked, her tongue in my ear. Dom rolled her hips and put my hand in her crotch. "Dom make number one boom boom with GI sodjer."

"Maybe later, Dom," I said. It had been at least thirty seconds since my last refusal. The Smith & Wesson Mark 9mm in my left pocket rubbed against a leech bite. I moved the pistol so the muzzle pointed toward the silver ball chandelier that hung from the ceiling. The six-inch-long silencer was stuffed in the breast pocket of my fatigues next to the garrote.

"You *ba de*? Nancy boy?" Dom asked. Dom jerked away. I might be infectious.

"No, Dom," I said. "Just a little tired. Here's a hundred p. Go get that drink you ordered."

Dom took the money and kissed me on the cheek. "*Cam on*, sodjer," she said. Her black stiletto heels tapped on the broken linoleum as she swayed toward the bar.

A staff jeep flying Democratic Republic of Vietnam flags from the antennas pulled to the gate of Colonel Hoang's headquarters. The two guards saluted and opened the gates without inspecting IDs. In the back of the jeep, an ARVN general with braids on both shoulders stared straight ahead through his gold-framed sunglasses.

My jacket was assassin. Killer on command. Didn't think about whose head got the specially designed Super Val subsonic cartridge blasted into their skull. It didn't matter. The enemy was behind every bush, in every hootch, and riding every bicycle in 'Nam. Even the South Vietnamese couldn't sort it out. The head of the Saigon government, Nguyen Cao Ky, thought the commander of I Corps, General Thi, was plotting a coup. Ky sent troops to Da Nang to liberate the city from the Viet Cong. While US Marines fought the VC outside Da Nang on Hill 327, dying to save the country from godless Communism, Ky's fighter planes strafed the city in an attempt to kill Thi and his loyal ARVN troops. The South Vietnamese soldiers fought each other more effectively than they did the Viet Cong. Warlords after a bigger piece of the turf. Da Nang wasn't the only place. My gut told me that Colonel Hoang was somehow doing the same and Liem was one of the victims.

Dom sat a Tiger beer on the table in front of me and sipped her Coke masquerading as bourbon. If all the booze I paid for had been real, Dom would be shooting her fish ball lunch on the linoleum. Instead, she twirled the little red umbrella that floated in her glass.

The beer washed down two more Dexedrine tablets from my pocket. One morning, after coming back to base still high from a handful of Dex and a successful op, I looked into my reflection next to the field shower. The mirror was a pie plate nailed to a bamboo post. My dull, blue eyes were covered in a sheet of glass that stared back at me. A tic threatened to pop out my bulging eyeballs. Cheeks writhed like they were full of baby snakes. I looked down a tunnel filled with a kaleidoscope of black-haired heads. A hollow thousand-yard stare. At my hootch, I used the fighting knife to shave a ball of opium. Shaking hands made it hard to light the pipe. It took two bowls to come down.

The uppers made the scabs on my legs itch. I used the handle of the Gerber fighting knife strapped to my calf to scratch.

"Why you watch *gia loc*?" Dom asked. House. "You no rike Dom?" She put her arm around my back.

"Looking for buddies," I said. "Sure, I like you." I glanced at Dom and played with the bone ring from Viper's finger in my pocket.

"Good ruck to you, GI," Dom said. She raised her Coke in a toast. A blob of eyeliner made the lashes on her right eye form a tar ball of black hair. One of her front teeth was brown, and steel glittered from her molars.

Two drunk marines stumbled into Holleywood, arms draped on the other's shoulders. A table and chair crashed to the floor as they made their way to the bar.

"Semper fi, comrade," one of the marines said to the bartender. He saluted without his hand getting anywhere near his forehead. "Gimme one a' them fuckin' bottles of piss you gooks call beer." He slapped his hand on the wooden bar.

"Make that two buffalo pisses, Uncle Ho. Ricky-ticky," the other marine said. He leaned both elbows on the bar, legs wobbling like he had run a marathon.

Time to di di mau. I came into Holleywood for the view and the quiet. Two rowdy jarheads and the MPs wouldn't be far behind. I couldn't risk it. I handed Dom another 100 p and stood to leave.

"No reave, sodjer," Dom said. "Go back room good boom boom." She pulled on the sleeve of my fatigues.

"Gotta split," I said. "Take the money and buy yourself another drink." I patted the back of Dom's hand and started toward the door.

"Hey, Cummings," one of the marines said. His finger was pointed in my direction. "Lookee over there. A boonie rat turnin' down pussy. Now ain't that just like them army girls. What unit you with, young lady, the asshole First? The bend-over Butt-allion?" He slapped his greens with his palm.

"Naw, Barbosa," the other marine said. "When real fightin' men come around, he's gotta turn tail and run home to Mommy." He drained the

Tiger in one long swallow and put it gently on the bar. "Uh-oh, Cummings. I think he's gettin' a blue veiner looking at two of America's proud and brave."

Dom strolled across the pitted floor to the marines, hands pushing up her breasts. The Beatles sang, "She ruvs me, yaa, yaa, yaa."

"Now here's a gook gash with good taste," Cummings said. He pulled Dom to his chest and nuzzled her hair, not her mouth. Barbosa ordered another beer and threw me a kiss. "Bye, sweetie," he said.

Didn't matter if the bars were named Holleywood, Sin City, or Pussey Galores, they were all the same. Drunken, horny grunts trying to forget, even for a second as short as it took to leave their buddy's white brain matter on their filthy fatigues. Ready to fight the evil blooming in their chests.

A bar in Cần Thơ. Three boonie rats just in from the bush. "Jenkins was the best," one grunt said. "The best LT we ever had. Not sayin' much with all the other baby fuckheads we got before."

Another said, "Aw, fuck. Just one more a' them West Point faggots. Thought his spit-shine shit didn't stink till that sniper tore off the back a' his head. Beggin' for someone named Claire. Fuckin' asshole."

A few minutes of arguing and toasting the lost friends before the fight. From across the room, I watched the first marine break his beer glass on the counter and try to rip out the eyes of his buddy. Seconds and the view in the bar was of flying chairs and fists. The way we honored our dead. Before the MPs arrived to stop the wake, I di di'ed.

Outside, the street was still alive with traffic and people. I had another few hours to kill before dark and no seconds to waste teaching drunk marines good manners. Time to do a walk-around of Hoang's place.

On the hard-packed street, two small boys ran by. Flip-flop sandals slapped the clay. Smudges of dirt covered their skin and torn shorts. One of the boys stopped and turned back to me, a bamboo stick in his hand. He pointed it at my head and shot. I raised my finger and shot back. The boy fell to the ground laughing. I helped him up and gave him a 25 p coin. "*Cam on*, buddy boy," the boy said.

Behind the building, a grove of scarred palm trees and poinsettia bushes hid my recon. The French shutters on the walls of the building were open, and ceiling fans pushed the dense air around. A parade of US and ARVN soldiers, along with a few businessmen, passed the windows. Sun-faded bullet holes made the walls look like saltine crackers.

Mosquitoes rose from puddles below the palm trees and bit my face. Another way 'Nam sucked my blood. In-country. The World. Once I heard a raggedy-ass, two-tour grunt returning from a week-long bush patrol say he "couldn't find The World on any fuckin' map" he'd seen lately. Besides, he'd "been in-country all day." 'Nam was the reality. The military ordered the troops to bring in body counts. If it used to walk or breathe and was Vietnamese, it was VC. Count 'em. My talent was to sneak up on VC and jumble their brains, a useful skill when I got back to The World. The CIA could collect on their training by sending me to other places where our way of life was threatened. Maybe sail to Cuba for another shot at Fidel. Or his wife.

A Vietnamese man with one arm and one leg used a bamboo crutch to walk down the alley behind Hoang's building. A pair of khaki shorts went to the thigh and a ripped tank top hung past his waist. He kicked off the sandal on his remaining foot and sat in the shade of the wall facing me. The man started to count the change in a dented metal cup in his left hand. It wouldn't be long before he spotted me.

I didn't want to grease him. I moved further into the bushes.

The man took a package of Tip Top tobacco out of his pocket. With his one hand, he rolled a smoke and lit it, leaning back against the wall and closing his eyes. Could be he lost his limbs to a "Bouncing Betty" land mine. The VC ones that sent shrapnel flying upward and made you a few legs lighter. Bouncing Betties littered the trails and roads of the Delta. Or maybe he stepped on a coconut shell loaded with gunpowder and holding live cartridges that ripped off his leg and severed his arm. Hell, it could have been a thousand ways. *Innocent* wasn't in the vocabulary of 'Nam. Bloody limbs were a mainstay in the diet of a Vietnamese rat.

The rain started. Not the drizzle I saw in my hometown of Seattle. Real fucking rain. The kind that drove you into the ground like a tent peg. The kind that didn't make a little pitter-patter noise, but roared like you were standing inside Snoqualmie Falls. There were no drops. Just a million rivers that made it impossible to see if the one-legged man was still against the wall across the alley. I di di maued from my hiding spot to a restaurant I had seen on A Do Road.

During my carp and rice dinner, I kept Colonel Hoang's face in my mind. The afternoon's recon had provided a picture of a stocky man with a mustache and shaved sidewalls who smoked a cigar and constantly scratched his jaw. A streak of pink skin showed through his black hair where a bullet had grazed his skull. Hoang smiled with teeth so perfect they had to be false. His visitors treated him like the conquering warlord he was, bowing in and out of his office. I had to blend in for the next four or five hours and hope Hoang stayed at the office during the monsoon.

* * *

The ARVN guards at the back of Hoang's building were huddled out of the rain under the porch by a louvered door. I had jumped the wall an hour ago and watched them smoke and laugh. I crouched behind a cement and marble fountain that must have once held a cherub spouting water. Now the cherub was headless and pitted with bullet holes, a bent copper pipe sticking six inches above the shoulders of the statue.

Lights flickered through the slats of the windows. Brief shadows made me guess that Hoang was somewhere on the third floor, in bed at 2 a.m. I made a final check of the Hush Puppy, knife, and garrote and crawled through the mud to a corner window. The Gerber easily popped the latch. Any sound was muffled by the rain that had long ago soaked through to my skin.

A formal dining room had everything but chairs to sit in around the twenty-five-foot-long table. The tricolors of the Democratic Republic of Vietnam covered the wall on the left, and across the buckling mahogany tiles, an open double door led to a hallway lit by wall lamps. The minutes passed, and I got used to the dim light. Framed oil portraits of Vietnamese in military uniform appeared between the windows. The smell of wet, soggy clay and mildew filled the building. In the corner, steady drops from a leak spattered onto the floor.

At the double door, I watched as a guard made his rounds, disappearing up the winding staircase. He carried an M16. A Colt semiautomatic hung from the guard's polished leather holster. I followed him, making sure my boots didn't squish on the marble stairs, Hush Puppy in my right hand.

The guard went down the second-floor hall. I climbed the stairs to the third. A long tapestry ran the length of the hall. Yellowed bell shades covered the few lights that burned. Alcoves held gold-painted Buddhas, candles, and small flower vases.

The handle on the third door to the left turned without a click. I stepped inside the room that I figured held the sleeping Hoang.

In the corner, a table lamp with a flowered shade gave muted light to the bedroom. Next to a window cracked open a few inches, a man slept in a canopied bed. The mosquito netting was curled in a ball high on the frame, not draped over the four-poster. A gold-plated Beretta dangled from the back of a wooden chair by a holster filled with 9mm caliber ammo, and a colonel's uniform was hung over a mannequin that stood on a metal leg. On the bedside table, a mug with a pair of dentures sat next to a stack of files and reading glasses.

I slid across the room and pinched Hoang's nose. When he opened his mouth, I shoved in one of his freshly cleaned black socks from beside his polished brogues, grabbed the Hush Puppy, and shot him in the hand. My arm barely felt the buck of the pistol. The bullet went through the flesh and lodged in his satin pillow with a *phhffupp*.

Colonel Hoang opened his eyes and tried to sit up, but the Hush Puppy pressed to his forehead wouldn't let him. Grunting sounds came from his mouth. He tried to grab the bleeding hand that flopped on the red-stained pillow.

"Do you understand that I'm serious, Colonel?" I asked, my lips six inches from his ear. "Nod your head yes and quit squirming, or the next slug goes into your brain."

Maybe it was the Dexedrine, but everything in the room was crystal clear. No chatter cluttered my head. No bodies mocked me from behind my eyelids. No doubts leeched my soul. I was a professional trained to "terminate with extreme prejudice." Another night at the office, but I didn't want Hoang to know he only had a few minutes to live.

Hoang nodded his head up and down. His eyelids were opened wide enough to disappear into his skull. The bleeding hand laid still, a dime-size hole in the middle of the palm.

"A few days ago, outside Vinh Doc, I had to shoot a dog," I said. "Felt bad. But it only lasted a few heartbeats. Do you think I'll feel any worse after I grease you?" I moved the Hush Puppy from his forehead to his balls and shoved hard. "Answer me." The end of the pistol's barrel stopped at Hoang's tailbone. First rule of interrogation. Make 'em know who's in charge.

Hoang bobbed his head side-to-side and moaned.

"*Im lang*," I said. Quiet.

Hoang's legs and good arm were pinned to the bed by the weight of my body on the thin blanket. I took out the Gerber fighting knife and held it in front of his eyes. The light from the lamp reflected off the sharpened blade, and the knife at Hoang's ear nicked a lobe so Hoang would feel the blood drip.

"Back at my hootch," I said, "I've got a string of ears hanging from the rafter like cloves of garlic. Twenty-three of the black beauties. One for every gook I've wasted." Telling this lie wouldn't mean anything to Hoang's next incarnation. "If you don't want yours to make twenty-four, you better tell me the truth. Okay, papa-san?"

Hoang's chin touched his hairless chest when he moved it up and down.

"Now that we're buddies," I said, "I'm gonna take the sock out of your mouth. If you make any loud noises, your balls will say hello to your asshole. Got it?"

Hoang nodded again.

The Gerber slid back in its sheath. I pulled the sock from Hoang's mouth and grabbed a handful of his greasy hair.

"I was sent to kill a woman named Liem," I said. "You know her?"

"No," Colonel Hoang said.

"I don't have time for this shit," I said. "I'll give you one more chance. Do you know Liem?"

"No."

Hoang's leg jumped when I shot him in the thigh. My hand was over his mouth and nose, pressing his head into the pillow. Hoang wouldn't bleed to death. It was only a flesh wound. The Hush Puppy was back at his balls.

"Last chance, Colonel," I said. I took my hand away from his mouth and gripped an ear. "So far, I haven't done much damage. But that's gonna change in a flash. Who's Liem?" Blood smeared my finger as I squeezed the knife wound.

"She's Jimmy Ky's *ba giao*," Hoang said. Mistress. Hoang closed his eyes and sucked air between his toothless gums. "Vice President Ky's son."

"Why have her killed?" I asked. "Ky's got lots of mama-sans around."

"Ky wanted bigger *hoi lo*," Hoang said. Bribe. "No more money left in *den cho*." Black market. "Americans taking all profit. How much you want, long nose?"

"But why kill Liem?"

"I not know. Ky say she VC. Maybe trade. More of the *den cho* for cadre leader."

"You had Liem killed for no reason other than to keep the *hoi lo* coming?"

"Americans taught us well."

"Was Liem VC?"

"Not know. Not matter."

"Did you have us ambushed?"

"*Vang*," Yes. "But Viper said okay."

"*Nay*?" Why?

"Said you getting chickenshit. Not trust you."

The end of the silencer scraped on Hoang's teeth as I jammed the muzzle six inches into his mouth, the *phhffupp* sound muffled by his tongue when I pulled the trigger. Hoang's eyes were open in death. His legs jerked twice, and his body relaxed.

The room filled with the shit smell that was a constant in the ritual of assassination. Except Liem.

The sheet on Hoang's four-poster hung over the edge, almost touching the crimson rug. I bunched the corner of the sheet into a ball and took the Zippo lighter out of my pocket. Every boonie rat in 'Nam carried a Zippo. If you couldn't set a bamboo hootch on fire with tracer rounds, the Zippo came in handy. I lit the sheets and went quietly out the door.

On the ground floor, voices came from a back room. Cigarette smoke drifted down the hall. I stayed close to the stucco walls, the Hush Puppy pointed toward the voices. The wet fatigues and Dexedrine caused my teeth to chatter. In the meeting room, the window was still ajar. I shoved the pistol into my webbed belt and climbed through. As my feet hit the mud, the rain increased. Maybe it would put out the flames that leaped from Hoang's bedroom window before the building burned into the clay.

The deuce and a half hit every pothole and mortar crater in the road between Vin Khe and Bien Ha. Springs on the truck chassis were MIA. Uncle Sam didn't splurge on the comfort of grunts. That was saved for officers who ate crème de menthe–topped ice cream on tables covered with white linen and china on glossy sampans anchored in the Son Sai Gon River.

A soldier sat next to me on the plywood that tried to pass as a seat, fondling an M26 grenade.

"Hey, man," the grunt said, "what's it like out in the bush?"

Clean uniform, polished M16, short hair, wide-open eyes, stiff body, and the quiver in his voice marked him as a cherry. He didn't have the Indian hunter, slew-eyed, unshaven, exhausted, "I've been in beaucoup hell" look of a 'Nam boonie rat. It took a few days to blend in.

"Keep your head down and you'll be okay," I said. "Stay close to the medic just in case. Make sure he's your buddy." I leaned back against the steel walls and shook my head from side to side. Fuckin' dumbass cherry questions.

My beard was years and thirty-four murders ahead of the soldier's smooth cheeks. I scratched a jaw that was covered in a layer of Delta mud. Sweat coated my body like rifle oil on an ArmaLite. The jarring of the deuce and a half made me slouch forward again or risk back injury from the steel sidewalls of the bouncing truck. Back injuries weren't a ticket back to The World.

Miles of rice paddies stretched to the horizon. Occasional islands of palm trees and thickets dotted with hootches were all that broke up the landscape. The road was busy with convoys and peasants in dirty pajamas and sandals carrying thatched baskets on their heads. Bicycles and motorcycles slalomed between M48 Patton tanks and M113 armored cavalry assault vehicles. Chieu hoi leaflets fell from the sky through the window of an army 0-1 single-engine Cessna out for a day of VC spotting and propaganda.

"You seen any action?" the cherry asked. His teeth were obscenely white. Not the yellow that came from months of C-ration Camels and toothpaste that went unopened.

My boots were caked in Delta clay the color of ripe pomegranates. I rubbed the bush boots against a green rivet in the truck bed that had shaken loose and stuck up two inches. The red mud came off in wads that seeped to the bed like fresh turds.

"Action?" I asked. "This ain't *The Green Berets*, and I ain't John Wayne. Don't be so anxious to get your dick in the paddies, soldier. The leeches don't give a shit if you're an FNG, cowboy."

A fucking new guy on his way to the Great Adventure. An innocent in the land of the insane. Grunts dying to take the same festering rice paddy they took yesterday while snipers picked them off one by one. Dead buddies that resulted in the slaughter of women and children. Agent Orange making lush jungle trees stick characters.

"Sorry," the FNG said. "I've only been in-country a couple days. Goin' to help fill out a Second Battalion squad at Bien Ha. I can't make sense of anything. The army recruiter said I'd be a clerk-typist." His chin fell to his chest. The quiver in his voice infected his whole body. Or maybe it was the jiggle of the springless deuce and a half and this pothole of a country.

Comforting the cherry would make me feel like a phony-ass, oily undertaker. Worse even. A medic in the bush telling a grunt with his shredded intestines in his hands that he'd live to see his sweetheart.

But this cherry had dimples. Round, perfect, concave ones in the middle of both cheeks. My grade-school nickname was Dimples. The girls loved to tease me about them. If there wasn't a beard covered by mud on my face, you could see them now.

"Forget what your momma told you," I said. "There ain't no rules over here. You'll be lucky to have clean underwear once a month. Beat your meat every chance you get. Goin' blind might be a blessing. Keep the pencil and paper in your supplementals and write home as much as Sir Charles lets you. Mail call is the only lifeline you can trust. Whatever you do, if you get a can of grape Crush, hold onto it. It's worth double its weight in piasters." The smell of the truck's fumes made me cough. I wiped my mouth on a crusty sleeve. "Oh, number ten important, if you've got a sharp can opener, guard it like your balls. Or give it to me."

The cherry looked at me as if I'd jumped the concertina wire at the Long Binh prison psycho ward. He gripped his M16 hard enough to turn his clean, white hands red.

Me giving advice was like Richard Speck telling the local grade school kids how to be good citizens. This cherry had an 18 percent chance of being killed or wounded, or, with more luck, a 56 percent chance of seeing one of his friends go down. But that was for all of 'Nam. If he humped it in the boonies for a tour, his shot at going home in one piece was worse than the odds of a back-row car winning the Indy 500.

The kid couldn't be more than eighteen. He looked fifteen. At twenty-three, I looked forty. The black grunt sleeping across from us had to be a granddad. Not even the jolts of the truck or the roar of tanks made him open his eyes. Dog tags hung outside his dusty fatigues along with a carved-metal peace sign attached to a roach clip. But his huge Wilt Chamberlain hands never left the strap of his M16.

"Okay," I said. I made little mud turd cakes with the toe of my boot. "There's only a few rules that'll help you survive. Number one, cover your ass. Number two, cover your buddy's. When you find yourself in Pinksville, keep that M16 on full rock and roll." I squished the mud cakes so they spurted out under the soles of the bush boot.

Puss from the gook sores ran down my legs and into the top of my bush boots. The flimsy socks I wore had vanished into the slime of the monsoons and the green crud between my toes. I rubbed my fatigue bottoms even though I knew it would just cause more bleeding and infection. Sometimes the itch made me want to rip off my fatigues and scratch to the bone.

The deuce and a half jerked to a stop at a thatched lean-to alongside the muddy road. A small boy ran up to the truck, his hand barely able to hold the frosty red can. "Coca-Cola, GI?" he pleaded. Two mama-sans sat in the hut out of the light rain, a tub of Coke on ice between them.

Ice in the middle of kilometers of rice paddies. When the sun popped through the clouds, it was over a hundred degrees and the humidity was close to 100 percent. But these mama-sans had ice. When the Hueys dropped beer on ice to a squad in the boonies, the ice that was left was smaller than a baseball. Ice was a letter from The World. It was like finding a dropped grenade in the middle of the brown water of a paddy.

"*Vang*, baby-san," I said. "*Hai, lam long*." Yes. Two please. I turned to the cherry. "Drink's on me, soldier." I handed the boy ten piasters for another Coke and gave it to the cherry.

The black grunt still hadn't budged.

The driver and his copilot argued with the mama-sans over whether they could use their worthless MPC scrip. "*Khong*," the black-toothed mama-sans clucked. No. "Piasters."

Two burned-out jeep seat frames sat next to the lean-to, out of the drizzle. Someone had thrown grass mats on top.

"Grab a seat," I said to the cherry. "Those grunts will be a long time trying to con the mama-sans out of a coke." I walked toward the bent, blackened chairs, the newbie and his M16 right behind. The baby-san sat in the lap of one of the old women and stared with round eyes while he picked his nose. Gook sores ran from the baby-sans ankles to his thighs. Some were scabbed over. Others dripped yellow puss.

The twisted springs poked through the grass mat and into the butt of my fatigues. The cherry sat next to me, M16 between his legs and Coke in his hand.

"Has anybody but an REMF wanted to know your name since you've been in-country?" I asked.

"No, now that I think of it," the cherry said. He looked at a gray sky, the color of the Hush Puppy Super Val bullets in my belt. Rain dripped from the edge of the thatched roof and pooled at our boots.

"Do you know why?" I asked. The Coke was still cool in my hand. I took a hit and watched a bulldozer wheeze and rumble by on the road followed by a squad of engineers in jeeps.

"No," the cherry said. The corners of his mouth were turned down, and there was only a hint of dimples. The frown made him look like he had been asked the meaning of life. Or why the fuck we were in this godforsaken hellhole.

"Because they don't want to know," I said. I watched a girl in a conical hat and gray pajamas lead a water buffalo through a paddy to the north. "It ain't no frat-house hazing. Even having your name in their heads makes a bush rat a little responsible for you." The girl stopped and fished something out of the mud. It looked like a big piece of shrapnel. "Besides, you remind them of what they were at the start of their tour. An innocent with a clean slate. They can never go back there."

The wind blew the garbage and diesel smell through the hut. I blew my nose on the sleeve of my fatigues. "Too much blood. Too many green LTs ordering them to die for some useless swamp. Too many buddies in body bags. Too much skin melting in napalm ooze. Too many nightmares. Believe me, they're more scared of you than you are of them." The sky above the girl was the color of her pajamas. "You're someone they'll never, ever be again."

The cherry took off his unchipped green helmet and put it on his knee. The leather strap still smelled like cowhide rather than sweat.

"I don't get it," the cherry said. "No one's ever been scared of me."

"Look," I said. "It ain't you. It's who you are. You're their conscience. Sitting here, you can't imagine what they've seen. And done." I crumpled the empty Coke can and threw it in the muddy water of the ditch behind the lean-to. "They didn't teach you shit in AIT. The cute marching songs about 'killing Uncle Charlie' are just that. Silly songs to get you to want a taste and do what you're told. But nothing can prepare you for what you're gonna see. I talked about rules. There's really only one. Live long enough to get on that Freedom Bird home. And don't look back."

The sound of distant VC mortars came from the south. The Type 63s made a *pop* sound different from the *blam* of the US M1s. Traffic on the road came to a halt. Soldiers spit tobacco into the mud and lit Camels.

The cherry jammed his helmet on his head and looked for a place to hide. His jaw worked from side to side with the grinding of his teeth.

"Relax," I said. The cherry's pants felt soft and clean when I patted his knee. Not like the stiff crust of my fatigues. "Those mortars are at least two klicks down the road." I leaned back in the seat as far as I could without tipping into the bamboo of the hootch.

A Loach scout helicopter flew down the road toward the fighting, trailed by three Cobra gunships. The 20mm cannons pointed south at the sound of the mortars and rifle fire. A copilot who manned the 7.62 miniguns waved through a cracked windshield. Bullet holes dotted the undercarriage of the Cobra.

At least the day's light rain kept the dust away. It was either the fucking rain or the fucking red dust.

"Isn't the procedure to take cover?" the cherry asked. His M16 was across his chest. He scanned the horizon as if the Indians were about to ride over the hill and blow away his wagon train.

"Where you from?" I asked. A puddle of water formed in the bottom of my helmet. Pieces of leaves and rice floated in the pool. Or maybe it wasn't rice. I poured the black soup onto the packed clay.

"Lacrosse, Wisconsin," the cherry said. "How about you?" He sat back down in the steel chair and fastened his leather chinstrap.

"Seattle," I said. "Grew up there. Went to the University of Washington to play football and chase pleated skirts." A piece of thatch stuck from the mat on the frame. I cut the piece off with the Gerber and broke it into little chunks with my fingers. "Got thrown into the slammer for helping shut down the interstate to protest this police action. The judge gave me a choice. Army or jail time. I was a quarter away from a degree in Asian studies. Figured it was time to get my learning someplace other than a book." Lies came easy here in the Kingdom of Mirrors, and this cherry didn't need to know about the Colonel. The rice kernels on the clay crawled toward my boot. I used the fighting knife to squash them into the dirt, one by one.

"What unit are you with?" the cherry asked. "You don't have any patches." The canteen that hung on the cherry's web belt was dented and chipped. Everything else on him was new. The pile of used canteens next to the processing center outside Ton Sen Nhut was smaller by one. The shrapnel scars held their own horror stories.

"On every base in 'Nam," I said, "there's a sector you don't go near. You don't talk to anyone going in or out. You don't sneak a peek. You don't ask questions. You don't want to know." I didn't tell the cherry that the few files on my black ops were marked in red EYES ONLY OF THE DIRECTOR and went back to Langley chained to the wrists of couriers in civvies and reflecting sunglasses.

Traffic on the road started to move. "Saddle up," the deuce and a half driver said. He carried three Cokes in his hands, and the mama-san pulled at his sleeve. The driver brushed her away and kicked an empty toward the other mama-san, who squatted in the mud, eyes raised to the gray sky. The baby-san held onto the woman's arm.

On my way to the truck, I handed a hundred piaster note to the mama-san and bowed. She snapped the bill at both ends, and the creases on her face turned up in a black-toothed smile. She cackled, "*Cam on*, GI, *cam on*." I knew the money would be split with the local VC chief. But what was left would feed these three for a month. Maybe the Charlie that extorted the Coke sellers would be my next assignment.

The cherry climbed into the truck in front of me. His M16 caught on the steel tailgate and dropped to the clay.

Mud coated the rifle and smeared my fingers when I picked it up. "Gotta learn to take as good care of this as your dick," I said. I slid the rifle onto the bed of the deuce and a half. The cherry grabbed the ArmaLite and hugged it to his chest.

The black grunt still slept on the plywood seat, but he had turned his face to the sidewalls of the truck. A rabbit's foot caked in dirt was hooked to his belt. A clenched Black Power fist was drawn on his fatigue shirt, and curly hair covered the ripped collar.

In a cloud of blue smoke, the deuce and a half moved. The cherry sat next to me, wiping at the M16 with a red bandanna. The canvas canopy over the truck bed kept the increasing rain off our heads. Black clouds joined gray where heat lightning strikes zapped the paddies to the north. Loaches and the Cobras raced back to their base.

The road to Bien Ha gave me two choices. Check out the snake pit I opened by greasing Viper and explain that my AWOL was caused by an ambush that had killed my entire squad. Or go rogue. Die at the hands of cowboys, not Indians. Only twenty-eight days to get my ticket and the one chance of riding the Freedom Bird was to wing it. Maybe Viper was expendable. There was no way to link me with Colonel Hoang. I closed my eyes and tried to act like the black grunt, but green eyes kept me from sleep.

The *whoosh* of a Soviet RPG flying over the deuce and a half canopy brought me back instantly. The rocket-propelled grenade exploded on the other side of the road, knocking two peasants off their bicycles. Bananas and tangerines littered the highway next to wheels and blood.

The truck driver slammed on the brakes. Before the deuce and a half stopped rocking, I was on my belly in the mud, scanning the grove of trees two hundred yards across the paddy. A puff of smoke and another grenade headed our way. M16s opened suppressing fire on the trees. AK-47s answered.

"Where are they?" the cherry asked. His hip touched mine in the mud. The cherry's rifle was pointed toward the palm and bamboo trees, but he wasn't shooting.

An M60 started a steady burp, and pieces of the distant trees flew into the air. The second grenade landed within ten yards of the truck. The tires nearest to the impact blew up in a haze of black. Burning rubber and cordite smell mixed with the smoke from the explosions. AK bullets pinged off the steel body of the deuce and a half like slot machines paying off. The black grunt rolled to the ditch behind us and fired a burst from his M16.

"Keep your fucking head down!" I yelled at the cherry. His head was moving quickly from side to side, and his helmet was drooped over his left ear. The shaking of his body rattled the dog tags that hung out of his fatigue neck, close to the sucking clay. The dimples were gone, and his skin turned the white of M34 phosphorous grenade smoke.

The muddy road where we lay was flat. Nothing to crawl behind and hide.

Before I could shove his face into the mud, the cherry jumped up and ran toward the truck. A grenade made a direct hit on the deuce and a half, blowing pieces of the cherry's upper body into the road next to the peasants.

I kissed the mud and pulled the helmet tight to my skull. The last thing I saw was pieces of green fatigues floating on the wind. AK rounds whizzed over my head, making a *thuuth* sound when they hit the mud. Grenades landed in the paddies and exploded with a boom, muffled by tons of water, rice shouts, and slime.

A mudpack of clay plastered my eyes shut. The taste was just like the muck at Benning, but I was twelve thousand miles from there, and this wasn't a drill. I pushed down on my helmet with both hands and waited.

Two minutes and it was over. Not even enough time for the 105s to start up from Bien Ha. The paddies were so quiet I could hear the mosquitoes.

Flames billowed from the truck. Soldiers crawled out of the ditch and from behind trucks and AVs.

Mud and blood pulled at my web boots when I walked across the road toward the burning deuce and a half. It had been knocked fifteen yards to the side by the RPG and lay half-submerged in the ditch water.

The black grunt stood next to the two truck drivers and looked at the blood, bananas, tangerines, and body parts on the road. M16s hung from their hands. One driver had his helmet in his armpit and bowed legs far apart.

"That cherry makes it a fruit cocktail," the grunt said. "Don't mean nuthin." No one laughed.

Thank whatever God brought us here, I didn't know the cherry's name.

The heat oozed from the jungle floor. Over the last eleven months, the Phoenix masters sent me to places where frying my brain was one of the more benign risks. Today, Vishnu must have been apologizing for the torrent of last night by putting the drying cycle on nuclear, mixing it with humidity thick enough to paint the walls. Mekong Delta hot. This kind of heat, Pantini said, "Don't matter if I got the squirts, the fuckin' heat melts it before it can get outa my asshole anyway." In our off-limits Phoenix sector of the camp, we called it "asshole heat" in memory of Pantini. He died when a gook sapper made it under the wire, after a grunt on perimeter fell asleep, and threw a satchel charge into Pantini's hootch. An "asshole number ten" day was the worst, and we were approaching that level now.

Back at the base, Comer hadn't been around to greet me. No interrogation over Viper's death. No time. Too many gooks to grease. Viper's temporary replacement, Martand, handed me a piece of paper, watched while I read the message, and lit it up with his Zippo when I finished. "Good fishin', troop," he said and walked out the door, the holster of his Colt scraping the bare knee of a stubby leg. He was one of the little people more suitable as a tank jockey, where big people took up too much space—not another phony-ass macho Phoenix spook in Bermuda shorts and flowered shirt.

Now I crouched next to a Hmong scout, surveilling the hootch on the edge of a vil three klicks from base, the leaning hut supposedly covering a tunnel entrance and the home of a suspected VC sector lieutenant. At least that's what the Martand-delivered orders read.

Late afternoon and we were waiting for the asshole day to be replaced by a few-degrees-cooler asshole night. Wasting the gook LT in daylight wasn't recommended procedure and, usually, not my style.

During the few breaks in the walk to this muddy vil, I found out my escort's name was Dang. Hmongs, Hoa Haos, Nungs, and Montagnards passed through my days in 'Nam like bottles of 33 beer, more commonly known as Tiger Piss. The Phoenix brain trust didn't want agents getting tight with scouts. Or, in the paranoia that defined 'Nam, let too many "yellow-skinned motherfuckers" know our faces. Dang had spent most of his twenties fighting for the Americans in South Vietnam. His English was passable, but there was no way I would ever be able to predict his mind. The Hmongs fought and died for totally different reasons than grunts. They hated Vietnamese more than anything, except possibly the Chinese, mainly because the Viets had pushed whole clans into the mountains and tried to starve them when outright massacre wasn't enough. At least the Hmongs didn't detest Montagnards, Nungs, and Hoa Haos—the tribes tolerated each other as oppressed brothers fighting the same enemy. For now.

The afternoon started to turn bronze in the fading sunlight. Battalions of mosquitoes came out for the last feeding. A soft breeze made the ferns and elephant grass where we hunkered wave innocently, like they didn't conceal two assassins. The monkey chatter increased, calls to come home for the night screeching in the trees. Mama-sans lit cooking fires and hung pots filled with rice and water over the flames, masking the smell of festering jungle. Two girl baby-sans splashed water on each other from a mud puddle not evaporated by the day's scorching heat and ran behind a hootch, laughing.

Night brought a few new dangers. One, I hated nearly as bad as the fucking leeches. Kraits. The black-and-white-banded killer was fifteen times more deadly than a cobra and hunted at night, not daytime. In the bush, these fuckers liked to crawl into sleeping bags, boots, and tents. Tonight, at least they wouldn't nail me while I was napping. The grunts called them "step'n a half" snakes, because you only got one and a half steps until you dropped dead.

Dang could have been dead, already suffering rigor mortis. I couldn't even see him breathe only inches from my face. It must have been history and survival that made the hill people so disciplined. Grunts could get stoned, swap lies, and cook in the middle of a night bivouac, no matter how close Charlie was. I never knew if it was a death wish, stupidity, or rebellion. But the result was a cargo hold full of body bags leaving Da Nang.

A few hours and I would enter the hootch behind the cooking women. Papa-san might not be sleeping, but the intel said he would be spending the night. Maybe a vacation, since VC duties were more often carried out after darkness fell.

At times like this, I sometimes passed the time composing letters never mailed to my mother. If it wasn't that, I couldn't stop the memories. Once, arriving at the door to our house in Fort Lewis after a little league game, a jeep full of base MPs slid to a stop. The sound of gunfire came from the backyard. Rushing around the narrow space between houses, we found Mom with the Colonel's Colt shooting at empty bottles of gin lined up on the fence. Garbage was scattered all over the yard. In the hand without the pistol, she held a nearly empty bottle of Gordon's. She wore only her lace pajamas, and her hair looked like the cats had combed it. Weaving, she aimed and pulled the trigger, most of the bottles safe from her drunken aim unless they were unlucky. She was babbling. "Fort Ord, Fort Dix, Germany, Fort Meyers, Japan…," a litany of all the places she had lived with the Colonel. But, between every location, she said, "Charlotte," and fired. Charlotte, my never-to-see-the-light baby sister, died two years before from "complications" at delivery. Now, no chance I'd ever have a little sister or brother. Mom ignored the order of the MPs to "put down the gun." That time, she was gone for three months. One of the Colonel's most often used words in Mom's presence was *hysterical.* It came to describe most all of the few sentences she spoke around him. It was the Colonel's firm belief the only reason we didn't address him as "general" was because Mom manifested her hysteria every day the sun rose.

No one else to fool. The darkness in my soul couldn't hide behind bowls of opium or bottles of Jim Beam. Or any of the other mind-altering substances available within yards of the plywood door of my hootch at the base. Earlier, I had decided that I wasn't going to let the Rand computer, Comer,

Martand, or anyone order me to murder another Vietnamese, innocent or guilty. No more lies. No more illusions of patriotism. No more debt to the Colonel. He was repaid with the corpses of too many. But the play had to go on for the days left in my tour.

Time to write.

Dear Mom,

I'd address this to the Colonel, too, but I don't really give a shit. You can tell him I made him proud yesterday and he can stop being afraid his little girl will embarrass him. I murdered a man in his bed because he helped send me out to grease a guiltless woman. Lost count of the silenced bullets I put in his body. Stopped the imminent invasion of our shores by these heathen bastard Buddhists.

Wow, the sights and sounds of 'Nam. Now I'm watchin' two little girls play tag between bomb craters. Kinda like kindergarten recess. You remember those years. We were in Frankfurt, and I was in base school. The Colonel made me learn to iron my slacks and polish my boots before I double-timed it to class. One day he came to visit and gave all us kiddies a lecture on growing up strong so we could give our lives in the noble fight against the oncoming yellow horde. Fuck, sometimes I get mad and hope someone will fire a mortar up his ass. But it'd probably jam on the thirty years of bullshit he's swallowed in the army. Time ta move on, troop.

The ruins around here are groovy. Easy to see from a klick away through the matchstick jungle, burned crispy black from napalm. Just wish I could enjoy them in the daylight. Maybe I would appreciate the glory of the fallen empire more than putting a silenced bullet in the head of a woman during a monsoon. Fuck, it rains here. That time the Nisqually flooded and the Colonel made me stand guard outside with my toy rifle in case of looters or a sneak attack, it was just a sprinkle compared to the Snoqualmie Falls downpour we get in serene Viet Nam. Anyway, he made me a lady killer. Oops, I meant man.

Now, I'm hunkered down in the grass. A spider as big as the Colonel's Silver Star just crawled by my face. I'm trying to count his legs, but I don't want to take my eyes off the vil too long or some crazed VC might blow my head into the banana trees. The guy next to me has two legs. For now. His family is dead. Wife and daughter raped in front of his eyes. No wonder he'd rather kill Vietnamese more than eat a rice and warthog dinner back at his village in the mountains of Laos.

Have a drink on me, Mom, if you're still able to pour without spilling or dashing to pray in front of the porcelain altar. I truly miss the heartfelt talks we never had. I really miss the Colonel. Here, I have to think and even make a decision. With him, I was too fuckin' stupid to do that. Must be growin' up. Already lived longer than some of the kids I blew away. Shit, I'm rambling. I'll sign off for now. I'd end with an "I love you," but those words are insubordination in the Morgan quarters. Give my regards to the Colonel. Tell him to go sit on his bayonet and pretend he's on the Tilt-A-Whirl. Sweet Dreams. Don't mean nuthin'.

Midnight and I wanted this act finished. Motioning for Dang to stay behind me, I moved toward the hootch. Not even the mangy dogs stirred. The VC ruled the night, but it must have been a holiday. If there was a tunnel entrance in this hootch, they were using another exit tonight. Or, surprise, the intel was wrong.

No rain. Foot and animal traffic had muddied the clay. The temperature fell twenty degrees. I sweated anyway, drops running down my back not able to absorb into an already-saturated fatigue shirt. Smoke from the evenings cooking floated above the trail between huts, lingering coals looking like fireflies. No stars in a land where humidity and napalm formed clouds that usually blocked the view. Except for the calls of a few night birds and the distant artillery, silence.

The door hung from rope hinges and was pushed to the side. Back against the bamboo wall, I peeked inside, Dang behind-and-faced into the vil. One room about the size of the canvas-covered end of a troop transport. Dirt floor. An old blanket strung from twine closed off one corner. Metal cups and plates on a bamboo-legged table, next to spoons and knives bent out of shrapnel, an unlit candle in the middle. Pajamas and straw hats scattered around mats on the floor that held two sleeping baby-sans. Woven baskets against the walls, underneath, the usual place for a tunnel entrance.

Stepping through the doorway, I made my way slowly past the baby-sans to the curtain and gently pushed it aside with the barrel of the Hush Puppy. Back in The World, I might have been some kind of master artist or craftsman. I was at the top of my business, and my trade was sneaking in the night. Not even a cockroach would know I was near. No one moved, and the sleep breathing was louder than any movement I made.

Two people on the mat in a space smaller than a single bed. A shelf above with another candle and pictures propped against the bamboo. Too dark to see if they were of this couple's wedding or ancestors. Burlap bags hung from nails in the wall, a jagged window above. A thin blanket on top of the motionless bodies. Only enough room to bend over and I could reach past the woman to the night's victim. Her long, black hair was splayed across a pile of clothes bundled for a pillow. Putting my hand over her mouth, I touched the barrel of the pistol to the skull of her husband.

"*Yen nao*," I hissed. Quiet. "*Su may man dem nay.*" Lucky tonight. Four eyes wide open. Invaders in the night. Nothing new to these people in the middle of a war zone. No training told them to be silent. It was natural.

The Hush Puppy was nearly soundless. Designed for the Navy SEALs, it could be used underwater. But I wasn't swimming. The Mark 22, Model O, held twenty-two green-tipped Parabellum bullets that discharged through a five-inch suppressor. The projectiles were heavier than normal 9mm shells, slowing down the velocity and making the discharge subsonic, eliminating the snap of a supersonic firing. When the bullets entered a head, they flopped around inside, turning brain matter into red-and-white custard. Only a few hundred had been manufactured by Smith & Wesson. And I held one to the forehead of a now-shivering, accused VC. But the Hush Puppy did make noise, and Dang would expect to hear it. I took the barrel off the man's head and pointed it out the window. The first *pphhuupp* was followed by the second, one beat later. I stood and smiled down, tipping the brim of my bush hat. "*Co dep ngay.*" Have a nice day, I whispered, and stepped silently out past the still-sleeping baby-sans.

At the door, I nodded at Dang, and we disappeared into the bush. A few more days and no one would die only because someone ordered me to kill. This papa-san would lay low for a few days, knowing he was marked for death, long enough for me to finish my plans and climb the stairs to the Freedom Bird.

Hanoi Hannah had a voice you just wanted to fuck. Let the soft tenor wrap you in the cocoon of that voice. Shoot your wad in the silky smoothness. Explode a billion rounds in the crater of her throat. The semen's song of Vietnam.

"GI?" Hannah asked, a Dionne Warwick ballad in her tremor. "Do you know who your girlfriend is out with tonight? Parked by the reservoir, listening to Johnny Mathis in a cool Mustang. Does his hand fumble before it unsnaps her bra? Is she nervous? Is she thinking of you? Tonight could be her night. And this one is for you, GI."

The lights in the hootch flickered from the concussion of the 105s firing artillery support for a platoon pinned down in a swamp to the north. Dirty cotton shorts were all I wore in the evening heat that was only slightly cooler than the hundred-degree days. The legs of my cot squeaked when I shifted my weight, a shrill insult to the mellow sound of Johnny Mathis singing "Chances Are" over Radio Hanoi. The words came to me in stereo provided by the fifty transistors across the base at Bien Ha tuned to the same song. I closed my eyes and wiped the sweat that puddled on my chest.

"GI?" Hannah asked. Now she was Roberta Flack singing "Killing Me Softly." "Did you hear what your brother soldiers did today in Ohio? Shot down students walking across the quad at Kent State. Maybe *Stars and Stripes* will print the picture of the young girl dying in the arms of her friend, a pool of blood at her feet."

My eyelids hurt from squeezing them closed so tight. "Jesus fucking Christ," I moaned to the empty hootch. The pillow made of an old Arrow shirt stuffed with useless civvies didn't scream when I punched it.

"Did you kill anyone today? Was it a woman? Or a little girl too?" Hanoi Hannah asked. "Will tomorrow be the same? Have you been in our beautiful country forever?" Hannah played "For Once in My Life" by Stevie Wonder.

The *whup whup* of a helicopter landing on the private pad next to the hootch came through the louvered windows. Comer was the only one who used the pad. He flew a UH-1 chopper without military insignia, just a drawing of a crisscrossed set of pistols. The little prick must be here about Viper. Or bringing his replacement.

The night's light show of flares, rockets, artillery explosions, and tracers outlined the small, thin man who walked through the bamboo door. He was Mickey Rooney short and tried to be Charles Bronson tough in his tight jeans, snakeskin boots, gold-buttoned, long-sleeve cowboy shirt, silver belt, studded hip holster, and Stetson hat. The stupid reflecting sunglasses he wore were useless in the dim lantern light of the hootch. All Comer needed was a pair of spurs, a lasso, and Shirley Temple to be in the movies.

"Home from the range, Morgan?" he asked. Comer's voice was a baritone croak. He must have spent hours in front of a mirror practicing to make it sound more like a bear's growl than the squeak he was probably born with.

Phoenix operatives weren't officially in the military. I didn't have to salute. Or even get up. I rolled to my shoulder and rested the side of my head in my hand. "Just bedded down the horse and hung up my saddle," I said.

Comer was followed into the hootch by the most dangerous man in Vietnam other than Westmoreland: Molar, the Toolman. Dangling from his throat was a leather necklace adorned with yellow and brown teeth. Molar was a collector. On the buffalo hide beside the teeth, Molar hung a carved silver pair of mini-pliers, a symbol for his tool of choice when he pulled a souvenir tooth from his victims. By the number of teeth on the leather, Molar must have killed more than a hundred Vietnamese. He worked Saigon.

Comer stepped aside to let Molar through the door. The cleats on the soles of his boots tapped on the uneven floorboards.

"You know this cowboy?" Comer asked. His arm stretched to touch the shoulder of the six-foot-four-inch Molar, dressed in sockless tennis shoes, Bermuda shorts, and a flowered shirt. A handlebar mustache curled around the corners of his mouth.

Molar's long fingers caressed his necklace. "Sure, he knows me," Molar said. "We were in special ops school at Benning and did a little jungle training in Panama." Molar's hand moved to brush his mustache. "How's the conscience, Morgan?"

From the black transistor radio on the spool table, Hanoi Hannah whispered, "GI, why you fight this war? Nobody at home wants you to. They spit on you when you get back. They won't look you in the eye. Your sister may be killed because you're here. Who will you talk to about what you've done? Will your sweetheart love you more for the babies you've killed? Listen, GI." The slow guitar of "Bridge Over Troubled Water" beamed from Radio Hanoi.

"Turn that shit off," Comer said. "I wish we would nuke that bitch."

Comer sat in the canvas-back director's chair across from me. Molar rocked up and down on the balls of feet behind Comer.

The cot squealed when I sat up and moved the radio out of Comer's reach. Dirt on the floor scraped my bare toes. Lanterns flickered with the continuous artillery fire, and my framed picture of Janis Joplin at Winterland jiggled on the wall. The night air was filled with the smell of gunpowder from the 105s, Cambodian Red, diesel and gas fumes from the petrol dump, jungle decay, and the latrine behind the hootch.

Comer twirled his pearl-handled revolver and asked, "Who do you think greased Viper, Morgan? The dinks? ARVN? A jealous husband?" He moved his hidden gaze from my eyes to the silver pistol. "Or maybe it was you." Comer looked back at me. "If the ARVN hadn't found the bodies of your squad on the trail, you'd be the prime suspect. Even if your story can't be proven, must believe we don't kill our own kind when there's enough gook savages here to waste. Right, Morgan?"

Simon and Garfunkel still sang, "Like a bridge over troubled water/I will lay me down."

Molar crossed his hairy arms on his chest and smiled. His canine teeth hung over his lower lip when he grinned. They were pointed to the side rather than up and down.

Sometimes I thought I lived in a Zap comic book full of sadistic cartoon characters. No real world would have a dwarf cowboy flying his own Huey and twirling a pearl-handled revolver while he chatted about wasting little people. Or a skinny giant in unlaced tennis shoes with dog's teeth who collected the molars of his victims and hung them from his neck.

Gotta lay off the acid. This was real as death could be.

The Colt .45 semiautomatic was in my hand next to my thigh, out of sight of Comer and Molar. Jungle humidity was hard on the bore of the Hush Puppy and silencer. They were stowed in my footlocker with the garrote. But the Gerber fighting knife was under my pillow. A new M16 leaned in the corner alongside an ammo belt and grenades.

"You got that number ten right," I said. "Don't matter how many I waste, you just keep me going out for more." The pebbled handle of the .45 was rough against the sheen of sweat on my hand. No-slip grip.

"You know we don't handle things like the army," Comer said. "Keep it inside the Firm. No pussy investigators, prosecutors, defense counsels, court-martial." He cocked and recocked the firing mechanism on his Smith & Wesson. The pistol made a click when the arm touched the breech. "If you're guilty, there's no court of appeal. It's summary judgment to the back of the head. Get my drift, Morgan?"

I scratched my balls with my left hand while my right pushed off the safety on the .45. Every chamber was filled with dumdum shells, not available to GIs, but standard issue for an assassin. One bullet into any part of Comer's body would take a team of surgeons to fix. If he lived.

Molar's hand slowly moved to his back. He surely had a pistol in the waistband of his Bermudas since he wasn't wearing a shoulder holster. Molar probably had a little Beretta in his pocket by the pair of pliers he never left home without.

"Loud and clear," I said. "What are you doing in the boonies? Got a top-secret mission for me? Want to swap lies around the campfire? Or just try to tighten my asshole with your threats? You know as well as me that 'Nam is a better place without the stink of Viper. Besides, it's hard to shit a killer you created who don't give a shit."

Could have been all the Cambodian Red I smoked that night. Or the remnants of an opium afternoon. But Hanoi Hannah's sultry voice was making my dick hard. "Hello, GI," she said. "What are you thinking about? A walk on the beach holding hands with your lover? Taking her home and slowly undressing her on the rug in front of the fire? Sharing a glass of wine? Kissing her firm breasts and making love all night? Tomorrow, there is a sniper in the trees who will make sure that dream never comes true. Instead, your lover will get a call from your mother that two uniformed men have just left her porch with condolences from the president. But tonight, relax GI, and listen to Dionne Warwick sing 'I'll Never Fall in Love Again'."

"That bitch is funny enough to make me stomp my Stetson," Comer said. He put his hat on the knee of his jeans and leaned back in the chair. "Can't figure why all the grunts listen to that bullshit. Thought you were a cut above the herd, Morgan." Comer took the reflecting sunglasses off and wiped them on the sleeve of his cowboy shirt. His eyes were the clear blue of the water above the reefs off Vung Tau. The pistol was back in the tooled-leather holster.

Molar stuffed his hands into the pockets of his shorts and relaxed his legs. He smiled at me like I just escaped a trip to the firing squad. Molar winked.

"Helps make it through the boredom and loneliness of hot nights," I said. I scratched at an itching gook sore on my calf, careful not to break the scab. This one was healing, unlike most of the others that were still open and oozing. The doctors called the sores "skin ulcers." The smallest nick and the infection began eating flesh. Like the tension that caused stomach ulcers to feast on the inside of most grunts. Hell, that's what the Rolaids in the C-ration supplementals were for.

Sunglasses went back on Comer's nose. He played with the cowboy string tie that hung from his collar. His fingernails were uncut and dirt filled the ends. "Got a new trail boss for you, Morgan. Saigon's getting too small for the Molar. Gonna transfer him to your ranch so he can ride herd."

The cleats on the soles of Comer's snakeskin boots were dull in the yellow light when he stretched his legs out to their full two-foot length. He took a small cheroot cigar from a can in his breast pocket and lit it with a wooden kitchen match on the silver of his belt buckle.

The pointy grin on Molar's ugly face widened, and I shook my head.

"Now ain't that sweet," I said. "Orders from another psychopath." A tic started the corner of my eye jumping. "When you gonna get that most of the people we grease don't have a damn thing to do with this police action? They're just people who didn't suck the right dick at the right time. Not a fucking thing to do with military targets."

Comer coughed and took out a red bandanna from his jean pocket. He wiped his nose. Gold circled the carved skull in the middle of the ring on his finger.

"Hello, GI," Hanoi Hannah said. "I'm worried about you. The Fourth Division has you in their sites. General Giap's troops have you surrounded. Sappers are shoving Bouncing Bettys under the wire around your camp. There's a shortage of crutches back in The World. Too many 'Nam brothers need them. What will you use to walk? I heard that the stock price of the wheelchair companies went up 50 percent. Maybe you should invest so your legs can bring part of profit. Lay back now and enjoy your last night with toes. Listen to a song by Blood, Sweat, and Tears."

David Clayton-Thomas sang, "And when I die, when I'm dead, dead and gone, there'll be one child born in our world to carry on, to carry on."

UCLA. Hanoi Hannah must have gone to school there. No East Coast or Southern accent, just a laid back nondistinct California dialect. Sometimes she dropped a word like all the English-speaking dinks, but she could talk the talk of 'Nam like a grizzled vet. Maybe she combined acting school with her language studies and psychology classes.

The radio was out of Comer's foot-and-a-half reach, but he tried to grab it anyway. I got there first and put the transistor in the lap of my sweat-moist shorts without showing the .45. Comer's hand went back to the pearl handle on his pistol.

"Don't make a cow turd what that bitch or you say," Comer said. "Our job is pacification. What better way to pacify the gooks than by putting them in their bedrolls for a long sleep? Old Molar here is gonna make sure you wrestle plenty of dink steers."

Behind Comer, a lizard crawled slowly up the plywood wall hunting for one of the flies that dive-bombed the nearby lantern. The gecko's tongue snapped in and out like he was using it to scout the trail. Through the door, flashes from the 105s reflected off the steel concertina wire that bordered the off-limits Phoenix sector of Bien Ha. Comer's Brut aftershave mixed with the other 'Nam firebase and hootch smells.

No one had used the dead man's cot in the hootch for months. Viper had his own. Molar slid the canvas-topped cot next to Comer and sat. A scar that looked like a pink zipper ran across Molar's tanned knee.

Back in the world of Zap. The three of us sitting within five feet of each other, heavy-duty firepower at our fingertips, being oh so civil, when the slightest move from any of the psychopaths would bring a shitstorm to the hootch.

"Remember that mission you were sidesaddle on with me, Morgan?" Molar asked. "Shit, with you along, podner, I got two extra teeth." Molar jiggled his necklace. "Never seen anybody better with a garrote than you. Fitted them Cu Chi Charlies with a bow tie so quick they couldn't even fart. Smooth, man." Molar ran his index finger across his throat. "But them dink fuckers shit their pajamas. Smelled worse than the latrine at a titty bar in Saigon."

The cot squealed like it enjoyed Molar's stupid joke as much as he did.

Smoke from Comer's cheroot made little Os when he leaned back and puckered his lips.

"You're a true professional, Morgan," Comer said. He cleared his throat and spit on the floor, the cheroot smoking in his hand. "Admit it. What other rodeo could you ride that gave the satisfaction of this one? Where else could you cut any bronc out of the herd you wanted? It's like Gunfight at the O.K. Corral here. And you're Wyatt Earp with a Hush Puppy."

The tic in my eye was about to do permanent damage to my face. Sweat dripped down my side from my armpits. It wasn't fear.

"Won't do any good to argue morality with you two cowboys," I said. "I've only got twenty-five more days in-country. Just give the orders and save the bullshit for the brass that appreciates your act. I don't give a rusty fuck if it's Molar or you sending me out."

The radio in my lap tickled my groin like a vibrator.

"I got a letter today from GI," Hanoi Hannah said. "He writes, 'Dear Hannah, I'm here at the Veteran's Hospital outside San Francisco. The doctors say I'll be able to feed myself soon. The nurses claim they don't mind changing my bedpan and I'm no bother. I do miss my feet and my right arm. Sometimes, I remember how I used to pitch in the little league games and play tag with my sister. She brings me flowers and Hershey Kisses when she visits, but she hasn't been back for over a month. I know it's a long way from San Jose. At night, I think about your voice and how you told us how terrible the war was for everyone. I wish I would have listened. Even if I deserted to Sweden or Denmark, I'd be better off than being spoon-fed my dinner and trying out plastic feet. Be well and I hope the B-52s aren't over your head.' That nice letter was signed by Corporal Marvin Brantley, Americal Division, Serial Number 8369934. Thanks, Marvin. Here's another Dionne Warwick song dedicated to you. I hope you recover soon." The sound of "Do You Know the Way to San Jose?" came from the transistor.

The gecko caught a fly and made it a one-swallow meal wrapped like Pillsbury dough in his curled tongue. Somewhere, outside the concertina walls, the Southern Cross helped guide the B-52 jockeys making their way from Thailand to Hanoi on Operation Linebacker.

Comer stood and wiped off the seat of his britches.

"You don't have to worry about the way to San Jose, Morgan," Comer said. "Tomorrow you're gonna di di mau to Cần Thơ." He tightened the cowboy string tie and patted his revolver. "I gotta saddle up. Molar will fill you in. Adios, muchachos." Comer strutted toward the door and signaled to the chopper driver to crank it up with a wave of his Stetson. The cheroot still burned in the corner of his mouth.

Molar stood. The cot toppled on its side against the wall, and the thin blanket from some dead man fell in the dirt.

"Gonna be fun, eh, Morgan?" Molar said. "Reveille at oh six hundred hours. Keep that Hush Puppy greased. I got beaucoup plans for it. I'll be bunking in Viper's old hootch." Molar walked the few steps to the door. The teeth around his neck clicked together. He vanished into the night still lit by artillery fire and flares and the sound of Comer's Huey taking off for Saigon.

The leather sheath on the fighting knife poked the back of my head when I lay back down on my pillow. I lit the roach of Cambodian Red in the C-ration can ashtray.

Books. I used to read books before I went to sleep. A ritual. Now books just scared the shit out of me. Books said things like: "The soldier, involved in the defense of his country, is the most honorable man. Willing to risk his life for the continuing cause of freedom and to assure that generations to follow will not be subjected to the yoke of tyranny, he stands as a beacon to all." Or: "There is a dark secret in every man's heart. Hidden until the time he is confronted with unspeakable evil. Then, he must choose the direction correctly or he will be lost to the blackness forever."

I never knew when a written line would ambush me. Sneak up. A sapper in the wire. Books weren't worth the risk. Just like going in the jungle on a moonless night. Too many punji stakes.

The smoke from the joint drove away some of the flies. I put my hands behind my head, the radio on my chest, and closed my eyes.

"It's time to say good night, GI," Hanoi Hannah said. "If you're still wondering what your girlfriend did tonight, I can tell you that she didn't miss you. She'll be dreaming of someone else when she goes to sleep. But, maybe tomorrow she'll answer your letter from two months ago. It will start, 'Dear John, I met the most wonderful man. He is against the war in Vietnam and has shown me the truth. I feel I can no longer love anyone who fights in that war. I hope, someday, we can be friends. Sincerely, Mary.' Now, rest your head on your poncho and let the sound of Simon and Garfunkel take you back." Radio Hanoi shut down for the night with "Homeward Bound."

I was glad I didn't have a girlfriend to remember. Only green eyes and an innocent cherry with dimples.

Flies covered the gook sores on the monkey's gray back. He was perched on the shoulder of a bearded GI in a dusty vil off the road to Cần Thơ southwest of Saigon in the Mekong.

Some of the monkey's sores were scabbed over, and others were shiny yellow and pink. When the monkey scratched, strands of wiry hair from the clumps that peppered his skinny haunches formed a gray cloud in the hot afternoon breeze. He was tethered at the neck to the soldier's wrist by a white nylon cord from an F-4 Phantom parachute. The monkey squeezed a green banana and screeched at Luong and me as we walked across the packed dirt of the vil to the crooked hut. Luong was my newly assigned Montagnard scout, a hill tribe mercenary working with the Americans for little pay other than the chance to kill Vietnamese. Lots of Vietnamese.

A peace sign was painted in white on the back of an army fatigue nailed to the bamboo wall outside of the hootch. Above the symbol, a sign made of an old C-ration box read TUNNEL RAT RETIREMENT VILLA. The hootch was blackened from fire and was the only one in the vil with a fresh thatched roof over the door. Green ammunition boxes were stacked against an outside wall with yellow flowers growing from the top box in each pile. An upside-down, webbed GI helmet sat on the clay next to the ammo boxes, white flowers blooming from the red dirt inside.

A shirtless American soldier in sandals and tiger shorts leaned against a pole that supported the palm roof, smoking a joint and petting the monkey sitting on his shoulder. The GI's hair hung down his back, and his brown beard matched the tan of his chest. A scar like a thin outline of Laos ran from under his shorts to his left nipple.

The soldier flashed the peace sign at Luong and then scratched the bright-red rash in his armpit.

The strap of my bush pack scraped against my upper arm. I pushed the pack higher on my shoulder, walked behind Luong, stepping around broken pieces from a clay water vase, and approached the soldier.

A naked baby-san waddled to the soldier, bony hips moving side to side, and hugged the soldier's thigh. A mangy, brown-and-black 'Nam dog yapped at the boy's heels.

The soldier patted the baby-san's black hair and said, "Okay, Tran, it's *ban*." Friend.

Ear against the soldier's leg, the baby-san squeezed harder and watched Luong and me. Dirt was smeared across the little boy's bulging belly, and his feet were the brown-red tint of Delta soil. Gook sores ran up his bowlegs from his ankles to his knees.

The soldier moved his hand to the baby-san's arm and held it. He wore a ring carved in green jade that reflected the tropical sun that pierced the ragged palm trees surrounding the vil.

Scrawny chickens searched the clay for rice kernels and maggots. Charcoal burned in a cooking fire next to the damaged hootch closest to the rice paddies. The blue smoke drifted through the vil, mixing with the smell of buffalo and human dung, boiling grease, and rotting fruit.

Two pigs rooted in a pile of garbage behind the soldier's hootch. One of the pigs limped on three legs, a white scarf tied around his neck. WIA was painted in black on the pig's haunch. Wounded in Action. Two Purple Hearts were pinned to the scarf.

Luong swatted at three brown-and-black chickens with the barrel of his M16 and walked across the packed earth to the soldier.

"*Chao*, Vietnik." Hello, Luong said. He locked his right palm and thumb with the soldier in a hippie peace handshake.

The monkey tried to hide behind the GI's head and made monkey whimpers. The soldier flipped the roach on the clay, pulled Luong to his chest, arm around Luong's back, and hugged the ex–Kit Carson scout.

"Hey, zipperhead," the soldier said. "How goes the war?" The soldier patted Luong's jungle fatigue and the full ammo belt crisscrossing his back. "You still a strack trooper? Won the fuckin' Medal of Honor yet?"

Luong let himself be hugged, but the grenades on his chest and the M16 in his hand kept them three inches apart. This was not the traditional greeting of a Montagnard.

A crumbling stone pagoda to the left of the hootch was going back to jungle. Thick vines were woven between the heaps of gray rock like threads of fat creeper snakes. Orchids grew from potting soil made of decaying vegetation that covered the shrine.

The baby-san stared up at the two friends with wide-open black eyes. Flies feasted on Tran's sores and the trail of dysentery that stained his thighs yellow.

"Number ten good, Nick," Luong said "Kill many, many dirty VC." Luong moved to the soldier's side and pointed to me. "Nick, this Morgan. We on trail to Cần Thơ."

Nick's bare chest was indented with the rectangles of Luong's MK2 pineapple grenades. The white of Nick's left eye, above a Furry Freak Brother smile, was the red of ripe passion fruit.

"Welcome to my pad, Morgan," Nick said. "This here's Tran." Nick looked down at the baby-san and gently pulled the boy's ear. "The ape is Lyndon. Smokes more dope than LBJ. Has bigger balls. Damn straight." The monkey dropped his head onto the white hair on his chest at Nick's touch. "Don't need to prove it by wasting kids though. Come into the hootch and share a doobie. Even got a few warm Tiger beers."

"Nice to meet you, Nick," I said. We gripped hands in the peace shake and stepped toward Nick's villa.

Inside the hootch, Nick rolled joints of Laotian Green. Lyndon was tied to a parrot's crossbar perch, and the monkey scampered back and forth on the three-foot bamboo runway.

My pack held a half dozen Hershey bars that I scavenged from C-rations back at Bien Ha. The monkey let me scratch his neck in trade for a piece of the chocolate.

"Don't see why the grunts call the VC 'monkeys,'" I said. Lyndon pressed the wiry fur on his skull into my hand. "This little guy is too cute to be insulted that way."

Lyndon's tight muscles relaxed as I rubbed, and he hunkered lower on the bamboo runway.

After Tran finished his half of the candy bar, he laid down on the grass mat, sucking his thumb and staring at the new giants in his world.

Nick, Luong, and I sat around a table made of empty cardboard C-ration cases stuffed with chunks of bamboo for support and covered by a smooth piece of door from a downed Huey. The chairs were eighteen-inch-high rounds of dark hardwood polished by years of rice farmers. A picture of Grace Slick fronting the Jefferson Airplane in concert at the Fillmore Auditorium hung from the bamboo wall next to a psychedelic poster of Moby Grape. The bed in the corner was a thatched mat of elephant grass with a GI-issue green blanket on top. Roaches and Camel butts filled an ashtray made from a coconut husk. Slanted eyeballs were carved into the hairy outside.

A rat poked his black head through a hole in the bamboo slats near Tran's head.

"Dat ra," I hissed. Out. The rat pulled his pink feet back and turned tail. "I hate them ugly fuckers. At least they speak dinkese."

I watched Tran's thin cheeks move in and out from the meal he made of his thumb. Tran was a poster boy for all the guilt-trip charities and antiwar jingoists back in The World. Perfect. Pitiful and beautiful at the same time.

"Why did they make you a CAG ghost?" I asked Nick. "And how are you still alive?" An M16 rested against my shoulder, butt in the clay of the hootch floor. The pin on one of the smooth grenades pinched the skin on my chest. I pushed the M26 closer to my arm and took a hit from a joint.

"Blows my mind, Morgan," Nick said. He fired up another number and passed it to Luong. "Should be KIA by now. The survival rate of Civilian Action Group guys is worse than traitor's row at Long Binh. I think the Charlies figure a peacenik in the hamlet is better than a rat in their tunnels."

"Used to visit two ex-grunt CAGs in a vil outside Bien Ha," I said. The floppy brim of the Aussie bush hat drooped in my eyes. I hung the hat on the barrel tip of the M16. "One day, a squad of marines found their heads on bamboo poles in the middle of the vil. The crows had picked out their eyes, but their dicks were still in their mouths."

Luong passed the number back to Nick.

"Ain't our government sweet?" Nick asked.

Nick took a long hit on the joint and held it in. Smoke came out from between the gaps in his yellow teeth, and he hissed, "I crawled down moldy tunnels with just a flashlight, a knife, and a Colt semiautomatic for six months. Got booby-trapped, stabbed, shot at. Could have gone back to The World twice with my Purple Hearts."

Nick flicked the ashes of the joint on the clay floor and ground them hard with his calloused bare feet. "But when I didn't, and refused to crawl in again, they made me a CAG. If you don't like this war and won't do their asshole shit anymore, you got a better chance of dying than if you're humping it in the paddies. There it is."

When Nick leaned back on the hardwood chair, a centipede crawled further back under the mahogany round. Nick's tanned brow was squeezed tight and furrowed with ripples like paddies in the wind.

"And if I said I was scared, they might have reassigned me. Sent me to the chaplain. But I told them I wouldn't fight at all. That the war sucked and we were killing the wrong people. Should be Westmoreland."

Tran jumped at the sound of Nick spitting on the floor. The pool of saliva wouldn't sink into the hard clay and formed the shape of a swamp turtle.

"The fucking LTs wanted me to grease women and kids. If they were in the tunnels, they were VC. Those kids didn't have a thing to do with whether a grunt got blown to Hanoi. Or took another vil for a day. Nuthin's gonna win this war. And I ain't gonna kill anymore, even if it means dying in this dusty ghost vil. There it is."

Nick closed his eyes, neck covered by a brown beard from the chin that was now drooped to his chest.

I set the rifle on the clay floor and touched Nick's knee. The muscles on his leg were tight as the leather wrap on the handle of my Gerber fighting knife.

"Both of us have done things that won't go in our scrapbooks, Nick," I said. "At least you've got the courage to stop. That makes you worth more than a thousand Westmorelands."

The burnt-grease smell of the cook fire came through the door on a gust of wind.

Nick's body was in a Mekong coma.

The bush boots on Luong's feet bounced up and down on the laterite clay. His black eyes blinked faster than I could fire the M16 on single shot.

"You number ten tunnel rat, Nick," Luong said. "Smoke many, many VC. Old squad miss you." Luong smiled from a mouth filled with the filed black teeth of the Montagnard hill people.

Luong was five-foot-two, the perfect size for a tunnel rat. The tunnels were usually only two feet wide and the same height. A scar ran across Luong's forehead and onto the front of his skull. No black hair grew from the pink ridges of the scar. The ARVN fatigues hung loosely from his hundred-pound body.

Tunnel rat scars usually were on the upper body, running from the head down. That was the direction that the bullets came from when the rats crawled into the darkness.

Nick opened his eyes, reached out and ruffled Luong's remaining hair. The tip of the little finger on Nick's hand pointed out instead of straight up, and the nail was black.

"Don't hassle it, Luong," Nick said. "I haven't defected to the NVA." Nick scratched the scar on his chest with the crooked finger. "Remember the bitch tunnel outside Cai Ba?" Nick asked. He handed me a joint, took a slug of Tiger, and grinned at Luong. "I went point. You were on my heel. This one held every trick the VC had. The first was the fucking snakes. Them green bamboo ones tied to grass vines. If I hadn't seen the creepers, them suckers would have made us stiff as JFK's dick." Nick pushed the long brown hair out of his eyes and gripped it in a ponytail behind his neck.

A cockroach crawled across the dirt headed toward the brown clay rice jug sitting against the slats of the bamboo wall. Luong crushed it with his bush boot.

"Many dead VC in that one," Luong said.

The rash under Nick's armpit looked like an advanced case of tropical measles. White peas surrounded by bright red circles. Nick scratched with the bent finger.

"The fuckin' VC love to leave rotting corpses by the entrance," Nick said. "Drag the dead ones down the hole. Think the smell will keep tunnel rats out. Flesh ripens fast in this humidity." He pinched his freckled nose and stared at me. "Our orders were to bring back a fucking body count. Had to crawl past piles of them, counting, 'One, two, three, another dead VC.'"

Nick pushed the pool of spit in the clay lazily with a filthy toe.

"So what's your MOS, Morgan?" Nick asked. "You don't have any insignia on. Look sterile to me. Like a spook. Sometimes, they used to send Luong out with the SOG assassination squads for some night action. Is that your jacket?"

The lips of Nick's smile were covered by mustache hair but couldn't hide the cynical grin.

I fingered the Hush Puppy Super Val bullets in the pocket of my fatigue pants. Phoenix operatives were surrounded by an aura of secrecy and evil. Nick knew it. Luong played a small role. But there was no way I could explain it to a man who had risen from the Dead Zone and spit in the face of the machine.

Trickles of sweat soaked into the back of my fatigues. I watched the monkey pick fleas from his armpit.

"We're doing recon in Cần Thơ," I said. "More like R&R than any Special Operations Group business."

The monkey watched me like there was a bamboo snake winding its way up the pole.

"What happened after you got by the snakes and bodies?" I asked.

The deformed nipple on the left side of Nick's chest was a straight line with a small pink bump. He rubbed the scar with the palm of his hand.

"That tunnel was the number ten worst," Nick said. "Had to be careful that we didn't land in a punji pit. The VC put trapdoors in the floor. If you fall in, the punji stakes are sharper than a KA-BAR and smeared in gook shit."

The hotter the afternoon, the more Luong's head scar turned red. Today, it was the dark-wine color of wet Delta clay. Luong touched the crescent shape of red that marked his hairline.

"*Vang*," Luong said. "VC dig holes in side tunnels and wait. When rat go by, they stab in head with sharp bamboo pole or choke with wire."

One of the scabs on Nick's leg made the outline of a leech. But it was dried brown and flaky, not wet and black. Nick rubbed it.

"We had a rule," Nick said. "Never fire more than three shots in the tunnels without reloading. The VC knew you'd be out of ammo and be in your face. And no rat was ever, ever left in a tunnel. We always brought them out. Dead or alive."

The monkey squatted on the perch, black toes wrapped around the pole, scratching his pink balls. Milky ooze dripped from the corner of his left eye.

The roach burned the tips of my fingers yellow from C-ration Camels. I pinched the roach and watched the ash and Zig-Zag paper float to the clay floor.

"Don't know how you guys could crawl into those tunnels," I said. "I don't have the cojones for it. Heard of a system up by Cu Chi that was like a city. Hospital, theater, nursery, wedding chapel. Everything a gook in Saigon would need."

The baby-san sighed from the mat. A corner of the GI blanket was stuffed in Tran's mouth, replacing his thumb. Nick watched him suck for a few seconds and walked to the sleeping mat, calloused feet quiet in the dirt. He covered the baby-san with the bottom of the green blanket and stroked the boy's head.

"Di nam tot, Tran," Nick whispered. Sleep well.

Nick backed up to his chair, eyes on Tran, and sat.

"Once I greased a VC riding a stationary bicycle in a tunnel," Nick said. "He was pedaling a generator that ran the lights in the operatin' room next to him. The sweat ran down his back like a monsoon. Could have been in the Olympics. Waited for an hour and watched from a side tunnel." Nick sat forward and crossed his thin arms on his chest. He stared at the green fungus between his toes. "You know, the VC don't have the luxury of anesthetics. The doc was sawin' off legs and arms and sewin' intestines back into stomachs while the patients bit down hard on a piece of bamboo. It's amazing how tough the zipperheads are. There it is."

Nick's hair brushed across his bare shoulders with every back and forth shake of his head.

"We got medics carrying enough morphine to last a gook *bac-si* a year," Nick said. Doctor. "They'll shoot you up for an infected hangnail."

The bent finger caressed Laos on Nick's side.

A fly the size of a dime landed on the lip of my beer bottle. I swatted it away.

"Do they really have a Bob Hope–type show that goes from tunnel to tunnel singing opera?" I asked.

Nick looked up and sat back on his hardwood stool. The lid over his red eye was beginning to droop. Maybe ringworm.

"Never saw that," Nick said. "Did see rooms with little stages that could hold a couple hundred dinks. If they put Dante's 'Inferno' to music, it would be perfect. There it is."

In the trees outside, a family of monkeys howled and scolded. Lyndon froze and stared out the hole in the bamboo wall that served as a window.

Tran was asleep. Only his cheeks moved with the continued sucking on the GI blanket. His knees were tucked to his chin. The smell from his corner of the room and the dark stain in the blanket below his butt made me reach for another of the joints on the tabletop.

Luong's fingers couldn't make it all the way around the pineapple grenade that he fondled. The bush campaign hat was stuffed into the ammo belt that crisscrossed his chest.

No ice in this vil. The Tiger beer was warm, but tasted cool when it went down my throat.

"Didn't see any mama-sans in the vil," I said. "Or papa-sans. Where is everybody? You the babysitter?"

"Mama-sans are in the paddies," Nick said. "Papa-sans are too old to work. Probably chewing betel nut and dreaming in their hootches. The young ones got drafted by the VC. You know, Uncle Ho wants you."

"What about Tran?"

"He's a war orphan. Parents got under an Arc Light mission. Not even a finger was found."

"So you adopted him?"

"Kinda. His uncle lives here, when he's not away doin' somethin' else I don't wanna know. Mostly at night though." Nick winked. "I suspect he might be doin' the same thing as you, Morgan."

"Heard a rumor about orphans. Seems there's an underground back to The World. You can buy a baby-san cheap and cure the guilt of shopping at the mall while your cousin bleeds out in a paddy across the ocean. The story says sometimes they ain't even orphans. Supposed to be run by somebody high up the government ladder. Sellin' kids is supposed to bring a thousand bucks a head to the bosses. You hear anything about that?"

"Damn straight," Nick said. "Wouldn't mind if Tran got a chance to go to the Big PX too. His life expectancy ain't too long here. And no mama-san or papa-san to miss him."

"Yeah, but I also heard some don't make it to The World. At least not the one we know. A lot of them are shipped to places where it's sand, not jungle. Or the girls get to be raised by madams 'til they sharpen their skills. Or not. There's always a high price on virgins, no matter how many times they get sold that way."

Luong's head moved back and forth between us, trying to follow the words. Once in a while, he even smiled, believing we cracked a joke. Tran turned over with a sigh, while Lyndon watched me like I was a huge banana.

"One thing we imported to this lovely land is a refined form of capitalism," Nick said. "Make a piaster any way you can. If that means sellin' babies, there's gotta be a market. I only wish I could blow up the shit of the dude who's supplyin' it."

Fingernails jammed with red. A layer of red on the crumbling pagoda. Green uniforms turned red brown. People transformed from yellow to sickly orange. Red gook sores and rashes next to blood scars from the leeches. Bamboo leaves drooping with an inch of red powder only washed clean by the monsoons that caused the mud to flow lava red. Like some god had thrown a blanket of blood over the world.

The point of the shiny Gerber fighting knife easily picked the red clay from my nails.

"What are you supposed to be doing here?" I asked. "Is this the army's try at the Peace Corps? Show the peasants how to plant rice in between the mines and booby traps?"

"I'm teachin' community action and awareness in order to enrich the lives of the South Vietnamese civilians," Nick said. "By my example and instruction, the villagers will soon see the superiority of democracy and the American way. There it is."

Nick lit another joint with a Zippo lighter, took a drag, and handed it to me. When the smoke was gone from his lungs and drifting into the haze of red dust that clouded the air, he chugged the last swallow of his beer.

Clay now gone from my red-stained fingernails, I started to whittle a piece of bamboo into a toothpick.

"No comment on that bullshit, Nick," I said. "Aren't you afraid?" I stopped whittling and watched the scar across Nick's ribs move when he swallowed. "You're out here in the boonies alone. No razor wire, claymores, or sand bunkers to protect you in the night. No radio to call in the arty."

On the back of Nick's right hand was a crude boonie-made tattoo of a peace symbol. He wiped it across his mouth, the beer in his left hand.

"Fear?" Nick asked. "Don't have the courage to show fear. To cry in the arms of a buddy at night covered by our ponchos. I let it eat at my stomach like the worms in the tunnels and try to smoke enough dope to keep the ghosts in their graves."

A full Tiger beer sat beside the empty bottle Nick put on the table. He flipped the lid with his C-ration opener and watched a stooped papa-san walk slowly from a leaning hootch across the clay yard.

"My DEROS is in thirty-eight days," Nick said. "It'll be a miracle if I make it back to The World. But I'm not going into another tunnel or greasing another Vietnamese even if they promise to evac me tomorrow."

Outside the doorless hootch, the vil looked like hundreds of others I had seen all over the Delta. Ghost towns peopled by orange skels with horrid skin ulcers and bloated bellies. Scabrous animals pecking or rooting in the clay for any meal, rotten or not. Craters from the B-52 Stratofortress Arc Light missions and M105 rounds that filled with muddy water and mosquitoes, but gave the skels a place to shit when the dysentery allowed them to make it that far. Hootches rebuilt a hundred times and blackened from the last Zippo assault. Brown clay jugs of water and rice next to cook fires that stank of burnt, decayed flesh and grease. Rats the size of toy poodles that feasted on a steady diet of dead flesh. In the distance, rice paddies and water buffalo working in fields of brown water that reflected the tropical sun and were home to millions of leeches, snakes, booby traps, and untold diseases.

Poverty. War. Peasants. Shrunken leathery breasts on black-toothed, pajamaed mama-sans trying to get one more meal from their empty teats. Bulging-eyed, malnourished baby-sans with outtie bellybuttons that look like the knots on orange balloons about to burst. Toothless papa-sans too old and weak to hump AK-47s through the bush. But still strong enough to stuff the C-4 from unexploded bombs in booby traps disguised as canteens, rice jugs, discarded rifles, dead GIs, and dolls. Vacant stares of hate on pocked faces resigned to generations of war. Everything covered in a film of red dust or mud.

MIA were the young men and women. They were fighting a war of liberation against the American imperialist aggressor. If not, they were shot.

The bamboo toothpick was sharp and strong. I put the toothpick in my mouth.

"Gotta di di mau to Cần Thơ, Nick," I said. I stood and slung the strap of the M16 over my shoulder. "Good luck. Hope you make that ride on the Freedom Bird."

I squeezed Nick's hand and the bent finger pressed against my palm.

The vacant thousand-yard stare came into his green eye. Nick's red eye was almost closed from the infection. Little tremors made his tanned skin jump like he was firing a pig machine gun. He put his other hand over mine and squeezed hard. One bare foot scraped slowly in the dirt. He looked over my shoulder at Tran and then back to me.

"Keep your head up and eyes in the trees," Nick said. "Don't mean nuthin'."

My throat was numb. Like the night I swallowed ten tranqs from a medic's pack. I nodded.

Nick stepped to Luong and hugged him, M16 at Luong's side, closing his eyes and locking his hands behind Luong's bandoleer. White puss formed a teardrop in one corner.

"*Tot suc khoe,*" Luong said. Good health. They stepped apart and joined hands in a peace shake.

Tran woke to the chatter of Lyndon and ran to Nick's side, wrapping himself around Nick's bare knee. Nick rubbed his hand through the black stubble on Tran's head.

"Peace, brothers," Nick said. "Stop by on your way back. The resort's always open." Nick untied Lyndon and the monkey jumped on his shoulder.

Tran's little hand in his palm, Nick led us out of the hootch. Sleep nuggets were in the corner of Tran's eyes the same color as the puss in Nick's. A fly buzzed Tran's face, and Nick flicked his hand to shoo it away.

Lyndon wrapped his tail around Nick's neck, his black eyes scanning the palms.

The packs and ammo belts that covered Luong and me squeaked softly from behind Nick and Tran.

The papa-san squatted in the clay, a bamboo pipe in his mouth and a conical grass hat on his gray head. Ribs pressed tightly against his orange skin. A white film covered the black of his eyes, and he swayed to a tune no one else could hear. Calves thin as corncobs ran to thighs covered by baggy, torn gym shorts that said OLYMPIC TEAM. Luong and I walked past the papa-san on the way to the trail leading through a tangled hedgerow and into the jungle.

At the trailhead, next to a dozen burial mounds dotted with white rocks, we turned and waved to Nick, Tran, and Lyndon. Nick flashed the peace sign. Tran stared with wide-open black eyes. Lyndon scampered from one of Nick's shoulders to the other.

The first to die was the monkey. The snap of a round from an AK-47 bounced off the palm trees, and Lyndon fell to the clay, nothing above his neck where a monkey head used to be.

In a second that seemed like a year-long tour of duty, Nick dropped to the ground and rolled into a ball covering Tran. The nylon cord on Nick's wrist jumped from the death convulsions of Lyndon, who lay headless thrashing in the clay. Blood pooled next to Nick's shoulder. His ankles were crossed and his arm pulled Tran tight to his chest.

More shots came from the trees on the far side of the vil.

Luong and I dove behind the burial mounds and returned fire with our M16s. The hedgerow danced with AK-47 rounds. Clouds of dry clay rose when the bullets hit the graves like horses' hoofs on the plains.

A Soviet RKG-3 stubby grenade flew end over end into the middle of the vil. The grenade's flight was slow motion in a background of smoke and jungle. I thought I could count the rotations before it exploded in a cloud of dust and bamboo splinters. Two VC in green pajamas ran around the papa-san's hootch in a zigzag line through the smoke. They sprinted across the open ground, firing their AKs on full automatic. The VC on the left dropped the barrel of his Kalashnikov toward Nick and Tran and kept firing. Nick's body jumped with every bullet that hit his bare back and legs.

I took dead aim and shot the VC in the heart. Luong lit up the one on the right with a short burst. Both VC tumbled to the ground, AKs thrown to the clay, sandals flopping.

Smoke and cordite smell filled the air, but no more rat-a-tat of AKs. Dead silence.

The papa-san was chunks of bone, gym shorts, and flesh.

Nick was motionless in the long R&R.

The cry of a baby-san.

Luong and I waited. After a minute, I motioned Luong forward with my hand. We walked to Nick, eyes scanning the far tree line, M16s on rock and roll.

Holes leaking red dotted the flesh from Nick's thighs to his neck. The wounds were the size of the end of Nick's bent finger and mapped a trail to the next meaningless tunnel that Nick would never have to recon.

Trickles of blood ran to the clay. The flies were already feasting.

Lyndon's body was still, pieces of his skull in Nick's hair.

A black-haired head turned crimson from blood popped up from below Nick's chest. Tran wiped the blood from his eyes and howled. While Luong watched the tree line, I scooped up Tran and we backpedaled toward the path.

The firefight was over in less than two minutes.

We were on the road to Cần Thơ with a war orphan and memories of another wasted GI who missed the flight on the Freedom Bird. But this time I knew his name.

The bunker was a B-52 crater a boonie rat had shoveled army straight before Luong. Tran and I used it as an NDP, night defensive position. The walls were flat laterite clay baked grenade hard by the tropical sun. During the monsoons, the tight bunker would fill with water, leeches, and mosquitoes, drying out only after days of evaporation. Now, after a week of rainless days, the bunker held fleas, ants, centipedes, and spiders.

Artillery fire from 105s shook the ground, but no loose dirt fell into the hole. The barrage was a few klicks to the east and outlined the scarred trees on the horizon. M60 machine guns were easily heard over the pop of M16s, Simonov carbines, AK-47s, and the occasional mortar. Fire made orange devil's tails and black smoke in the palm trees across the paddies below what would be the Southern Cross.

Tran was asleep wrapped in my poncho sucking his thumb. Luong had fed the baby-san pound cake and tuna fish from a C-ration meal while I kept lookout. My M16 rested on the clay pointed down the path to the east. On the other sides, miles of stinking booby-trapped paddies made a quiet assault less likely.

A rat ran in front of my face. I swatted it with the barrel of the rifle, grazing the rat's pink tail and sending it toward a paddy with an angry squeak.

"How did you get to be a VC, Luong?"

Luong crawled across the bunker the size of a Volkswagen bug and squatted next to me facing Tran. He pulled the knees of his jungle fatigues to his chest and rested his chin on top.

"NVA come to village outside Pleiku," Luong said. "Take family in the night. Shoot papa-san and mama-san. Take me and *nguoi vo* to camp. Make wife cook and me scout to find other Degar hiding in forest."

Degar was the name the Montagnards gave themselves. The Vietnamese called the ethnic Degar "*mo*." Savages. The GIs called the Degar "Yards." Montagnard was the Degar name for the forests they were fighting to keep after centuries of occupation.

The Starlight II Scope was in a hard-plastic case in my pack. The snaps and color made it look like the black case held a flute. German Starlight scopes were used by grunts in 'Nam to capture the light of the moon and stars and amplify that sky's light to watch in the dark. Everything seen through the lens was a black shape outlined in a field of green. The CIA researchers at Fort Monmouth had made a lighter, more effective scope only available to Phoenix operatives, perfect for assassins who lived in the dark.

I unsnapped the case and put the Starlight next to the M16.

"You have any baby-sans?" I asked.

Luong's webbed belt held a dozen grenades. Most were the common M26 tin can variety. Luong also carried two Willie Pete white phosphorous and two CS gas grenades. He handed me one of each to add to the pile of weapons that grew on the lip of the bunker.

"*Khong*," Luong said. No.

A brief flash of artillery lit the gold cross that hung from Luong's neck. The cross was strung on braided copper wire liberated from a radio cable. Luong fingered it in his right hand.

"You a Catholic?" I asked.

Luong kissed the crucifix and shoved it under the top button of his fatigue.

"*Vang*," Luong said. Yes. "Missionaries come to Central Highlands two hundred years ago. Many Degar Catholic, but still worship forest animals too. Even believe in circle of life. French like Degar better than dirty Buddhists."

The Smith & Wesson was in its holster, the silencer in my pocket. I laid the pistol next to a magazine of regular ammo for the M16.

"What happened to your *nguoi vo*?" I asked. Wife.

"NVA *hiep*," Luong said. Rape. "Many, many times. Make me watch until I show NVA Degar brothers in forest. She *tu van* with bamboo knife to heart." Suicide.

Luong took the cross out from his shirt and squeezed it. His head sank to his chest and his lips moved, eyes closed. The scar on his head jumped with every word of prayer.

The back of Luong's shoulder trembled when I touched him. Flesh thin as my poncho covered his bones.

A CS gas grenade rolled in front of my eye from the cache on the foxhole lip. I pushed the grenade back and watched the flames make serpent outlines above the tree line.

"I'm sorry, Luong," I said. Breathing was hard in the humid, heavy night. Luong's story added to the wet cotton in my lungs, and I gasped for air.

Fucking war. Vietnamese who thought Montagnards were savages to be treated like enemies invading land the Degars had occupied for a thousand years. Forcibly relocating gentle forest people to foul, crowded cities so they could live in cardboard shacks next to the dump. Americans like me who took advantage of the hatred and despair so the Yards would kill other Vietnamese for us. And walk point on patrol as human mine sweepers.

Tran sighed and slurped on his thumb. The sound of a baby-san sucking on a Tootsie Roll Pop at the base PX back in The World.

Luong tucked his poncho tighter around the baby-san's feet and swatted at something I couldn't see.

Maybe ants. I hoped they weren't fire ants—that meant we would have to move. Better a black-nosed spider. They were harmless. Tran would tell us soon enough.

"My life is kill VC," Luong said. "Many, many VC. Only way for me to get to heaven and be with *nguoi vo*. Must free her soul."

The sniper rifle's scope had a detachable Redfield-Leatherwood 3-9 power auto ranging telescope, giving the rifle a nine-hundred-yard effective range. The scope was wrapped in oilcloth and sat in my pack next to a box of .308 Winchester ammo used when the modified M16 became a long-range killing tool. I took the scope and the bullets out and began to unwrap the oilcloth.

"What was your village like?" I asked. "I haven't been to the Central Highlands."

The bandoleers of M16 magazines on Luong's chest weighed almost as much as his hundred-pound body. He loosened the straps but didn't take the ammo belts off.

"Village called Darlac Haut," Luong said. "In mountains. Many big trees in mountains around Darlac Haut. Live in long houses on stilts made of hardwood. Thatched roofs. Carve many saints and animals in walls."

Combat-ready grenades had their pins bent for quick release. I used my left hand to twist the metal pin on an M26.

"How do the Degars live?" I asked. "Who does what? Back in The World, the men work, and the women stay home and have babies. Or go out and burn their bras."

Luong's M16 butt was chipped and dented. He picked off a jagged piece of plastic on the handle.

"Everyone share food, clothes, drink. Women watch baby-sans. Men hunt wild pigs and mountain deer. Women cook. Weave beautiful clothes. String necklaces and bracelets in many colors. Make other jewelry from silver and brass. Many villages grow dry rice, maize, bananas, and coffee. French teach some to grow rubber trees. Not Darlac Haut. Only hunt and grow rice. *My le* country." Beautiful.

To the northwest, across the paddies, the foothills of the Central Highlands began. The foothills were a hundred klicks away, but Luong smiled when he looked in that direction.

The XM21 scope was unwrapped and lay on the oilcloth next to the rest of the growing arsenal. I picked up the Starlight scope and scanned the paddies. Pointing it at the flames would blind me for minutes.

"How long have you been a Kit Carson scout?" I asked.

Through the scope, the world was green with forms of distant palm trees in black. Paths on top of the clay dikes made dark, straight lines dividing the paddies.

The metal fasteners on the canvas cover of Luong's canteen snapped softly. He took a swallow and touched my shoulder.

"Drink, Morgan," Luong said. "You answer question now. Why you fight?"

Water the temperature of spit still felt good going down my parched throat. After the drink, I sectored the horizon with the Starlight.

"My old man was a colonel," I said. "It was the thing to do in my family. A long history of warriors. Went to college and thought about running away. But the ghosts captured me."

A night breeze brought the shit smell of the paddies to the bunker. The villagers rotated the paddies, using one for a shit field per year and planting it the next. We must have been close to the shit field. I wiped my nose on the arm of my olive fatigue.

The leeches didn't just stay in the water. Somehow, they made their slimy way cross-country in search of blood. I hated them worse than the rats, snakes, and the hordes of mosquitoes that infested the Delta. At night, when leeches sucked onto your skin and you couldn't use a cigarette to burn the bastards off, you had to drown them in bug juice. Worst case was a knife. I took a plastic bottle of insect repellent out of my pocket.

Fucking leeches. Most of my gook sores were the result of leech wounds. The sucker's saliva carried an anticoagulant that kept flesh bleeding for up to six hours after the leech had filled his belly with blood. If you didn't treat the wound right away, it would become an oozing gook sore in a day next to the boils that festered on your thighs. I covered my face with bug juice, keeping the bottle handy against a leech attack, and wished there was a grenade big enough to blow the black belly off every leech clear to Hanoi.

"I don't know why I'm still fighting, Luong," I said. "No one in my family has been raped or murdered. No one has mortared Seattle. No one has been relocated to Walla Walla. But people I touch lately seem to get shot. Like Nick. Don't know how much more I can handle."

The Gerber fighting knife was in the leather sheath at my waist. I put the knife on the berm of the NDP next to the Redfield sniper scope.

Luong snapped his canteen back into the canvas. Flames from the continuing fire in the trees reflected in his black eyes.

"What your vil like?" Luong asked.

"Rains a lot in Seattle," I said. "The city is on an inlet from the Pacific Ocean called Puget Sound. Hills and lakes surrounded by trees. It's green all year around. Lots of birds. You know, Luong, birds are one thing I miss in the Delta. Rarely see any. I guess they don't dig napalm. You know a leg they call 'Kentucky' back at Bien Ha?"

Tran grunted. Not in alarm, but the sound of a baby-san learning to exercise his voice even in a foxhole and asleep. His skinny, yellow fingers opened and closed as if he was trying to hold a silver rattle.

Luong knelt beside Tran in the hard clay and stroked his head. The green plastic poncho squeaked when Luong's knee rubbed against it. He moved back next to me and touched the polished walnut butt of the sniper rifle.

"Think went on night patrol with Kentucky squad," Luong said. "Maybe he RTO?" Radio telephone operator.

The flames in the palms and banyans were dying. No more small-arms fire.

The paddy stink mixed with the smell of burning trees and hootches and the body odor of two unwashed soldiers.

Through the Redfield scope, I could see black forms backlit by the flames. The VC were picking up the dead and heading to the tunnels before a sweeper team was sent in.

"That's the grunt," I said. "Know why he's called Kentucky?"

"*Khong*," Luong said.

"Kentucky's squad scorched a vil by Cẩm Thông," I said. "He found an injured crow. First bird any of the boonie rats had seen in months. Kentucky took the crow with him and nursed it back to health. Fed it C-rations and plucked its flying feathers when the crow got better. Named the crow Free for the Freedom Bird 727 that flies grunts home. Back at Bien Ha, Kentucky taught Free to say 'motherfucker' and 'slope asshole.' And smoke dope. Man, that crow loved to get loaded."

The cigarillo can that held the stash in my breast pocket wasn't there. I patted the fatigue anyway, but the weight of the can was a phantom. Like a grunt with a blown-off leg still thought he could feel his missing foot.

"Took Free into town and insulted every dink he could," I said. "Kept the crow tied up on a perch outside the sandbag door to his hootch. One morning he woke up and found Free skinned and hanging by his neck from the perch. A note was nailed to the crow's pink body. It said, GI DIE. His buddy, Mallincrot, asked him if they could barbecue Free and if Kentucky thought it would taste like chicken. Kentucky said Free would probably taste better than the Kentucky Fried Chicken he got back in The World.

Ever since, the grunt's been called Kentucky. No one remembers Kentucky's real name."

The shapes in the vil had disappeared, and the 105s were silent. Time for the artillerymen in this sector of the Delta to bag some z's or get loaded.

The plastic magazines for Luong's M16 still hid his chest. He unhooked two and set the black magazines next to his rifle.

"*Giac ngu*, Morgan," Luong said. Sleep. "I watch for VC."

A black-nosed spider crawled from the oil-rag wrap of the Redfield scope. I flicked the spider away with fingers stained brown-red and began to pack the riflescope.

"Can't sleep, Luong," I said.

Luong loved to touch the walnut handle on my sniper rifle. Must have reminded him of the hardwoods of his Central Highlands home. He rubbed the stock with his right hand while his left was around the trigger guard of his M16.

"Believe in Jesus, Morgan?" Luong asked.

The Redfield scope fit easily in my pack alongside the C-rations and a mildewed copy of *War and Peace*. I stroked the book.

"I'm a living testament against the old line that there's no atheists in a foxhole, Luong," I said. "Maybe there was a time when I believed. No more. No God would let the shit that happens here go on. I've seen too many faces in a death look that didn't say they were going to a better place. Besides, if there was a God, how would I ever be forgiven?"

In the dim light, Luong's gold crucifix was still visible. He stroked it like it was the butt of my sniper rifle.

"Jesus forgive you, Morgan," Luong said. "Go see priest. He tell you."

The fires were just a flicker on the eastern horizon. I held the Starlight scope to my right eye and searched the paddies for movement.

"There was a chaplain at Bien Ha," I said. "They called him Shakey. Not Padre, like every other chaplain in this fucking place. Shakey dropped to his knees every time a mortar round popped anywhere near the base. The grunts used to get off on yelling 'incoming' just to watch Shakey make the sign of the cross while he groveled in the clay. Kentucky liked to toss a grenade and have it roll against Shakey's boot. Jesus, Shakey would shit his fatigues and hiss, 'Holy mother of God,' with his eyes closed tighter than Pat Nixon's legs."

The black-nosed spider was back. But this time he was in the clutches of a centipede. I crushed the centipede with the bottom of a Willie Pete grenade and brushed the two bugs down the mounded clay that was the lip to our night bivouac.

"Shakey was no advertisement for religion," I said. "Got so bad, Shakey's teeth were falling out and he was afraid to wash his fatigues because a visiting Bishop had blessed them. Lucky pants. Sent him back to The World on a mental."

Maybe Luong understood what I said. Maybe not. My stories weren't for Luong anyway. War stories fueled the insanity of 'Nam. They were the gallows humor that kept me and most others from pulling the pin on an M26 and eating the grenade.

Luong added two more M16 magazines to the pile of weapons. Now I could see the hump of his breastbone.

"Priest in my vil French," Luong said. "Priest stay until NVA set him on fire in church. Burn all *dem*." Night.

If we came under attack, the arsenal in front of Luong and me and the extra ammo behind us were enough to defend against two squads of VC. Until the Chicom M63 mortars fell. The only thing that kept the good guys on the winning side of the scoreboard in this war was superior firepower. While the VC packed old Russian and Chinese rifles that crumbled in their hands, we had the best ordinance that the American military industrial complex could provide. And profit from.

Tran was a child of war. No squealing like an American brat. Death was the sentence for loud noises in the dark. Tran whimpered. The sound of a lost 'Nam puppy cowering on the side of the road, frightened by the Patton tanks that rumbled by.

I watched Tran's yellow hands reach again for something that wasn't there. No mama-san to share a meal from her shriveled, empty breast. No papa-san to tell him stories about the generations of rice farmers who had cultivated the land while centuries of soldiers came and went.

"Maybe he's hungry again," I said. "You didn't feed him much the first time. Most of the baby-sans have stomach worms, so they get hungry fast."

The M16 barrel pointed downhill when I set it in the clay.

"You watch," I said. "I'll feed him."

Luong handled the Starlight scope as if it was booby-trapped. His hands turned the scope slowly side to side, inspecting the hard-plastic cover. The scope inched toward his right eye.

"Vang," Luong said.

Tran's black eyes were wide open. His jaw worked up and down, chewing on his thumb. The poncho was pulled below the waist of his naked body, and he was in a pool of piss and diarrhea.

Black eyebrows formed perfect crescents at the base of Tran's forehead. His cheeks were yellow bomb craters. Not the chubby pink of a Gerber baby. But his skin still felt smooth and soft against the roughness of my clay-stained fingers.

Even in the dark hell of this hole, Tran smiled at my touch. The dirt caked on my face made it hard to smile back. But I did. No way to stop the reflex. Something like napalm warmed the inside of my chest.

I picked Tran up and laid him on the shoulder of my flak jacket. The baby cocktail puddled in the clay from draining the poncho. The paddy and fire smell was now joined by the odor of dirty diapers that Tran never wore.

If there weren't ants before, they would soon come to soak up the slop. Maybe even a few wet, black leeches that made the trek from the paddies.

The filthy sleeve on my fatigue served as a rag to wipe Tran's bottom the best way possible in the night in a foxhole somewhere in the shit of the Mekong Delta.

Tran continued to suck his thumb and watch Luong while I made an assassin's effort to take care of the baby-san. Tran grabbed my ear under the bush hat and pulled no harder than the tug of a heavy earring. It tickled. This smiling thing was getting serious.

The rank air sucked through my yellow teeth, and I searched my pack for the P-38 can opener, a grunt's most valuable tool when he was in the boonies, after his M16. A bent or broken P-38 meant having to beg for a working opener from other grunts who would want to make a deal for pound cake or peaches. Or use a KA-BAR that caused the food in the olive-colored cans to spill on the clay, risking a wound that would become an oozing gook sore in a day.

"This detail ain't in the Phoenix program handbook," I said to Luong.

The P-38 easily opened a can of applesauce. The old bent spoon from my pack that had seen countless C-ration meals fit just fine in Tran's little mouth. The coolness of the spoon on his gums made Tran slow to let go for another bite of applesauce. I moved the spoon around in his mouth and gave him time to enjoy the treat. There weren't any other foxholes calling our name.

A rare cloudless night and the Southern Cross glowed bright above the horizon. Not an artillery shell, mortar, or rifle disturbed the silence. The moon reflected on the brown water of the paddies broken by the clay banks of the dykes. Only embers remained in the burned vil. A breeze that dropped the temperature to a cool eighty-five degrees blew the stench of the bunker into the stink of the paddies.

A shooting star flashed across the northern sky, a white tracer marking its path.

Tran was soft and gentle and falling back to sleep in my arms. His black eyelids would close slowly and then snap open. I rubbed my hand on the thin black hair of his skull.

Luong was focused on the trail, the M16 in his hands and the Starlight scope next to him.

My teeth chattered. It seemed as if everyone I touched died. Part of it was my MOS. Innocent women with green eyes and unknown enemies. Liem. But the stench of death that covered me must attract the grim reaper even when I wasn't his tool. Nick. I didn't want Tran and Luong to be the next victims.

I sang softly to Tran. His eyelids fluttered less.

"All along the watchtower, the thief he kindly spoke, 'There are many here among us who feel that life is but a joke.'" Hey, it was the best I could do. At least I wasn't singing the Jimi Hendrix version, even though he was a member of the 101st Airborne.

The pack made a decent pillow for Tran. I laid his head on the nylon and wrapped the baby-san in the poncho.

Luong moved over a few inches when I joined him at the lip of the bunker. I touched the smooth butt of my rifle for reassurance, but left it on the clay berm and held on to an M26 grenade.

"You ever cross paths with a leg named Baby Huey?" I asked Luong.

In the light of the moon, any silhouettes would be easy to see without the scope. Luong continued to scan the distance with his black eyes.

"*Khong*," Luong said.

The normal cures for the fears weren't available in an NDP without risking being found by VC who wouldn't hesitate a heartbeat to bayonet a baby found with two enemy soldiers. No pot. No tranqs. No acid. No whiskey. Just stories.

"He was in the Second Battalion out of Chu Li," I said. "Baby Huey was on patrol near Hoa Vu when his squad found a tunnel complex. The LT picked the Baby's number to go down the hole. Baby Huey was over six feet tall and covered in pink fat that hung over his web belt and out the buttons of his fatigues. He was dumber than a banyan stump and smiled all the time like he was back in Iowa at the soda fountain drinking vanilla milkshakes. Baby Huey went in shirtless, headfirst. Got stuck. Three grunts pulling for five minutes on each leg couldn't get him out. All the time he was stuck, the grunts could hear his muffled voice yelling, 'Don't pull off my pants, don't pull off my pants.' On the last pull, the grunts got some help, and Baby Huey's pants came out before him. He was wearing pink-and-black bikini shorts. The patrol serenaded Baby Huey with 'Itsy, witsy, teeny, weeny, pink and black polka-dot bikini, was all that covered Baby's tunnel today.'"

Luong hadn't moved. His face held the intensity of a soldier that knew danger was closing in.

I touched Luong's thin bicep. He still didn't look at me, but stared straight ahead into the darkness like a bird dog with an M16 pointing to a duck.

"American music not your thing?" I asked. Luong never sang along.

Flea and mosquito bites were some of the tiny wounds that became gooey sores in the humidity and filth of the Delta. Maybe it was Nick's monkey. My neck and head itched worse than from the case of lice the medic had treated two months ago. I scratched and squirted on more bug juice.

"*Im lang*, Morgan," Luong whispered. Quiet. "Someone coming."

Luong's shoulder touched mine. The muscles on his upper arm knotted, and he sank lower in the bunker, eye on the sight of his M16 aimed across a paddy to the east.

The magazine in my M16 was in tight and on rock and roll. Quickly, I checked it anyway, barrel alongside Luong's rifle.

The shadows that moved slowly across the paddy dike three hundred meters north were VC. Their silhouettes were dark against the moonlight reflecting from the brown water of the paddies sprinkled with new stalks. A dozen gooks. Heavily armed, silent, and headed in the direction of Firebase Amazon near Dieu Ban.

Luong's hands and knees made no sound on his crawl across the bunker toward the sleeping Tran. If the baby-san made as much as a whimper, Luong would quiet him.

The Starlight scope gave a black profile of the VC and magnified even the smallest detail. The leader carried an AK-47, a rucksack, bandoleers of beer-bottle grenades, and canvas ammo pouches. All the Charlies wore sandals, bush hats, and dark pajamas loose at the ankles like black bell-bottoms. Bamboo tubes of rice held tight by leather thongs hung from their necks. Half the squad had white bandanas tied around their throats in four-square Boy Scout knots.

Two of the VC held RPG-7 Type 69 rocket-propelled grenade launchers and enough grenades to melt an attack force of M48 tanks. The grenades each had four knifelike fins that opened out as soon as the projectile was clear of the tube, giving the grenades the accuracy to penetrate a tank from five hundred meters. The RPGs were as long as the VC that carried them were tall, and almost as heavy.

A Charlie in the middle of the line packed a Chicom RPD machine gun over his shoulder. His chest was crisscrossed with 7.62 cartridges, and he was bent at the waist under the load that must have weighed over a hundred pounds.

The VC behind him balanced a piece of metal on his head that looked like the frame of an old plow converted as a base for the machine gun.

The rest of the soldiers were loaded with backpacks, spare ammo, grenades, and AKs. Loaded for bear. Or long noses.

One of the VC limped and was having a hard time keeping up with the man or woman in front of him. A rip in his pajamas showed a skinny leg bandaged from the calf to the thigh and covered with a dark stain.

My breathing was slow and silent, and my face was blacked out by greasepaint. The same for Luong. The wild card was Tran. I looked over the shoulder of my camouflage fatigues at the baby-san and Yard.

Luong squatted next to Tran, who was asleep wrapped in my poncho, sucking his thumb. An M16 was at Luong's side, and he flashed me the peace sign with calloused fingers.

The VC continued walking on the dike trail, heads as high as the weapons would allow. The limping gook stumbled, a ray of moonlight reflecting off his mouth like a silver tracer. The ray was magnified a thousand times in the Starlight scope and blinded me for a few seconds.

A three-quarter moon was in the eastern sky. Cloudy yellow halos surrounded the stars, making them look bigger and softer. The lingering smoke from the earlier hootch fires mixed with the smell of the shit field, Tran's dysentery, and the earthy smell of damp clay. A night mist rose from the paddies, making the VC even more phantomlike.

The sound came first. It was a low-pitched hiss joined by a soft whir. The one that kills you is the one you don't hear. Tonight, the 105 round sprayed the shit out of the VC squad, who didn't hear a thing until it was all over and their blood fed the rice shoots that had grown in the paddy for a thousand years.

A heartbeat before impact, I jerked the Starlight from my eye or the rays from the blast would have been more than painful. The paddies lit up like a forest fire from the explosion of the C-4.

Marking and spotting flares were fired from trees to the north. No need. The first round was a direct hit. Even without the scope, I could see there were no more VC on the dike. But the mortars kept up for another minute, accompanied by M60 machine gun and rifle fire.

It must have been easy for the grunt RTO to call in the arty with such precision in the dark. He only had to move his coordinates a few hundred meters south from the firefight earlier and he had a bull's-eye.

Concussions shook the clay, and Luong held Tran to his chest. The baby-san's black eyes were open almost as wide as his mouth, which screamed something I couldn't hear. Tran's hands covered his ears, and his bare feet kicked Luong's ammo belt.

A warm hug in the middle of 'Nam rice paddies. My father, the Colonel, wouldn't hug me if it meant a star on his shoulder. At least he didn't make me salute. I wasn't afraid of crying for fear of giving away my position to the enemy. Only hearing another scolding lecture on the need to "be a man in a world full of pussies." I watched Luong hold Tran to his chest.

After the firefight, the absence of sound was almost as scary as the fury of the bombs. From ear-crushing waves to dead silence. I could almost hear the chirp of baby birds on a spring morning in the Cascade Mountains. But there weren't any birds. And the trees were on fire.

Tran made soft, gurgling noises while Luong bounced the baby-san on his shoulder. Tran's head swiveled slowly side to side. The leisurely scanning movement of a GAU-2A minigun turning on its pod in search of targets and firing rounds per minute. But Tran didn't have any weapon but his innocence.

I tossed Luong one of the canteens on my web belt. He unscrewed the metal cap and tried to give Tran a drink. The baby-san kept his lips closed tight and watched the flames in the distance.

No survivors. At least none that I could see move. No patrol would risk going out in the night to count the bodies. Or carry the pieces away. That would wait until the morning sun rose on the stinking paddies that now soaked up body parts as protein. But the day belonged to the grunts.

The walls of the bunker were flat and smooth and pocked by worm and ant holes. Luong sat, back resting against the clay, and patted Tran's butt. He softly sang some Montagnard lullaby. The sound soothed Tran. His black eyes fluttered a few times and closed.

Mom sang bedtime lullabies to me until I was three. By then, I had a little green uniform and size-five kids' combat boots, along with a Daisy air rifle that the Colonel had wired a plastic bayonet onto. I ran around the house in uniform, my head covered by a camouflage helmet. My playthings were metal toy soldiers, tanks, and deuce and a halfs. The Colonel told Mom to stop the "fucking pansy-ass singing" before she "turned me into a fruit."

The M16 would be my security blanket for the night. Sleep would be impossible so close to a kill zone. I set the (useless for now) Starlight scope on the clay and put both hands on the ArmaLite.

Luong stroked Tran's black hair and watched the fire from the mortars burn to embers.

Another long night of sentry duty filled only by boredom combined with the fear a sniper with a night scope might have me in his crosshairs.

The letter I had been writing for over a year to my old man, the Colonel, replayed in my mind. One day, I might put the words on paper and send it. For now, it was enough to know I had good intentions but not courage enough to use the free mail service given to grunts. Assassins too.

The normal "I miss you" schmaltz was insubordination to the Colonel, so I didn't give him any of that. He never gave it to me either, since he didn't write. I was a man doing a man's job. Not a kid like everybody else in these fucking swamps fighting a war made by old men for reasons long-ago forgotten.

I did my best writing when I smoked a couple OJs—opium-soaked joints. OJs came wrapped as Camels or Marlboros and looked exactly like the real deal. A pack of twenty cost ten bucks. Tonight, I only had my memory to work with, and I didn't need a pencil since I'd never get around to anything but fantasy.

Dear Colonel,

They call infantrymen in 'Nam grunts. Or boonie rats. Or legs. Last week I saw Kawolsky's leg. It reminded me of a baton at the Fourth of July parade in Woodinville, the way it twirled end over end against a background of blue sky. Chunks of flesh and bone flew off like the flashes from a sparkler. The red of his blood, the white of his skin, and the blue of the sky, was a real Old Glory. Like the flag you wear stitched on your VA campaign hat.

Kowalsky stepped on a toe popper land mine. Missed his toes but took his leg. When Doc zapped him with morphine, the last thing Kowalsky screamed was, "Doc, find my fuckin' leg. Find it, goddamnit. I know you can sew it back on. My old lady don't want no one-legged gimp in the house."

Buffalo wasn't as lucky. He earned his Purple Heart the hard way. Went to collect a souvenir ear off a dead VC. Booby-trapped with a 105 round. The explosive power of a 105 in a man's face is something to behold. No more reason to save shaving gear from the C-ration supplementals.

Grunts. Can't figure that one. Could be from humping a hundred-pound nylon and aluminum pack in the jungle all day. But grunting ain't the sound I hear or make. It's more of a "fucking motherfucking cocksucking asshole pack" sound. Don't make that grunt sound when I shit either. Don't need to. It runs out on its own, real quiet-like.

Visited a vil a few days back. Wasn't on the map and won't ever be. No tour buses stopping to snap photo ops. Lots of crispy critters lying beside burned out hootches. The napalm jelly that didn't torch off covered the clay like Vaseline. A mama-san who must have been out taking a shit was the only dink we found alive. You know, when we liberate one of these vils, the locals give us this look. It isn't welcoming and friendly. It's more of a "if I get the chance, I'll roast your balls on a sharpened bamboo stick" look. And here I heard we were winning hearts and minds. Headquarters calls a pacified vil an "oil spot." Be better if the REMFs called it "meltdown."

Oh, back to Kowalsky. He was medevaced to Da Nang Hospital. Put him in the White Lie Ward. Seems his leg wasn't the worst of it. The doughnut dollies promised Kowalsky he was gonna be okay and on the next Freedom Bird back to Fort Lewis. Hey, maybe he'll look you and ma up.

Just joking. He's dead.

Man, is the jungle here fucking beautiful. Lush green trees. Wild orchids. Banyans bigger at the butt than an Oldsmobile. Fruit that drops ripe and juicy into your hands. Meadows filled with ten-foot-tall elephant grass that sways in the wind like wheat in a field outside Spokane. Monkeys swinging from limb to limb and chattering monkey talk. Butterflies in glorious greens, blues, and yellows. B-52 craters the size of the gym at Mercer Island High School. Stick forests a few weeks after the Agent Orange fertilizes the leaves. Pointed black snags and fat stumps from trees given a coating of napalm. Fertile soil so full of shrapnel that a mine detector is useless. It never stops pinging.

Man, I can't wait to see the jet setters make 'Nam the next undiscovered hot tourist spot. Hey, I forgot the white sand beaches. Man, you can see for miles from your own personal guard tower. You'll feel safe because of all the razor wire and claymores surrounding you and the M60s aimed at the jungle. Catch a gorgeous sunrise over the black smoke of the shit detail burning the slit trench in diesel. The smell comes off your clothes after a couple washings. Think I'll use the Yashica 35mm I got in Bangkok on R&R to snap a few pics of this place. Make up a brochure when I DEROS. "Visit friendly, scenic Vietnam."

I knew you'd ask what I do for fun since I kicked mainlining. Now I mostly just mellow out behind a few tokes of opium. The zips get the good stuff right out of the Golden Triangle. Don't worry, the CIA is getting most of the profit, so it's dollars well spent. Margolis scored some windowpane acid. I'm telling you, those flares and howitzers are trippy at night behind a couple hits of windowpane. If I gotta pay attention, the medic just slips me a few Dexedrines to put a little edge on. But I really get laid back with a half-dozen Quaaludes. The juicers think I'm a soul brother the way I stagger around. At least I don't chuck my cookies on my bush boots like the beer freaks. A lotta guys just smoke dope. I think that's for pussies or when there ain't something more kick ass on the base. But there always is.

In your war, I wonder if there was honor. Blowin' away a few Krauts must have made you feel good. Cappin' gooks just leaves me empty. Sending home a snapshot of you holding up a dead Jerry, cigarette in his white lips and you smiling, captain's bars on your shoulder. You know, the picture in your "War Album." Now that should have given you a woody even knobbier than looking at them black-and-whites of Ava Gardner's legs I found in your drawer. Anyway, did you feel that you'd sacrificed for God and country? Keeping the world safe? A real patriot?

I greased a woman the other night. She was sleeping when I pushed her out of bed and into the garden. Put a silenced bullet in her brain next to a clump of white orchids. The ants got there before I could di di mau back to base. She was beautiful. Innocent too. But I didn't find that out until later. Hey, it was orders and in my brief. Was I honorable?

Sometimes when I'm a few tokes over the line on the opium pipe, I think about courage. What I mostly do is hump around in the boonies to get from one place to the other so I can hide in the bush until dark and sneak up on somebody and put a bullet in their heads and slink back to base to get loaded and wait for the next victim's name to be imprinted on my soul. The Hueys fly over my head, full of body bags, dripping red out the open doors, the metal grating on the deck so slick with blood you can't stand up. Did those wasted soldiers have courage? Did they meet the enemy face to face and the better man won? How the fuck would I know? It ain't my style.

I hear there's lots of stories back in The World about the lack of discipline among the troops in 'Nam. What a crock! LT Marinovich went against the boonie code. Kept sending a man down the tunnels, not just tossin' a grenade in the hole and callin' it sanitized. Made his squad flip a coin for honors. Tuesday night, after several warnings, he was sentenced to death by fragmentation grenade. The M24 rolled into his laager while he was readin' a letter from his wife. There was a color picture of her. Pieces of the Kodak moment were smeared in blood to the part of his arm they found in the bamboo tree the next morning. Don't break the rules if you can't pay the dues.

There was a general in town last week. Top made the troops turn in their filthy, ripped fatigues for new ones and stand at attention while the general landed in a cloud of dust from his own private Huey. The rotors didn't even stop turning before he was on his way. They stood proud and brave and at attention in the hundred-degree-plus oven of this shithole while he pinned a medal on Sergeant Ripperton. Phoenix agents like me just got to watch, snickering from our sector of the base. The opium sure helped. The grunts got their old fatigues back too.

Mail call is a big deal here. If we're in the bush, the Hueys drop the bags with the Coke on ice and ammo. I sit on my pack suckin' on a J and watch my buddies stand in a crowd nervous as a sapper in the wire waiting to see if the girl back home wrote and their name will get called. Sad to see some of them slink back to oiling their M16s and brooding over the lack of a note from The World.

There's a downside to getting stoned in the middle of a war zone. My mind sometimes goes on a bummer thinking about things like the Gulf of Tonkin Resolution. Stars and Stripes *wrote that it's been rescinded. Now the Pentagon says they have the constitutional right to wage war since the president is the commander in chief. Shit, makes me feel better that I'm greasin' women under the authority of the commander in chief and not just some fuckin' resolution.*

Luong touched my shoulder. The shock of his fingers made me jump hard enough to knock one of the M24 grenades into the bunker.

"Okay, Morgan?" Luong asked. "My turn guard."

Through the greasepaint and the mist of the night, the whites around Luong's black eyes were sharp and bright. He left his hand on my shoulder.

The M24 sat against the ankle of my bush boot. I picked it up and put it next to the stack of ammo in front of me.

"Just writing a letter," I said. "Only a couple hours until daybreak. I'll stay up too and take care of Tran. Maybe sing him 'Amazing Grace.'"

Tran's little fists were clenched tight, and he shadowboxed with a dream warrior. The poncho was slick and had slipped to his feet, showing the bulge of a malnourished belly filled with last evening's C-ration pound cake. Tran's head moved from side-to-side as if he was trying to fight against the battle with his tiny neck, black eyebrows scrunched in a frown.

Water had seeped into the bottom of the bunker during the night. The water would be sucked into the air by the day's tropical humidity, but Tran, Luong, and I would di di mau at first light, leaving the banana spider that wove a silver web above Tran's head to catch a long-legged insect's meal of mosquitoes and flies.

I moved two meters across the bunker and picked Tran up without disturbing the spider. Hated the fucking things. Spindly, spastic legs thinner than the wire on my garrote below a hairy, black body long and thin as the 7.62 bullets for my M16. But I was scared to kill one and be infested by nightmares of falling into a punji pit, bleeding to death on the shit-soaked stakes, and covered by fucking banana spiders bigger than Tran's head. Eight-inch legs tickling my face, mouth sucking my blood. Visions of Liem were enough.

Tran's chin rested snugly on the shoulder of my camo fatigues, cheek nestled against my neck. He tucked his arms, fist still closed, under his belly and pushed his knees into the bandoleers on my chest. Little slurping sounds came from his mouth, and dribble wet the start of the beard above my collar.

"Amazing grace, how sweet the sight," I sang. I patted Tran's bare back to the rhythm of the only lullaby I could think of.

Tran shivered in the eighty-degree coolness of the Delta night and made short hissing sounds from his baby-san-toothed mouth.

The silhouette of Luong's head and shoulders was outlined above the rim of the bunker against the morning light. The barrel of his M16 was pointed toward the tree line to the north where the remains of the VC squad were already being processed as feed for the next rice harvest.

The song calmed me as much as it seemed to soothe Tran and the spider that barely flicked a long leg to the peace movement anthem.

* * *

Shades of milky blue rose on the eastern horizon over the shadows of palm and banana trees. Smoke still came from the hootches burned in the night's firefight across the paddies. Mosquitoes lifted from the brown water in hordes of gray.

The fuel pellets easily ignited in the old C-ration can I used for a cooking pot. I added a chunk of C-4 to make the stove hotter and burn longer. The blue flames were low and hidden by the rim of the laager and the early dawn light.

Tran was on my knee, watching me add the dried eggs and pieces of ham I had mixed in the bowl made from another C-ration can shaped to fit above the flame. He tried to grab the handle of the Gerber fighting knife with his little fist, and I put the Gerber in its leather sheath. Tran sucked his thumb with short breaths that moved his belly against my fingers. A ball of snot blocked his left nostril like a green nose plug.

The cowboy coffee would have to be sacrificed for Tran's meal. Luong and I would survive on the Dexedrine that helped us get through the night.

Sunlight streaked the paddies with gold and silver over Luong's head. Nylon cord tied the flaps of Luong's Aussie bush hat, tilted to the side of his head, exposing the scar under his hairline to the sun's rays.

A chemical smell of the fuel pellets and C-4 joined the stink of Tran's diarrhea and the shit fumes off the paddies.

The old, bent spoon from my ruck was too big for Tran, but he tried to use it anyway. I guided his hand into the C-rat plate filled with warm scrambled eggs and ham and then somewhere in the direction of his drooling mouth. What didn't make it between his lips fell to the clay bottom of the bunker.

Fat earthworms started their morning search for food and crawled toward the eggs, which had turned pink in the soil.

With the hand not holding the spoon, I reached for the medpack in the ruck and took out a tube of antibiotic ointment that I used on the ulcers that dotted my leg. I sang "The Itsy, Bitsy Spider" while I softly rubbed the ointment on Tran's shiny gook sores.

The bent spoon fell to the clay, and Tran whimpered at my touch. His back pressed against the M16 bullets crisscrossing my chest, and his bare butt pushed on my knee. But he didn't cry.

Packing a ruck and holding a baby-san was a class not given at Special Ops school. One hand balanced Tran on my knee while I stowed the cooking plates, poncho, fuel, and spoon tight against the copy of *War and Peace*. Everything had to be arranged perfectly. No metal against metal. A clang in the bush was a siren that called death by AK. I gave Tran a drink from the canteen before I hooked it to my web belt.

The syringe of morphine hung from my neck on a leather thong. Tran saw the sun glance off the plastic tube holder covering the needle and grabbed for the "sweet sleep." His little fist wrapped around the tube and headed toward his mouth.

I gently took the morphine from Tran's hand and stuffed the dope through the V-neck of my camos. The back of my collar had "77" stitched into the green cotton. No insignias or name anywhere on my uni. No dog tags. No wallet. No letters from home. No military ID of any kind. If my corpse were found, the big Rand computer in Saigon would sort out who was in the body bag. Or not.

The sun made shadows through the palm trees over Luong's right shoulder. On the back of his neck, a mosquito was still as a sniper.

"Want some *do an*, Luong?" I asked. Food. "Tran ate the eggs, but Morgan's Café has peaches covered in gravy."

The bandoleers that crossed Luong's back moved slightly on top of the sweat stains of his bush uni. Luong was an expert at being perfectly still. Blending into his environment. Becoming a log or a lump of clay or a rock. Luong could stay motionless and undetected in the middle of a hamlet for hours.

"*Khong*," Luong said. No. "Need to di di soon, Morgan. Get to Cần Thơ and leave baby-san."

Tran reached again for the leather thong that held the syringe. His black eyes wide, he watched to see if it was okay.

Tiny fingers. Crusted in dirt and puffy on the top. I squeezed his hand softly and held it to my chest.

"*Khong*, baby-san," I whispered and smiled into those bottomless black eyes that held the battles of a hundred years. "GI need *thuoc* to keep us both alive." Medicine.

The morphine had to do. No RTO. No medevacs would come for a dust-off. No doc to hold intestines in. No buddies to carry me back or mourn my death. If I was wounded, the morphine might be the only thing that kept me moving.

The little head on my shoulder weighed less than a frag. I stroked Tran's hair while his bare butt rested in the elbow of my arm.

"Luong," I said, "you're right. Pack up. We gotta hump it for Cần Thơ and find someplace for Tran. I'll watch."

Luong moved to the back of the bunker, and I took his place, Tran still cradled in my arm. My right hand touched the trigger of the M16.

The sun was high enough to send tracers of light through the upper limbs of the banana trees. Thick fog rose from the paddies and died after billowing upward for a meter. The day was already warm enough to heat up the decay of the Delta. The smell of rotting garbage and boiling fish oil greeted the morning. Nothing moved on the horizon other than the gentle sway of the palms and the clouds across the sky.

Luong finished packing the ruck with the Starlight scope, grenades, and ammo. He helped me put the ruck on my back while I held Tran. Luong stepped out of the bunker and took point, Tran and I on drag.

"Back humpin', Tran," I said. "We're off to find you a home."

It would be a daylong hump, sticking close to the trail, not on it. Every approaching sound would require us to vanish in the bush until we were sure it wasn't a patrol, less likely as we got close to Cần Thơ.

Morgan, Luong, and a baby. A fairy tale. Death was my life, and now I was risking it to save a war orphan in a land overflowing with parentless babies. But I couldn't get rid of the daily scene of mama-sans standing in the dust beside the road. They weren't selling Camels or Chiclets. They held up dead babies, already blackened by the sun, flies swarming. Rumor was the infants were drugged and rubbed with charcoal. This was another drama that fit perfectly into the sense of guilt, never far from any grunt's conscience even if they had done nothing evil. They had seen the beast and the mama-sans with the corpses made more piasters than one's selling their bodies or Coca-Cola. Now, my donation was saving Tran.

The red ball was packed-clay slippery in the humidity from the sandaled feet of peasants and VC. The speed trail wound through groves of bananas and chest-high grass. We were a klick from Cần Thơ and already had passed black-toothed mama-sans carrying baskets on their heads who scolded us when they saw Tran in my arm. Soldiers were a part of their life and history. But a grunt with a baby-san was another matter.

Ahead, the jungle ended, and hootches became thicker until the suburbs joined the city of Cần Thơ.

"*Dung lai*, Luong," I said. Stop. "I better do some recon before we walk into town with a baby on our shoulders."

Luong slipped into the grass. Within a meter, he was invisible even to me. No blade was flattened or even rustled. Luong moved quiet and unseen as a bamboo snake. I followed. Tran was asleep, head pressed against my neck.

In the distance, the whine of motorcycles and honking of jeeps drifted across the fields. A pig squealed, and roosters crowed. The *whup-whup* of Hueys signaled the presence of the army on the far side of town.

Luong squatted in the grass and took off his bush hat, wiping his brow with the sleeve of his fatigues. His M16 rested against his thigh, barrel pointed to the tips of the saw grass.

"You have plan, Morgan?" Luong asked. He picked his teeth with a piece of bamboo. The gaps in his mouth were black around the filed points of his incisors.

I held the sleeping Tran with one hand and wrestled my pack next to the M16.

"We'll feed Tran," I said. "Then I'll probe Cần Thơ. There's a couple European women there who run an orphanage funded by USAID. Really, it's drug money from the spooks, but the nurses will know what to do with Tran. I won't let anyone sell him. You *dung lai* here with the baby-san."

C-rations that Tran could eat were running low. I sorted through the ruck with my left hand and moved the pork and beans, meatloaf and gravy, and beef slices aside. There was only one more tin of applesauce and one of peaches left. I used the bent opener to pry off the top.

The fucking mosquitoes attacked along with an army of flies. Fresh blood and food were all they needed to form a buzzing cloud in the little bivouac we made in the saw grass. Before I woke Tran, I smeared more bug juice on my hands and face.

Mosquitoes and flies didn't bother Luong. He opened a leather pouch of cooked rice and added a few drops of fish oil from a plastic bottle covered in bright Montagnard writing that showed a fisherman pulling in a net filled with carp on a river sampan.

The repellent fit snugly back in my ruck next to the silencer for the Hush Puppy.

"Maybe you should feed Tran," I said. "Give you a chance to get to know him better. Establish a little trust. I'll di di to town."

The saw grass smelled ripe and wet from yesterday's rain. Some of the tips held seed buds like wheat in the fields of The World and waved a golden salute in the tropical breeze.

Through the grass, we could see the trail. But no one could see us.

Luong set the leather pouch on the ground and put the fish oil in his pack. Flies crawled on his forehead and fingers.

"*Vang*, Morgan," Luong said. "Tran eat *gao* with peaches." Rice. He reached for the baby-san with a smile that reflected the overhead sun off the sharp points of his teeth.

I moved my hands around Tran's ribs and gently passed him to Luong without letting the baby-san's head flop onto his chest. Flies landed on Tran's butt and legs and began to feed on his gook sores still glistening with ointment. After Luong had Tran in his arms, I swatted at the flies and covered the baby-san with my poncho.

"Tran sleep," Luong said. "Feed baby-san when wake up."

I stood, leaving the pack and C-rations on the ground. The bandoleers on my chest slipped easily beside the ruck. I dropped my frags next to the extra ammo, but kept the M16 and two cartridges in my fatigue pocket.

"Won't be needing this arsenal," I said. "If I get in an ambush, it won't save me. Don't think I'll get jumped this close to town. You keep it. Take good care of Tran. Should be back in a couple hours. Regular signals. *Cao biet*, Luong." Good-bye.

Luong patted Tran's back and flashed me the peace sign.

The saw grass barely moved as I stepped through onto the red ball trail, visions of a sleeping innocent in a land of death putting speed into my mission.

The old two-story French villa in Cần Thơ that housed the USAID orphanage was on Hoa Tao Street. Apple Blossom. Rainwater from leaking gutters had stained the white stucco walls with brown designs. Termite and bullet holes made the building look like a huge, off-white dartboard. In the middle of the wall facing Hoa Tao Street, a red cross was painted beside the three concrete steps that led to a screened front door. The mesh was torn and hanging to the cement.

My M16 was propped against the wooden frame of a stall selling Chiclets, Hershey bars, Pez, and Coca-Cola, and I leaned on a torn sign that read BEST PRISE FOR GI.

The mama-san who sold me an ice-cold Coke for 5 p wore a conical straw hat to shade the afternoon sun. Her soiled, gray pajamas were buttoned to her wrinkled neck. Two baby-sans tossed stones and played hide-and-seek between her scarred legs. The sandals on the mama-san's feet were worn out, and her white heels showed through holes the size of the Medal of Honor in the rubber.

The street was busy with oxcarts, mopeds, Citroens, Jeeps, and pedestrians dressed in pajamas, jeans, or colorful ao dais. There were no Vietnamese men older than seventeen or younger than forty-five in sight unless they were on crutches. The Saigon government had caved in and declared a universal draft demanded by Johnson. Vietnam's finest were the same ARVN that often di di'ed when the action got hot.

America's finest were part of the street scene. GIs stumbled in and out of the bars that lined the packed-clay road while white-helmeted MPs watched and chatted with young women wearing satin dresses slit to midthigh. All the soldiers carried M16s, and most had Colts strapped to their waists. I was no more out of place than Nixon at a Quaker retreat, sipping a bottle of Coke through a straw and smoking a Camel.

Gasoline fumes were stronger than the smell of overripe fruit and fly-covered pork that hung from the booth two down. Neither the perfume of the bargirls nor the sweet smell of orchids and hyacinths could win against the blue smoke that billowed from the unmuffled exhausts of the motorcycles and cars.

The door to the orphanage opened. A redheaded woman stepped out, long, fine hair flipping up in the afternoon wind. She was followed by a Vietnamese woman carrying a diapered baby-san with only one foot. The mama-san bowed and walked down the steps.

Standing tall, the redhead waved and watched the mama-san blend into the crowded traffic. The pale, white arms that were crossed on the redhead's chest pushed up breasts that stretched the fabric of her white cotton blouse. She wasn't smiling.

I field-dressed my Camel and set the Coke bottle on the ground. With the M16 in my right hand, I threaded my way between mopeds and walked to the orphanage door. The metal handle was only held by one screw and nearly came off in my hand.

The redhead sat behind a scarred, wooden desk in the middle of the room under a ceiling fan that barely moved the mushy humid air. She wrote with a Bic pen, but looked up with the sound of the screen door's creak.

"No guns allowed," she said. "Park them against the wall." She pointed to a sign next to me that read WEAPONS. A bamboo basket for pistols sat on a C-ration crate, and the wall was nicked at the height where an M16 sight would touch the plaster.

The air in the room was dense and heavy. I wiped the sweat that was suddenly beading on my forehead.

"That's against the orders of the day for Cần Thơ, ma'am," I said. "Supposed to be armed at all times."

The pale, white skin on the woman's cheeks turned red. She pointed the Bic at me, and her brows pushed together in a frown.

"I'll have none of that," she said. "I don't give a farthing about any 'orders of the day.' If you want to come in, stow your weapons over there. Or take them out in the street with you." She moved the barrel of her Bic in the direction of the WEAPONS sign.

The woman spoke with an Irish brogue. Her chin was square and masculine below full lips that were light red without the need of lipstick. Rounded cheekbones surrounded a perfect nose that was slightly turned up. White teeth showed as she talked. Full, black eyebrows ran above green eyes that seemed to see through me and into Hoa Tao Street.

My bush boots made crackling noises in the grit-covered floor on my way to the weapons storage. I leaned the M16 on the wall and unhooked my holster, lightly dropping the Colt in the basket. I turned back to the woman.

"Name's Smith, ma'am," I said as I walked across the wooden floor toward the woman's desk. "Yesterday, we got caught in a firefight about five klicks from here. We were in a vil when the VC ambushed us, killing all the civilians. Except one. A year-old baby-san named Tran. We've got him hidden out. Before I hand Tran over to anyone, I want to know what's going to happen to him."

The woman sat back in her rattan chair. Bamboo weave protested with a squeal. She tapped the end of the Bic on her forehead and inspected me for tics and lice.

Dirt and sweat. No mud-covered pig in a vil rooting in the garbage smelled any worse than me. The stains under my armpits didn't end before they disappeared under my web belt. I could season the beef strips in my C-rats with the salt caked on the liner of the bush hat I held in my right hand. I used to be as pale-skinned as the woman. Now I didn't know if my face and arms would ever be anything but red from clay dust and sunburn. At least I had washed off last night's bug juice and black greasepaint, which made me look like a raccoon.

The redhead laid down the Bic on a small stack of files and folded her hands.

"I'm Colleen O'Hara, Mr. Smith," she said. "Or is that Private? Corporal? I don't see any stripes or a name tag. But you seem like officer material. Tell me more about the baby-san. Pull that chair over." Colleen nodded her head to the left.

Against the wall, a metal folding chair sat listing to the side, padding on the seat ripped and showing gray steel. I unfolded the chair and put it in front of the teak desk. I sat down, careful to keep my weight on the right side.

"First, I know what happens here," I said. "USAID thinks it's a great idea to win hearts and minds by paying Vietnamese to adopt war orphans. Not bad propaganda back in The World either."

I stroked the rim of my helmet, keeping my hands from going AWOL.

"But the cash really comes from the CIA and is used to pay bribes and hush money," I said. "The kids are made slaves. Or worse. I don't want that for Tran. What I want to know is that he's going to be well taken care of."

The ceiling fan clicked and wheezed on every rotation. It was moving slowly enough that cobwebs formed on the blades.

Windows on the walls away from Hoa Tao Street were louvered and the slats were open. Outside, the leaves of banana trees scratched the wood. Behind Colleen, a closed door held a sign reading PRIVATE in red letters. *RIENG* was written just below. USO posters were spread around the walls, mostly showing happy uniformed soldiers who looked like Fred Astaire dancing with WACs who looked like Ginger Rogers.

The sound of baby-sans crying came through the door marked *RIENG*. The muted noise was joined by the clicks of mama-sans talking in rapid fire Vietnamese.

Colleen continued her recon. Her head nodded up and down, making decisions. The tightness of her gorgeous face said she was finding more questions than answers.

"Now, laddie," Colleen said, "how do you know all that?" She smiled, and a dimple sucked in on her cheek.

I touched the handle of the Gerber fighting knife in my pocket. There was no way Colleen or General Westmoreland would get me to stow it while I was in-country.

"Let's just say that the boonie-rat network knows all," I said. "There's not diddly that happens in 'Nam without the smoke signals passing it around. If it don't happen, it gets told anyway. Don't mean nuthin'. I'm a good listener."

Colleen's Irish smile infected me like a case of the giggles. I smiled back.

"By the way," I said, "is it Miss O'Hara or Mrs.?"

The rattan chaired creaked again. Colleen sat back and crossed her forearms on her chest, but the leprechaun smile stayed.

"Well now, Mr. Smith," Colleen said. "Why would I be tellin' you that? You won't say what your rank is. It is Mr. Smith, now isn't it? Not Lieutenant? Or agent?"

A small hole above the knee of my bush fatigues showed the whiteness of the skin not exposed to the tropical sun and ever-present mud and dust. I played with a loose thread of the once-green cotton.

"Okay, Miss O'Hara," I said. "Let's not go down that trail. I'm here about Tran. I don't care where the money comes from or why. Only that Tran's looked after and not sold into slavery. Or that some South Vietnamese politician gets a piaster richer by selling him someplace else."

The dimple was gone. Colleen's face changed as fast as the weather in Dublin.

"We do the best we can with what little we have, Mr. Smith," Colleen said. "Before any child leaves this building, we run a background check on the adoptive parents. But we're depending on intel provided by the military and the Provincial government. And the CIA. Do you trust any of them?" She slammed her hand on the desk, and the sound was the crack of an AK. "You don't know me, but I'm insulted you'd even suggest I'd sell babies. Who do you think you are?"

The hole in my pants was now as big as the bottom of a Mike 2 grenade. I thought I was going to ask the questions.

"We've made a whorehouse of this whole country," I said. "For centuries, the foundation of Vietnamese society has been the family. Now, that's burned away like the jungles we bomb with napalm. Kids are sold on the street. And out the door of orphanages. Used to be that a thousand piasters fed a family of five for a year. It takes a thousand today to feed one person."

The right side of my butt was cramping from sitting off balance in the crooked steel chair. I shifted to the left and felt myself tipping toward the floor.

"And there's no men around for support," I said. "Unless they're cripples. The teenagers younger than seventeen run in gangs and terrorize anyone who has a rice bowl to cook in. It's the baby-san mafia. What they don't steal, the corrupt local government and VC tax collectors get. I'm not blaming you. I said it before. My mission is about Tran. What can you do? And how can you be sure?"

Red hair covered the tops of Colleen's shoulders and thick strands hung to the peaks of her breasts. She twisted the strands with her left hand.

"Thanks for the lecture, Mr. Smith," she said. "With that and ten piasters I could buy an M16. It's a buyer's market on Hoa Tao Street. We don't sell babies here. In fact, it's just nearly the opposite. We pay for them to be adopted. But I still want to know more about Tran. Where did you find him and how? Where's his mother?"

Firefights. The sound was a mad minute louder than standing inside the jet engine of a B-52. But I never heard it. My focus was on the targets and saving my ass. The noise was drowned by blood and severed arms. Nick's body jumping at the hit of every AK round.

Somehow, an ant had gotten into my filthy sock. I squished the little red biter and took a deep breath without looking at Colleen.

"We were rappin' with a CAG ghost named Nick in the vil where he was TDY," I said. "Just as we were leaving, the VC ambushed from the palm trees. He was holding Tran. Nick curled up around the baby-san and took all the bullets."

I hung the hat on my knee, covering the hole, which was now the size of a Coke bottle bottom.

"We made friends with Tran through the afternoon," I said. "He seemed to be Nick's adopted son. Everybody was killed but us. We hid behind some grave mounds at the edge of the vil. Grabbed Tran and di di'ed. Didn't see any mama-sans around. I figure they got greased, too."

A gecko poked its head through the louvers on the window to Colleen's right. The little green lizard's pink tongue flicked in and out in search of a mosquito, and his bugged out eyes studied Colleen almost as intensely as I watched the striking woman.

Wrinkles formed on Colleen's forehead, and her green eyes turned up the temperature on my face hotter than a pound of burning C-4. She tapped the Bic on the stack of files. Colleen's stare had me locked into her sights.

"So you don't really know if Tran's mama-san is dead or alive?" Colleen asked.

Ham and lima beans were the most hated meal of all the shit that passed for food the US government gave to boonie rats, much of it left over from the Korean War. Ham was supposed to be a dark red when cooked and lima beans white. Ham and lima beans in a C-ration can were a solid gray and smelled like they had been aging in the tropical sun since Dien Bien Phu. The taste and texture was worse than chewing on a letter from The World. Fruit cocktail was number ten best, and no boonie rat without a serious head wound would trade a dozen ham and lima beans that were number one worst for a fruit cocktail. Colleen was a fruit cocktail.

The ant bite itched, but Colleen's eyes were causing a tingle to start somewhere else. An itch that hadn't been scratched in months and had been MIA since I wasted Liem.

The bent folding chair was causing me to feel off balance and dizzy. Maybe it was the dense, hot air. I stretched my bush boot to the left and tried to straighten myself.

"The vil was home to an American grunt," I said. "We killed a couple of the VC. Charley's brothers will want revenge. If the mama-sans were alive, they're paddy food now. Or packing supplies on the Ho Chi Minh Trail. But you can check yourself. The vil is called Do Lai 3 on the topo maps."

The left hand that held the Bic to Colleen's mouth was ringless. There was no telling white circle around the tan of her ring finger. Colleen chewed on the tip of the Bic and tapped her other hand on the table.

"We will," Colleen said. "Why don't you bring Tran in? The bush isn't any place for a baby-san to be without a mum. We can take care of him here."

One of the buttons on the chest of my fatigues had gone missing. I tried to close the breach with my hand and felt the sweat on my body.

"What are you going to do with Tran?" I asked. "Let's say his mama-san has joined her ancestors. I want to know exactly what happens next. I'm not bringing him in until you tell me."

Freckles dotted Colleen's cheeks. The brown spots were barely visible, but they seemed to be getting darker. No makeup covered her face. Colleen didn't need any. She was refreshing. A cherry-vanilla ice cream cup the Hueys dropped into the LZ sometimes during resupply on holidays. Or after a successful op with a high body count.

Colleen nudged aside the pile of files and took a form from the top desk drawer. She held up the paper.

"We fill this chit out," Colleen said. "On it are queries that it seems only you can answer for Tran. The bottom half is a report for the army medics who come by every few days. No totty is released without a physical. Before we put the kids out for adoption, we try to get them healthy. If you couldn't tell, there's a nursery and infirmary in back. Will you help me fill this in?"

Colleen smiled, the dimple a small mortar crater on her cheek, and pointed the Bic at me, the other hand on the form.

Days of rain, mud, and brown paddy water turned my feet white and wrinkled as soaking in a bathtub for hours. A hint of pink was at the bottom of every crease where the skin hadn't rotted off. The pink off-white of Colleen's face. With no wrinkles. I lifted my toes and felt bone on leather.

"You get intel on the Vietnamese parents?" I asked. "Maybe I can give you a hand."

"Those chits are confidential," Colleen said.

"So is Tran's location," I said. "But I'll bring him in if you tell me where he's going. Don't want you to pay his new parents and they sell him back to some gook official. Maybe I've got sources I can use."

"No can do, Mr. Smith."

"Well, it seems we're stuck like the Paris Peace talks, Miss O'Hara."

"At least let us take a gander at him. For medical reasons."

"I've compromised too many times in this hellhole. Tell me who his new mama-san's going to be. Or you'll never see him."

"What alternative do you have, Mr. Smith?"

"It's Russian roulette here anyway. Maybe I'll di di to Saigon and see if I can get Tran adopted back in The World. For no money. Some of the baby-sans are getting on the Freedom Bird."

"Well now, Mr. Smith. Won't your unit miss you? Won't your commanding officer think you're AWOL? Or is your brief 'need to know'?"

Colleen dropped the Bic on the desk next to an ancient black telephone with no dial and put her chin in her hands, elbows resting on the teak. Her whole face smiled like she had found a pearl in her fish ball.

The only sounds came from the clicking of the ceiling fan and the *bleets* of moped horns on Hoa Tao Street. Exhaust clouds drifted through the louvers and formed a layer of blue fog at the top of the room. The walls were molding in the constant tropical humidity, and the smell joined the orchid bushes outside the windows, fighting a losing battle with the traffic fumes. I watched Fred Astaire twirl Ginger Rogers around a ballroom filled with happy soldiers and thought about Bic pens. One of the stories that circulated in the firebases was about a grunt with chest wounds who couldn't breathe. Under attack and lacking the proper instruments to vent the gagging solider, the medic stabbed the barrel of a Bic into the man's throat. I could never look at a Bic again without seeing it dangling from a bleeding grunt's neck.

The times when I didn't wear boots in the boonies, I was on a black op. I became Vietnamese. I could walk with the stooped shuffle of a barefoot peasant, leaving no tracks but toe prints in the clay. In a pajama top and a conical hat, head bowed, not even the VC could tell I was a white devil. I could stand next to a hootch in the shadows and VC five feet away didn't know I was there until the Gerber or the Hush Puppy gave them a wake-up call. Or the shitstorm exploded from one of my escort's M60 pig machine guns.

Several methods were used for questioning VC. One was terror. Like hooking electrical clamps to a suspect's balls. The wires led to a hand-cranked field phone. One turn on the crank and the lines lit up, causing the suspect's back to arch and his eyeballs to pop out. It was called the Bell Telephone Hour. Another method was silence and isolation. But this method took patience, in short supply in the bush. Colleen and I used method two.

At Benning, I was taught to show no fear to a prisoner. Always be the one in control and powerful. The giver of life. Or taker. But Colleen's stare made the itch spread from my feet, a sensation like laying my poncho on an anthill for a night bivouac.

The green fluorescent dial on my Navy SEAL watch read 4:21. I had to get back to Luong and Tran before dark, when the VC quit their day jobs and came out of the tunnels to take the night.

Relax, Morgan. Or Smith. Float in the land of opium dreams. Escape to a world of red hair and freckles rocking in a hammock strung between the green palms of China Beach. Hear the sound of emerald waves lapping on the white sand, and feel a ripe coconut breast pushed against your shoulder, fingers tracing the Delta through the hair on your chest. The touch of moist lips on your cheek and a knee pressed tight to your thigh. Let the smell of a woman fill your nose.

Green eyes darker than the pebbled skin of the gecko watched me. Colleen must have played this game. Or been trained well by whoever she worked for. Most of the white civilians in 'Nam had some cover to cloak them from their real mission of gathering information for one of the ABC intelligence agencies.

The watch read 4:25. Colleen's chin still rested in her hands, and the power was shifting faster and more real than the Domino Theory.

The skirmish was over. But I hoped the battle had just begun. I pushed the leg that had gone to sleep against the floor and straightened myself in the leaning chair.

"Okay, Miss O'Hara," I said. "Let's deal. I'll bring Tran in. You do your med workup. I'll be around. When you send him out, you agree to tell where he went."

The short sleeves of Colleen's white blouse stopped just below the curve at the edge of her shoulders. She raised her arms straight above her head and shook her hands awake. Through the gap in her sleeves, a thin bra covered breasts the size of moped headlights.

"Deal, Mr. Smith," Colleen said. "I was askin' myself how long it would take. For a tick, I thought you nodded off."

My left side was numb from keeping upright in the bent chair. I stood, careful not to put too much weight on my leg.

"One more thing," I said. "I'll be back with Tran before dark. Then I'd like to continue rapping. I'm not dressed for a candlelit dinner, but maybe we can grab a beer somewhere."

Colleen tried to rub the wrinkles out of her blouse top with her right hand. The left smoothed long, red hairs that were sticking to the side of her head.

"Bring Tran in, laddie, and I'll see about that," Colleen said.

She came around the desk and walked me toward the WEAPONS sign. Her leather sandals squeaked below bare toes with a hint of old white nail polish. A skirt fell below Colleen's knees and didn't cover calves shaped like Wilma Rudolph's. A rope belt was tied loosely around her slim waist, and the ends hung to the top of thighs that showed through the cotton dress.

Maybe the Dexedrine, but tremors stopped me from snapping the steel buckle on the web belt holding the Colt. The canteen that was usually next to the pistol was what I really needed to help the dryness in my throat.

"All a twitter, soldier?" Colleen said. The dimple in her cheek was infecting the side of her face. Freckles around the craters turned the red of her thick hair. She touched the elbow of my camo fatigue.

Colleen's fingers shook gently. Like Tran's hand when he tried to hold the morphine tied to my neck. But her feel was the heat of the tropics. Hot enough for me to spontaneously combust.

The goddamn buckle wouldn't snap. My fingers were numb and as useless as the leg that was still asleep. Colleen's smell, musk with a trace of lavender, made my good leg feel it wouldn't keep me standing much longer.

A swish of cotton and Colleen was in front of me. White teeth contrasted with the red lips turned up in a smile that was about to break out in a laughing jag. Her hands moved toward my waist, and she bent over.

"Let me help you, soldier," Colleen said.

The last woman I touched was Liem.

Giao te. Fuck. Worse than Mother zipping up my fly before I went off to the army's nursery school at Fort Lewis. I slid an inch back and dropped my arms to my sides. The muscles in my stomach tightened like Cassius Clay was about to punch me and a current from the Bell Telephone Hour ran to my groin.

The back of Colleen's head gave a glimpse of a white neck dotted with freckles thicker and darker than the crop on her face. Just above her, a fat fly lumbered like a loaded B-52 and tried to find a landing strip in her hair. I swatted the fly away, afraid to continue looking down on the beautiful woman fumbling with my web belt.

"Stand still, soldier," Colleen said. "I don't have all day to mess about."

I couldn't see the smile that must be on Colleen's face, but the curve of her back rocked with laughter, and the touch of her fingers on my waist played Roberta Flack singing "Killing Me Softly." A peek down gave a view of the tops of freckled breasts that disappeared into a bra rimmed with faint sweat marks. Cleavage dark and inviting as a warm night on Au Tau beach.

Heavy breasts. Two of my favorite words in English. Almost as good as *Freedom Bird*.

The metal on the belt clinked together, and Colleen stood, rubbing her fingers. Green eyes stared into mine, filled with Irish cheer.

"Off you go now, Mr. Smith," Colleen said. "Bring me that baby-san."

I pushed the belt higher on my waist and checked the buckle.

"Thanks, ma'am," I said.

A moment in time in the middle of a war zone where everything stops. Green eyes locked into mine tighter than banyan roots to the jungle clay. Smiles disappear and are replaced by something indefinable. But more electric and filled with promise. The only noise the M79 thumper in my chest.

Colleen stepped aside, almost stumbling in her sandals. She caught herself with the back of the bent chair.

The elbow of my fatigues brushed against her bare arm. I took two steps to the M16. The handle was cool and reassuring. Not a mystery like this Irish witch. I let the rifle hang from my hand parallel to the wooden floor.

The mock salute from Colleen was sloppier than even the most grizzled cynical boonie rat. Fingers bent, Colleen's cupped hand bumped the top of her nose.

"Cheers, Mr. Smith," Colleen said. "I'll think about that pint while you're fetching the baby-san."

Phan. Shit. There was no way I could stop myself from smiling back at this redheaded Irish beauty. Just like I couldn't resist Tran's coos and the surprising tug that his touch brought to a soul burned by the dead. Maybe Colleen could save us both.

The M16 was in my right hand. I saluted with my left. The sunburn on my face caused my smile to bring a sharp pain to my cheeks.

"Thanks, Miss O'Hara," I said. "I'll be back with Tran in a few hours."

Colleen still held her cupped hand loosely below her forehead, and her white teeth were surrounded by her smile. She was perfectly at ease, shoulders slumped and legs bent.

"Don't mean nuthin', troop," Colleen said. "Just saddle up and ride 'em hard."

The laugh started somewhere deep in a place that hadn't been touched since the coughing fit after getting bazookaed with Fralich's M16 barrel two months ago. The Cambodian Red seared my throat and caused me to spray the mouthful of Bud all over Fralich's bare chest. His hand-carved leather peace sign dripped with beer that seeped into his skivvies.

I stood in front of this saluting beauty, tears running from my eyes and stomach feeling the knotted pain of laughter. And relief. Maybe her spirit would be my Freedom Bird.

The lump in my stomach made its way to my throat and lodged like a betel nut. I turned to the ripped screen door and pushed it open.

A convoy of olive-green jeeps and deuce and a halfs filled with ammo crates and C-rations was passing on Hoa Tao Street. Dust covered the grunts riding in the open trucks and formed clouds that hid the stalls across the road. The sun was almost to the top of the jungle canopy that grew on the distant hills.

I stood on the cement steps while the dust settled on the mopeds and pedestrians.

My feet hurt. The thin ragged socks under my bush boots were bunched in the toes. It was a hassle to keep pulling them up. After a few days in the mildew between my toes, my socks were as rank as a greased VC left in the jungle for weeks. And came apart just as easy. I wiggled my big toe to move a clump that was pressing against the bone and leather toe and looked back at the orphanage.

The last glimpse of Colleen through the torn mesh was a stunning red-headed woman smiling and watching me walk down the steps to Hoa Tao Street. I gave Colleen the two-fingered peace sign and headed south to fetch Tran feeling like I was under an Irish spell.

Shit. I couldn't translate the zaps to my nerves. Not even a krait slithering past or a squad of NVA appearing like wraiths in the mist made the back of my neck twitch like this Irish witch. I couldn't just pass it off as being around a white woman for the first time in nearly a year. No other had ever gotten into my skin like Colleen. Maybe there was a "no fly zone" that Tran penetrated and now was open for traffic. Maybe it was the way the corner of her mouth turned up just like Mom's. Maybe it was the wild hair that made me think of faraway lost worlds. Maybe it was that I couldn't remember ever feeling this way and certainly not this quickly. More likely, it was just 'Nam, a place where any harbor that could possibly be safe cried out to be entered. Whatever the reason, a sense of purpose and hope—dead for months—returned and made me forget, for a moment, Liem's eyes.

* * *

Only a few mama-sans were on the red ball, most already back squatting in front of cook fires stirring the night's variation of rice. The ones I passed balanced elephant grass and bamboo baskets, filled with stalks or Coca-Cola from the black market that thrived in every city in 'Nam.

By the time I reached Luong and Tran's bivouac, the sun was well below the horizon, and I could imagine the first stars of the Southern Cross through the humidity and smoke haze.

"*Hoa binh*," I whispered to the green, eight-foot-high wall of grass. Peace. It was the password that Luong and I used to keep from mistakenly unloading a magazine of M16 bullets into the other.

"*Chien trauh*," Luong said, just barely louder than the breeze that made the elephant grass sway in the evening wind. War. If he hadn't answered, tracers would light the night.

Only a slight rustle in the grass and I was standing next to Luong and the pile of weapons. Bats swooped over my head, looking for a sunset meal.

Tran smiled at me, drool in the corner of his little mouth, and clenched his tiny fists. He was propped on Luong's thighs, bare butt pressed against a fragmentation grenade.

Luong started to his feet, never taking his hand off the M16.

"You louder than *con voi*, white devil," Luong said. Elephant. "I hear you coming for half klick."

I took Tran and nuzzled the baby's neck. Tran kicked my flak jacket and made cooing sounds.

"Saddle up, troop," I said. "Gotta find this baby-san a new mom."

The M16 rested against the rice paper wall of the Chinese restaurant on Thom Cai Street. Fragrant flower. Luong kept most of my arsenal, except the Hush Puppy, which poked under the back of my camo fatigues. A Willie Pete M34 white phosphorus grenade was in my pocket. The kind of grenade that not only provided a smoke screen, but would light up the bamboo walls in this place quicker than a napalm cocktail, letting Colleen and me di di in the white haze. Anyone unlucky enough to get phosphorous on their skin would feel the jelly burn a hole to the bone. And keep on burning to the other side.

The Irish witch sat across the table, green eyes sparkling like Burmese sapphires in the candlelight. A sneer close to a smile bent her lips and pushed her dimples into squished craters.

"You must be expectin' Giap's Second Division armed like that," Colleen said. She could see the spoon on the grenade hanging from the outside of my pocket.

The pin on the M34 jabbed my thigh and made me feel as uncomfortable as Colleen's stare. I pushed the grenade lower in my pocket.

"The only reason this city isn't off-limits after dark is because we're ordered to be armed at all times," I said. "After the last incident here in friendly Cần Thơ, I'm surprised grunts are allowed in at all. But where would the REMFs go at night if the city were shut down?"

I leaned forward, elbows on the pitted Formica table, and stared at Colleen.

"Two weeks ago," I said, "the MPs found a supply clerk from the base crucified on a lamp post on Hoa Doa Street. They took his eyes."

Colleen had changed out of her nurse's uniform and wore a purple ao dai painted in hyacinths. A white orchid was pinned to her hair, contrasting with the deep red of her braids. She fingered the orchid and the smirk disappeared like VC down a tunnel.

"Well, laddie," she said, "you surely know how to get to a lady's heart. It would be nice if we could forget the war for the eve'nin'. Make believe we're on Regent Street for a nice side of mutton."

The red clay under my fingernails was as much a part of me as my rotting toes. Now the red was darkened by a mix of greasepaint and rifle oil. I picked at the nails on my right hand with the plastic sword toothpick that used to hold the umbrella in my Singapore Sling.

"There's nothing I'd like better," I said. "But there's the matter of millions of VC trying to kill us as well as their own countrymen. Did you find a home for Tran?"

A few minutes after sunset, Luong and I delivered a sleeping Tran to the orphanage, where the baby vanished through the back door of Colleen's office in the hands of a clucking mama-san. When I handed Tran over to Colleen, he instantly put his head on her shoulder and closed his eyes. She stroked his head and cooed in Tran's ear.

Luong waited near a hedgerow that marked the north border of Cần Thơ. Tonight's op wouldn't begin until well after midnight, and his recon would be good enough to write the death warrant on another target.

Rice paper napkins were next to the plates, and their slightly brown tint was darker than Colleen's skin. She picked up her napkin and rubbed it between her fingers, looking down at the painted French plates, a holdover from colonialism.

"Not yet," Colleen said. "But we have someone in mind who would be better than one of the refugee orphanages."

"We've got a deal, ma'am. As soon as you find out, you're going to tell me."

"At the end of the day, I don't know how much difference any of it makes."

"Why do you say that? Something change in the last few hours? Looks to me like you're letting this place get to you, too."

Colleen's head rose, and a quiver started in her shoulder. A small tear formed next to the lash in her right eye.

"Wanted so much to have an nice evening out and put this place aside," Colleen said. "Got less chance of that than the Queen mum bein' next month's centerfold."

The half of me that was Irish was under the spell of this woman who spoke a lilt right out of the streets of Londonderry. The other half was the normal reaction of a soldier in a distant land enjoying the rare presence of a beautiful woman. I tried to smooth my hair, but it was full of red dust from the day's march and sweat from the tropical sun.

"What is it?" I asked. "Does it have anything to do with Tran?"

Colleen rubbed her eye and picked up a fork that must have been liberated from an army PX. The US MILITARY stamp was still on the handle.

"No," Colleen said. "We got an intelligence report today that most of the widows who take in the kids get their pensions knicked by the local ARVN commanders. They sell the extra rice chit we arrange for them. Many of the tykes are starving. It just seems there's no end to the mischief here. Makes Belfast look like God's own."

"You shouldn't be telling me that, Miss O'Hara," I said. "I'm not going to let it happen to Tran."

"And that may not even be the worst of it," Colleen said. "Now, the drums are beating that it might be the son of the vice president selling babies. Nothing much we can do but our jobs with what we have. I've filed an official complaint. In triplicate."

Fucking Ky. Now, he was connected to two women I knew. One was dead and the one across from me was drowning in his swamp. Now I was afraid for this spunky Irish lass. You didn't mess with someone like Ky unless you had a battalion to cover your back.

"I think we may have done better for Tran," Colleen said. "I'll know more tomorrow. As sure as one lives and breathes, this place is arsed-up."

Nothing I could do about Ky. For now. But his was a mounting debt that had to be called before I rode the sweet bird home. I took a sip of the drink and changed the subject with the grunt way, a story.

"Back at the base," I said, "we adopted a local kid to clean up for us and run errands. His left foot was gone, courtesy of one of Uncle Ho's mines.

Called him Festus because he limped around with the stump stuffed in an old tennis shoe filled with dirt and tied tight to his ankle. Gave him a few p most every day. He never stopped smiling and loved to sing 'Proud Mary' and have us join in. His teeth were already rotten at ten years old, and he couldn't have weighed thirty-five pounds. Don't know if he had any parents alive, but one day I was coming back to base and I saw a mama-san slapping him and pulling at the pockets on his ratty shorts. He never wore a shirt. The old bitch was screeching. *'Tien bac, tien bac.'* Money. I went over and pulled her off. She tried to scratch my face, and I shoved her down, put Festus under my arm, and hightailed it for our tent. Festus never quit bowing and thanking me, and he cleaned the place spotless. He left before dark. The next morning, his good foot was nailed to the gate, still in the tennis shoe. Never saw Festus again. See why I don't want Tran goin' down that trail?"

Armed soldiers, mostly officers, drank Tiger beer at the bar and ate at the wobbly tables. After a glance at me and a second of thought, they all knew what a dirty boonie rat with no insignia on his camo fatigues casually eating with a beautiful woman meant. And they didn't want to know anything else. I couldn't have been any more obvious as a Phoenix or SOG agent if I got up with my Hush Puppy and put a silenced bullet to the back of the barkeeper's head.

The smell of *nuuc luan* fish sauce overpowered the smell of the exhaust from the cyclos on the street and the sweat from the march. A night in a bomb crater didn't make the aroma any sweeter, and, with a few day's beard added in, I wondered how Colleen could stomach having dinner with me.

Colleen watched me like I was in line for a command inspection. She put her fork down and folded her hands together on the edge of the table.

"That was a bad patch for you," Colleen said. "But I have to live with it every day."

The waiter put a heaping plate of river lobsters on the table and two bowls of rice. He bowed and walked away, a pair of dark slacks several sizes too big for him dragging on the linoleum and covering all but the soles of his rubber tire sandals.

My beard itched, and I scratched softly, always afraid that some incurable skin rot would make it slide off in my fingertips.

"Enough, please," I said. "Tell me how a woman like you got to Cần Thơ."

The tear peaked out of Colleen's eye again, and she looked down at her hands, clasping the napkin tight enough to turn her fingers red.

"Seems as if I traded one war for another," Colleen said. "At least here, I don't know the people bein' killed. And doin' the killin'."

The rice in the wooden bowl was still steaming. I scooped a spoonful on Colleen's plate and mine and then dropped a lobster on top.

"You were involved in the Troubles?" I asked.

"No way of escapin' it," Colleen said. "Like here, there's always someone who wants you dead."

"Then why would you come to this shithole?"

"I couldn't do any good in Belfast. Thought maybe here I could help someone."

"How did you get to the orphanage?"

"Answered an advert in the *Irish Times*. Sounded about as far away as I could get. Never wanted any babies in Belfast. Not another one for a crazed bomber to blow up. But here, babies are everywhere. And needin' help."

The ceiling fan turned slowly through the dense night air, working as hard as a sternwheeler on the Mississippi. On every rotation, the fan clicked. The sound was like snapping my M16 to full auto.

GIs were filling the restaurant, and the jive-assing was getting louder in the bar, directly related to volume of Tiger beer being chugged.

One supply clerk yelled, "How the fuck would you know, you fuckin' pussy. If Charlie walked in here, you'd get slivers in your dick divin' under the bar." His buddies slapped him on the back of his spotless fatigues and they called for another round.

"Damn straight!" the soldier next to the clerk kept screaming, leaning into the REMF so he wouldn't eat any of the cigarette butts on the floor.

Old Spice aftershave joined the smell of fish sauce and spices. But nothing could overcome the burnt, dead stench that draped everything in 'Nam.

Colleen and I picked the meat out of the lobsters and chased the bites with spoonfuls of rice and swallows of cold beer. She didn't look at me, but I marveled at the thick cleanness of her hair.

The *nuuc luan* was spicy, and the beer helped cool my mouth. I took a swallow and noticed that Colleen was looking at me, green eyes mirroring the candlelight.

"We've started down the wrong trail from the beginning," I said. "Maybe we could just rap. Tell lies like the grunts over there." I nodded toward the men at the bar.

The smile lost in the jungle of Belfast returned to Colleen's face. She put her spoon down on the table and wiped her hands.

"Not bloody likely," Colleen said. "Couldn't escape it there. Can't do it here either. Back in the pubs, all we talked about was the Troubles. Here, it's just a more clinical way of killin'."

Lobster shells were piled high on my plate next to the rice. I dropped another on top and stared at Colleen.

"You've seen your share of misery," I said. "But we've got a deal. Tomorrow morning, I want to know where Tran is going. By the way, my name is Morgan."

"Roger that, Morgan," she said. "Let's toast to Tran. And all the wretches who don't have mothers in this place you call a shithole."

Colleen raised her Tiger beer, and we clinked the brown bottles together.

"How is it possible that you have the slightest interest in a baby-san, even if you did save him in a firefight?" Colleen asked. "Why are you responsible? There's thousands more just like Tran."

There was napalm burning the inside of my mouth. Now, the heat from the blazing fish sauce moved toward my chest. I took another hit on the beer.

"I've seen grunts bend over to tickle a baby-san and end up in so many pieces the medic only put the bigger parts in the body bag," I said. "I watched a smiling little girl toss a grenade in a command jeep, killing two lieutenants on the road outside Saigon." I scratched at the stubble on my face and tried to keep eye contact with the witch. "All the way here, I asked the same question you did. Only thing I come up with is that a cooing, helpless baby is the same all over the world, even if his daddy works nights for the VC. The baby-san is innocent." Colleen's eyes were sited in on me like a Starlight scope, and I felt the crosshairs. "I'm not innocent. Maybe there's still a little place in my heart that makes me human. Tran touched it. Part of it is the guilt that every grunt carries and never leaves. Like his P-38 or M16. If I do something noble in this hellhole, there might be a chance. In the next life anyway."

Humping through the mud, eighty pounds of gear digging into my shoulder, I didn't feel any heavier than now. My head nearly slumped to the Formica.

Colleen slid forward in her chair and touched my forearm. I was afraid to look at her.

"Morgan," she whispered, "I've heard lots of stories and seen more than I ever wanted to. If there is any action that can be 'noble' in this country, it is what you have done and are doing to save Tran." She sat back, putting her hand in her lap. "Enough," Colleen said. "We just keep getting into the horrors. Tell me the tale of Morgan in The World."

From one dark side to the other. The past was only a touch lighter than the present, but at least it might get me away from the vision of babies and body parts. I closed my eyes and tried to figure where to begin.

The Colonel was burrowed into my memory. I told Colleen just enough to give the picture of an army brat raised on marching orders and parade-ground discipline who never had a home other than a temporary posting. A graduate in Asian studies with an education perfect for America's plans for the "yellow plague."

A boy who joined the ROTC to defend his country from imminent invasion by the heathens, the real reason to satisfy a father who expected him to become a man someday and not the sniveling punk he thought his son had become.

But I didn't tell her what my real jacket was. I was trained in disinformation as well as ten ways to kill in less than five seconds. With my bare hands. But she knew. She was part of the drama, no matter what her stories were. There were no innocents in 'Nam. Except baby-sans. I told her I was part of the pacification program in the outlying villages and that's where I met Tran. There was no need to hide the cynicism. Everyone in 'Nam was a cynic. It led to statements like, "We burned the village to the ground to save it." Or the campaign I claimed to be part of to win the "Hearts and Minds" of the peasants when all they wanted was for us was to di di back to the US of fucking A so they wouldn't have napalm raining on their conical hats.

Colleen pushed her plate away and slid back her chair.

"Walk me to the orphanage, Morgan," she said. "I'm knackered and have an early wake-up."

The waiter was watching us from behind a false paper wall painted in scenes of the islands off Vung Ta. I waved him to the table and asked for our bill.

By now, the desk jockeys in the bar were polluted. All eyes turned to attention when Colleen stood and walked toward the door. I was right behind, M16 in my hand.

The drunkest REMF was the bravest. And most foolish. He swayed against his brother clerk and raised his beer.

"Check them headlights," he said, pointing the bottle at Colleen. "They could light up the jungle brighter than a battery of M60s."

Nobody joined his slobbering laughter. It was unspoken that I could unload my M16 into them and there would be no court-martial. Military rules didn't cover Phoenix operatives. Maybe I'd be sent back to The World. Or to some remote outpost in Central America. No LBJ. One hard look from me and a hissed "Shut your fuckin' dumbass mouth" from his buddy, and the clerk looked at the polish on his never-muddied boots.

Colleen went through the door, not acknowledging the remark.

The street was still alive with cyclos and the occasional oxcart. Outside, no longer shielded by the smell of fish sauce and cooking meat, the smoke burned my nose. The high-pitched whine and beep of the mopeds overrode the night sounds of Cần Thơ vendors still hawking their trinkets. Traffic smog now hid the moon.

Children, who never slept until the last grunt staggered back to the base, clutched at my fatigues and begged, "GI, GI, want fucky-suck? Coca-Cola? Chiclets?" I kept up with Colleen's quick pace and tried to ignore the ragged kids.

At the steps to the orphanage, Colleen stopped and turned to me.

"Good night, Morgan," she said. "Tellin' lies is what we all do best here. And you're a pro."

Colleen stepped toward me, and I put the arm without the M16 around her waist. The kiss lasted longer than the time took between hearing the hushed thud of a mortar tube and the impact. Her lips were full and moist and brought back long-forgotten memories of partings in front of a university sorority house. Her breasts pushed hard against my fatigues, and I worried that she would feel the KA-BAR in my pocket.

No way I wanted this to end. I pulled her tighter and felt something long lost and only newly rediscovered with Tran.

After ten seconds, Colleen pulled away.

"Might have to go to confession now, Morgan," Colleen said. "See you in the mornin'." She climbed the three steps and opened the battered screen door, disappearing inside.

I was frozen on the steps for a minute, the war completely fragged. All too soon, I touched the Hush Puppy and headed toward Luong for another night of murder on command.

If there was a health department in this shithole, the shack Luong and I stalked would have been condemned before the next monsoon. Or be floating in a B-52 crater. The roof of palm leaves patched with pieces of scavenged tin leaned close enough to the mud to take a drink. Old Coke cartons were jammed between bamboo poles to form soggy walls that stank almost as bad as the slit trench behind and the pit where the day's burnt garbage still smoldered. At least what the pig didn't eat.

Tonight's brief was to wax another local VC leader. But if Cong officers lived like this, Uncle Ho didn't have wooden teeth. The dude probably pissed off somebody who knew somebody who had a friend that could get anybody's name in the Rand computer back in Saigon, even if it was for farting at the wrong time.

Another hour and we'd grease the dogs that slept under the servant's wing of this mansion, the only dry place in the rain and fog that oozed out of the jungle. But first, it would be wise to find out if the marked papa-san wasn't going out for night duty. Or if his baby-sans had dysentery that kept them shitting through the wee hours.

Luong was next to me, and his every breath communicated all I needed to know. We packed enough artillery to blow this hootch to Cambodia, and Luong was eager to waste any Vietnamese that wasn't a Montagnard. His RPG touched my shoulder and was more than enough to scatter anything inside the flimsy hut.

Too many letters to the Colonel. My thoughts were on *Stars and Stripes*, the USMVN answer to the *New York Times* that was more like a comic book written by Westmoreland and War, Inc.

Months beyond a year in this tropical hellhole, propped up through the day with jars of bennies. And the night. Grooving on the color of tracers crisscrossing the sky and the melody of mortars and artillery *whumping* to the beat of the Pentagon. Screams in my rare nights when sleep came, only possible with Jim Beam, weed, opium, or Quaaludes to let me close my eyes to the faces imprinted on my eyelids. Heads with perfect round holes in the back. Women's heads. Men's heads. Babies. Bloodless holes the size of a dime that always gave a vision clean through the skull to a death smile that said, "I forgive you." I couldn't forgive me.

Fuck it. Don't mean nuthin'. No mood to write more whiney brain chatter to the Colonel. Do some story composing for *Stars and Stripes*. Hell, I always wanted to be a journalist.

SLEEP DISORDERS ROCK
VIETNAMESE VILLAGES

(Saigon, June 24,1970—Exclusive to *Stars and Stripes*) Liem Tran, a recent graduate of the Sorbonne, slept peacefully in her bed outside the small hamlet of Cu Thi. Her day had been spent working in the nearby orphanage devoted to amputee war victims, all under the age of twelve. But this night would be her last.

Like ten others in her village over the last year, she would be discovered in the morning, dead from a mysterious new virus that leaves those infected with a fatal hole in the head.

"At least she died without pain," said Dr. Quan Duc Yuen, the local tire merchant and butcher responsible for critical care in the village. "None of the victims of this fatal disease appear to have suffered."

Dr. Yuen spoke off the record to *Stars and Stripes*. "There have been numerous sightings of strange machines flying in the area at night. I believe that we are the targets of some type of extraterrestrial activity aimed at making monkeys the dominant species in this country. There is no other way to explain both the deaths and the behavior of the local leadership."

Dr. Yuen asked not to be officially quoted or identified, but *Stars and Stripes* has found that Dr. Yuen lives at 14 Yo Don Street, between the Chiclet distributor and Luc's Cyclo Shop. He is five feet one inch tall and has a distinguishing mole on his left cheek shaped like Che Guevara's head. At last count, three long white hairs curl from the mole to below the collar of his pajamas.

Contacted high above the Ia Drang Valley in his unmarked black Huey Command gunship, General William Westmoreland said, "This is a very sensitive top-secret issue. I cannot comment, but I have high-level intelligence operatives attempting to verify this classified information. The peace-loving people of South Vietnam should be assured that I will not rest until we find the cause of this pandemic. The undercover operatives who work out of Second Battalion, based in Cu Thi, have been designated to carry out Operation Simian under the command of Colonel Yu Tu Monk at ARVN headquarters and will spare no effort. His agents can be seen investigating the claims wearing colorful masks imported directly from Indonesia by US Military Command, Saigon. Of course, all the information I have given you is 'need to know' only and any breach of security will be punished by immediate shipment stateside."

Colonel Monk can be reached in Cu Thi over channel 6 of Military Command Radio, codename "Chimp," password "Ringtail."

The rain changed from the sneaky kind that didn't drown out all sound when it pounded on the banana leaves. The kind that made you think, "This ain't no worse than a regular Seattle drizzle," while it soaked everything you wore down to the shriveling white skin. Now, the rain was the typical eardrum-shattering sound of M60s at close range. Wouldn't be no need to creep up on this terminal gook. We could drive a tank through the puddles all the way to his bamboo door, and he'd still be sleeping the sleep of a thousand Buddhas.

Rainwater dripped from the brim of Luong's bush hat and ran down the bandoleers on his chest. There was a slight smile on his face, and I could see the outline of the black stumps of his teeth. Whenever he knew there would be dead Vietnamese near in ricky-ticky time, the grin was sculpted in place. He'd give up the betel nut, food, the chicken bone and snakeskin amulet on the thong around his neck, the crucifix, everything, for the chance to waste a Vietnamese over the age of twelve. Now, I knew he stared unblinking at the shack, fantasizing about the night's meal. I had to watch that he didn't lob a grenade into the hootch when we were di di-ing.

The leeches would be falling from the trees by now. It wasn't just water that was running under my poncho and down my shoulders. The slimy cocksuckers were sure to be feasting on my back and legs. It always seemed like they knew exactly when to attack. Times that I couldn't strip and use the bug juice, Zippo, or a KA-BAR to peel off the bastards. Once, on patrol, we took a helmet and the squad filled it with writhing leeches picked from our bleeding bodies, dropped in a little C-4, and danced to their snap, crackle, and pop. "Bloodsucker Rag," we called the jig.

The green dial on my Navy SEAL watch read 3:13 a.m. Almost time for creep and weep, but there were enough minutes left to write another *Stars and Stripes* article about this wonderful adventure.

WESTMORELAND:
WAR OVER IN NEXT FEW DAYS

(Saigon, June 24, 1970) On Thursday, MACV ordered squad leaders in all operating theatres of Vietnam to begin counting ammo issued to troops as presumption of "confirmed kills."

General "It's my War" Westmoreland, said, while dining at the officer's club in the old Imperial Hotel in Saigon, "The American taxpayer has paid billions of dollars to train the most effective fighting force in the history of the world. We must assume that every bullet expended has led to the death of an enemy. Soldiers under my command are disciplined and patriotic. They would not dare sacrifice valuable resources unless they were assured of hitting their target."

According to sources at Command Headquarters, the immediate result of this new order was a body count yesterday, the first day of this new policy, of 7,356,783 North Vietnamese or Viet Cong KIA and 14 US. There were no civilian deaths. The second part of the new directive stated, "Casualties will no longer be listed, but reported as KIA."

General Westmoreland commented, "It is traitorous to think that the best soldier's in the world would not hit within the kill zone for every shot fired. My soldiers are taught to kill, not to wound. I will no longer allow these honorable fighting men, nor myself, to be insulted by claims that they cannot fulfill their mandate. I predict, at this rate, the war will be over within the next few days."

Only a few minutes now. There was no letup in the intensity of the rain, an always-welcome cover to the *phfffupp* sound of my Hush Puppy. I might be able to get away tonight without murdering the papa-san's mother, who, if she had survived thirty years of war, would surely be sleeping with the children. The Vietnamese family structure and custom called for the mothers to live with sons and be caregivers until they reached their death karma.

My mother lived in Sedro Wooley, north of Seattle, in a mental hospital run by the state of Washington. The Colonel had her committed and said, "That weak woman is the only reason I haven't gotten my first star." Sometime after I was born, but earlier than my first memories, she went AWOL to the land of Gordon's on the rocks. When she was sober, the kitchen floor was spotless and the meals were charcoal. She didn't stray far from the ice trays. The Colonel ate his meals on the base, and I scrounged at the neighbor's, where touching wasn't a sign of an imminent descent to sissiness. A handshake and salute passed for intimacy in our family. Maybe I'd write her a letter, but I didn't know if Thorazine impaired reading comprehension.

The dogs hadn't moved over the last few hours, except to scratch themselves, and the pig slept in a growing puddle. Staccato rain was the only noise. I touched Luong on the shoulder and pointed to the hootch, signaling him to follow.

No need to crawl through the mud. We could use the darkness, bushes, and contours of the ground for cover. Not even a sentry ten feet away would see or hear us moving slowly across the little swamp of open space.

Two minutes and we were beside the hootch. The threat was the dogs. I was already holding the Hush Puppy in my right hand, aimed toward the dog at my feet. Luong held a KA-BAR to the throat of the other. I looked at Luong, lowered the silenced 9mm, nodded, and fired at the base of the dog's skull. Luong slit the throat of the one he knelt above, grabbing the dog's muzzle as the blade sliced through like a piece of hot shrapnel. There wasn't a sound from either dog, and the only movement was a few inaudible kicks.

Our night vision was good enough to see forms of bodies lying on straw mats in the darkness of the hootch. This family didn't have much. A cooking pot, a few dishes and cups made from old C-ration cans, standard for the "best china" across 'Nam, a small altar with a Buddha, pewter bowl for incense, a rice basket, and pajamas hanging from pegs in the bamboo wall supports. We stood hunting-tiger still, breathing shallow and silent, just like the good-ole-boy instructors at Langley had taught me. It came naturally to Luong.

The highest point in the hootch was the place of honor. Papa-san would stay dry and away from the snakes and scorpions. It was as futile to wonder what crime this supposed VC commando had committed as it was to wonder why old men sent boys out to die. It was him or Leavenworth for me, if I survived the interrogation. It was different if I waxed a few of our own in a bar. That could be written off as "boys will be boys" or a psychotic moment much desired by Phoenix. Failure to follow orders to murder would be treason. And I could already be on the list for disobeying in a hootch just like this one. I moved slowly toward the sleeping Charlie, Luong on drag in case one of the baby-sans was foolish enough to cry. We were both on full rock and roll, but would only need a waltz to vaporize this scene. My Hush Puppy cut through the dark in front, and I knelt beside the man who could have been anywhere between twenty and fifty.

Scars that looked like Frankenstein's monster's ran across the VC's back. Or the local pajama maker had stitched the wounds. Greasy, black hair touched the bottom of his neck, reflecting what little light seeped through the cracks in the bamboo walls. His head rested on a pillow made of an old burlap rice sack, and his breathing was the ragged sound of past bouts with pneumonia. Next to him, an old mama-san snored lightly, covered only by a sleeping ao dai. I gently pressed the Hush Puppy to the back of the VC's head.

VC? Was this pitiful old man really a VC? Now wasn't the time to hesitate, but recent missions seemed to make me a killer for hire, not an instrument of war. It was days since Liem, and I couldn't get her death smile from my psyche. The trigger on the Hush Puppy was filed so that the slightest touch caused someone to die. With pressure softer than a heartbeat, I moved the trigger. The 9mm jumped in my hand less than the bounce of the papa-san's head on the burlap. The bullet went into the pillow, not a millimeter from his skull. I covered his mouth with my hand and pushed down, holding hard and staring into his wide open eyes.

From the corner of the hootch, a baby-san began to whimper. He was sitting up and watching me with charcoal eyes, his mouth open. Luong turned and aimed his M16. Without taking my eyes off the baby-san, I pushed the barrel of Luong's rifle toward the clay floor with the Hush Puppy. No one else in the hootch moved, but I sensed they were awake.

"*Ben ngoai*," I hissed at Luong. Outside. "*Bay gio*." Now. I had to make it appear as if another gook was dead with a hole between his eyes, if only for a few days. There was no way in the dark Luong knew this target still lived.

Without a glance back, Luong nodded slowly and stepped out, his slump looking like someone had stolen his fish ball dinner after days in the bush without food.

Slowly, I turned back to the man, who was as stiff as one of the grunts in a body bag on the Da Nang tarmac.

"*Bien mat*," I whispered. Disappear. "*Hay ongba chet*." Or you're dead.

Standing, I watched the baby-san and moved silently toward the bamboo door. This baby-san and his family wouldn't be fatherless and would survive to smell the paddies being warmed in the morning, not acceptable behavior in the Phoenix unpublished handbook. The chance these civilians would raise the alarm and risk Luong and me being greased was a death sentence I was willing to risk. I slipped through the door, vanishing quickly into the jungle, only the squeal of the roused pig and the *thwap* of raindrops on the banana leaves echoing around us. The box score was two walks and fifty-plus strikeouts. It was the eighth inning.

The morning dawned bright in Cần Thơ, the sun breaking through the black dragon clouds that promised an afternoon return of the monsoons. Luong was renewing bonds with some of his Hill Tribe brothers, and we were scheduled to rendezvous at 1700 near the gate to the base. Trips home weren't veiled in secrecy, and we could hitch a ride on a deuce and a half down Highway One, not really worried about orders or schedules as long as the mission was accomplished. As far as Phoenix new. At least I didn't have to bring back a fresh ear for proof, though many others did. I was eating breakfast at Le Petite Cần Thơ, not wanting to join any of the grunts for base chow. Today, they were too full of macho stories for me to dig the bravado or the runny, white scrambled eggs. Luong and I had marched through the night storm and bivouacked a klick outside town under our ponchos, scraping leeches from our bodies while the rain thwacked on the plastic. I was killin' time until Colleen's elegant legs climbed the steps to the orphanage across the street.

The rice on my tin plate was mixed with powdered eggs, green onions, sprouts, and some brown meat that I didn't want to know. I washed it down with a local homebrew that tasted like DuPont Chemical's finest. A mixture of fermented rice, water, napalm, and C-4. The meal was delicious and spicy. I called for another beer, and my mind drifted to the first woman I thought I loved and didn't kill.

Homecoming at the University of Washington meant that ROTC cadets like me would have to run the gauntlet of abuse served up by the fringies and other protest warriors as we paraded through the celebration in our dress uniforms. Eggs, oranges, and rotten bananas were the favorite ammunition, serenaded by "baby killer." Of course, the oranges had already been drained of the vodka injected into them. In the late sixties, even the quasi-military ROTC still had enough redneck support from east of the Cascades to guarantee a few fights broke out in the bleachers. T-shirt-wearing, muscle-bound, shit-kicking wheat farmers stomping on longhaired peaceniks. For this Saturday's game with UCLA, I was ordered to carry the flag into the stadium because I had questioned the captain's use of the words "slant-eyed gooks" in class the week before. Being flag bearer was a punishment these days. No decent co-ed wanted to boink someone they had just seen smeared in banana jelly and named "kiddie raper" in front of sixty thousand people. Not until she made up her mind if she was for or against the war anyway.

Monday, in Asian Studies 315, I was putting books in my backpack. Aly, the frizzy-haired co-ed who gave the most passionate arguments against the Domino Theory and had never said "groovy" about me, swished across the room in her paisley granny skirt and stopped.

"I saw you on Saturday at the game," she said.

Aly's brown eyes blazed against the background of her tanned skin, freckles, and curly, shoulder-length hair. She hugged her textbooks against a braless chest that didn't hide the size of her breasts under a loose, tie-dyed top.

"What does it feel like to be part of a killing machine committing genocide against innocent peasants?" she asked.

The scent of patchouli oil filled my nose, more accustomed to the stuffy lecture hall smell. Students mumbled softly on their way out the door to the next class. I glanced up at the clock and saw I only had eight minutes to get across the quad to my Advanced Deviant Behavior seminar. I slung the pack over my shoulder and let myself drown in those brown eyes.

"Not cool," I said.

Aly put her hand gently on my arm.

"You have time to rap over a cup of java at the Student Union?" she asked. "I really want to get into your head and see what would make someone believe what you do."

One of the ROTC classes tried to prepare us for torture. They taught about jamming bamboo slivers under fingernails and pouring Coca-Cola down noses, along with even more gruesome torment. Of course these were "war crimes" and only discussed under the guise of "what not to do" with a wink and a grin. I couldn't imagine the pain, but there was a force in Aly's touch that nearly knocked me to my knees. My tongue was in a knot tighter than the cuffs around a VC prisoner's wrists.

"Uhhh," I said.

"Not so tough, are you, ROTC boy?" Aly said. "Come on. I don't have scabies."

She pulled at the sleeve of my denim shirt and tugged me toward the classroom door.

Following orders was something that had been scorched into my auto-response mode. I trailed behind. Deviant behavior would just have to wait.

In the student union, we solved the war and dissected Ozzie and Harriet lifestyles, the pigs, acid comedowns, Gandhi's death, the military industrial complex, and Hoover's love of dresses. She described her life as the little sister of two Idaho farm boys. It was the start of trips to uncharted universes. Months later, both of us longhaired byproducts of sex, politics, weed, hashish, and hallucinogens, Aly left for the Chicago Democratic National Convention. And never came back. My head was filled with patchouli oil even as I stepped onto the bus for OTC.

Across the street, now blue with cyclo fumes and buzzing with the angry beehive sound, Colleen opened the screen door to let in a shoeless mama-san dressed in a ragged, orange ao dai. Colleen must have used the back door to the orphanage or come in before I started my breakfast. Her long, red hair was pinned behind her head with ivory chopsticks, a morning flush still on her dimpled cheeks.

Colors. 'Nam was full of tints. The brilliant orange clouds, a combination of napalm and jungle that quickly turned to oily black. Brown. Monsoons mixed with the clay, leaving the ever-present brown-red coat that stayed even when it dried. The black of the monster-fucking flies that tried to crawl in my mouth and covered corpses only a few minutes dead. Two women with green eyes, one a dead anomaly in a country of black eyes. The other a gorgeous import. The color that haunted me was red. The red that comes from an open wound and drips from legs sawed off by a claymore turned against the wire. The small circle of red that grew like a cherry stain on Liem's forehead after the *pphhuupp* of my Hush Puppy. But green was the hue of the live 'Nam. Fucking green everywhere. A jungle canopy so thick and vivid green that it was impossible to gauge distance. Watching a wall of green, trying to catch a silhouette in black, exposed enough for a kill shot to the head. Sometimes I thought I would always dream in shades of green, the color stamped on my nightmares. Now, I stared across the busy brown dirt road and marveled at the pink on Colleen's cheeks.

The last of my beer drained, I dropped a few piasters on the Formica table, grabbed my M16, and headed for the orphanage, dodging mopeds, taxis, rickshaws, pedestrians, oxcarts, and bicycles.

Inside, the sign to stow weapons remained on the wall. I leaned my rifle next to the bamboo basket for handguns, breaking the rules by keeping my Hush Puppy and KA-BAR.

Colleen squatted next to a naked baby-san sucking his thumb and nudged the boy toward the door in the back. She looked over the boy's skinny shoulder covered in weeping scabs and grinned at me. A wisp of hair behind Colleen's left ear waved in the wind from the fan. The gecko was in the same place on the wall as yesterday, tongue out to catch the day's meal of mosquito.

"Hello, cowboy," she said. "Sleep well?"

The hardwood floor was swept clean, and, walking toward Colleen, I watched the mud still caked and dry on my boots fall to the uneven boards in little brown clots and wondered why this Irish witch made so jumpy. I had faced squads of VC in the bush and escaped ambushes that aced every other comrade, leaving me alone and on the run. Never was I as scared as watching the smile light up Colleen's face.

"Just groovy," I said. "My poncho and a foxhole make the Rex look like a trailer in the Appalachians. Any word on Tran?"

Colleen stood and smoothed the cotton of her skirt.

"Our goal is to relocate the orphans as quickly as possible so that they can assimilate in a family and community environment," she said. "Babies are the easiest. Early this morning, we sent Tran to a local village. Duc Lo. A family there has been asking for weeks to adopt an infant. I'm going to visit tomorrow. Would you like to tag along?"

There was no ETA for Luong and me. Nobody to make us burn shit for being tardy. In fact, I didn't exist on any military roster. When I walked through the towns of 'Nam, few made eye contact. When I went into the bush to carry out orders, no REMF waited to check me off a list on return. I might not come back from a mission that never happened. Only the ones left alive in a hootch, barber shop, or vil knew of my visit.

"Sure," I said. "What time do you want to di di? I can get a jeep. Tomorrow, I want to visit Tran."

She touched a wisp of red hair on her forehead.

"Only one cockup," Colleen said. "Got another rumor. Seems this Ky fellow was upset by my complaint. Supposed to make an unannounced visit anytime." She smiled and took a step toward me.

No coincidences. Now, Ky was coming into my life in a big way. Soon, he might replace the other nightmares. I smiled back.

"Don't hassle it," I said. "What you're doing here is good and can't be mixed with evil."

We were close now. So close I could see the steel fillings in her back teeth. And feel the heat from her skin, even though it must have been pushing a hundred in the room.

Colleen moved nearer and touched the arm of my mud-caked fatigue.

"Now aren't you the perfect gentleman," she said. "I was going to take a cyclo, but a spin with you would be better. What are you doing now? Want to go for a ride if you can get a jeep so easily? You must have some clout around this place to do that."

"No problem," I said. "I'll ETA in a half-hour back here."

Two hours later, we were at the ruins of a Buddhist temple being slowly eaten by the jungle. Roots from the banyan, banana, and bamboo trees pushed through the blocks of limestone around the base and spread up the walls, making the temple look as if a giant green octopus was sitting on top. White and pink orchids bloomed from cracks in the stone. A crumbling, ten-foot-wide stairway led to a dark opening surrounded by carved Vietnamese lettering. The sun shot beams of light through the high, green canopy, and the ever-present smell of decay seeped from the jungle floor.

I parked the jeep on the well-used trail and helped Colleen with the army-issue canvas rucksack she packed. No one was in sight.

"This is one of my favorite spots," she said, stretching her arms and pointing to the door at the top of the temple. "If no one is around, I love going up there."

Still in Indian country, my M16 was in my hand. We climbed the stairs and entered the darkness. It was at least twenty degrees cooler inside than the hundred-degree day of the jungle.

"Turn around," Colleen said. She fumbled in her rucksack, which I had carried up the steps.

Even though the day was the typical monsoon gray, it was brighter than the blackness of the chamber. The space smelled of incense and mold. My eyes slowly adjusted, and I saw a raised altar in the middle of a ten-meter-square room carved out of the hillside. Empty niches for offerings and statues were dug into the walls every few meters.

The snap of a match and the room was lit by a candle Colleen took from the pack. Limestone pieces had fallen in piles around the room and water dripped slowly from the ceiling above the rubble, but the area around the altar was dry. Vietnamese hieroglyphs displaying elephants and warriors covered the walls.

"Don't you feel like you're the first white face in here?" Colleen whispered.

I turned to her. There was that Irish grin on her face, mouth surrounded by freckled cheeks. The "all business" look was gone, replaced by something I couldn't recognize. The change was as eerie as a tiger in the bush, the jungle suddenly quiet.

She moved closer, and I touched her face. She slid the straps of the rucksack off my shoulders and put her arms around my neck.

"Well, laddie," she whispered, "this is a dream I've had ever since I first came here." She kissed me. Hard. I could almost hear the grinding of a tank as it tried to turn sharply on packed clay. The soft feeling of her breasts went through my fatigues and the spot between my legs was immediately as hard as the KA-BAR in my belt. I was never one to make the b-girl scene. Aly was my last. And that was years ago. War was my life, not romance.

Within seconds, we were naked on the altar. Our shadows waved on the walls, the images pushed by the slight breeze from the jungle. I could hear the sound of monkeys in the trees outside, my mind too trained to be completely lost. Yet.

Colleen was on her back, laying on the fatigue top I spread on the pebbled surface. My mouth was on her left breast, tongue flicking like a cobra on her nipple. The little mole between her breasts was perfectly round, and I licked it, too. My other hand held the weight of her right breast, and she reached to stroke my cock. Ivory hairpins dropped to the stone, and her hair fell over the end of the altar in a canopy of red. The jungle noise was replaced by her moans, and the aroma of decay was masked by the musky woman smell.

Heat. In 'Nam, the only respite was the rain. As soon as a shower ended, payment was due. The temperature went from ninety-plus to well over a hundred in moments, the air saturated and smothering like someone had soaked your fatigues in gasoline then lit you on fire. It was hard to breathe, the air so heavy you could weigh it. Air conditioning was reserved for officers, not assassins. There was no escape, even at night. Now, the room temperature was reaching that of the jungle outside. Or it could just be me.

Our bodies slid easily together, greased by sweat and need. She spread her legs and pushed me inside her. My knees scraped on the rough stone, but there was no pain, only the feeling that my soul was being taken by the moistness of Colleen. I moved in and out to a rhythm set by the pressure of her hands on my back. Eyes wide open, she stared at me, unsmiling, with a look of intensity and purpose that I had only seen in combat.

The days were many since Aly, and now I needed discipline. That was something drilled into me by months of training and the reality of motionless nights when even a blink could mean a sniper's bullet to the head. The waves of feeling kept me on the brink with every thrust. Colleen moved easily under me. The pace of her movement was increasing at the same rate as mine. I pulled out and put my face between her legs, fingers spreading her lips and tongue searching for the right spot. I knew I was there by the moans that became a yes. My hands went to her nipples, squeezing gently and rolling them in my fingers. Her hips pushed hard into my face and arced above the altar. Seconds passed with the smell of her filling my nose and her juices washing away some of the ever-present jungle taste still in my mouth. She bucked firmly and stayed with her mound in the air, my tongue inside her. She screamed a long "Nowwww" and pushed my head away. "Get inside me *now*. I need you." Colleen grabbed at my butt and pushed me into her. There were no more gentle thrusts. She slammed her hips into me and pulled me harder inside, hands gripping my back. "Shag me!" she screamed. "Harder." The feeling started somewhere near my toes and moved quickly to my cock. Discipline was gone, and years of Aly loss resulted in an orgasm that knocked us off the altar, writhing in a pile of clothes on the limestone floor of the temple.

"Crikey, you Yanks are good for somethin'," Colleen laughed. We were rolling on my fatigues, Colleen's face blushed and grinning and me hoping neither of us got stabbed by my KA-BAR.

"We'd better di di, Colleen," I said. "We may have alerted every Cong in the province."

I helped her up and brushed a spider web from her hair. We dressed, and she blew out the candle, helping me get the rucksack on my shoulders.

On the way back to town, we passed a few pajama-clad peasants whose unsmiling faces didn't keep Colleen from waving. We talked about home, and she told me of an alcoholic father on the dole and a mother so enmeshed in Catholicism that she couldn't leave a loveless, abusive marriage. Admission to university and escape from Belfast to the jungles of Vietnam. I told her about the Colonel and a mother whose afternoon tea was gin and tonic. But nothing about what my true role was in this police action. Mostly, we talked about Tran and what the future might bring for a war orphan in the horrors.

In Cần Thơ, I dropped her at the orphanage. We made plans for tomorrow and parted with a handshake. I watched her climb the steps to the orphanage, her blouse untucked at the back of her skirt, traces of limestone dust in her hair. I drove away to return the jeep to the motor pool and meet Luong for the night's bivouac in the jungle, the first bars of "Danny Boy" a whistle on my lips.

In the morning, we shared a breakfast of GI issue franks and beans, prepared by Luong. He used a bag of Montagnard spices, C-4, and my helmet. We listened to the jungle awaken. Crickets and horned frogs battled with the buzz of mosquitoes. I offered him a Lucky Strike and smoked while we drank cowboy coffee and spit out the grains. Sometimes, I missed the comfort of a cot and runny eggs in the mess line. Not today. The taste of Colleen was still on my lips, and I would be seeing her again soon.

At the orphanage, the old mama-san swept the floor with a broom made of dried rice stalks tied to a bamboo stick. Her graying hair was wrapped in a bun, and the wrinkles on her face gave her a permanent smile. The ao dai she wore was a patchwork of tattered, faded flowers, held around her waist by a nylon cord that looked like it came from the rigging of a 101st Airborne casualty. She hummed an unrecognizable tune and didn't hear me slip through the screen door.

"*Tot buoi sang*, mama-san," I said. Good morning. "Colleen?"

The mama-san made another stroke, adding the prize to a small pile of rice kernels and dirt. She leaned against the broom handle and said, "Missy Caween di di. Pham Bien. Pham Bien." She flicked her hand as if to shoo me away like one of the always-circling flies. I could see finger bones covered with saran wrap.

I knew Pham Bien was a small vil about five klicks east through the paddies and one that Colleen said might be a possible home for Tran. I put the butt of my M16 on the hardwood floor.

"Tran?" I asked.

"Pham Bien. Pham Bien," she said. She started to sweep again. The rice stalks rubbing on the teak floor made the sound of crushing bone-dry flowers in my fist.

"Ky?" I asked. "*Ong tham?*" Did Ky visit?

"*Vang*," the mama-san said. "*Hoi sang som.* Missy Caween *di di yang*!" Yes. Early this morning. Colleen left quickly.

Fuck. I didn't know what a visit from Ky meant for Colleen, but he wouldn't have come with a bouquet of orchids. Time to find her. And Tran.

"*Cam on*, mama-san," I said. Thank you. But she was already turned away, her bare feet sliding toward the door at the back of the room.

On the street, I motioned at Luong to follow me. It only took a nod. He was in the shadows of a bicycle shop, fronted by three rickshaws and a Motorola sign taller than any Vietnamese. We were never seen together in a city. In fact, we were never together unless someone was about to die. Or was already dead.

Even before eight in the morning, the street was crowded. The whine of cyclos and the clouds of blue smoke that trailed every bike blended with the smell of pork boiling in grease. It would be at least a klick outside Cần Thơ before the noise and aroma of the city cleared our nostrils. I didn't have to glance back to know that Luong was behind me as I threaded my way through the women in ao dais and men in pajamas or khakis. In ten minutes we were on the outskirts of Cần Thơ, heading east on the dike of a rice paddy. Soon, we would have to take to the tree line. A lone GI followed by a Montagnard would raise questions and present an easy target. For now, I was still on an altar in an abandoned jungle temple, enjoying the sun on my back and the sound of gentle waves and wind rustling the rice stalks.

No jeep this morning. Didn't want the news to get back to Comer I was alive and taking joyrides. Yesterday, it took a few packs of Camels and a bottle of Johnny Walker to "borrow" a jeep off the books for the afternoon. If I would have needed it again today, the price only went up by an extra pack of Camels.

To take my mind off Colleen, Tran, and Ky, the walk gave me time to write a letter. One, like all the others, that would never be put on paper. This one was again to my mother. Colleen gave the pages to me. Love was an emotion that I found ironic in 'Nam. The fantasy was of Colleen and me in a loft somewhere back in The World, struggling to make our way, happy and content in our love and lust. A new adventure for both. Talk would be of the day's experiences, carrying out the garbage, and what to make for dinner. Simple. Not whose hootch I would sneak into that night or how she would find a home for a legless orphan. Had my mother ever felt "love" for the Colonel?

Mother, I'm here in the middle of a war zone, and I need your advice. You never talk about how you and the Colonel met or anything of what was and is in your heart. We never had any mother-son talks. I think the Colonel must have told you that everything I needed to know, Uncle Sam would teach. What I saw was a woman who laughed only after her husband smiled, granting permission. A salute. A woman who retreated to her room and the fifth of gin hidden in a Bon Marché hatbox on the top shelf of her closet. Yes, I knew. A woman who shook my hand, while at attention, like the Colonel. Not a hug. A woman who never kissed her husband. Not that I witnessed. You stood tight as the cords on a trip wire. But my letter is for guidance, not to give a litany of whimpers. The Colonel said the army would "make a man even out of a sissy whiner." Me. Well, I'm here. I don't know if I'm a man or not. What is a man supposed to feel when he puts a silenced 9mm between the eyes of a beautiful green-eyed woman and watches her brains explode into the mud? Patriotism? What does a man feel when the heat of a woman's slick body makes the tropics an understatement? What is a man supposed to do when every thought is on her thighs around my neck, the smell of her riper than the scent of the decaying jungle? Did you ever love the Colonel? Were your dreams filled with visions of the Colonel perfectly hanging his perfectly pressed uniform on a chair and sliding between the starched sheets, still in his perfectly pressed skivvies? Did that thing that feels like a mortar attack assault your heart? And what does it mean? Here, the grunts say, "Don't mean nuthin'." But that's just an easy way to avoid the question. And the horror. Cynicism veiled in nonchalance. It means everything. Yesterday, I made love to a woman who won't leave my mind. I've only known her two days. When I think of her, there is this sensation of a million needles poking around in my stomach. My heart seems to weigh more than a grenade. Sometimes, my knees feel like they do after a thirty-klick forced march in full combat gear. When I look at the red clay trail in front of me and scan the tree line for nasties, everything is as vivid as a close-up color snapshot. There's beauty here. I never realized it before. I know it's her. Did you ever have those thoughts? What do they mean? I'm asking for your help, Mother. I'm lost in an uncharted world.

The letter was harder than others, whipped out on my mind screen with cynicism and pain. Too many thoughts of Colleen and Tran interfering like an early-morning wakeup call with a garbage can lid. A note like this, questions of an unknown feeling like love, were as foreign to me as a trip to Paris. Never the receiver, and only a taste of what love might bring. Never a chance at being around a child. I wondered what was happening. Was I finding a can of grape Crush in the middle of a firefight?

We slogged through a flooded paddy and stepped into the jungle. I lit a Lucky, and we took turns burning the leeches off our legs while artillery fire in the distance blocked the sound of the breeze in the palms. Luong handed me his canteen, and we rested for a few minutes. It was only a few klicks now to Pham Bien. And Colleen.

Black smoke danced in its own wind above the scorched earth that was once Pham Bien. The sight of flames and smell of burning bamboo reached us before the sound of AK-47 fire. Luong, in the lead, stopped and silently pointed across the rice paddy to a woman running toward the muddy water, her hair burning, silent screams coming from her open mouth. A few meters from the dike, her arms flew up and her back curved inward, shot by someone shrouded in the smoke. She fell on the bank and rolled to the bottom, legs digging the dirt in a last spasm.

Trees and elephant grass had given cover for our approach. Now, we waited, M16s on rock and roll. The horror wasn't new. I had seen the burning of small vils and execution of rice farmers many times, the perpetrators NVA, Vietcong, ARVN, or the devil dog Americans. It didn't matter who was responsible for the massacre to a dead Vietnamese. I knew what we would find.

During the years of following the Colonel to postings around the world, I groomed a mask I believed served me. Its value became even more important when I landed in Da Nang for my first tour of duty. If that little tingle in my heart began to twitch, I shut it down. Post haste. History had shown me that it was a lie and led to pain the Colonel, Mother, or the US government were incapable of repairing. Later, viewing the aftermath of a mad minute, I was glad there was no way the horror would open the armored scars. Thanks, Colonel.

There was no chance to cross the paddies undetected between our hiding spot and Pham Bien without crawling through the muck of the paddies. It would take Luong and me minutes of eating sludge to make our way to the slaughter I knew awaited. But someone would pay. Hopefully, Colleen's role as a neutral aid worker would give her a pass. I doubted it.

As we got closer, the urge to pick myself out of the stinking mud and run to the vil, M16 ablaze, and blow away the bastards who did this, began to eat at me like a jungle tick. After five minutes, the only sound from the smoke and flames was exploding coconuts. No screams. No wailing. No shots. That was the bad news. The good news was it was over.

No one in black pajamas or dirty olive-green fatigues had shown their faces on the paddy side of the vil. That meant the butchers had probably di di'ed in the other direction through the islands of jungle. And saved my life. I had disabled parts of my psyche, but blind rage was still the answer I gave all too often. Consequences, like a bullet through my chest, didn't enter into the picture. Not even halfway across the paddy, I stood and headed in. Luong tried to pull me back, but I pushed him down into the slime. Dung covered every part of my jungle fatigues and filled my nose with the stench of buffalo shit. But the perfume I smelled was anger.

The first casualty was the burning woman with a bullet in her back. Face up on the clay, smoke still drifted from her head. The hair from a quarter-inch mole on her right cheek was the only thing that kept her from being completely bald. Ants and centipedes were already attacking a pool of blood that leaked from under her left armpit. Her pajamas were nearly burned away, showing buckling skin, blackish red, and oozing over most of her body. A pocket of flesh on her stomach still smoldered as if it were phosphorous jelly. Eyes wide open, her lips moved slowly in prayer. I shot her between those black eyes with the Hush Puppy.

The flames in the vil hadn't died down. Bamboo crackled, and every few seconds a pole would explode with a high-pitched *pop* that couldn't be mistaken for an AK-47 round. Two dogs ran through the smoke, tongues nearly hanging to the ground and eyes filled with madness. When they saw us, both dogs turned and ran back into the inferno. Now, the smell was a Saturday afternoon barbecue. The world had turned peach and black, as if I was looking through a night Viewfinder with an orange filter.

The bodies were everywhere. Some in the open by the well or on the paths that crisscrossed the vil. Others were still burning in hootches. Almost every body had been shot in the head.

Luong was right behind me. He tried to grab my arm and pull me into the jungle. He wasn't crazed. Any dead Vietnamese filled his appetite for hatred, no matter what the flavor.

Body after body, all women, children, or old men. No sign of Colleen. Maybe she was late or had left before the massacre. Yeah, and maybe LBJ was a loving grandfather. There was no need to check faces, she would be easy to identify by her size alone. Tran would be harder. I had already rescued him once from a scene almost identical to this. Second chances didn't come down the trail often in 'Nam.

The mantra in my head was "Don't mean nuthin'." Three words, the anthem that defined this police action, added to my armor. It must have been VC or NVA that did this, because I had heard the easily recognizable *pop* of AK-47s, not the *chunk* of M16s. It meant that Colleen might have been the target. And Pham Bien paid in blood for cooperating with foreign white devils. And, somehow, Ky was responsible.

We had gotten as close to all the burning hootches as the flames allowed, and I turned over any charred baby's body that might be Tran. I used my Hush Puppy on two of the unlucky survivors. The path at the far side of the vil led into a thin canopy of trees. A few meters down the trail, I could see a blackened lump the size of a mortar shell.

Intuition. No one had the knowing of a grunt in the middle of a firefight. Every sound, every sight, every smell was magnified beyond any sense of proportion. The world was a 3D movie on your eyelids, playing at full volume on a concert-quality Marantz high-fidelity system. And you'd read the plot. It always ended badly.

I stooped to touch the smoking bundle. A breeze blew some of his ashes toward the trees. When I stroked Tran, there was no softness to what little flesh remained on his bones. I tried to turn him over, but his little body felt like it would crumble at my touch. There was no blood. I could see a bullet hole in the back of his skinless head. Dead before they shot him.

Luong stood above me, his eyes searching the tree line for gooks. The violent deaths of children, even the ones he loved, were a part of Montagnard life. It was one of the reasons that he and his brothers were some of the fiercest and most merciless fighters on earth. His life's goal was to kill as many Vietnamese as possible before he met the gods. But, now, Luong bent down and gently touched Tran. I swore there was a tear in his eye. No fucking way that was possible.

It was hard to get my hands under what was left of Tran. I slid my arms as gently as possible beneath his body and moved him to a spot under a banyan tree a few meters off the trail. The ground was covered with a layer of rotting leaves and brush. I swept it to the side and dug into the clay with my entrenching tool while Luong stood sentry. Every few seconds, Luong looked back and watched me dig. The thick roots around the banyan made a tomb that fit Tran perfectly. I covered his body with clay and gathered a few rocks to put over the grave.

The Colonel and Mother weren't churchgoers, and any religious bent I may have held was lost the minute the 727 touched the ground of 'Nam. The myth that there were no "atheists in a foxhole" was pure bullshit. God and Jesus, along with LBJ and Westmoreland, were the most cursed beings in any 'Nam foxhole I ever experienced. I took off my helmet and bowed my head. I remembered meeting Tran and rescuing him from a firefight when his adoptive parent had died with Tran in his arms. Now, Tran was dead. I remembered the way he sucked on my fingers and kept quiet when a VC patrol passed close by. I even remembered Luong smiling at Tran's grin. Mostly, I remembered Colleen ruffling his thin hair and tickling him under his chubby chin. I couldn't summon a prayer. Only memories. Don't mean nuthin'.

No Colleen. Not among the smoldering corpses. Kidnap was an often-used NVA and VC tool, and they must have thought this red-haired woman might buy a few more AKs or vials of morphine.

On the trail, Luong pointed to boot tread marks, a giveaway it was regular NVA troops, sandal-wearing Viet Cong, who carried out the massacre. At least a dozen NVA had gone this way, and the length of their strides told us that they were moving fast. A daytime action like the massacre of Pham Bien would surely draw the interest of any American troops in the sector. If we didn't catch them quickly, they would disappear with Colleen down one of the thousands of tunnels to wait for the night. After they put some distance between themselves and Pham Bien, they would stop leaving tracks. Luong and I followed at a trot.

Ky. The further we went into the bush, the more I was convinced the evil was his. Beyond the slaughter, it meant he was working with the NVA. It was their signature we followed, and he must have ordered it done. Certainly the NVA were capable of massacring a vil, but it usually wasn't their style. They used the "kill one monkey" strategy of Phoenix on their own people, kidnapping or forcibly enlisting those of fighting age. Not torching every living soul.

The trail stayed in the trees, winding around rice paddies. After a few klicks, the terrain became slightly hilly and the jungle canopy thicker with fewer rice paddies. Monkeys chattered in the limbs, warning their brothers and sisters that more of the ugly men who walked on two legs were near. The men who carried death in the sticks in their hands. It was already near one hundred degrees and 90 percent humidity as we climbed the first of a line of rolling hills more like large mounds. Sun occasionally broke through the trees and cast shadows that seemed to hide a million gooks. No wind penetrated the thick growth, and all normal precautions were ignored. I kept up the pace.

At the base of a banana tree, Luong, on point, motioned me to stop. During the chase, we had leapfrogged whenever the slightest hint of danger came up. He raised his nose to the canopy and sniffed. I did the same. Cheap tobacco. They were close.

Pointing to the right and left of the trail, we slid into the jungle on opposite sides. Slowly we moved toward the smell, using trees, ferns, and low palms to hide our progress. The jungle was quiet, another sign that they were easily within range of an M16.

There wasn't time to lay a planned ambush. We would be outnumbered, and any second they might disappear down one of the thousands of Alice in Wonderland holes camouflaged in the country. My guess was they were celebrating a successful massacre and kidnap before they descended into darkness. We had to stop them getting into the tunnels.

Five minutes later, I heard the low murmur of voices speaking Vietnamese. I gently pushed aside a palm frond with my M16 and counted fourteen men squatting on the clay or leaning against an ancient termite mound at least fifteen feet high. And one woman. Colleen's hands were tied with bamboo vines. She was barefoot. There were scratches on her legs up to where her shorts ended just above the knees. Her khaki blouse was ripped and dark spots the size of C-ration cans covered her clothes. Black soot was smeared over her face and her red hair was a few shades darker. The closest NVA soldier jabbed her every few seconds with the barrel of his Kalashnikov. Colleen's green eyes were closed, chin on her chest.

At another time, I would have been overjoyed to encounter fourteen dinks together, all within range of a few well-thrown grenades. Full of victory and slaughter, this squad must have forgotten their training. But now, there was no way I could loft a grenade into the nest.

I often marveled at the way Luong became invisible in the bush. Then, reading my mind, he would appear like a Montagnard ghost at the very moment I first needed him. Now, he was ten meters away behind a palm, staring at me. Using my hands, I made clear that we would open fire at my signal, working the kill zone out from Colleen. If any NVA ran to the jungle, we would use the grenades. Luong knew I would target the NVA to Colleen's right and he would take those on the left.

Before I could shoot, the NVA who had been prodding Colleen moved to the base of the termite mound a meter behind him and brushed away the dirt. There was a trap door. He said something to the other soldiers, they all laughed, and he dropped below the ground. No more time.

My M16 was on semiautomatic for accuracy rather than to lay down a field of fire. I shot the man closest to Colleen in the head, immediately aiming at the next soldier. On Colleen's left, NVA tried to shoulder their AKs or headed for the jungle. Only one made it. I could see all this in panorama without a thought or hesitation. On the right, I shot five soldiers, including one who dropped to his knees and pointed his rifle at Colleen. I caught a glimpse of black pajamas escaping behind a banana tree and wasted several shots that pinged off the bark. When I turned back, the muzzle of an AK appeared out of the tunnel opening, pointing at Colleen, standing in the same spot, frozen, her eyes still closed. I screamed, "No!" and ran out of the bush. Before I could reach her, the AK fired and she fell to the clay, the back of her blouse instantly turning red. Luong got to Colleen at the same time as me, took another step and dropped a fragmentation grenade down the hole.

He turned back and squatted, scanning the jungle and switched his M16 to automatic. The ground shook with the explosion and chunks of the termite mound broke off, smoke billowing out of the tunnel.

Over the last month in-country, I often longed to eat the barrel of my Hush Puppy, no silencer needed. A bullet through the brain just like the victims I had killed in the blackness of night. Especially after Liem. Now, I held Colleen in my arms and kissed the blood that leaked from the corner of her mouth. I vowed on Colleen's soul that I would kill the NVA responsible and Ky before my tour ended. Liem, Tran, and now Colleen meant a death as painful as possible for Ky. And it didn't matter if I ended up a rotting corpse nourishing the rice shoots. A bounty was already on my head, and I didn't care if someone collected the reward. I would leave a body count of dead gooks that would make Phoenix smile.

My pack felt heavier than Colleen when I lifted her over my shoulder. I walked to the trail. Before he followed, Luong dropped another grenade into the hole. There would be more hidden entrances to the tunnel complex within a few hundred meters of our position. Soon, NVA would be crawling up into the sunlight to kill us. Now I had a mission, but first I had to bury Colleen.

Two klicks east of where we found Colleen, I stepped a few meters off the trail into a patch of wild orchids and laid her down beside a rubberwood tree while Luong stood sentry. The sun was directly overhead, cooking the jungle to a boil that smelled like a stew of rotting bananas. Flies as big as malaria pills fed on the dried blood that coated Colleen's blouse and tried to drink from the sweat on my face. I brushed away a blanket of decaying leaves and started to dig my second grave of the day. This one would be bigger.

Two women in the last three weeks. One died at the end of the barrel of my silenced 9mm. The other might as well have. I condemned her to this hole in the jungle clay. Death followed me like the stink of a latrine. I should have had one of those red skulls that marked the chemical warfare canisters sewn to my face. The first woman entered the spirit world after she freed my soul of any blame. Or so I believed. Liem was a genetic freak in a land of black eyes who I never met anywhere other than the dark. But Colleen, those emerald eyes brilliant in the sun, exposed me to a light that hadn't burned for years. If ever.

Love. Months ago, I read a poem written by a dead VC to his girlfriend or wife back home. It was translated by an ARVN lieutenant assigned to intel.

You call to me
Every moment of every day.
Distance can't keep us apart
When destiny drew us together.

I'll hold you for eternity
As long as you keep calling.

Most Vietnamese could quote the work of their country's poets, who wrote flowery lines about love, family, and the beauty of the mountains and jungles. Or wrote their own verse. The poorest peasant could break into a sing-song chant that even a white devil soldier could tell was poetry. It was culture unknown to most eighteen-year-old draftees only in 'Nam because they couldn't afford a bus ticket to Canada. For some reason, this poem wormed its way into me and attached itself like a leech. I didn't understand it then and wanted to own its longing. Brief moments with Colleen had opened a feeling that was only known to me in words. She would never call again, but I would hold her for eternity.

It took me nearly an hour to dig a grave deep enough to hold Colleen. She had told me there was no family or loved ones who cared if she ever returned from 'Nam or I would have risked carrying her body to Cần Thơ. I dropped the last of the clay over her and spread leaves and rocks on top.

When I finished, Luong turned to head back toward Cần Thơ. I touched his arm and pointed in the direction of Colleen's murder, the opposite way. I didn't wait for him to protest. Luong didn't anyway, just looked into my anger and nodded. If we didn't meet any of the pursuing NVA on the trail, I would stay near the tunnels until the rage was cleansed.

Love may have been Indian country to me, but fury and revenge were friendly territory. Viper was the latest casualty. Colleen's killers would be the next. Slowly, we made our way toward the tunnels, staying a few meters off the trail, hidden in the bush.

It was only the scrape of a sandal on the clay. Enough to make Luong hold his palm up for me to stop. I was already crouching behind a Durian tree, M16 in one hand and the Hush Puppy in the other. Three gooks were moving down the trail. In a glance, I saw two carried AKs and one an M16. Bottle grenades were tied to their wastes. One wore the uniform of the Viet Cong, dirty shorts, and T-shirts. The two NVA, black pajamas and checkered handkerchiefs around their necks. I signaled Luong. We had done this so many times that another ambush was as natural as dysentery. Before they reached us, I signaled Luong to take the last NVA with his knife. He moved a meter to our left and stood still as a cobra. I would grease the first two with the Hush Puppy. No noise to alert their comrades or stragglers.

The lead VC fell to the ground with a small bullet hole just above his right eye. No blood spattered the jungle, just a red circle like an ink stain. Before the dead VC touched the clay, the second dink stopped and began to raise his M16. He was dead by the time the rifle reached his waist. The third was already gagging on his own blood from the blade of Luong's knife. Luong's hand covered the NVA's mouth from behind, a smile on his Montagnard lips. He dragged the soldier into the brush, legs in their final death mambo. Within seconds, the bodies were hidden, no trace of the killing on the trail. The jungle had only heard two *phupps* and a slight groan from Luong's victim. We were moving immediately, the three dead soldiers not even a distant memory.

This time, at the termite hill, Luong stood behind a marabou tree, on the opposite side from where I squatted in a thicket. They must have wanted us badly to come out of the hole in daylight, usually the kingdom of the grunts, when the VC were fucking, sleeping, and eating. The tunnel entrance had already been repaired, but more likely, abandoned. The VC dug tunnel entries in a triangle, approximately fifty meters equidistant. We had already scouted the area, finding no other trap doors. Not surprising, since the VC had mastered concealment to such a degree that you could swear you knew the spot where a VC disappeared and not find it for hours. A two-hundred-pound bomb could fall directly on the slanted entry and the damage would be contained to the first ten meters, usually a water trap anyway. Through a system of layered bamboo, dirt, and husks, the passages were nearly impregnable. We didn't find any trails other than this one either. With nightfall, the VC would creep out and begin the mayhem of darkness. We would wait for them here.

"GI number ten. Number ten pussy. Fucky-fuck number ten. Number ten sister virgin." Number ten. The mantra of Vietnam heard in every town. Colleen was number ten. Now, number ten would be the number of VC dead before I would di di from this killing ground. Luong knew and was only disappointed that it wasn't ten more. Ten dead VC or NVA wouldn't nearly equal one Colleen.

Discipline was the one gift the Colonel had given me. It always had a touch of respect and honor. Those traits began to fragment the minute

I stepped onto the tarmac in Da Nang. I was a trained killer in an insane asylum called 'Nam. Rules and regulations were trite, stupid, and dangerous. The only rule that mattered was getting through your tour with your dick still attached. And your buddy's. Hair, uniforms, salutes, drugs, rules of engagement, noncombatant rights, all the normal rules of war were forgotten. My orders were only complete with the words "terminated" written with red grease pen over the photo attached to a classified file back at the rear. But I never said "terminated." "Greased" was too perfect, even if it meant a body bag trip to The World for a maggot like Viper. There was no discipline. Only survival. And revenge. I popped a yellow jacket and waited for the night.

Darkness comes early in the tropics, especially when there is a canopy of jungle to block the sun. Fruit bats were making their early evening dives to gather bugs. The few birds had gone to nest, and a slight breeze rustled the palms. The temperature had dropped to a cool eighty-five degrees. Somewhere near, a tunnel vent released the faint smell of cooking rice and fish balls. A firebase in the quadrant was beginning its nightly shelling in an attempt to keep from being overrun. Two black-and-orange centipedes tried to crawl up my boot, and I crushed them with the butt of my M16.

Everyone had limits. While mine were expanded by my job description, there was a line I wouldn't cross. That line led underground to a world inhabited by poisonous snakes tethered to vines, sharpened punji sticks smeared in shit, hidey-holes in the walls manned by dwarf assassins waiting with razor-sharp bayonets, ink-black water traps that had to be swum to get further into the tunnel, trip wires ready to set off grenades that would imbed my skull fragments into the packed laterite clay, and scorpions, centipedes, and rats hungry for my flesh. The tunnels were nearly always the same, like some demented engineer had written a nightmare manual. Always around a meter wide and nearly two meters high. But I had only heard this from tunnel rats. Even if I were ordered to descend into this hell, I would refuse. If pushed, the officer would take his last breath while he watched the frag roll across the floor of his bunker. I would rather get an extended holiday in LBJ, Long Binh Jail, than face the underground world. Or die.

Luong and I had discussed strategy in our own language of grunts, hand signs, pigeon Vietnamese-English, and eye movement. If one VC approached, we would let him go. He was the scout, soon to be followed by his comrades. If three or four showed their blackened faces, we would take them out as quickly and quietly as possible and await more of their brothers until the body count reached ten. Plus a few more if necessary. Not less. But if a bigger squad came in our direction, we would have to follow silently and work our way from back to front, a much more dangerous plan. In order to be successful, noise would be the enemy.

The first sound was a muffled cough. Close-quarter life in the tunnels caused many VC soldiers to die from tuberculosis, rather than a bullet or Arc Light bombing. My eyes had already adjusted to the darkness, and I counted four VC coming around the termite mound. Again, I would take the first two or three and Luong would grease the rest.

The outcome of the action was much the same as the afternoon's. I stepped from the bush and shot the first two in the head. This time, Luong used his Hush Puppy, since his KA-BAR might not have been fast enough. We dragged the bodies off the trail and went back to waiting. It was over in seconds. The cicadas resumed their symphony while I hummed "Sympathy for the Devil" under my breath. There would be more.

Relationships were not part of my history. Like a foolish romantic, I let the dream of a future blank out the madness that surrounded me. Colleen was an ice-cold bottle of Bud on a blazing afternoon in the Delta. A long shower next to the latrine, washing off weeks of red clay that seeped into every sunburnt pore. A shot of morphine to take the edge off. She wasn't a letter from home. I didn't read the few that arrived. I sent them back to Mother unopened marked RETURN TO SENDER. ADDRESSEE LOST. The Colonel and Mother were my only role models. Relationships led to barrenness tolerated only by Jim Beam and sleep and obedience. Career came first. I knew the Colonel laid on top of Mother and ordered her to conceive a soldier. This was not a land that cultivated hope. For a mad minute, I ignored everything and dreamed that there was a future. A future with a green-eyed Irish lass. Now, she was buried in the bush, and I awaited a chance at vengeance.

The last VC in the line of eight limped. He was struggling to keep the assigned interval of five meters between each gook. Luong would take care of him first. We would leapfrog the rest, using our knives, a hand over the mouth, to kill the remaining soldiers. Worst case, if discovered, we would have to open fire with M16s and grenades. But we were professionals. Luong moved from behind the marabou tree, and I passed next to him just as I heard his KA-BAR swish across the limping VC's jugular.

A talent I had learned and mastered was silence, a major requirement of my career. Luong didn't need any practice. We could sneak into a bedroom with a dozen sleeping Vietnamese in the other room and guards patrolling, snuff the target, and steal into the night without even awakening the dog. I didn't hear the VC's body hit the ground or any final prayers or gurgles. I could feel Luong's black-toothed grin behind me. The next man was now fifteen meters ahead, and his silhouette was almost hidden in the darkness. At least they were forced to go slow. As quickly as possible, I reached him and slit his throat with the knife in my right hand, palm over his mouth with my left. His weight sagged against my fatigue blouse, and I eased him to the clay. Luong stepped around me without any acknowledgment, his sense of purpose defined by the burning of his village and rape of his eleven-year-old daughter. I felt rather then heard the next VC slump to the ground. I would have to pick up the pace to stay with Luong. Three down and five gooks to go.

The VC in front of me had stopped and faced back in the trail. He whispered, "Nguyen. Nguyen." I stooped to appear five-feet-tall rather than six and murmured, "*Hien tai.*" Here. When I was in front of him, I buried the knife into his throat, reaching behind to catch his fall. Luong silently loped past. This time, there was noise from Luong. It was a grunt and the sound of metal on metal. The VC must have heard me stab his comrade and put his AK up before Luong could waste him. I screamed "*Xuong!*" Down. Every fifth round from the M16 that had been strapped over my shoulder was a tracer, and the jungle was immediately lit by beams of green light. Before I could take aim at the furthest VC running away down the trail, I saw Luong throw a grenade. I hit the ground firing. Smoke filled the trail, and branches fell from the tree line, but no return fire. We counted four more dead and one escapee. I had an idea Colleen might not approve of this revenge, but I didn't care. It was for me.

We couldn't take the trail any farther. We slipped into the bush. In an hour, we found a small cave made by the roots of a huge banyan tree and bivouacked for the night, cutting brush to hide behind, neither of us sleeping, and my thoughts only on dead possibilities.

The base camp had taken artillery fire for the last two nights. Luong and I passed through the gate in late afternoon, after sleeping in the bush, laagered a few klicks from Colleen's grave. Alongside us, a line of filthy grunts, eyes on the clay, stumbled like they had just received their "Greetings from the President" letter. One soldier, a crimson-stained bandage across his forehead, dragged his right leg and was supported by two other grunts. We blended in, just as dirty and tired and numbed by the pointless conquer of a small patch of clay that would have to be retaken again tomorrow. And the cost of that dirt in lives.

Soldiers moved ammo to the howitzers, cleaned M16s, patched bunkers, burned turds, and sat on sandbags, shirtless, smoking C-rat Camels, dog tags dangling on their chests. No one made eye contact as we crossed the camp to the Phoenix compound, a no-man's land that spooked the grunts even more than Charlie crawling through the wire in the night. At least they knew what Charlie was up to, rather than the voodoo image groomed by Phoenix. Rumors were that Phoenix assassins were not limited to suspected VC targets. That any who violated the whimsical rules might not wake up from the nightmare that surrounded them.

Luong went to the thatched-roof huts reserved for Montagnards, and I entered my barracks. Comer was waiting, the little shit's snakeskin boots spit-shined, not a speck of dust spoiling their gloss. The belt buckle on his Levis reflected the late-day sun that came through cracks in the plywood walls. Today, he wore a striped cowboy shirt, fastened at the neck with one of those silly string ties. He looked ridiculous, a white Stetson hat topping his skinny five-foot-tall body. The other agents were out slaughtering suspected VC, because no one else was in the barracks. Comer's black unmarked helicopter must have been parked behind the barracks. I hadn't noticed it on my way in. He touched the pearl-handled Colt on his hip.

"Home from the range, podner," he said. "Wrestle any steers while you were on the trail?"

Not even the sight of Doc trying to hold in the wormlike coils of oozing intestines leaking from a gutshot grunt made me more nauseous than this dwarf. I dropped my pack beside my cot and rested the M16 next to it. I didn't put away the Gerber or Hush Puppy. He might be Mickey Rooney size, but he could shoot out a burning match at the distance between us.

"If you mean did I complete my mission," I said, "the answer is yes. Does the phony cowboy bullshit make up for the fact that you're shorter than the gooks you order me to grease? And uglier than the toothless milky-eyed mama-san begging for p outside the gate?"

Comer's smile was evil. No joy. No love. No hope. Dead. His eyes were blacker than any Cong I had seen. His twisted grin could make babies scream in terror.

"Ten paces behind this shithole at high noon?" he said. "Is that the way it's gonna play, Morgan?"

Nothing I would have liked more than to fill his scrawny hide with 9mm slugs. The Gerber was still strapped to my waist, and the handle was cool on my fingers.

"What the fuck do you want?" I asked. "Tell me, then you can mount your chopper and ride on outa here."

He flipped the string tie hanging from his neck.

"Well, podner," Comer said, "I think you been in the saddle a might too long. How about a week in Bangkok? Meet some a' them purty señoritas."

"Jesus, Comer. You ever seen a drunk grunt after the Hueys dropped a load of Bud, spewing his shit further than your tiny dick can piss? When you talk that way, I feel just like that grunt. Talk fucking English."

"Well, son, your brain must have gotten boiled in the sun for you to speak to old Comer like that. Too much more of it and you'll be hitchin' a ride back to The World in the cargo hold with a plastic wrapper holdin' yur body parts together."

"You can't stop. All right, just tell me when the plane's taking off. Then you can quit ruining another glorious day in Vietnam."

"As soon as you stow your gear. You don't even have to put on clean fatigues. But, first, a few questions."

"Yes, he's dead. Not even a whimper from his dog."

"Ain't that sweeter than a waterhole on a Jewwlie roundup? I ain't interested in that. One dead gook is the same as another. Got a few doubts about you, though. You were supposed to be back at the ranch two days ago? Where you been. Chuggin' tequilas down on the border?"

"We ran into a little trouble. Since I don't have a black Huey to fly me around, and you wouldn't give me a jeep, we had to hump it on foot. If you ever got your boots dusty, you'd know."

"You're saying there's Indians out there? Well, hell, boy, we better circle the wagons." Comer chuckled, the grin showing his crooked teeth, yellow from the cheroot that was always in his mouth. "Quit your whinin' and tell Comer more."

"What the fuck do you want to know? We got ambushed. Twice. The target wasn't in when I rang. We had to recon until he came home." There was no way I would tell Comer or anyone about Tran and Colleen. Or the targets still breathing.

"I think you lie more than a Mex'cun cattle rustler," Comer said. "When I send you out, boy, part of the orders is that you report back in the time I give you. Not spend it at the saloon. Followin' my command is how you earn your paycheck."

"I don't suppose you can read, Comer, but *Newsweek* just ran an article about how the Thai and Philippine soldiers you and your kind have been trumpeting here to fight the red tide are paid twenty times more than a grunt. Two hundred times more than they get to defend their own countries. Now, who do you suppose foots the bill? All they've been doing anyway is sitting around their camp drinking Tiger beer on ice, compliments of Uncle Sam. Another PR lie about the same as the pacification program. Don't talk to me about paychecks."

"That fuckin' commie Fulbright and his fat, Jew-boy mouth. We had to send those cowboys home after he leaked the story. But, hey, it worked for a while." Comer tipped the bill of his Stetson. "You're trying to change the subject on me, Morgan. Ain't gonna work. You were only going a few klicks. Can't take that long. You moonlightin'?"

"Yeah, Comer. I hire myself out on the side as an assassin. What I do for you is my patriotic duty. You know, grease a gook for Dick. That's what I get. Dick."

"It's a trust issue, Morgan. Ever since Viper got wasted, I been wonderin' what your role was. Maybe I oughta talk to that buddy of yours, Luong. But them Yards are tougher to make talk than a deaf Comanche. I suppose it wouldn't do any good to call his balls on a field telephone. Make his nuts jump before I added one of his ears to my necklace."

Unlike most of the REMFs, I knew Comer could and would kill. For all his stupid bravado, he was more than willing to back the words. I had seen it and often wondered how anyone could smile while the knife went in. His brief wasn't only to direct our group. He was our example. And instructor. I hated him for it.

"If you so much as breathe on Luong, I'll hunt you down, Comer. You won't enjoy having some of the tricks you taught me used on your slimy body."

"What's wrong with us, Morgan? We never seem to ride the same trail. We just dance the Texas two-step. I won't touch a black hair on that Yard's skull. Not because of your threat. He's the best roper in the camp. And so are you. On the other hand, I could sure use that reward out on your head. Need another hat. This one's gettin' sweat stains on the band." He took off the Stetson and rubbed the inside.

Guys like Comer always had an agenda, and it was harder to find a tunnel entrance in the dark than figure out what they wanted. Or why. I sat down on the cot and started to untie my red boots, caked in the mud of Delta clay.

"Vietnam is a better place without Viper," I said. "Even someone like you has to admit it. What do you want, Comer? I told you what happened on the mission. The target is terminated. I don't know anything about Viper other than he's in hell. It's time I catch some z's."

I laid down on the cot, hands behind my head.

Comer put his hat back on and walked across the room closer to me.

It was getting dark. A breeze blew through the open door and the cracks in the walls. Flies circled, and the gecko sat unmoving in his regular post on the ceiling. One of the other agents had pinned a picture of a white woman who must have been his wife or girlfriend to one of the wooden beams with a bayonet. Her eyes were gouged out. He had used a red grease pen to scrawl DEAD on the bottom of the photo. Comer touched the picture and smiled.

"Another Dear John letter," he said. "I pray that you boys can learn to adjust to civilian life when you get back to The World. You know, understand that love is what makes the world go 'round." Comer laughed so hard his Stetson fell to the dirt floor when he doubled over.

"Shit," he said, "you boys are always good for comic relief, something sorely lacking here."

Dead. Dead. Dead. I wanted to kill this mutant runt more than riding the Freedom Bird out of Da Nang. I was taking orders from a stunted psychopath. Not even the crispy black skin of a napalmed baby made me want to puke more than this mutant. I closed my eyes so tight I thought they might weld permanently shut.

"Hey, Morgan," Comer barked. I opened my eyes. "Don't get bucked off your horse now. At least I taught you cowpokes skills you can use for the rest of yur life. You know, if the little lady rides in someone else's saddle, you can silently kill her with your bare hands in less than five seconds. Ten different ways. Or is it twelve?" He held his hand in front of his face and began counting on his fingers. "One, jugular. Two, eardrum. Three . . . oh shit, who cares? That's enough to grease even a Mormon's herd."

Early in my tour of 'Nam, Comer held a class that combined use of the garrote and interrogation. He didn't need a dummy. Comer had a suspected VC officer who hadn't been forthcoming with the address of his bunker complex. He demonstrated the right amount of tension needed to sever each finger, then a hand, while an ARVN translator laughed and told us "Charlie lose tongue." Comer unbuttoned the VC's fly and wrapped the wire around the prisoner's cock and balls. Within seconds, everyone in the camp heard that the bunker was two klicks south, beside a burned-out water well. Comer had compassion and left the VC his privates. But he did show us how too much force led to a messy decapitation, warning us that a head falling on the ground made an unacceptable thud.

One thing I had learned. How to control my breathing and heartbeat. Lots of practice in trenches and dark rooms. It took all my willpower to slow down. And not imbed the Gerber in Comer's eye.

"Enough, Comer," I said. "No more questions. No more jokes. You've got ten seconds and then I'm outa here. You're gonna have to use that Colt to stop me." I sat up and swung my legs off the cot.

Comer tapped his hat down on his head.

"There's a bird leaving for Da Nang at 1900 hours. From there, you're booked on a flight to Bangkok and the pleasures of Pat Pong. Don't come back here. Report to me in Saigon in a week. They've got some hot chili cooking for us. They don't want to use local talent. Get cleaned up and wear your civvies. Adios, muchacho." Comer tipped his hat and walked out the door. Within minutes, his Huey was cycling and he was gone.

The Phoenix program headquarters were in an old French mansion in the palm trees on To Do Street, near MACV, Military Assistance Command Vietnam, and a few blocks from the American embassy. I rode a cyclo to the building, winding through streets that smelled of rotting fruit, burning shit, gas fumes, sweat, and flowers. My driver looked like any of a hundred of my victims, except he had only one arm. A buddha on a chain swung from the frame that held the plastic roof over the passenger seat. Stickers covered the sides. Most of the signs read COCA-COLA, but one said VISIT LA JOLLA. SURFER'S PARADISE.

Consistent with the spook state of mind, no guards were in sight when the cyclo stopped in the courtyard. Of course, they were everywhere, but it took time and effort I didn't care to use to spot them. No sentry at the door. If anyone uninvited tried to enter, a shitstorm would hit. The shutters were open, and white-laced curtains covered the windows. Orange rust stains from overflowing gutters streaked the cream-colored stucco.

I gave the driver 20 p and walked up the five steps and across the porch that fronted the mansion. One step through the door and I was greeted by "Welcome to the ranch, Morgan," from Comer. "Step into my corral." I missed the tail who must have called ahead. Today, Comer wore the Levi's and snakeskin boots, but had ditched the Stetson and cowboy shirt in favor of a short-sleeve top. Must have been the head spooks didn't like his act.

The floor was hardwood, and Comer's boots clapped as we walked down the hall toward the back. Ceiling fans kept the humid air moving. All the windows were open, but most of the doors lining the hall were closed. I didn't see another spook before we entered the last door on the right. Molar sat in a wicker chair next to the gunmetal-gray desk. He looked up from a folder he was reading. I thought the necklace made of VC teeth must be stashed in his pocket alongside his set of mini-pliers. Like Comer, he was in more acceptable clothing today. The Hawaiian motif was replaced by khaki pants and white shirt. He still didn't wear socks.

"Hello, Morgan," Molar said. "Good to see you again." He winked.

The lies were already starting. My job was to do what they ordered and stay alive long enough to kill them both before I rode the Boeing back to McCord. That would be tough, since they were probably about to give me just enough intel to make their target dead, and me along with him.

Comer moved around me and sat behind the desk.

"Grab a seat, Morgan," he said, pointing to another chair in the corner.

There were no books. No pin-ups. No paintings. Nothing on the walls. Just a desk stacked with files and a black phone with no dial. An open window was behind Comer, and a hint of breeze blew through the curtain. I slid the chair in front of the desk and sat.

"How was Pat Pong?" Comer asked. "Did you catch Tai's act at Pussy Heaven? She does amazing tricks with those Ping-Pong balls."

Sweat. At least in the bush, you didn't have to put up with air heavy in exhaust fumes and rotting garbage that settled on every surface including your skin. I wiped the back of my hand across my brow.

"Tell me what you want me to do," I said. "I saw your cowboy show before, and it doesn't deserve an encore. You can skip that and playing the gracious host too."

Molar laughed. Comer didn't.

"You heard of Air Marshall Ky?" Comer asked. "The vice president of this here democracy?"

"Yes," I said. "I read *Stars and Stripes*."

"After publicly urging us to nuke the North, now Ky's saying that we're only here to defend our interests. Those don't coincide with Vietnam's and our presence should be greatly reduced. I wish he were in the murder book. But he's not the problem. It's his son. Jimmy Ky. He heads the local version of the mafia in South Vietnam."

Let me count. Maybe six sentences without any cowpoke jargon. The brass must of tired of it and ordered Comer to quit. And now Ky was the topic, as if he left my mind for a millisecond over the hours in Bangkok. But Comer couldn't know it. Cowboy knowing was a myth as false as the Domino Theory.

"Surprise. You mean there's crime in Shangri-La?" I asked.

"Now this is just rumor, Morgan. But, yes, I think there is." Smiles all around. A little male bonding. Good for the soul. I wanted to jump across the desk and drive his nose into his brain with the heal of my palm.

"It seems Jimmy," Comer said, "an old friend of Phoenix, has been siphoning off money meant for the Golden Triangle. Now, that's not so bad. We're making a fair profit already. Enough to buy a share in Evergreen Cargo to transport the goods. And pay your salary." Comer lifted a file from the top of the stack. "But, now he's buying up arms and ammo stolen from bases all over 'Nam. Stockpiling them somewhere we want to know. He's gone so far as to have his boys ambush convoys. Try to blame it on Charlie. Gotta think he's in cahoots with the NVA too." He handed me the file. "Take a look. That's all the intel we have on his movements. First, we want a location for the goods. Then we want him to disappear. Forever. But make it look like it was VC work. Don't want to piss off the vice president."

I took the file but didn't open it.

"Why me?" I asked.

"Because you're the best," Comer said, looking toward Molar. "Except him. But Jimmy knows Molar, and it would be tough for Molar to get close."

Saigon wasn't my turf, but I had been here often enough on "special detail" to know the sights. Before the arrival of five hundred thousand Americans into Vietnam, the city was considered "the Paris of the East," with the Song Sai Gon River substituting for the Seine. Now Saigon had become the whore of Asia. Guns, dope, watches, jewels, little girls or boys—anything—could be bought on the crowded sweaty streets. Sex. Especially sex. At every glance, sex blasted at grunts in from the boonies and the lucky soldiers stationed in the city. Dancers wearing only sequined G-strings and halter tops beckoned from the open doors of the thousands of bars. Vietnamese men passed out little cards, written in English, touting the "clean hostesses" inside. But Saigon had developed its own incurable strain of clap,

Heinz 57, that left thousands of American cocks with a drip like a faucet missing a gasket. I opened the file.

Jimmy Ky was the child of power. And now diplomacy. In a country with no more rule of law, his climb to the top of the local crime syndicate was simple. Helped by his dad, the general, and the long association with Chinese Tongs in the Vietnamese underworld, Ky had murdered his way to mob chieftain. Now, he was the don of the South Vietnamese mafia. He took over from the French Union Corse gang after LBJ mandated the buildup of US forces. Nor did it hurt to have an army to fight the battles for you. ARVN troops were used whenever a few more M16s were needed. Or a tank. His entourage included street killers, dope dealers, bomb experts, pimps, military officers, and politicians. One of Ky's specialties was controlling the market for marijuana joints, rolled in his factories and disguised perfectly as cigarettes, cellophane seal, tax stamp, and all. They were dipped in opium and could be bought at every bar and street vendor. He had been an ally of Phoenix and the CIA, cooperating in assassination and extortion. His sins were ignored as long as he was the house pet. This unwritten agreement was well-known throughout Saigon and gave Ky even more fearsome power. I wasn't as interested in his background as how I could kill him. I flipped to a page marked TOP SECRET.

Ky lived in a well-guarded mansion just down Tu Do. He didn't have to drive far to meet his masters. Most of his time was spent in offices above the Sporting Bar, also on Tu Do and in the middle of the busiest commercial section of Saigon. The Sporting Bar was the hangout for Green Berets and LURPs. The location of Ky's headquarters beneath a Special Forces retreat was another indication of his entanglement with US objectives, whatever those might be. I memorized the little information inside the folder, embedding the picture of Ky in my mind, and looked at Comer.

"I'll need Luong," I said.

Comer was picking phantom dirt from behind his fingernails with a gold-handled knife and inspecting the nonexistent results.

"Can't see where that would help, Morgan," Comer said. "He's a Yard, and they don't get along well in the city. They're hill people, more at home boiling the brains of their enemies in cooking pots." He looked at Molar for support. Molar nodded.

"I won't be able to do this alone," I said. "You know that."

"Molar here can help," Comer said, pointing the knife.

Sure, when Ky was entering a dreamland that he would never escape, I'd join him at the hand of Molar.

"I have to know when I give an order, it'll be obeyed," I said. "Don't think Molar would listen to his own mother, let alone me. With Luong, I don't have to say a word. Just a look and he knows. There's something magic about the Yards, especially when it comes to killing flatland Vietnamese."

The Montagnards had inhabited the Central Highland mountains for thousands of years. And the Vietnamese from the lowlands had been trying to exterminate them for just as long. The Yards had joined the French and now the Americans to help revenge the atrocities that had taken place at the hands of their whiter neighbors.

The sound of Jesse Colin Young singing "Come on, people, now, let's get together . . ." drifted through the open window from Armed Forces Radio playing in a nearby office. Comer dropped the knife into the right-hand desk drawer.

"The Yards are demon worshippers," Comer said. "Molar only kneels at the altar of pussy. That's more Christian." Comer nearly slapped himself on the back with his humor. "Can't trust any a' these goddamn gooks anyways."

"But I can trust a ghoul who wears a necklace made of his victims' teeth?" I asked.

I wondered if business meetings all around the world were being held with this amount of fun, all parties concerned armed to the teeth with knives, pliers, pistols, and garrotes, violent death only a smile away.

Molar was proud of his necklace. He took the teeth out of his pocket and fondled them like they were a prayer mala.

"You know what would complete the set, Morgan?" Molar asked. He held up the necklace and pointed to an empty space. "You."

One on one, I believed I could take this guy, but Comer surely had the girly little Derringer under his sleeve. I would be dead by the time the Gerber went through Molar's neck and the tip reached the other side. I turned back to Comer.

"Luong could sneak through the window behind you and you wouldn't even notice," I said. "It doesn't matter how many men Ky has guarding him.

If I tell Luong to kill him, Ky should be designing the burial urn for his ashes. Are you going to bring him in or not?"

Comer's eyes and sharp nose reminded me of the rats that made their home in the bunkers back at base camp. When the artillery started, the monsters would dash through the clay, looking for any escape, running over our bodies like we weren't there. They were bigger than dachshunds and a million times nastier. If the rats were hungry, or the monsoons drove them earthward, no toe was safe. On the other hand, an infected rat bite was a free ticket back to The World.

The chair squeaked as Comer leaned back and clasped his fingers behind his head.

"Whoever you want," Comer said. "If little ole Molar here intimidates you, I can't help that, son. Just finish the job. Remember, we want to know where the munitions are first. After that, you and Luong can party on Ky's balls for all I care."

It would be harder to ditch Molar and his team than avoid detection by Ky's men. At least I knew the Phoenix mercenaries would be lurking in the palm trees. I couldn't trust Molar within ten feet of me. From this point on, he was as much of an enemy as a sapper in the wire. If this was a legitimate op, Comer would never agree to using a Yard in Saigon, but Molar could now get two sets of teeth rather than one.

"Then call him in," I said. "I'll do some recon in the meantime. Where do you have me billeted?"

"For a valuable man like you, Morgan," Comer said, "only the best. You're at the Majestic. Don't get too cozy with the army spooks and news-rats. That place has more rumors than fleas. Luong oughta be here in a day or two."

Not even a childhood of saluting the Colonel, the reflex groomed further in ROTC and officer's training, would make me lift my hand to my forehead. I stood, dropped the file on the desk, and walked out. No one wished me a good day.

It was hard to be a white man in the bush and be taken for anything other than what I was. But in Saigon, there were newsmen, missionaries, colonialists, expats, thrill seekers, businessmen, and soldiers in civvies to blend with. Easy to go unnoticed. I spent the rest of the day watching the entrance to Ky's mansion. For cover, I used the back seat of a Renault taxi that I rented by the hour, staying at the end of the queue of other cabs, a block down Tu Do.

The street was a constant stream of traffic. Cars, cyclos, Honda 50s, an occasional oxcart, and pedestrians of every color fought for a place. Soldiers in from the bush were the loudest, making their drunken way from one whorehouse to the next, sometimes a b-girl on their arm. The Vietnamese women wore colorful ao dais, the hookers with slits running up their thighs and high heels clicking on the sections of sidewalk that had concrete. The men were dressed in standard-issue black or khaki trousers and white shirts, sleeves rolled up on their forearms. Palm trees lined both sides of the street, and parrots squawked in the limbs, fighting to be heard over the noise of two-cycle engines. The exhaust fumes left a blue cloud that settled on every surface. I fought the need for sleep. It had been weeks since I had caught more than an hour or two of z's. During the few days in Bangkok, I couldn't drown the memory of Colleen with gallons of Jim Beam. And the days were the same as the nights. What I ached for was a pack of Jimmy Ky's opium-laced joints. Riding the dragon always made me dream.

Visitors came and went, drivers waiting for their passengers in the turnaround inside the gate. Twice, ARVN staff cars with South Vietnamese flags flying from their antennas arrived, staying only a few minutes. The Fords that carried the officers were always escorted by jeeps loaded with sunglasses-clad, unsmiling soldiers holding M16s on full automatic. A white man in a Mercedes sedan, wearing a tan tropical suit, was inside the longest. Two Chinese women and several Vietnamese male civilians also made court appearances. A nervous man who smiled, bowed, and opened the doors greeted them all. Behind him, two men carrying AKs watched. Occasionally, I saw the curtains of one of the second-story windows being pushed aside. Sentries. Counting the greeters, the guards in the windows, the men who patrolled the gardens and the man on the roof behind the chimney, there were eight. I wouldn't know how many were inside until I found a way in. I didn't see Jimmy Ky.

By seven o'clock, no more cars were arriving. It was dark, and I had the driver make a circuit of Ky's complex. Ten-foot walls topped with razor wire protected all but the front side. No problem. I hadn't seen dogs other than the neighborhood shorthaired scabby mongrels that were everywhere in 'Nam. Dogs were more of a hassle than a challenge anyway. I told the driver to take me to the Majestic, stopping on the way to haggle with a vendor over a pack of Lucky Strikes.

The Majestic overlooked the river and the hundreds of thin boats that plied the water, the vendors selling fruit, vegetables, grenades, and fish balls. Sandbags protected the front, due to the accelerating bombing campaign of the NVA. A hotel a few blocks up Ton Duc Thang Street had been destroyed a few nights ago, resulting in the first casualty in 'Nam for the BBC. Huge ceiling fans kept the heavy air moving in the lobby. Bouquets of orchids and hyacinths sat on the counter and on tables spread around the first floor. I registered under the name "Larry Colton," an alias that Comer always used for me when I was in Saigon.

After a shower in my room, I went to the bar for a nightcap. The perfect mix to relax me was a couple Jack Daniel's on the rocks and one of Ky's cigarettes just before I turned the lights out, if I could lift my hand to the switch. Food was a problem. Too many C-rats and base chow made my system rebel at the thought of chateaubriand. Behind the bar was a tropical garden, ending in a boardwalk that ran along the Song Sai Gon. Candles flickered in the breeze created by the fans and the louvered open doors. There were lots of drinks with umbrellas sitting on the tables. But the hardcore newsrats drank their whiskey straight. Real campaigners. Willing to stick a pen in the face of a wounded grunt and ask him, "Does it feel lucky to be alive when your buddy is lying beside you with his intestines in his helmet?" America needed the answer. And these guys were tough enough to tell the story. The reptilian part of my brain identified with these snakes. The human side wanted all these pussy vampires to spend a few weeks in a napalm hell. I sat at the bar and listened to the newsies swap stories, sipping my first Jack, staring at the gilded mirror and the reflection of a man whose hair was graying at twenty-three. Not a bad guy. Needed to visit the barber. Didn't smile much. That scar made him look a touch dangerous and sinister. Eyes of an undertaker.

The pseudo Hemingways played the game, drinking their whiskeys neat and telling macho stories, recording the horror from another colonial outpost for dispatch back to The World. But the real danger was vicarious, lived through the sunken eyes of grunts forever mutilated by Vietnam.

The most boisterous reporter wore a tan catalog ammo jacket, the pockets bulging with film canisters, notebooks, water bottles, a tape recorder, and toilet paper. A dusty bush hat sat on the bar next to his whiskey. He hadn't shaved in a week and constantly massaged the stubble. A Camel was never far from his lips. The other wannabes were mesmerized by his every word, like the bullshit was coming from the mouth of the Dalai Lama. I couldn't help thinking about leeches. They crawled into your fatigues and lived on your blood, hitching a full-bellied ride until they were burned or cut off. I wanted to do the same with these bloodsucking hollow men. Put them in my helmet, add a chunk of C-4, torch it with my Zippo, and watch their bodies shrivel in the flames, crackling like frying bacon.

"Watched an evac Huey take off from a hot zone outside Ben Tre," the guru said. His bush fatigues were still stained with mud. One persona these assholes liked to fake was the grizzled grunt. "When the chopper tilted to avoid the trees, blood ran out like a dam burst on the Red Sea. All of a sudden, two arms and a leg slid into the palms from the open door. The leg still had a boot on and twirled like it was in slow motion all the way until it bounced on the ground."

Nods of understanding all around. Yes, they could picture the scene and wished they could have gotten it on tape. But that's all it was for them. A photo op. One of thousands that went clickless every day. At night, choppers ferried them back to their beds in the Majestic, while the grunts living in the firestorm couldn't go home.

Another whiskey for me and the rage might drown. I ordered one more on the rocks.

"Two days ago, a few klicks from Tan On, I saw some ARVN baptize a Cong," the professor said. "It was a joint op with some Airborne troops. The vil was deserted except for women, children, and old men. When they used flamethrowers on the hootches, a Charlie, wearing only a loincloth, ran from the fire. The way they look at it, if he's of fighting age, he's either VC or knows where they're hiding. Guilty. They started to interrogate him. Nothing. There was a big clay pot in the center of the village for storing water. The ARVN officer had two men grab Charlie by the hair and hold him under the water. Every time they pulled him up, the officer would scream in his ear. Nothing. Down again, increasing the amount of time he was under water. I could see the officer getting more pissed. Finally, he took his Colt from his holster and shot Charlie in the ear, leaving his body in the pot. The Airborne guys just watched. Don't think Charlie found Jesus."

The asshole turned to me. I was the only one not worshipping at his altar, and he needed the validation. A faded movie star making a comeback in a lousy flick, reading *Variety* and begging for a good review.

"Haven't seen you around before," he said. "What's your jacket?"

These limp-dick fuckers loved to use gruntese. Made them feel there was a slight possibility they could be men. I watched the ice melt in my drink. In contrast to this chickenshit's filthy fatigues, I was showered, shaved, and dressed in slacks and a white shirt.

"Just got in," I said. "Gee, I'm pleased to listen to fellas who know what the real story is."

This fuckface couldn't tell sarcasm from an M16. He smiled.

"You're American?" he asked. "Not one of those tourist Aussies or Brits?"

"Red, white, and blue. That's me."

"Bravo," he said and clapped me on the back. "Me, I'm a reporter for the *New York Times*. Name is Runson." He offered his hand.

"Morgan," I said. "Frank Morgan." I squeezed until I felt the bones scrape in his knuckles, a smile of pure innocence on my face.

Runson tried to pull away, but I held him tight. He struggled to smile, a hint of fear sparkling in his eyes.

"That's a strong grip," he joked, pulling harder and beginning to panic. I let him go.

"Must be all that nonpasteurized milk back in Kansas," I said. "Hey, you heard any good rumors?"

Runson rubbed his hand, then dropped his fingers to his side and shook them to get the blood flowing. He studied me like I was the map coordinates for his next artillery barrage. After a few seconds, he put his elbows on the counter.

"Buy me a whiskey, and I'll tell you about what I've been working," he said.

The bartender was a young Vietnamese, probably only here and not climbing from a tunnel because he was a spook. And no white face would know who he reported to. I ordered a round for Runson and another for me, ignoring his fan club.

"Got a lead on a local big shot running drugs out of Laos," he said. "Nothing new for this part of the world, but he's got connections with the CIA." He took a swallow of his fresh whiskey. "Hey, Frank, this is a long tale. You got any plans?"

I moved my head from side to side.

"No," I said. "That sounds incredible. I'd love to hear about it." I pointed to an empty table in the corner. "Let's move over there so I can hear over all this racket. I'll buy you something to eat."

I was using my best humble-college-sophomore-talking-to-his-esteemed-teacher voice. Visits to places like this and observation of gonadless fuck-wads like Runson gave me the intel that reporters were always looking for a free meal. Between a chance to have an innocent offer of adoration and free dim sum, there was no way this jerk could refuse.

"Be glad to," he said. We picked up our drinks and walked to the table.

Behind us, the open windows showed sampans on the river over a deck and mahogany railings. The smell of lavender blew off the water, scented with the ever-present hint of raw sewage. Tips of palm fronds nearly tickled our faces. Candles lit all the tables, and only a few were occupied, genteel sub-dued murmurs the opposite of a mad minute. Waiters in white shirts and bow ties carried platters of fried rice, spring rolls, and steaks to some of the other patrons, white linen napkins over their forearms. I set my drink on the table.

"Please tell me more," I said.

Runson sat straighter in his chair and cleared his throat. The lecture was about to commence.

"Well, it began a month or so ago with a chat I had with a man at the bar. He was so blitzed, I had to lean into him to keep him from falling off his stool. Claimed he worked for Air America running heroin out of Laos. I did a some background checking and interviews. Even talked to a few Hmongs working as scouts through an interpreter." He took another swallow of whiskey. "A little history. The Hmongs originated in China and fled from the genocide and enslavement of a series of dynasties, especially the Ming. When they reached Laos, Cambodia, Burma, and Vietnam, the good lowland farming regions were already populated, forcing the refugees to find homes in the mountains where subsistence was nearly impossible, leading to people known for their hardiness. And lack of fear. These guys are tough. I was afraid I might get my throat slit if I asked the wrong question. Not smiley people." Another swallow and he waved at the bartender, holding up two fingers. "Anyway, existing on what little they could grow in the rocky soil and hunting, they were continually in the middle of whatever war was happening around them. The French had trained the Hmongs and used them against the tribe's primary modern enemies and torturers, the Vietnamese."

Much of this I already knew from my university studies, but didn't want to push him for the information I really wanted. If he knew something about Ky, I would buy him all the drinks and chow mein in Saigon. I stared into his eyes, a student starving for his expertise.

"The high elevation villages of the Hmong meant it was fertile ground for the growing of superior grade opium," he said. "Without money to pay taxes, the Hmong began to substitute the plant for francs or piasters. The French saw profit and encouraged the Hmong to increase crops, using the money to support their ongoing fight to keep Southeast Asia a colony. When the French were defeated at Dien Bien Phu, the Americans were already there and had learned a valuable lesson. Drugs meant money. Since we were not at war with either France, Laos, Cambodia, Burma, or Vietnam, most of the Americans illegally on the ground were advisors or intelligence agents and needed to be funded 'off the books.'"

The waiter was at the table, standing patiently while this pompous asshole spouted his narrative.

"Do you mind if I order for us?" Runson asked. "I think you'll like it."

I grinned wider.

"Sure," I said. What I really wanted to do was stop the charade and stab him in his pretentious mouth with one of my chopsticks. Patience, Morgan.

He looked at the waiter.

"We'll take the cha ca," he said. He turned to me. "It's grilled minced river fish. The bones are taken out and the meat is put into saffron water. The fish is marinated in salt before it's cooked. They add mint, dill, shallots, and more. Delicious."

"Sounds great," I said.

Turning back to the waiter, he said. "Bring us a big bowl of pho ga too." Back to me. "That's chicken noodle soup. But none like you've ever tasted."

The waiter bowed and walked toward the kitchen.

"Where was I?" he said. "Oh yes, in the fifties, the CIA supported an unsuccessful and little-known war backing Chiang Kai-Sheck's Kuomintang in an attempt to retake mainland China. The KMT hid in nearby Burma, where they persuaded local Hmongs to grow poppies for drug production rather than food. Using incoming Civil Air Transport planes, run by Sea Supply, later Air America, the CIA transported food to Burma and weapons to the KMT. On their return, planes were filled with opium for sale and distribution in Taiwan and Thailand. This was all coordinated and subsidized by the CIA, the foundation for the growing career of the CIA as the world's biggest drug cartel."

Since I'd been in 'Nam, I heard the stories from Phoenix agents, transferred out of the mountains because their faces were too well-known or their junkie habits were becoming a problem. Dark tales of cannibalism, torture, murder, orgies, and devil worship. The CIA supported a Laotian mountain chief, General Yang Pao, from their secret base at Lang Tieng. Pao was Hmong and his men became trained killers while the women stayed home and harvested poppy bulbs. The Hmongs mostly fought for the Americans from a Laos. Their country was being saturated with two million tons of bombs by the B-52s that also dropped whispering death on Cambodia and North Vietnam.

When I was with Dang a few days earlier, I asked why he fought for the Americans. He told me, in his halting English, about "the promise." It was a CIA bit of false propaganda promising the United States would aid in the battle against Communism if the Hmong helped in the conflict. I knew the promise wouldn't be fulfilled, but any lifeline for the Hmongs was better than the present.

I brought my attention back to the professor.

"Things are starting to backfire. I've heard nearly 30 percent of the ground troops in 'Nam are addicted to heroin. Pilots for Air America are refusing to cooperate or hooked themselves, like the man who started my investigation. CIA agents are getting greedy, setting up their own operations. Small wars have broken out between rival chiefs over who will control the money. Dover Air Force Base in Delaware is now America's biggest entry point for heroin, the drugs smuggled in caskets and body bags or sown into the chests of dead GIs. The DEA enforce a policy of noninterference with Air America and the drug supply chain run by the CIA. None of the CIA officials will answer questions, so I have to get the information at the source. Here."

Dinner arrived, along with another round of drinks. Runson was getting close, and I was famished. But it still couldn't stop me from wondering what the fuck I was doing in this country. We were all killing ourselves, and it looked like my ride home wouldn't be in a leather seat either. First, Ky.

We ate. Between chopstick-loaded mouthfuls of noodles, I asked, "You said something about a local big shot. What's the story there?"

Runson was a hog at a pile of dead bodies. Soup dripped from a chin already stained brown by *nuuc luan* sauce. He wiped his mouth with his napkin, the turd color still on his beard.

"Yes," he said. "Seems the vice president's son, Jimmy Ky, is behind the drug supply line. Makes beaucoup bucks, and the CIA does more than protect him. They fly the dope in."

There it is. Ky. All trails led to his door. Just another guilty count condemning him to death. I was starting to think some higher power was prodding me in Ky's direction. But I didn't believe in higher powers, except those that could be found looking at the bottom of an empty bottle of Jack Daniel's.

Once, walking through camp, I passed a sandbagged hootch with a peace sign painted on plywood nailed to a two-by-four. Two shirtless grunts, hair well below their ears, were passing a water pipe. "Wanna hit?" one lazily asked, holding the smoking pipe toward me. When the grunt extended his arm, I could see the tracks. Looking at the other soldier, his arm was identical, a map of the Son Sai Gon River leading from the inside of his elbow in both directions and needle holes that might have marked targets on the day's action map dotting his flesh. I took a long, smooth hit. "Wanna listen to some tunes?" the first grunt asked. I nodded, holding the smoke in my lungs. Following them inside, I could have been in Haight-Ashbury. Tapestries hung from the plywood walls. Burning candles covered most of the surfaces, wax dripping into the dirt. Psychedelic posters were pinned wherever the tapestries didn't cover. Santana, in his curly, long hair, stared at me. Sticks of incense smoked from bronze holders carved with dragons. Another shirtless man sat on a couch made of sandbags, asleep. The same tracks scarred his arms. In the corner, two gigantic Marantz speakers flanked a turntable and a reel-to-reel tape deck. The clue I wasn't in California was the stack of M16s and grenades by the door.

The first man walked across the room and pulled an album out of its sleeve. He blew on the vinyl, then put it on the record player. He pushed a switch, and the needle made its trip up and down. Immediately, Steppenwolf screamed "Born to be Wild." The grunt turned to me and smiled, pointing to an empty seat on another couch. No chance to rap. The speakers were awesome. The grunt went to a corner and moved a sandbag, taking out a small, lacquered box. He sat across from me, seemingly forgetting I was still there. His entire focus was on what was inside the box. Reverently, he took out a bent spoon, a Zippo, a syringe, a length of plastic tubing, and a clear bag of brown powder, setting each peace gently on his thighs. I watched him cook his fix, fill the syringe, squirt a drop out the end, wrap the tube around his upper arm, cinching it with his teeth, and shoot the heroin into his arm. He leaned back, eyes closed, while Steppenwolf took him on a magic carpet ride. At the end of the album, I left. No one noticed. A few days later, I stopped by the hootch again. None of the grunts I met before were there, and all the hippie paraphernalia was AWOL. I asked the trooper nearest the door where they were.

"Fuckin' junkies," he said. "The LT caught 'em shootin' up. Sent 'em out on night patrol with Watson over there." He nodded at a bare-chested skinhead sitting below an American flag, cleaning his M16. A beer was beside him, and his biceps were bigger than the local cantaloupes, covered by homemade swastika tattoos. "Never came back. Watson said they just disappeared into the bush like ghosts. Didn't find their bodies." Watson smiled. That was my first week in 'Nam.

Runson was finished with the noodles and about to take the last few bites of his cha ca. The waiter brought more whiskey, and Runson was having a hard time guiding the chopsticks to his mouth.

"Don't understan' the stupid sodjers here," he slurred. "Killin' themselves with heroin. Can't figger it out."

Ten more whiskies wouldn't stop the anger. Enough of this prick who only lived off the deaths of boys much younger than him and whose biggest risk was getting a bad bottle of whiskey. I slammed my glass onto the table loud enough to make the arrogant slime jump and look at me. I could see he wasn't used to being disturbed or challenged in his safe haven, especially by a clean-cut young white man who he only suffered for the price of a free dinner.

"In journalism school back in The World," I said, "I'll bet some tweed-coated, pipe-smoking, shitbird professor told you, 'The pen is mightier than the sword.' You sucked right off his tit. Came over to find out if he was right and wet your dick in the blood of America's youth. Maybe win a Pulitzer and get your byline known to all the right people. Could be a book in it too." The Gerber was in my hand before Runson could blink.

"Take out your pen," I said to the bloodsucker, the tip inches from his nose.

Runson shrank into his phony ammo jacket like putting salt on a snail.

"Do it," I hissed.

He reached into his breast pocket and took out a gold-plated Cartier pen, probably one of the knock-offs sold on Tu Do.

I laid the knife on the tablecloth.

"Now," I said. "I want to see if you can stick that pen into my eye. I want to see how mighty it is. I want to know if you can do anything but serve up bullshit for these fresh turds who aren't worth the sweat of one grunt willing to die for his buddy."

The reporter tried to smile, but it came out like a five-year-old caught in a lie. Now I had the attention of the other newsies in the room. None of them moved. Probably their first taste of action.

Somehow this man must have witnessed enough death to figure he was mean and tough. Osmosis. He put the pen down on the table, sober.

"I don't have anything to prove," he said. "I've been out in the boonies. I've seen the horror. I've earned the right to tell it like it is. America needs to know. Now, finish your drink and leave me alone."

There was a cliché that I had thought was a myth, but I had experienced it enough to be a true believer. The room turned red. The reporter's ammo jacket was crimson, and the sweat on his brow was blood.

If I stuck the Gerber in the asshole's eye, I would spend years in LBJ or stand at attention in front of a firing squad. Even Phoenix couldn't save the ass of an agent who gouged the eye out of a reporter with witnesses nearby. Jimmy Ky wouldn't suffer from my hands. I wouldn't get to salute the Colonel again. Don't mean nuthin'.

With my left hand, I grabbed the collar of his ammo jacket and pulled it hard together at his throat. My right hand held the Gerber to his eye. Our noses touched.

"Fuck you," I screamed. "You don't know the truth. You write what Westie and the other zombies tell you to. You watch the blood seep into the clay. For what? To sell newspapers? So you feel like a man? Have you seen a woman die with a bullet between her eyes from your pistol? Have you had the power of life and death in your fingers?" I let go of his collar and put the Gerber back again. "Now, you've got three seconds to pick up that pen and show me you're not the dirtbag phony I know you are."

The reporter smoothed out the new wrinkles in his jacket. He didn't reach for the pen. Suicide wasn't his trip.

"You know I'm not gonna do it," he said. "You'd kill me. What I would rather do is buy you another drink and you can tell me what the real story is. If I have offended you, I apologize." There was no more childish smile on his face. But there was a tic above his right eye. He had been around enough to realize his life was hanging on the whim of a burnout who had seen and done too much.

Someone punctured the tires on my jeep. All I felt was the weight. The incredible weight of eyes that haunted every moment. I slumped my shoulders and tossed the last of my drink down my throat.

"No thanks," I said. "I think I'll turn in. You boys have a fine evening pretending."

Maybe it was the drugs. Mood swings. Days and nights of living on yellow jackets had just brought me to the brink of murder. And I hadn't even been ordered to. Maybe it was what I had become. I was having a hard time distinguishing that voice in my head from my master's like Comer. Phoenix had succeeded. I was a stone killer. And a man just came within a millimeter of death because he was a blowhard. There was one speck of conscience left. But the battle was nearly lost.

I took the stairs to my room and smoked a joint, sleeping through the night on dreams shaded green.

In the morning, after a breakfast of ham and eggs unlike anything the chow line at base camp had on the menu, I walked to the Sporting Bar. Soon, I would have to choose the best site for approaching Ky. Even at ten-thirty, Special Forces soldiers were drinking Tiger and Lucky 7 beer. Or maybe they had been there all night.

Saigon was an arms-free zone for all but MPs, but these soldiers must not have gotten the word. M16s, Colt pistols, M79 grenade launchers, and sawed-off shotguns sat on tables or rested against legs. Many of the men looked as if they had just arrived from a long-range patrol in the Delta, their fatigues caked with clay and their eyes still surrounded by black greasepaint. Most had no insignia on their uniforms, another sign they were under orders from the spooks, the bastard cousins of SOG, Special Operations Group.

As I walked through the louvered swinging doors, taking in the "don't give a fuck" atmosphere with one glance, I knew exactly what was going on in the heads of these men. They had crawled on their bellies through the mud, the least of their worries the snakes, leeches, poisonous spiders, malaria-ridden mosquitoes, and booby traps. Pushing aside a clump of rice or elephant grass, they never knew when a squad of VC or NVA would be waiting, smiling, and pointing an AK at their faces. Maybe even a battalion. A place like the Sporting Bar was one of the few sanctuaries they could go to forget the yellow men. Forget the bodies that played the pirouette of death caused by their rifles or the buddy who got his ticket punched by a trip wire hidden on the trail. Unfortunately, the Sporting Bar didn't make any of them forget. Gallons of beer only made them angrier and the stories more bizarre. The lifeblood of 'Nam wasn't the millions of dollars of supplies that were consumed every day. It was stories. If the stories stopped, the war would end. If the supplies stopped, the grunts could eat off the land. I had heard enough stories never to sleep again. Now I would have to listen to more to get the information I needed.

No one paid me much attention. In some ways, I felt like a comic book character. I would walk into any one of a thousand bars in Saigon. No one would seriously mess with me. Today, I wore khaki pants, loafers with no socks, and a short-sleeve, white cotton shirt. No beard, my hair over my ears, the tan, the scar, and creases welded to my face the only indication that I had been in the bush. The intuition these men had groomed after months in the boonies gave them the ability to smell death. I wore that like a neon sign across my chest. An unknowing cherry who mistakenly stepped into the Sporting Bar would be lucky to leave with only a few broken ribs. But I wasn't a green troop just in from Da Nang and seeking adventure. No words passed to communicate who I was. It was natural boonie rat knowing. I walked to the bar and ordered a Tiger. No one made eye contact.

Most of the light in the bar came from the door. Table lamps were twenty watt and covered with Chinese paper shades. A jukebox played Beach Boys songs at low volume. Later, it would get louder, in proportion to the drunk level of the grunts. The smell of fish frying in oil drifted from a beaded doorway that led to the back. Smoke curled around the ceiling and created a fog like the aftermath of an artillery strike. Cigarette burns scarred every table and the bar. Butts and roaches littered the floor.

The beer was ice cold. This was a hangout for Special Forces. If things weren't the way they wanted it or up to their expectations, a phosphorous grenade would have the bamboo walls burning in seconds, leaving the Sporting Bar another innocent but still dead casualty. I raised my beer to a soldier who was alone and hunched over a Lucky, his M16 leaning against the thigh of his torn fatigue pants. He nodded.

The typical conversation starter was, "Where you from?" This dump was different. Special Forces soldiers didn't give a shit. Dialogue would most often begin with things like, "You wearin' pink boxers, pussy? That tan came from China Beach, and you ain't foolin' nobody. I got mine from a month in the paddies near Long My." But I was different, too.

"My old man's a colonel," I said. "That's why I'm here. What's your story?"

The soldier had streaks of red in the mud on his face. His bloodshot eyes held the ever-present thousand-yard stare when he looked at me, not saying a word. Sometimes it took days for the mouth to be able to translate messages from the brain, after only saying things like "down" or "mortar" or "doc" for weeks.

"You're fuuucked up, man," he said, enunciating every vowel. "Nobody ever admits that their old man's an officer. You gotta be ready for a Section 8, talkin' that shit. Or willing to eat a frag." He drank a long swallow of his Lucky and called for the barmaid.

The b-girls in the Sporting Bar were older than the normal whores in the other bars. And they didn't harass the patrons with "Buy me drink, sodjer." They wore ao dais showing lots of flesh, but stayed huddled in the corner unless a grunt beckoned. This was a place for serious drinking. The serious fucking could be found most anywhere else.

I finished my beer in one long swallow and asked the barmaid for another while she was serving the grunt next to me.

"Don't make much difference how," I said. "Just when."

He turned his head full on. The red streaks came from a scalp wound that I hadn't seen and was still oozing and raw. Special Forces troops, fresh from a month of long-range reconnaissance in the boonies, often didn't wait to be mustered for a trip to town. They stole a jeep and went. Who would stop them? Not even Westmoreland. There were more unwritten laws in 'Nam that were honored than volumes of the Military Code. One was "Don't fuck with LURPs." It was a capital offense. More of the second sight told me this was a LURP, not a Green Beret or SEAL.

"You got that right on, man," he said. He clinked his fresh beer against mine.

"Hear you dudes hit some heavy action down by Ben Luc," I said. "That true?" The best way to loosen any grunt's tongue was a story. Especially one about him. Most wanted to talk about the fear without naming the beast. It had been inside their heads, eating the horror for days, if not years.

The LURP watched his reflection in the mirror behind the wall and waited for nearly a minute before responding.

"Shit," he said. "Never saw nuthin' like it. We laid in that fuckin' water for a week. Intel told us there was a fresh battalion of NVA meat startin' up in that sector. Got the info from ARVN scouts. If that ain't fuck all, don't know what is. The rain was so bad, couldn't a' seen or heard a fuckin' tank within five meters. By the time we finally saw Charlie, none a' us had any blood left from bein' sucked dry by them fuckin' leeches." He held out his arm and pushed up the sleeve of his fatigue blouse. His forearm was covered with puckering scars about two inches long, both from the leeches and burning them off. "Wrong day. Right Charlie. They showed their dink faces. We laid low until they got close enough to smell the shit in my pants. We opened up, and the artillery strikes came within a few feet of our heads. Them yellow fuckers had their own mortars back in the trees. Couldn't go forward or we'd be wasted by friendlies. Couldn't go back or the gook mortars would rip us new shitters. Ended up hand to hand. I'm the only one in my squad who made it back without ridin' medevac." He scratched at the sores on his forearm and looked at me. "I been wonderin' how they knew we were there. I think the ARVN set up the whole thing. All their troops were in the rear. Told us to go out there and had the NVA wait until we were nearly done anyway. Lost my best buddy, Corrigan. He took a bayonet to the kidney. Don't mean nuthin'." He downed the rest of his beer in one motion.

The war was beyond the comprehension of a kid from Omaha. The ARVN general he saluted had millions in a numbered Swiss account, earned from the black market drug trade, assassinations, NVA payoffs, prostitution, and a percentage of the wages of all his men. The ARVN scout he listened to was more often than not working for the VC and hated him more than any North Vietnamese. The crippled beggar in the street would knife him if it was dark enough and he turned his back. The whore he fucked might have razor blades in her pussy. The little girl crying at the sight of her mother being dragged away could be booby-trapped with C-4 sold to the VC by the master sergeant at the ammo dump. His green lieutenant would likely get everyone in the squad killed if his orders were followed. There were no innocents. Everyone was the enemy. Except your buddy.

The story was the same. Only the people who died were different. I motioned for the barmaid to come over and ordered two more beers. The LURP knew one was for him.

"You been in here before?" I asked.

"Yup," he said. "Been in-country nearly a year on this tour."

No introductions had been made. It was not done with grunts who were in the shit day after day. If I knew your name, I might have to feel something when your shit got scattered. I might even have to feel responsible in some small way. The load was too heavy.

The barmaid set the beers in front of us, and I reached for mine. There was a sheen of moisture on the cooled glass.

"Ever seen the guy who works upstairs come through here?" I asked. I figured Ky owned the Sporting Bar.

"Yaa," the LURP said. "Why ya' wanna know?" The look was like he was trying to decide if he should open the shirt of a dead VC. The booby traps were everywhere.

"A little business proposition."

"What would that be?"

"You don't want to know."

"I get that you work alone. You're a fuckin' spook. And I *don't* wanna know. Just makin' conversation."

"So, have you seen him? Thirties. Probably wearing sunglasses, tall for a gook, thin, and always has lots of bodyguards. Drives a Mercedes. Or gets driven. Wouldn't be surprised if he owned this joint."

"You gonna grease him? Need any help?"

"Naw. Just need to have a discussion."

"Right on, spook." He laughed, the first smile since I sat down. "Sure, I've seen the dude. Everyone here has. Sometimes, he buys a round. Never hangs. Disappears into the back, followed by a couple gooks tryin' to look mean. Gets lotsa visitors, too."

"Does he keep any schedule?"

"Don't know that. You can ask around. The times I've seen him, it was morning. Like now. By the time he left, I was too blind to see him. Or anything else."

The LURP looked over my shoulder.

"Goddamn," he said. "I think your buddy just walked through the door." He nodded behind me.

I chose this grunt and the spot on the bar because of the mirror. I could look without being too obvious.

One of the other SOGs yelled, "Hey, General. We're gettin' thirsty. How 'bout buyin' a brew for your best buddies?" That was met with cheers from the other grunts.

Jimmy Ky had been trying to make it across the room without having to slow down. Now he was caught. He stopped, held up his hand, and waved to the barmaid. When she got close, he said, "Bring these fine men a beer. On me." He spoke nearly perfect English. His entourage stood a step behind him, glaring at the grunts as if they could scare them. Not even with an M60 pig machine gun. The grunts cheered. Ky walked through the beads, followed by his bodyguards.

"Now ain't that one fine gook?" the LURP asked. "Whose gonna buy the free rounds when you waste him?"

"I never said anything about killing," I said. "What gave you that idea? Just business."

Again. I couldn't shed my skin. I was sitting next to a LURP who had probably zapped more gooks than me. The stench wafted from us like a slaughterhouse. He knew, and not a hundred Tigers could change his mind. He also knew what guys like me did. We were talked about in whispers. And avoided. He killed in firefights, meeting the enemy straight on, while I crept through the night in search of my prey. And it didn't have to be Vietnamese.

For the rest of the day, I drank with the LURP. No one else joined us. I counted a half-dozen visitors. In the afternoon, I staggered through the beads toward the back, acting as if I was too drunk to see that it wasn't the way to the latrine.

Three mama-sans tended to pots of frying grease and chopped fish and vegetables. A big pan of rice warmed on the gas stove. Dishes, bowls, and cups sat on metal shelves. A stairway climbed up the wall on the left. The door at the top was closed and one of the bodyguards, leaning against the railing, scowled at me, yelling, "Di di!" pointing back to the way I stumbled in.

When I came back to the bar, the LURP asked, "Find what you were lookin' for?" He finished another Tiger and looked away, smiling. I didn't answer.

Ky came down and left the Sporting Bar a few minutes before dark. Perfect. It gave me time to check out the back and get to the Majestic for another night of riding the dragon.

There was a message shoved under the door when I woke up after a night tripping to Puff dreams. Luong would meet me at the Ben Thanh Market at 0900. Of course the note didn't read that way. Comer loved to play a game that joined cowboys with spooks. "Stagecoach arrives by fruit stall oh-nine-hundred." Luong couldn't show his face at the Majestic, and I didn't think any heathen Montagnard had ever been allowed through the door by the Vietnamese management. A white man walking with Luong through the streets would attract immediate attention. At the market, we could camouflage our conversation for the short amount of time it took to give him a rendezvous point.

Two choices for meeting Ky, the mansion or the Sporting Bar. Ky wouldn't make the decision where or when he died. It was a question of logistics. And our survival. On the ride to the market, I decided my best work had been in the night. Scaling the wall at the mansion would be the plan.

Motorized and foot-driven cyclos fought with Renaults, Peugeots, jeeps, and pedestrians for space on Le Loi. I hired a pedal cyclo outside the Majestic and joined the morning traffic. The street was already a fog of blue smoke, and the air smelled of baking, rancid fruit, Son Sai Gon River sewage, and exhaust. A dog nipped at my driver's legs, and he barked back, careful not to offend the soul of the mangy bitch. Buddhist monks made their morning rounds in flowing, orange robes, knowing the believers would feed them without even holding out a hand. The few palm trees that still existed in this land of asphalt and smog looked as if they needed an emergency transfusion of clean air and water.

Stopped by an overturned fruit cart, we sat on Le Loi for ten minutes while the mess was cleared, mostly by young boys who stuffed their pockets with bananas and mangoes. On the sidewalk, a woman stood next to the cyclo. An umbrella shaded her from the morning sun. She wore a long, white coat that fell below her knees, slit up the side and showing her black pants. One of the legacies of the French period in 'Nam was the mix of French-Vietnamese blood that produced absolutely stunning women. She could have walked down the runway of any designer's show in Paris. Almost as beautiful as Liem, but black eyes. And alive. I waved to her, but she modestly turned her head down and stared at her flip-flops.

The smell of fruit and fish got stronger as we neared the Ben Thanh Market. Cyclos and taxis jostled each other in the make-believe queue on Le Loi. My driver stopped on the outside lane of traffic that was four layers deep. I gave him a few piasters. He tipped his straw hat and grinned in a toothless smile, turning immediately to battle the others for what might be the only fare for the rest of the day.

Few white faces were among the thousands shopping, and they were wearing military fatigues. Tough to make Saigon a tourist destination in 1970. The accelerating street-bombing campaign of the VC kept most visitors close to their hotels.

It was just before 0900, and I knew Luong was already here. All I would have to do is stroll through the stalls and he would make contact. He must have felt like he was covered in pineapple juice and lying on a nest of fire ants. Surrounded by this many Vietnamese, every nerve end in his body would be screaming to kill. Saigon was another world, inhabited by a million of his enemies, and he would stand out like a grunt with all his limbs in the amputee ward at the 36th Evac Hospital outside Saigon. He couldn't wear his traditional Montagnard clothing of baggy pants tied with colored cloth, blouse, and headband.

Two MPs walked down the crowded aisle toward me. At a jewelry stall, I was holding up a Rolex watch that cost the equivalent of a Hershey's with almonds. Dressed in civilian clothes, I wore khaki pants and a white, short-sleeved shirt.

"Sir," the one on the left said. "This area is not secure. Please be careful." He had three stripes on his shoulder. He was black and would have been in the heavyweight division in the battalion boxing team. The other MP was white and over six-foot-five.

I took off my sunglasses and turned to the MPs.

"Roger that, Sergeant," I said.

Both MPs, relatively relaxed for being in a city under siege, came to attention. Not the parade ground kind. The kind where you are leisurely swimming in the river and all of a sudden you see two red eyes barely above the surface and moving toward you. The kind that makes the muscles tense. It's called "survival instinct." I didn't think they were afraid, but some inner voice was telling them that death was very near.

The official response would be to demand my ID and pass. Neither one asked. We examined each other for a few seconds.

"Thanks again, Sarge," I said. "I'll keep my eyes open. You have a good day now." I turned back to the Rolexes. A minute later, I felt the MPs move away only by the drop in tension in the aisle. It could be a lifetime before the stink of doom and danger was erased from my soul.

The Vietnamese woman showing the watches didn't even bother to beg me to come back or start her "first sale of morning" pitch. She had seen the exchange. I walked deeper into the market.

The further I went, the more I was surrounded by Vietnamese and the staler the air. Smells of cooking fish and rice mixed with spices trumped all the other odors. The noise level increased, especially the women, shrieking, "*Mua re.*" Buy cheap. Someone touched my arm. It was Luong, dressed in the Saigon uniform of the day, black pants and white, long-sleeved shirt rolled up on his forearms. But there was no way to mistake him for a flatland Vietnamese.

A member of a proud and ancient culture, the man beside me was stoop shouldered and meek. I had never seen Luong this way, but he must have chosen subservience as part of his disguise. Of course, if he strode through this market, head high, challenging anyone who approached, in seconds, he would be another piece of meat decomposing on the ground. If I had to guess, probably half the men here spent the nights fighting as VC. Luong obviously did not belong.

I bumped into him, dropping the newspaper I carried on the ground. We both knelt to pick up the paper.

"Twenty-two hundred hours," I whispered. "By the American embassy. Twenty-four Tu Do. Palm trees in the back. Bring your gear." Luong barely nodded, and we stood, immediately pushing through the crowd in different directions.

On the ride back to the Majestic, I wondered which of the many eyes that followed me through the market were there at Comer's orders. I would be foolish to think I wasn't under surveillance. This op stank as much as the day-old corpses I came across after a firefight in the bush. I would play this one like there were two enemies, Comer and Ky.

A year ago, I landed in this country already filled with doubts, but answering some vague call to duty bludgeoned into me by the Colonel. Now, I didn't care about him. Nor did I have any misgivings about what killing sleeping Vietnamese did to advance the cause of America. It was useless. It was murder. We were losing this war as surely as the day would be hot and humid. Another suspected collaborator dead at my hand wouldn't do a single thing to win this police action except add to the misery that was at every glance. Ky would be my last. He deserved to die.

As we turned off Le Loi onto Dai Lo Nguyen, two old peasants in from the rice paddies were begging on the corner. I told the cyclo driver, *"Dung."* Stop. Each man was missing an arm. Crutches sat on the curb beside them. They were filthy, and brown rags covered the stumps. Gook sores oozed yellow fluid down their uncovered legs. One man's right eye was bulging, the lid closed. The other's left eye was milky with cataracts, and he tried to smile as I approached, his palm up. I gave them each a few piasters and escaped before the street kids could swallow me.

The response of the US military in 'Nam after an attack on American forces coming from any of the thousands of vils was to burn the vil to the ground. Often, whatever civilians remained when the troops came back became "casualties of hostile action." The survivors were moved out, and a new vil was built, usually including barbwire. The villagers were allowed to go home to new hootches they didn't want, guarded by ARVN soldiers who hated and tortured them. I had seen this response dozens of times and never understood why we would burn the village to the ground and then rebuild it. But, most of all, I remembered the old men who were beaten and interrogated. These two villagers were probably examples. They were too old to fight for either side. Any young men in the village would have to immediately escape to the VC or the Americans would assume they were already Cong, a death sentence. We were responsible for recruiting thousands of young men who didn't want to fight but had no choice. And thousands more old men who died or drifted to the cities to beg.

At the Majestic, I ate lunch and waited for darkness, cleaning and oiling the weapons in my room. Black greasepaint was added to the arsenal, and my Gerber was on my belt. At 2130, I put the weapons in my duffel bag and went out the back door.

In the bushes behind 24 Tu Do, I waited for Luong. Again, I knew he was already somewhere close by, watching. The Hush Puppy silently shot out the only streetlight on the block. Luong would slide next to me when it was all clear. It had been days since I composed a letter to Mom and the Colonel, and I hadn't told them about what happened to Colleen or Tran.

Dear Mother and Colonel,

Since I wrote you last, I think I fell in love, even without your guidance. And I didn't have to pay for it. Not in money anyway. You'll also be glad to hear that we nearly adopted a baby boy, Tran. Colleen and I spent an idyllic few days together, exploring the beautiful cratered countryside. Something was starting in a place inside my heart that I never felt before. When I looked at her, there was this prickly sensation like I had napalm inside my skin. When we made love on the altar of an abandoned temple, I thought I would come forever and the darkness was filled with my own personal nighttime artillery barrage. Oops. Sorry, much too graphic for Catholics or whatever religion outside the army you're following now. I found Tran in a vil that was under attack by a squad of VC. His adoptive father died while sheltering Tran from the AK bullets, curled in a ball with Tran the core. Colleen and I decided it would be better to place Tran in a home in 'Nam, so she went before me to meet the new parents in Pham Bien, a quaint little vil that is now ashes. So is Tran. Well, not quite. He was only burned bad enough to leave this layer of crusty potato chip black on his skin. His hair was burned off, and he looked like a baby barbecued monk. I buried him next to a tree with no crucifix to mark the grave. Do you think Father Mulcahey will say he gets into heaven? Colleen was kidnapped. No ransom. They greased her with their AKs when Luong and I came to the rescue. So, would you expect anything else? I couldn't rescue an infected toenail. This could be my last letter. Tonight, I'm staked out by the house of the son of the vice president of Vietnam. I'm going to kill him. Colonel, you'll be glad to hear I'm following orders. But I think command wants me dead just as bad as Ky. You see, I've gotten this reputation as a rogue. Damned if I know why. Could be that there haven't been only gooks who died from my Hush Puppy, M16, or KA-BAR. I have a suspicion that there might be a surprise waiting for me on Tu Do Street. Well, hell, it's been fun here in paradise. Don't mean nuthin'.

Through the second-floor windows, I saw a man patrolling the rooms. He stopped, lit a cigarette, and moved on. He carried an M16. Things looked pretty much the same, and no tightened security was obvious. Luong touched my arm. I should have jumped at this phantom, but I was expecting him to appear like a ghost in the mist. It was now well after 2200, and I signaled Luong to move behind another palm tree and wait.

By 0400, most of the lights were out in the mansion. Little traffic of any kind had passed on the street in hours, but I could still hear occasional riffs from a bass guitar coming out of one of the bars on Tu Do. The guard made his rounds, stopping every few circuits to peer from a window. There were no stars visible over Vietnam to guide the way. I motioned to Luong, and we crossed the street.

The wall didn't provide much protection for Ky. Certainly, more lookouts would be patrolling the grounds. Luong used my cupped hand to steady himself while he cut the razor wire. We both carried knives, a garrote, Hush Puppies, smoke grenades, and pistols taped to our fatigues so they were silent when we moved. Our faces were blackened with greasepaint, and our clothes were dark. As usual, all the tags were off our outfits and the serial numbers filed from our weapons. We were sterile, and only my face would identify me as a probable American. I didn't need to wear the penicillin bracelet, since I wasn't allergic. Luong disappeared over the wall, and I followed, using the top edge of the wall to pull myself up.

On the ground, Luong crouched beside me, staring at the glow of a cigarette near the corner of the mansion. I motioned him to go that way while

I covered the other direction. A dry fountain was between the house and me. I duck-walked to a point behind the marble and stayed down. Within seconds, Luong was back, and only the smell of the cigarette remained. There had to be more guards, and the dead man's buddy would be around soon.

Every mission was a close call. Luck played a role. It only took someone having a sleepless night to mean Luong and I would have to shoot our way out if we wanted to live to kill again. Once, I had stood in a target's hootch for minutes, listening to the rhythmic breathing of the man and his wife. When I moved toward the sleeping mats, something brushed my forehead, and I jumped back. The man must have known he was on the list. He had tethered scorpions from the bamboo ceiling. It wasn't the bite that was the threat. That would be painful, but I would make it. They were hissing scorpions, dangling as sentries. The scorpion made the sound of fresh Coca-Cola being poured into a glass, and the papa-san and mama-san sat up. No choice. I couldn't risk the mama-san's screams. Two *phuupps* from the Hush Puppy, and they were dead.

A cooling breeze rustled the palms that bordered the house. Lilac petals fell from the bushes, giving the impression of a night snowstorm with gigantic flakes. A rainsquall passing through just after midnight made the grass smell fresh and masked the usual scent of Saigon. A car drove by on Tu Do, sounding as if its muffler had been shot with an M16.

I wanted to sanitize the rear of the mansion before moving to the front. Tonight, we would have to use more force than normal. It was too risky to rely on stealth alone.

A man came around the left corner of the house carrying a rifle. When he was close, he stopped and whispered, "*O dau anh*?" Where are you? He looked toward the far corner of the mansion and took a slow step in that direction, M16 now at his shoulder. In two quick strides, I was behind him and the Gerber sliced through his neck like it was made of chocolate ice cream. I pulled him into my chest and eased his body to the grass. Luong helped me move him into the bushes.

At the front corner of the house, the Mercedes that delivered Ky to the Sporting Bar was parked on the gravel turnaround. A jeep marked MP drove by, the two riders out to enforce the midnight curfew. I nodded at Luong to neutralize the man standing at the wrought-iron gate. He knew by my signal that I would take out the guard on the entrance steps at the same time. I hesitated for a second, listening, knowing that something didn't feel right, but there was nothing obvious. I touched Luong on the elbow, and he moved toward the gate, using the shadow of bushes for cover.

Sliding along the wall of the mansion, I couldn't see the guard, but I could see Luong's profile. By the time I reached the steps, the man at the gate was being pulled behind a lilac bush. I cleared my throat, knowing the sound would bring the front door guard to me. The guard whispered "*Cao*?" Fox. It was a common name. "*Cao*?" he said again, and I heard him start down the steps. The barrel of his rifle poked around the corner. I was crouched low on the grass and drove my Gerber up into his stomach, moving the blade toward his heart. Ribs broke with a muffled *crock*. I grabbed his rifle before it hit the concrete stairs, letting his body fall over my shoulder. After he finished his death dance, I carried him across the narrow patch of grass and laid him in the bushes.

The front door was unlocked. Inside, a long hallway led to a stairway at the back. Muted wall lamps lined the hall, and all the doors were closed. A Manchurian weave runner covered the hardwood floor all the way to the end. Paintings hung on both sides above narrow tables topped with flower vases decorated with Chinese art and characters. Someone had been smoking a cigar in the last few hours, and the smell couldn't override the burning kerosene. Luong gently closed the door and stood behind me. Not a sound in the house, but there had to be more guards than just the one patrolling upstairs. I pointed to the doors on the left, and Luong started down that side. I took the right.

All of the rooms were dark and empty. Luong and I arrived at the bottom of the stairs at the same time. No sign yet of the man on the second floor.

Stairs. I hated them. Old houses in the tropics suffered from the heat and humidity, warping the wood faster than in colder climates. No matter how slow and careful, I still had to shift my weight. At any time, the boards might creak, and I was dead. The climb required as much focus as walking through a minefield, especially with a guard due to appear at any moment. Give me a one-story clay floor hootch any night.

First, I pointed toward Luong and the door, then at my chest, and, finally, up the stairs, indicating to Luong to stay here and watch the front while I went hunting on the second level. I tried to stay to the wall side of the stairs rather than the middle. It took minutes to get to the top, and my right hand was slick from sweat caused by holding the Hush Puppy in front of me. I would have been easy to spot in the dim light on the stairway, and the guard wouldn't give me a chance to explain.

This hallway was carpeted too and lit only by more wall lamps turned low. Doors were both to my right and left. No noise, but the smell of Old Spice and kerosene lingered in the air. I crouched behind a three-foot-high lacquered vase and waited for the guard to make his rounds. He must be on break. We had been in the house nearly five minutes.

A door opened to my right and a man carrying a Remington pump action shotgun came into the hall. He wore black pants and a white shirt, the Saigon uniform, but he had on brogues instead of sandals. I waited for him to get near, stood, and circled the garrote around his neck from behind, giving just enough pressure for him to know that any struggle would leave him wearing a red bow tie. "*Khac dan ong*?" I said, my lips touching his ear. Other men? With one hand, I took the shotgun and rested it against my leg. He didn't say anything, nor did he try to fight. I pulled the garrote tighter, and blood warmed my fingers. "*Khac dan ong*?" I asked again. He pointed to the door on the right at the end of the hall. "*O dau Ky*?" I asked. Where is Ky? He tried to turn around. I loosened the garrote enough for him to point behind us toward the door on the left at the other end. Bringing my free hand up, I twisted hard and heard the wire squish through the flesh on his neck. Blood shot from his throat, and I let him collapse to the rug next to the shotgun.

At the top of the stairs, I motioned Luong to come up. I didn't need to tell him to be quiet. When he was beside me, I put my mouth by the side of his head and whispered, "Guards in that room." I indicated the room on the right and turned back. "Ky is there," pointing to the room at the opposite end. "We have to grease the guards first. Then Ky." Luong nodded and followed me.

The only worry was that the frame had warped and there would be a squeak when I pushed the door open. Both Luong and I had our Hush Puppies out and Gerbers in easy reach. No sound and we were inside. Faint light came through the open window. Four cots lined the walls, and a man slept in each one. I stepped to the right, and Luong immediately went left.

The room smelled of fish balls and bad breath with just a hint of Brut. A fan in the far corner pushed the stale air around the room. Clothes were piled next to each cot, and more shotguns leaned against the wall. Empty Lucky beer bottles and teacups sat on an end table between the cots. The remains of a rice dinner formed a greasy design on a page of newspaper. I reached the first man, put the Hush Puppy to his head and fired. At the same moment, I heard the familiar *pphhuupp* of Luong's silenced pistol. I swiveled to the next man and shot him the face, hearing Luong do the same on his side of the room. Not even a moan.

Luong trailed behind as we walked down the hall toward Ky, checking every room on the way. They were all empty.

At Ky's door, I signaled Luong to wait outside. I slowly turned the handle, pushed open the door, and stepped inside. Closing the door, I let my eyes adjust to the darkness and slowed my breathing. After a few minutes, I could see two forms through the mosquito net that covered a king-size, four-poster bed. I crept across the rug. Ky was on the left, and the long black hair of his date was splayed over the pillow on the right. A Colt pistol sat next to a flask of water on the bedside table, flanked by a fifth of scotch. Clothes were scattered around the room. I could see my reflection in the mirror of the vanity that held bottles of perfume, lotion, and pills. I didn't have much experience with expensive perfume, but the room had the scent of money and sex. I pushed open the netting on Ky's side and shoved the Hush Puppy in Ky's ear, nudging him awake.

"Tell the woman to get in the closet," I said. "Now. And tell her not to say a word." I pushed hard enough for Ky's head to turn toward the woman. He slapped her on the shoulder and hissed something in Vietnamese I couldn't understand. I knew a fair amount of the language, but it had to be slow. Or my choice. Ky's tonal rhythm was more like rounds being fired from an M60 pig machine gun. The woman looked at Ky, the gun, and into my eyes. She jerked the sheet off, jumped out of the bed, naked, and hurried to a louvered door a few steps away. She had high, small breasts, and I could see the darkness at the top of her legs. The woman closed the door behind her and whimpered.

Ky was watching me. I pressed the Hush Puppy harder against his head. When he turned away, I put my left hand over his mouth and shot him in the right knee, holding tight so he couldn't scream. He bucked on the bed, and I moved the Hush Puppy to his eye, shoving it hard enough in to feel the silenced barrel move his socket deep into his head.

"Quiet," I said. "When I take my hand off your mouth, you're going to answer my question. No shouting. There's no one to rescue you anyway. Understood?"

I put the Hush Puppy to Ky's throat. He nodded, and I took my hand from his mouth. He stopped moving.

"Good," I said. "Only one question. Where are all the guns and ammo you've been buying up and hiding? Don't start by denying it or I'll shoot your other knee, then move up."

Ky's bucking had caused the sheet to come off most of his body. He was naked, and there was a dragon tattooed on his chest, fire spouting from its mouth. He was hairless except on his head and groin. He didn't just sit behind a desk or ride in a Mercedes. Taut muscles showed that he probably practiced some form of martial arts. I guessed a Chinese flavor. His eyes showed no fear, and the rate of his blinking had not increased, even with the pain in his useless knee and the pistol at his throat.

"I do not know what you are talking about," Ky said. Perfect English. His breathing was regular, and he acted like it was just another night in peaceful Saigon.

I shot Ky's other knee.

This time, Ky didn't buck. He grimaced and inhaled, eyes still on me for just a split second before they turned to the door behind me.

"Whoa, podner," Comer said. "Slow your gait or you'll get thrown."

I kept the Hush Puppy hard against Ky's throat and looked toward the door. Comer and Molar were standing next to each other, shotguns aimed at my chest.

"Get the light, would you please, Molar?" Comer said. Molar walked to a table lamp and switched it on, the grin on his mouth like a butcher slicing up Grade A filets to take home to his wife.

I twisted my body toward the bed so I could see the two spooks, never lessening the pressure on the pistol at Ky's throat. He was beginning to tremble, shock not far away.

"Where's Luong?" I asked.

Comer chuckled and took a step closer to me.

"That injun' di di'ed when I told him to skedaddle," Comer said. "Pulled rank. Besides, he wanted to live to kill a few more of his gook cousins."

Too many times we had saved each other's lives to believe this bullshit. Luong was either dead or waiting for the right time to smoke these two. He was my only chance. He must have been confused when they showed. Just enough for Luong to hesitate. At least, that was my hope. I moved my left hand slowly toward the pocket that held the smoke grenade.

"You can see this mission is nearly over," I said. "Jimmy was about to tell me where he's hidden the guns."

Comer stepped to a chair in the corner and sat down, the shotgun never wavering from my chest.

"Don't let me slow your roundup," Comer said. "Let's hear what Mr. Ky has to say."

"Not before I know why you're here, Comer."

"Seems you've strayed a few klicks off the trail, son. I can't prove it, but I'm sure as hell positive you waxed Viper. And let some dinks live who should be under a tombstone. You oughta be in LBJ or in front of a firing squad."

"So this was all a setup?"

"Just good planning. You know, kill two birds with one shotgun. Makes it easier to ride the range when the Indians are dead. Now, I want to hear from old Jimmy there before he checks out. Looks like he's losin' a bushel of blood."

"Then what? We gonna walk out of here like we're buddies?"

Comer was decked out in his cowboy shit, minus the Stetson. His jeans covered the top of his snakeskin boots, and his pearl-buttoned shirt was tucked under his silver belt buckle. He waved the shotgun at me.

"Boy," Comer said, "you got three seconds to ask Jimmy again. Then we can rap."

The Hawaiian shirt that Molar wore hung over the waist of his Bermuda shorts, and the buttons were undone, showing the tooth necklace on his hairy chest. He wore Converse All Star basketball shoes. His face wasn't sweating, but his stink filled the room. Molar took a step toward me.

"Make that one second," Molar said. "I can't wait to grease this asshole."

Molar's brains splashed on the mirror. Luong was in the doorway, firing his Hush Puppy. Before Molar toppled to the floor, he pulled the trigger on his shotgun, the flechettes going just over my head and into the louvered closet. The woman shrieked, and there was a thud. One of the barbs must have grazed my head. Blood leaked into my eye, and I staggered away from the bed.

When I turned, Comer was crawling across the rug, trying to aim his shotgun at Luong.

Luong fired at Comer, the round hitting him in the leg. Luong looked over my shoulder and yelled "*Du oi.*" Down.

I felt the bullet go into my arm at the same time I heard Ky fire the Colt. On my way down, I pulled the pin on the smoke grenade. By the time I hit the floor, I had thrown it into the corner.

Luong was now firing at Ky, who was rolling off the bed. No way Luong would let Ky survive. He knew who was really behind Tran's death. And Colleen's. He kept firing, and Ky's body danced one last step before it dropped to floor.

Comer turned toward me.

The grenade went off with a bang, and smoke immediately filled the room.

Before I was completely sightless, I fired two more rounds in Comer's direction and heard him grunt. I could vaguely see Ky's lifeless body, but the sound was as deafening as standing next to a howitzer in free fire.

Someone grabbed my good arm and began pulling me toward the door. I started to cough, but let Luong lead the way, the dizziness already making it hard to stay conscious and the blood and smoke blinding me.

On the steps outside, we both stopped to breathe before we stumbled toward the gate. Ky didn't breathe any more. If Comer wasn't dead now, he would be soon.

Luong dragged me into the bushes across the street. Smoke from the grenade made me cough, and every hack caused the wound in my arm to send lava toward my shoulder. I sat on the clay and put my head in my hands, trying to decide what to do next. Molar and Ky were dead. It was likely Comer was too. If he survived, there was no way I would live even a few more days. He would send a posse to find me. Luong and I would be the survivors of a mission gone critically wrong that had US fatalities never listed in the *Washington Post*. I raised my head and waited to see if anyone would come to the house. Explosions and gunfire in Saigon were more the norm than a soundless night. Luong crouched beside me, watching.

Now I was definitely rogue. Even though Comer had betrayed me, the Phoenix program would turn all its resources toward executing anyone who killed one of the highest officers in the spook regime. No Long Binh Jail. No firing squad. That didn't matter to me as much as seeing Comer bleed out. Besides, I would have time to make up a story.

Not even a jeep crossed in front of us. The neighbors might have heard the shots, and they would be keeping their heads down, hoping the violence didn't spread. Smoke still drifted from the windows of Ky's house, but no flames. All I could smell was the afterburn of the grenade.

A man staggered down the stairs, holding his stiff leg, his other hand on his stomach. He coughed and bent over at the waist, wobbling like one of the grunts on Tu Do after a twenty-four-hour binge about to chuck his dinner of fish balls. It was Comer. Alone.

Luong was right behind me, and I could feel his hand on my back steadying me as we crossed the street. Before Comer could stand straight, I grabbed his arm and pulled him behind a palm tree to the side of the turnaround. Hidden from the street by bushes, I kicked Comer in the back of his knees, forcing him to the clay and onto his back. His Levis were ripped at the thigh, and blood ran down the jeans in a steady red line. When he landed, Comer put both hands on his belly and didn't try to stop the fall. His stomach made the sound of squeezing a saturated sponge and blood oozed between his fingers. I pushed the tip of the Hush Puppy against his head and put my hand over his mouth, hissing in his ear.

"Why, Comer?"

It wouldn't be long before shock froze his mind or a passing MP noticed the smoke. Leaves, grass, and soil were still damp from an afternoon shower, and my nose was healing enough to smell the ripeness. The only sound was the ever-present boom of distant artillery.

Luong stood facing the road, his back to us.

Spit and blood from Comer's mouth wet my hand. He pushed against my fingers and stared at me in the dim light. I let him talk.

"You're a fuckin' traitor, Morgan," he said. "You wasted Viper. You've gone into the darkness." He groaned and tried to sit up. "Killin' is getting' to be fun for you. We can't have that. Gives us a bad rap." Comer coughed up a wad of phlegm and tried to spit. It sounded like he was a late-stage tuberculosis patient.

I pushed harder with the Hush Puppy.

"Viper deserved to die," I said. "He sent me out to kill an innocent woman. And I think you knew. Did you?"

Beams from headlights showed through the palms and made shadows on the street. Luong tensed, and we both looked at the house. No more smoke. The jeep passed without stopping.

Comer's eyes were starting to flicker. I slapped him.

"Don't go away just yet," I said. "Did you know Liem was innocent?"

"What the fuck do you care? She was just another gook cunt."

"Why did you have me grease her?"

"She wouldn't fuck the right colonel. Don't mean nuthin'."

"Did you know anything about Ky selling baby-sans?"

"Why the fuck does it matter to you? Ky was mixed up in lots of dirty business."

"Answer the question. Did Ky know about the babies? You were paying the expenses of the orphanages out of drug money."

"Ah, now, Morgan, how would you know that?"

"The babies. Ky."

"Sure, Ky knew how to squeeze an ounce of blood out of every dumbshit in this shithole country. That includes baby-sans."

"And you had a part in it?"

"Can't get me to confess to that one, Morgan. Why? You want one a' them heifers to ride home?"

I twisted the barrel of the Hush Puppy hard enough to make a sound on Comer's forehead like grinding my Gerber.

Luong was close enough to hear. He bent down, never taking his eyes off patrol.

"Sell babies?" Luong asked.

"Who the fuck you think you are asking me questions, monkey? I don't talk to greaseball slants unless they're servin' me a cold one."

"Sell babies?" Luong asked again.

"Fuck you, ape man. I bought 'em. Ky was the one who sold 'em."

Luong spit on Comer's face and stood up, back on patrol.

Nothing moved around us except smoke and the occasional drop of rain. I twisted the Hush Puppy again.

"You are one sick, evil asshole, Comer. What about the drugs? You know there's grunts out their shootin' up what you're sellin'."

"If it wasn't us, it'd be somebody else. Can't have an inventory if there ain't no market. Besides, what do think pays your salary? You're off the books, Morgan, just like all the other spooks runnin' around here."

The rain started. Just a few drops. Comer's body convulsed, and I knew there wasn't much time.

"Ky ran the drug trade?"

Comer's eyes flickered. I shook him.

"Answer me," I said.

He stared at the dirt.

"Right on. He did that and paid good greenbacks for the franchise."

"Did you get any of the money for sellin' kids?"

"You saw my new Stetson, didn't ya'?"

"Who else knows about tonight?"

"Nobody. Me and Molar wanted to slice you up for killin' Viper. And bein' a pussy. Ky was the cover."

"Did you tell anyone in Phoenix about Viper and me?

"Why? You afraid they'll get you for that murder, too?"

"Just answer."

"Maybe we can do a little horse tradin'. You know, I'll tell you if ya' let me ride on outa Dodge."

"The only trade is gonna be how quick you die."

"Not fair, is it, Morgan? You're gonna take my scalp anyways."

"No one else at Phoenix is in on it?"

"What the fuck, Morgan. To them, you're the best killer in the herd. But you're not gonna see your momma again. They're gonna hunt you down and kill you just like you did Ky."

I took the Hush Puppy from his forehead and shot him in the temple. I didn't want it to be a forehead shot and leave my signature. We dragged Comer's body into the house and dropped it at the bottom of the stairs.

Upstairs, Ky's lifeless body was in the room where Molar lay dead. I found Molar's necklace and ripped it off, planning to throw it away before some GI thought he found a righteous souvenir. We didn't have time to search the house.

Turning to leave, I noticed a drawer had come open on the nightstand during the firefight. A thick wad of hundred-dollar bills was wrapped in a rubber band next to a pile of jewelry. I grabbed the money, knowing Luong could use the cash. No need for me wherever I was headed, and the thought of taking payment for killing these leeches was absurd.

"Meet up outside," I said to Luong. "Watch for MPs or anyone else. I've got one more thing to do." I followed him down the stairs.

On the first floor, I used my Zippo to set the drapes in a front room on fire. When I reached the end of the curtains, a bulge formed the outline of something I couldn't figure out. I pulled back the cloth. Two young girls in skimpy nightgowns. Behind me, flames were lighting the dark and starting to crackle. Eyes stretched wide, the girls shrunk back and stared. Maybe ten years old. Max. Long, black hair. Bruises on their faces. Bare feet. Hands over flat chests. The heat was warming my back. I grabbed an arm on each and pulled the whimpering girls out of the room.

Outside, Luong and I both tossed grenades through the door and di di'ed for cover, each of us dragging one of the girls. The blaze and noise would soon bring the MPs or any other night patrol. The four of us disappeared into the bushes across the street.

Within minutes, flames lit the night on Tu Do. Smoke filled the trees. The rain picked up and fell from the branches of palms. I held my arms around one of the girls, trying to keep her dry. Luong held the other while we waited for the adrenaline to run its course.

"I'll take these girls to the Red Cross," I said. "No more orphanages. Even if Ky is dead."

Luong stroked the girl's hair.

"No, Morgan," Luong said. "I take home. Mountains. Family."

Never had Luong strung together this many words in English. I always knew he could understand, but words were as rare as a solid night's sleep.

"Are you sure?" I asked.

"Yes. Tran dead. Girls live."

Too many butchered lowlanders. Something must have changed Luong. I crouched closer to the quivering girl in my arms, hoping it would keep her a little warmer.

"I thought you hated Vietnamese," I said.

"Yes. Not girl-sans. Not *ham hiep* wife." Rape. "Not let girl-sans die." Luong pointed to my chest, then back at his. "You. Me. Same, same. War, not *cua chong toi*." Ours.

"How will you make it to the mountains with two little girls?"

"Americans think dead." He nodded toward the burning villa. "You tell. Me. Girls. Walk. No sweat, GI." Luong smiled.

The roll of bills was in my pocket, and I held it out it out to Luong.

"Here," I said. "This will help."

Luong looked at the money and shook his head.

"No, Morgan," he said. "That too many problems. Don't need in village. You keep."

Still holding out the dollars, I stared at Luong for a few heartbeats.

"Okay," I said, "but you earned it," putting the money back in my pocket.

I touched Luong's arm and passed over the girl I held. He was right.

"Go home to the Highlands," I said. "You've saved my life enough times. I'll tell them you died inside." I looked at the flames across the street, then back to Luong. "Take care of the girls and yourself."

This wouldn't be sealed with a hug. Luong's heart was buried somewhere beneath visions of torched Montagnard villages. Public displays of affection were taboo in the Montagnard culture anyway. He bowed and walked away, a girl under each arm. But something had changed since I watched him let Tran suck on his finger. My last view was their backs vanishing in the shadows. I headed for the Majestic.

In the morning, I walked to Phoenix headquarters. The house doctor at the Majestic had bandaged my wounds and gave me a few painkillers, allowing a few hours of sleep after a long shower.

Clean and groomed, I walked through the door into the bustle of a building on alert. Somehow, one of their family chiefs had been killed. I wondered who would replace Comer and Molar, but I didn't really care. I was getting out soon one way or another, and there was no more time to send me out into the bush. No way I would accept another assignment even if these fuckheads tried.

On the way to the late Comer's office, one of the familiar spooks, named Filgram, stopped me.

"Did you hear about Comer?"

"No," I said.

"He got killed last night. Him and Molar were over at Vice President Ky's son's place."

Luck. Sometimes the grenade bouncing into your foxhole didn't explode. Or the mortar at your feet was a dud. Comer must have been into it deeper with Ky than even I imagined. Couldn't tell anyone else at Phoenix his greedy schemes. No one was rushing to put me in handcuffs and haul me to LBJ. I wouldn't even have to explain about Luong. If I was right, nobody still alive even knew he was in Saigon.

"Any idea who did it?" I asked.

"Must have been a squad of VC. They burned the place after the shooting. Found Comer by the stairs with a bullet in his head. Not much else was left, but you could see the entry wound in his skull."

"Do you know who I should report to? Comer was my CO."

"Guess you better go see Williams. He's acting chief of station."

If there was one shitbird left in 'Nam I detested, it was Williams. He didn't have the cowboy bullshit act of Comer or teeth around his neck like Molar. But he was a Harvard grad, one of the hundreds recruited by the Company over the years. Harvard had a nickname. Langley North. And the arrogant assholes that came from there firmly believed their shit wouldn't burn in kerosene. It was made of gold. I walked down the hardwood floor toward the end where I knew Williams hung out, his office next door to a Rand computer.

No uniforms here. No salutes. Phoenix people like to believe they were fooling everyone. That's why every rickshaw jockey, cabbie, or cyclo driver in Saigon knew exactly where to go if you said "Phoenix." No address needed.

In all the rooms, fans turned lazily on the ceilings, and most desks held a smaller one, trying to keep the temperature of all the secrets from imploding. Men, and a few women, in chinos and short-sleeve shirts or lightweight skirts, hustled from room to room, clutching pieces of paper. Saving the world. Most windows were open, except in the front of the building where a sapper could toss in a surprise. Most of these personnel hadn't seen a firefight except on the news. The white walls and brown floors were scrubbed daily, and it smelled like chlorine. Enough electricity was used fueling the bright lights to keep the neon of the Pussy Parlor downtown going for a year. I walked into Williams's office and stood in front of his gray metal desk. He had his WASP face stuck in a file. I cleared my throat.

Williams looked up. He sat strack straight, the military jargon for stiff as a fucking pile of mortars. Or a prick from the Ivy League with a KA-BAR jammed up his ass believing he was better than anyone stupid enough to hump it in the bush.

"Morgan," he said. "I've been waiting for you to make an appearance. Sit down." He motioned toward a folding chair covered with a stack of yellow files, some marked SECRET in bold red letters. I dropped the pile on the floor and sat.

"I suppose you've heard Comer is dead," Williams said. "When did you last talk to him? Isn't he your case chief?"

What little was left of Williams's hair was peppered with gray. While his back was nearly as rigid as a dead gook forty-eight hours dead, his chin drooped, the victim of too many vodka tonics and beer. No evidence of a need to shave, it didn't seem like his face had hit puberty. His ears stuck out so far, no Gerber could have taken more than one easy stroke to slice them from his skull. Sweat stains turned the armpits of his collared white shirt gray. He was more dangerous than Comer and a fuck of a lot smarter. If I was going to escape LBJ, this dance had to be the pageant winner.

"Yes," I said. "Filgram just told me. Sorry to hear it." I looked at the floor and hesitated a few seconds before I lifted my face. "Last time I saw Comer was a few days ago. He sent me to the Majestic. Said to take it easy. I only have a few days left on my tour. He told me to check in here or he'd send me a message at the hotel. He said he might have something local before I go."

If Williams even had a whiff of how I really spent last night, the Colt I knew was at his waist would already be aimed at my head. He tapped his pencil on the desk.

"What about the bandage on your head? Where'd that happen?"

"One of my last missions. Got ambushed just outside the base. That's why Comer brought me in. This ain't no climate for healin'. Just keeps oozin' like it's a tube of Brylcreem."

"I seem to remember something about that in an action report. Weren't most of your Hoa Hao's killed?"

Somewhere in the piles on Williams's desk was an account describing everything about that day. And every day I spent in 'Nam. Williams was playing games, and I knew where he was headed.

"Yes," I said. "I hid in a hole. Covered myself with leaves and dirt. Lucky to make it back through the wire."

"Didn't you report to Viper?"

There it is.

"Yes," I said.

"What do you think happened to him?"

"Don't know. I was in the bush. Heard it was a VC sapper."

"That's the way it looked. But it could have been one of ours. Did he have any enemies beside the VC?"

"Can't say everybody loved him, but I don't think anybody hated him enough to cash his chit."

"There were some rumors you and Viper weren't the best of friends."

"Can't say we threw back a lot of stubbies together. But we had a professional relationship. You know, respected each other's skills."

If the bullshit got any deeper this old villa would drown. I had two things going. First, nobody really liked Viper. Williams was just going through the motions of a spook bureaucrat covering his ass. Following up in case there was some story he didn't pursue. If he had any proof, I'd be sweating a lot more than I was now. Or dead. Second, nobody knew I was out with Comer last night. No reports filed. Comer would only have written down his dealings with Ky if it could advance his position with Phoenix, not when it was growing his Swiss bank account. But the most surprising part of this chat was I still didn't give a shit. Steadily, over the last twelve months, the "I don't care if you blow my shit to Guam attitude" only got stronger. Now, I was slowly realizing Liem's murder made me as disposable as the bodies bulldozed into trenches by the Corps of Engineers if the VC weren't fast enough to retrieve them. But I did want Luong and the girls to make it to the mountains. I did want this Harvard prick to finish.

"Well, I don't know how sincere you are," Williams said. "But there's no evidence to contradict what you're saying. With the mess around here this morning, not much I can do but send you back to the Majestic until things settle. Get some rest, Morgan. There might be a problem I need you to resolve. We'll talk."

Williams looked down at the desk and slid a file in front of his face. I was dismissed. And it didn't piss me off.

R&R at the Majestic only lasted three days. My wounds weren't bad enough for more idle time. I was ordered into the Phoenix office, and Williams told me one more mission was required before I rotated out. It was in Saigon and involved one of ours.

Intel had tracked the leader of a group formed by an ex-Ranger captain, Anthony Donaldson. The clandestine squad was formed to help deserters use an underground railroad for escape to Thailand. Donaldson's nickname was "Rooster." Rumors of the "Westend Boys" were whispered at every base and camp in 'Nam. Their title was a combination of our commanding general's name and what they hoped would be his future. If I came back with his dog tags, I would be on the next Freedom Bird leaving Da Nang. If not, the unsubtle threat from Williams was "an after-hours Board of Inquiry that might delay your trip for a very long time." While I didn't much care about any late-night execution by Phoenix, Rooster sounded like someone I'd like to meet before checking out of this fucked country or getting a bullet in the back.

Donaldson was rumored to hang out above one of the filthiest bars in Saigon, the Last Hope, near the river and surrounded by tin shacks, rickety bamboo boardwalks hugging the water, sagging palm trees, and the smell of weed burning. Phoenix had infiltrated his group, and Donaldson was supposed to be at the Last Hope tonight.

Desertion was one of those topics the brass tried to squelch like the sanitizing of vils by killing every man, woman, and child. My job was to see a dead witness was better than a live one. At any time, there were hundreds of deserters hiding in Saigon, trying to get to Sweden, the Promised Land. MACV didn't want the troops to have any hope and certainly didn't want Walter Cronkite making the group a lead item on the six o'clock news.

At 2200, dressed like a grunt just out of the boonies, filthy and fatigues torn from having rolled in the dust behind the Phoenix Building, I carried an M16 into the Last Hope. The bar was in a dark alley off Ben Ham Tu Street, butting against the river. There were no sarcastic greetings, secret handshakes, or slaps on the back. The few grunts at the chipped Formica tables only glanced at me and returned their focus to the cans of beer in front of them. A Doors album played on a turntable in the back of the small, dark room, the sound coming from two twelve-inch Akai speakers with the felt covers ripped and hanging loose. A fan pushed the humid, smoke-filled air around the ceiling. It was well over ninety degrees even at this time of night.

The beer was cold, and the mama-san didn't smile when she put the can in front of me. No b-girls in this dump.

"No chit," she said. "Piaster." She meant no MSC, military script currency. I reached into my pocket and dug out a few notes.

All insignias were ripped off my fatigues, and there was no name tag. I picked up my can of Lucky and walked over to a table where two grunts sat, facing the door.

"What unit you guys with?" I asked, pulling out an empty chair.

Both were in civvies, but were unmistakably boonie rats by the hardness in their gaze and the way they stared through me into the jungle, scenes of fire and death playing a never-ending film on their consciousness. The man on my right took a swallow of his beer.

"Not a good question," he said. "Why do you want to know?"

"Just makin' conversation," I said.

"The rule here is the war doesn't come through the door. Stow it outside, troop."

"I'd like to stow it a lot further than that. You guys heard of Rooster?"

They didn't tense. Nobody would be in here unless they were looking to get out or were CID. I had been in too many firefights to have the smell of a cop.

Both the men wore khaki shirts and shorts. No shoes or socks meant they lived somewhere nearby. Probably in one of the lantern-lit rooms on the second floor I had seen from outside. The man on the left fired up a Camel with his Zippo.

"Rooster?" the man said. "Don't know no Rooster."

The M16 rested against my thigh. I took out the Hush Puppy and laid it on the table.

"Pay attention, assholes," I said. "I could have played this another way. Walked in with my M16 on rock and roll and blown you away. I wouldn't have spent a minute in LBJ. In fact, I would have gotten another commendation in my file." I touched the silencer on the barrel of the Hush Puppy. They knew what a Hush Puppy was, and it wasn't standard issue for a grunt. Only spooks. "Or I could have snuck upstairs and put one bullet from this in Donaldson's head." I patted the silencer. "Those were my orders. You know, a firefight in the streets of Saigon gets a lot of publicity, but a dead deserter bleeding onto his sleeping mat in a dump like this don't mean nuthin'." I sat back, taking the Hush Puppy with me. "You've got two choices. Either tell Donaldson I want to rap or I go home and say he wasn't in. That way, they'll be back with the flamethrowers to burn you and this place down. After they shoot you. No court-martial, boys. Bad PR."

If they were scared, I couldn't read it. Grunts get so used to fear that it becomes the natural state, and sitting in this bar facing one man didn't compare to listening to Charlie's taunts of "You die, GI" in the night.

The men glanced at each other, and the one smoking the Camel nodded. The other man got up, his chair scraping on the floor, and walked toward a beaded curtain in the back.

The remaining man flicked his package of Camels, and one smoke popped out. "Coffin nail?" he asked.

I took the smoke, and the man lit the end with his Zippo. RANGERS was engraved in the metal.

While we talked, the Last Hope emptied. Not in a rush, but the grunts who witnessed the conversation got the vibe and disappeared like tigers in the mist. The mama-san changed the record to Buffalo Springfield. Posters of Jimi Hendrix in his Ranger uniform were scattered around the walls. Smells of dead dogs and cats drifted from the river, and the cigarette smoke couldn't mask the stench. The windows were open only because there was no glass in the panes. One of the walls leaned outward, showing cracks in the wooden beams.

The man who left came through the curtain and motioned me to follow. I picked up the M16 and put the Hush Puppy into my pocket, nodding at the Ranger with the Camel in the corner of his mouth.

On the other side of the curtain, the man held open a door that led outside to a bamboo ramp that swayed to the waves on the river. Giant fern and banana leaves hung to the broken railing. Muted light came from reflections off the river and the lanterns inside the Last Hope. River sampans were moored to the walkway with frayed hemp ropes. After ten meters, we were at the bottom of a stairway that looked like it was only attached to the Last Hope by two nails and a roll of twine. The man started up, and I waited for him to reach the top, not believing the staircase could hold two of us. The man stopped and turned.

"Don't be scared, spook," he said. "But if you fall in the river, close your mouth." He opened a screen door and went through.

Inside, a muscled, shirtless man sat on a cot, the blankets untucked, holding a half-empty bottle of Old Grandad. RANGERS was tattooed on his right bicep and dog tags hung from his neck. An American flag was pinned to the wall, framed by pictures of Che Guevara and Bobby Seale. The room smelled of burning ganja, and a roach still smoldered in an ashtray made out of a twisted piece of shrapnel. Candles burned on an empty C-rat case table. A Colt pistol sat next to the candles.

The man who led me upstairs went back out the door.

Donaldson watched me and took a pack of Marlboros out of the pocket of his shorts. He lit one with a strike from a wooden match against the C-rat case.

"Have a seat," he said, pointing to a stack of ammo boxes, the only possible place to sit in the room other than the cot. He took a slug from the whiskey bottle and held it out to me. "Drink?" he asked before I could sit. Three steps and I covered the distance between us, taking the bottle in my hand and swallowing half of what was left. I walked backward until my calves touched the ammo cases and sat, leaning the M16 against the wall.

"All of the body bags that leave Ton Sen Nhut aren't filled with casualties from gook fire," I said. "Some of them won't be buried in Arlington. Some of them won't be listed in the statistics. Their records will disappear." The Hush Puppy was in my palm, and I could feel the coolness on my hand. "I was sent here to make you one of the 'Lost Ones.' The brass thinks you're a criminal. And a coward. You wouldn't still be here if that were the case. Nor would you have that tattoo." I nodded toward his arm. "Tell me why."

Donaldson laughed. The cynical sound of an innocent man raging at the hypocrisy of the judge.

"Ain't it sweet," he said. "The pogues order us out to kill baby-sans and list their burnt flesh in the body count. We spray Agent Orange on rice paddies so the locals will starve. We poison their wells so they can't drink. We rape their daughters for fun. Too many times I was ordered up the same hill just so my captain could brag that we had captured the high ground for the day. Too many times, I lost buddies to machine guns that were carried back up that same hill during the night after we left. And all for what? We ain't gonna win this war. All we're doin' is givin' the liars in Washington a chance to feel like men and help the machine churn out dollars." He spat on the floor and then drained the last of the Old Grandad, throwing the empty bottle on a pile of dirty clothes in the corner.

Nothing in what he said was untrue. And I could add pages to the list. Innocent women assassinated because they wouldn't fuck. Indiscriminant bombing of civilians. Denied incursions into neutral countries. Torture. And I had participated. No more. I emptied the Hush Puppy magazine and put the pistol on the floor.

"We could debate all night," I said. "But I agree with you. The facts are that you're a condemned man. The CID knows all about you. If I don't come back with your dog tags, I'll be dead. And that won't save you."

Donaldson laughed again and waved his hand in front of his body, indicating the whole room and his world outside the walls.

"And this is better?" he said. "I could have been in Sweden months ago. But I'm just crazy enough to want to help anyone else escape who wants to di di."

"How do you do it?"

"Fuck, man. Just zap me. You think I'd tell you. Maybe you want some of that blond stuff in Stockholm?"

"Maybe, but I'm more interested in you."

At some time, everyone meets a zealot. Could be they worshipped two-headed snakes, saving whales, or torturing their enemies. Occasionally, as was the case with Donaldson, they were the good guys and always seemed to have a candle burning inside, lit by the cause consuming their souls. But their eyes were clear, the vision of destiny already imprinted in their minds leading to a righteous solution to every question. Energy wasn't a problem when the path was clear. Donaldson was a fanatic on the road to salvation, the redemption of his soul the jungle highway to Sweden. He bounced his legs and talked.

Donaldson told me about his tour in the Highlands. About a lieutenant he fragged after the officer laughed while raping a wounded mama-san and shot her in the head when he came. In the language of gruntville, the lieutenant became a double veteran, "Kill 'em after you fuck 'em." Afterward, the lieutenant ordered the squad to burn the vil and shoot everyone still alive. About buddies killed by sniper fire and booby traps. About ambushes in the jungle where the only way their location could have been known was leaked to the Cong from ARVN scouts that guided them. But he saved most of his anger for the "lying shitbags at MACV and the scum in Washington." He crumpled an empty package of cigarettes and tossed it toward the near bamboo wall.

Most of the time I listened, having witnessed much of the same. And having many of the same beliefs. I flipped the wooden match on the hardwood floor and took a long hit on a Camel.

"Can't argue with you, Donaldson," I said. "Somehow, the army built a mold made of murder and insanity. The walls are so thick, not even a grenade can break you or me out. The plaster gets into your brain and short-circuits the rational parts. Covers your eyes so you only see what they want."

A box on the table. Prerolled joints. Donaldson lit up, sucked in, and passed it to me.

"Gimme a name, spook," Donaldson hissed, smoke drifting from the corners of his mouth. "I'll take responsibility."

Taking the spliff, I crushed out the camel on the floor with my bush boot.

"Morgan," I said. "Frank Morgan."

Donaldson held out his hand, still keeping the ganja in his lungs. No games. He wasn't a fat-cat, leech journalist. We joined in a shake that coiled our thumbs together and bonded our eyes.

A cloud of gray smoke and one long exhale.

"So, you gonna di di this shithole, Morgan?" Donaldson asked. "Go see your momma and check if the girlfriend still has you on the list?" He took back the joint. "How you gonna look them in the eye? When you're touching their skin will you remember the eyeball pouches made of gook hide? Get a job sellin' used cars? Go back to school and study the history of good wars? What's the plan, man?"

The smoke made dragons in the air when it came out of my mouth.

"Been in-country more than a day," I said. "Nearly a lifetime. Just like you. Never had this rap with anybody except my skull. Every second. Every glance. Every dead gook. Now, I don't know where home is. All I know is that the killin' has to stop. Let me tell you a story."

Donaldson slumped back in his chair. Before his next hit, he said, "Go for it, spook. Don't we all just eat stories? Take's up the time."

On the floor, more whiskey. I opened the bottle and swallowed enough the slopover ran down my chin.

"Rode the Freedom Bird over next to a grunt who told me there ain't no rules in the 'Nam," I said. "Took a couple winks and my first kill to know he was right on. Spent nights hunkered in the dark, waitin' for a Charlie to bliss out. Killed his dog and then left him leakin' oil from his forehead. But, one night, it was a woman. Supposedly a VC hotshot. Beautiful. Green eyes. Smiling. The ants couldn't drink her blood fast enough." I took another long swallow and passed the bottle to Donaldson. "Found out later I was ordered out 'cause she wouldn't fuck the vice president of the Democratic Republic of South Shithole's son. *Innocent* ain't in the vocabulary where I work. Had to grease a few white devils to compensate. Ones who stayed in the rear, gettin' free pussy and sluggin' down ice-cold Tigers while dumb shitbirds like us lost our souls. Met a CAG ghost and adopted his kid. Only had the baby-san a day and had to bury his ashes and the parts of his belly I could scoop into my bush hat in the clay. Fell in love. Is that an oxymoron in the Land of Burnt Flesh? Well, shit happens. Anyway, she was an Irish witch, and we spent an afternoon at her altar. Had to waste every one a' the slants who made her dance to their AKs. Took a while, but me and my Montagnard scout tracked them all to hell. Caught up with the old VP's kid a few klicks from here. Introduced him to my Hush Puppy and remodeled his knees before I left him smoldering in his villa. Found two little girls hidin' behind the curtains and a shitload of money. Couldn't leave the baby-sans on the grill. The scout's got 'em hopin' they'll make him forget watchin' some ARVN take turns on his wife before they stuck a knife up her pussy and turned left. While I was doin' my job, the brass showed. Took a lot a' persuadin' to make 'em stay. They're still there. Permanently. What I finally figured is it ain't us. Maybe we still got a shot at something other than this." I waved the hand holding the whiskey bottle around the room. "But I doubt it. In one a' my psych classes before I left The World, some asswipe professor said, 'The human spirit has an infinite capability to reconstruct itself, shedding the error of past mistakes, while letting the reborn person emerge.' Ain't that a hoot? I'll bet he never laid in the saw grass listenin' to a man he just gutshot scream for his momma through the night." Another hit on the bottle and I went on, boonie knowing pounding in my ears, saying Donaldson was worth saving, not me. "Now you, you've found a way to jam it up their asses while helpin' the best way you can. Me, the only answers came from the barrel of a pistol or the blade of a knife. Ain't gonna be no rebirth for me."

Outside, the sound of Bob Dylan feeling like a rollin' stone. A boat person yelling "*Xing ong!*" Move. Lanterns on sampans drifting slowly down the river. Palm fronds waving in the wind. The slats on the window drooping like sleeping soldiers. A breeze filled with the smell of fish oil and decaying animals. A creak from the rotting stairs. Inside, another suck on the doobie.

"Guilt," Donaldson said. "You ever think it's what got us here and what's gonna keep us from goin' home?"

"Yup," I said. "And some kinda fucked-up sense of duty."

"Right on," Donaldson said. "Some a' that 'duty' shit from this end a' the bunker, too. Signed up 'cause my half-brother came home to Omaha needin' to take a dump with a nurse holdin' him on the shitter. No way would my old man let me grow girly hair and hand out petunias on the sidewalk. Said, 'Boy, someday, you have to step up and be a man.' Well, I couldn't take a leak without movin' all the contraptions for my brother away from the toilet and couldn't sit at the dinner table without the old man's eyes comparin' me to the cripple. Pretty soon, the stares carried me down to the recruitin' office so I could come here and trade a few dead gooks for my brother's legs.

And my father's eyes. Didn't know nuthin' 'bout no Domino Theory or the Military Industrial Combine. Did know I couldn't watch my brother learn ta push his wheelchair up the ramp or listen to my old man 'tsk, tsk' and shake his head every time I walked into the room no more." He looked out the broken louvers on the window, the thousand-yard stare glazing his eyes before they shut. "Now, it's Beckman's suckin' chest wound I see and no way to patch it. The doc got popped by a dink machine gun, and I couldn't even crawl over to his medpack. We were pinned down. I watched Beckman die, the blood bubbling on his fatigues between my fingers. His last words were, 'Don't let me die in Turdville.'" Donaldson opened his eyes. "He wasn't the first. Or anywhere near the last. What are we gonna do, Morgan? Go back to The World and be Joe Citizens after what we did? And saw? Can you ever look a baloney sandwich in the eye and not remember it's the same color as some grunt like Beckman's intestines? Or pinch a little cousin's cute ear and not see a row of black gook ears hangin' in a base hootch?"

Not even the breeze off the Son Sai Gon could blow away the heat. Or the mood. Old fatigues piled in the corner were starting to smell like the base laundry before wash day. The poster of Che in his beret was beginning to spook me. Something about those eyes. Too many eyes, including mine. God should have built-in horror filters. I rubbed mine, and it didn't stop the movie.

"Me," I said, "it was more duty. Saw lots a' vets at the Fort on crutches, the bandages starting where their legs used to be. Sympathy isn't a big play around those places. More, 'if I look or think too hard, I might be next' attitudes. Learned ta recite the Uniform Military Code by the time I was ten. Started the day with a Pledge of Allegiance. Could name the Joint Chiefs of Staff before the last ten presidents. Lost any choice before I took my first breath." A gecko ran across the tin ceiling and disappeared behind a bamboo strut. I turned to Donaldson, who continued his stare out the window. "Ever think about forgiveness? Not of Westmoreland or Tricky Dick. Or the gooks. About yourself. Started with me, buried under a banyan tree, waitin' for a dink bayonet to slice through the dirt into my dick. Forgiveness took a sabbatical after I found out the girl Liem wasn't VC, just like I suspected. Revenge helped a lot. And lettin' a few innocents live, moves that coulda sent me to LBJ. The last coupla' days I figured there ain't no Freedom Bird home."

The roach was burned down to Donaldson's fingertips. No cinders or smoke left, its vitamins already lazily drifting in his brain. He studied me. No illegal smile.

"Fuck, Morgan," he said. "You're a tougher spook than me. It's not the people I greased. It's the ghosts of the ones I let die. It's not the dried ears or the wailin' mama-sans clutching dead baby-sans to shriveled breasts. It's Dornoff's arm sailin' over my head like a bloody baton. It's not touching a crispy critter with my M16 barrel and watchin' the husk of his body crumble like burnt paper. It's hearin' that shot from inside the tunnel, knowing it should have been me and not Jurgens. Yes, I gotta forgive. But I don't think I can forget."

The chair creaked, and Donaldson reached behind, bringing out an M26 grenade. He stroked it like it was a puppy and snapping the pin with his fingernail.

"You ever wondered what one a' these would taste like?" he asked, kissing the grenade. "Pull the pin and stick it in your mouth. Bite down on the steel and the metal tang would be your last sensation. No more conscience. No more smokin' bodies. A quick flight to freedom."

Sure, the same thought had beckoned me. More times than I felt love. And at this very moment. But I didn't want to tell it to Donaldson. He might pull the pin right now and send us both to hell in a million pieces. Something was making me want to live, if only long enough to make sure the assholes didn't win again and take Donaldson's skin. I set the bottle back on the floor and Donaldson picked it up.

"Hope," he said. "I know there ain't much hope to feel lookin' across a toasted vil to the smokin' horizon. But you gotta look into your soul and know it's in there. Somewhere in the dark. And it wants to get out and take you home."

I stood up and walked to Donaldson.

"Look," I said, my hand on his bare shoulder. "I'll make you a deal. You put down that M26, and I'll take your dog tags. We're about the same size. When the troops come to burn this place, I'll make sure they can't recognize the body. That there M26 oughta do the trick. Your tags'll make 'em think it's you."

A smile. A hand on my forearm.

"Muchas gracias, podner," he said. "But I coulda run a long time ago. I'm just gonna take a long bivouac here and do what I can."

"Not possible," I said. "Your choices are limited. So're mine. We can stay here and gripe about the unfairness of it all until they send a squad to grease you. Or you can move out. I have ta take your dog tags. And you gotta di di. I already died in this shithole. I wanna let you go, but they have ta think you're dead. You'll have to disappear. Your life's worth ten of mine."

He was wobbling on the cot. I wasn't fooled. Donaldson could have an Old Grandad IV attached to his arm and he would still think clearly. He would always be a highly trained killer, and, if he chose, I didn't know who would be quicker to grab their pistol and shoot. But it wasn't going to come to that. Instead, he took his hand off my arm, tore the dog tags from his chest, and threw them at me.

The ID jingled when I dropped them in my pocket. Donaldson got up and touched my shoulder.

"Bad deal, Morgan," he said. "Neither of us is gonna die in this shack." He gently pushed me back toward the ammo cases. "There's another way. Sit and listen."

I sat and Donaldson went back to the cot.

"I been in-country a year longer than you," he said. "Had lots a' time ta think. Did too much killin' ta go home. Started this railroad cause the scene was covered in blood every time I opened my eyes. Believed doing somethin' was better than pullin' the pin on the M26 I always carry. Just in case, ya' know." He smiled, fondling the M26. "Ain't gonna end up at the end of a rope at LBJ. Now, you got the same baggage I carried a year ago. It's gonna take time, but there's a reason you're still alive. You'll figure it out. For me, it ain't The World. My one regret is I can't tell my momma I'm alive." He looked down and scuffed his unlaced boots on the hardwood floor.

Choices. I made a bad one when I walked up the stairs to the Freedom Bird, followed by lots of corpses more. First, I was an innocent. But months of mindlessly following the command of Phoenix put the blame right on my soul. No more orders. No more killing. If it meant I would die from the orange of a flamethrower, don't mean nuthin'. And I didn't care about anything but one last gesture. Getting Donaldson out of the shit. I leaned forward and put my hands on my thighs.

"Don't know if what you say is true or not," I said. "Right now, what I do know is we're both dead if we stay here. You're dead if I don't bring your tags back or they're on somebody's burnt carcass, including mine."

"You got a death wish?" Donaldson asked. "Like I said. Neither of us is gonna die." He reached into his pocket and took out another set of dog tags on a silver chain and held them up in the wavering light. "One a' the reasons you're here is we had a traitor. Musta' been feedin' intel to MACVN. Came here actin' like a blissed-out junkie, wantin' ta' ride the rails to Sweden. One a' the boys you met downstairs greased him this morning when he pulled a Colt and started threatening. Kinda expected somebody like you. But not so soon. We hadn't decided what to do, but you made the decision for us." He tossed me the dog tags. "Take these too. You might need a little more evidence."

I put them in the pocket with Donaldson's.

"I guess you can see it don't matter much to me," I said. "I'll take the tags in just to give you some time. After that, I'm scheduled to head out. Maybe I'll be on the plane. And maybe not."

"Listen up, Morgan," Donaldson said. "We both greased people who had no reason to be killed. We both saw things that'll make dreams something only a bottle or a needle will cure. From what I've heard, you think we might be even but not equal. I ain't keepin' score. Do a few more smokin' bodies make you the winner? You got no call to do anything but heal. And you will. Maybe, someday, you'll thank me. Just like I'm thankin' you."

We both stood.

"You gotta di di, post haste," I said. "If they find out you're alive, it won't be for long. And me? Somethin' tells me the brass would love to see me squirmin' at the end of a bayonet."

Next to the dog tags in my pocket, the wad of money pressed against my thigh. I took it out and handed to Donaldson.

"Don't need this," I said. "Maybe it'll do you and your boys some good. It's blood money anyway, and no one knows it's missin'. I was thinkin' about droppin' it off at the orphanage. Ain't gonna keep it myself."

The roll filled Donaldson's palm, and he looked down, surprise on his face, turning the money around with his fingers.

"Stopped bein' paid by the Combine a year ago," Donaldson said. "None a' these deserters have any money, and it's been a struggle to get them out.

But I can't take no more death dollars." He tried to shove the bundle back to me, and I left my hands at my sides.

"No fuckin' way, Rooster," I said. "If you want to throw it in the river with the other shit driftin' by, it's your call. I ain't takin' it back."

The sound of the river was a gentle murmur at the door. I moved toward the steps, feeling Donaldson's stare like a sniper's scope between my shoulder blades.

"Hang on a sec, Morgan," he said. He put his muscled arms around me, turned me around, and whispered, "Thanks, buddy. Say hello to The World for me if ya' make it. I don't think I'll be goin' home."

"At least you'll be gettin' outa your luxury accommodations here," I said, waving my hand around the slanting walls of the filthy room and pointing the M16 at the floor. "I'm not sure if I want a way out of this lice-ridden shithole of 'Nam. But I ain't goin' nowhere 'til I escort you down the stairs, if we make it without fallin' in the river."

No performance now. Donaldson stood strack straight. Guard duty alone in the perimeter foxhole. Never losing concentration and all senses on bush alert. He studied me like I was a map of the day's action in the middle of Indian country. After a minute, he scratched the scar on his chest and pocketed the cash.

"The way I see it," he said, "I really got the choice of leavin' now. Or waitin' for the death squad to blow this joint to Cần Thơ. Maybe you're right. Ain't got no home left, but that ain't no reason to commit suicide in this fuck-all place. You neither."

Donaldson stepped toward an old rucksack under the cot and began to stuff a pile of molding clothes inside.

From over his shoulder, he said, "Can't refuse a cordial invite like yours. Been meanin' to see some new country anyways."

No nostalgic glance around the filthy room. Donaldson obviously had known for months his tour of 'Nam was destined to end in an unmarked mud grave or floating with the dead pigs in the Son Sai Gon if he didn't run. The risk was that he didn't care. Like me. But some light still burned in the Zippo of his soul, and he stood, hoisting the pack over his shoulder.

"You first, spook," he said, nodding toward the door.

At the bottom of the stairs, I heard him softly say, "Peace, brother." When I turned, I expected to see him standing, two fingers in a V, saluting another lost comrade. But he was gone, melting into the bushes like so many stories in this tortured land.

The Phoenix headquarters stayed open all hours. I laid Donaldson's and the other guy's dog tags on Williams's desk. Earlier, I read the spy's name was O'Malley and he was a Catholic. There must have been some catastrophe in a land consumed by them or Williams would be throwing back aged Kentucky Bourbon with the elite class who stayed at the Rex. I didn't say a word, while Williams turned the tags over in his hands.

The long stare was right out of the scene repeated every day all over 'Nam. The one where the cherry lieutenant said something stupid like, "We gotta take that bunker." Or "Jones, crawl down that hole." I didn't know if Williams was planning to shoot me and have my body thrown in the brown water of the Son Sai Gon. But the longer I gazed, the more I knew this man didn't want to kill me. Might get blood on his chinos. He just gave orders. If I walked out of this room without him calling the guards, I would have a pass, even if I didn't want it. Seconds went by and, if he made a move for the pistol at his waist, I would break my oath of no more killing. He would be dead before he got the Colt out of its leather holster. Donaldson had probably already vanished into the jungle, and I only wanted to give him a reasonable head start away from Saigon. If Williams tried to give me another mission, it wasn't gonna happen.

Finally, Williams blinked.

"So, Morgan," he said. "Where are the bodies?"

The room was brighter than this morning, ceiling lights making every surface glare. Two black phones sat on Williams's desk, polished like his English. Only two files were left and were stacked neatly in front of him. Pens, a pencil, and an eraser were lined up perfectly beside the documents. He wouldn't last an hour in the muck of the boonies.

My eyes never left his.

"In the river," I said. "You can dredge the whole damn thing if you want. You'll probably find a lot more."

More stares. He was deciding whether to believe me. But there was a risk. He knew I was a colonel's son. He knew any hint of killing Americans by Americans would be a major public relations blunder. He knew publicity about an underground railroad was something the news hacks would feast on. He knew it was probably better to forget the doubts and lack of bodies or his long career at Langley would be in jeopardy. Hell, he could always blame somebody else as long as the news was kept quiet.

Now, there was no reason to lie to myself. To live anymore by a creed unwritten by Phoenix, but nonetheless followed like it was a warped Bible of murder. To kill innocents at the command of psychopaths and Stetson-wearing dwarfs. To sneak around in the night, a Hush Puppy my guide to unending dreams of death shots to the forehead. To hear the *pphhuupp* sound that echoed in my skull. To smell that final shit of my victims, a stink I thought coated my soul. When I left Seattle, I believed I knew who I was. A young man off to war, fulfilling his duty to God, family, and country, a timeless story. Outside an abandoned rubber plantation, rain puddling beside her head and mixing with her blood, I realized I wasn't a patriot. Evil couldn't be shrouded by Old Glory. There was something bigger than the misguided slaughter of the guiltless in pursuit of an unwinnable war. The only regret I had was it took so many bodies in their death dance to make me understand, while men like Donaldson showed true bravery. The demons still bombarded, but I only had to get by Williams for them to start retreating.

Tonight, at Phoenix headquarters, there wouldn't be any heartfelt good-byes. No tears or pats on the back wishing me good cheer and lots of blond pussy. No "atta boy" for being the most lethal assassin off the books. Just like I carried the stench-ridden aura of stone killer throughout my tour, by my last day in country the executioners at Phoenix sensed I was no longer a believer. To a point, I had done what was required. Now, no more would die by the wire on my garrote. No one would twist as the Gerber punctured a lung. Any debts resulting from being born in America to a colonel and his walking-wounded wife were cancelled. And the corpses of those I killed had been honored with the bullets in Comer's and Ky's bodies. I was done, and I hoped sleep would someday come like the lazy white clouds over the Delta.

Williams looked down and opened the top file.

"Okay, Morgan," he said. "Dismissed."

The last time I felt like this, Comer died. And lots of others. Fucking "dismissed." But the pledge still lived. No matter how much I wanted to slice his arrogant head from his shoulders with the Gerber, and how another body wouldn't mean one more day in hell, I was finished. If I didn't know where the next days would take me, I did know the killing was over. I didn't move.

"I want on the next flight out of Da Nang stateside," I said.

Williams closed the file.

"Be back here at oh-seven-hundred hours," he said. "There's a chopper leaving then."

In the morning, a letter was handed to me before I stepped onto the Huey. It was from Mom and the first one I opened in twelve months. The chopper touched off, and I used the Gerber to slit the envelope.

Below, we flew past Armageddon. Smoke rose from cyclos, tanks, burning shit, cook fires, and bomb sites. Women bent over in rice paddies, water buffaloes close by. Lines of jeeps and AVs covered the mud roads, pushing aside the stream of peasants, thatched baskets balanced on their heads. Drooping palm trees struggled to stay alive in the rancid air. Not even the *thwop . . . thwop . . . thwop* of the Huey could drown out the boom of artillery. Beside me, there had been so much blood, the hoses couldn't wash it away. The stain in the metal looked like the faces of a hundred grunts.

Dearest son,

I haven't heard from you in a long time. I hope this letter finds you well. I know part of you is punishing me and your father, and I want you to forgive both of us. There are lots of things we didn't tell you. Your father doesn't believe in that kind of talk, but he loves you and so do I. We are still in the same house, and your room waits for you to come home, just like me. According to your father, it should be soon. When will we see you?

Love, your mother

The side where the door gunner rode was open. I threw the letter over his shoulder and watched it swirl away in the wind.

The Freedom Bird 727 from Da Nang was crammed with noisy grunts on their way back to The World. Stewardesses walked the aisles, moving quickly by the most drunken soldiers. Survival. A pinch or a grope was the limit these blue-uniformed women risked, while men with 365 days of horror decided if they were lucky or not sitting in the cloth-covered chairs. Or if wading through a rice paddy, mines hungry for a foot to touch the detonator and send a leg airmail to infinity was the reality their lives had become. Buddies in shiny green body bags roasted on the asphalt outside the Plexiglas windows and were not forgotten along with the ghosts who would haunt the returnee's doubts like pus-filled wounds.

Beer was the drink of choice. Hours jammed together would be filled with false camaraderie and stories, the fear of what awaited more powerful than a squad of NVA on the trail. Budweiser was the escape from the punji stakes of home poised at their hearts.

Many of the returning troops hadn't bothered to shower after their final days in the boonies, even if they were dressed in parade ground tropical unis ready for the band to greet them when they touched the long-awaited soil of the motherland. Most of their last hours were spent signing rotation papers, too drunk to stand without leaning on the grunt in front of them in the line. The plane smelled like a firebase latrine, even after numerous sprayings with Lysol. Periodically, the chorus of the Country Joe McDonald classic would break out and resonate in the plane "And it's one, two, three, what're we fightin' for? Don't ask me I don't give a damn, next stop is Vietnam. And it's five, six, seven, open up the pearly gates. Well there ain't no time to wonder why, we're all gonna DIE."

Beside me, a grunt who couldn't grow a beard if he tried seemed forty years old, and his eyes were the black of a dead water buffalo. When someone clapped, he jumped and ducked, trying to take cover behind the seat back in front of him. If he hadn't just ended a tour of Southeast Asia, he looked like he'd be finishing up his senior year in high school somewhere in Kansas. Between mortar attacks, he chewed phantom fingernails bleeding from the hundreds of bites that came before.

Since I had never been regular army, I didn't wear a uni. Along with a few days of growth on my chin, a khaki shirt, pants, and sandals were enough to signal most of the men not to talk to a spook without a name tag on his chest. The old jungle knowing told these hardened troops I was someone they didn't want joining the nightmares they already had. That wasn't me. Not anymore. Somewhere between a monsoon night, a green-eyed innocent, and this 727, I found out I wasn't the ruthless killer Comer and the others created. That conviction didn't stop me from ordering another cold Bud, but did make it taste better.

Looking around the plane, I didn't feel kinship with any of these men. We may have come over for relatively similar reasons of duty, honor, and adventure. Or because we were forced to by a system hungry for young meat. But most of these grunts had a home, even if it would have changed to something they couldn't imagine. Only the soldier beside me seemed too shell-shocked to celebrate.

"You gonna be okay, troop?" I asked the boy a few hours later, his arm beginning to tremble. He had refused anything to drink, and his eyes darted like fireflies around the crowded cabin.

Hearing my words, his gaze settled on a dirt spot scarring the knee of his uni. He wouldn't look at me. I knew he thought I was the sapper crawling into the hootch of his mind.

"Don't worry, soldier," I said. "I'm retired."

He began to pick at the stain, still not risking a glance, probably believing my eyes might be as vacant and dead as his.

None of us would ever be the same. Our rite of passage had been drowned in the blood of innocents. I could easily pick out the ones who had felt the terror of a night controlled by the VC. Or watched a buddy being loaded on a Huey, never to make the flight home alive. It was in the eyes. It was in the "don't give a shit" posture. It was in the warped wrinkle of a smile. But none of them had done what I did. Their orders were clear, "Kill or be killed," while mine were "Kill before they wake up." I didn't get where I would end up or who I might become. Only that I wouldn't be a murderer.

The Bud was dry, and I wasn't ready to join the grunts who now slept, ignoring the noise. For some, it was the first time out of a poncho in months. The stewardesses had turned down the lights and covered dozens of the men with blankets while they fought off the silly advances of those who wanted to drink their oblivion.

After a time, the party settled down, and the walls closed in. At least with the noise, I was enough distracted to only let the enemy invade the edges of my mind. Now the thoughts were of eyes and bodies and an unknown future. A life I didn't know if I wanted to live. Or how. Somewhere over Guam, I decided my first stop would be Omaha. Donaldson's mom needed to learn her son was alive. I owed him. Without his words, I would be a crispy critter in the ashes of the Last Hope.

The soldier alongside me didn't sleep. He fidgeted in his seat and swiveled his neck at every loud sound, rarely without a fingernail in his mouth.

"Don't worry, troop," I said. "The ghosts will fade."

I was beginning to think Donaldson was right.

I was twenty-three and had a whole life behind me. Don't mean nuthin' after all.